CHOOSING AGAIN

A WHISPERING PINES NOVEL

Kimberly Diede

ALSO BY KIMBERLY DIEDE

CHOOSING AGAIN

A WHISPERING PINES NOVEL

Kimberly Diede

Celia's Gifts Book 4

To Amber: always choose the paths that offer you laughter and light

"I am who I am today
Because of the choices I made yesterday."
—Eleanor Roosevelt

CHAPTER ONE

GIFT OF FORGOTTEN TREASURES

"*A*re we finally going to do this?"

"Yeah, Val, we're *finally* going to do this," her brother confirmed. "We're *finally* giving this cabin a complete overhaul so we can break this weird hold it has over Renee."

Val turned to face the sad little structure. Ethan was right—the cabin did have a strange grip on their sister. Not that she could blame Renee. Val shivered in the cool morning air as she took in the dismal scene: walls leached of color with shards of dirty white paint splintering off the trim; curled shingles on the roof, sporting clumps of fuzzy moss. Even the grass under her feet felt brittle, a stark contrast to the canopy of fresh green leaves and a sunlight-dappled sky above. Lawns stretching from one edge of the resort to the other were lush from spring rains. It was only here, around *this* cabin, where springtime had failed to evoke signs of rebirth.

Val shivered again.

She understood why Renee hated the run-down unit. Someone had dubbed it the "Gray Cabin," and aptly so. Ever since they'd returned to Whispering Pines as adults, the cabin had been the site of unfortunate—even *dangerous*—events. Events that lurked in a mother's worst fears. In Renee's case, some of those fears had come true.

Shaking off the jitters, Val fist-bumped her brother before climbing the wooden steps. Together she and Ethan would help the two of them start over—their stubborn sister *and* this sad little cabin.

All the furniture needed to come out. They'd rip out the flimsy, pressed-wood cabinets, too. A brick fireplace (the cabin's only interesting structural element, in Val's opinion) was getting a whitewash treatment. The back wall in the bedroom—the wall with the water damage that Renee said reminded her of blood stains—would be taken down to the studs.

Val and Ethan needed to be able to assure Renee that every last negative vibe was gone.

The whole family had been encouraging Renee to do something with the Gray Cabin. After the horrific episode when Val's niece Julie's ex-boyfriend-turned-stalker-turned-kidnapper stashed Julie's unconscious body on the bed in the back, Renee had locked the old cabin up tight and tried to pretend it didn't exist. Which was ridiculous, of course. There were only a handful of cabins at Whispering Pines as it was, and to stubbornly allow one of them to be out of commission was silly. Val was glad Renee was finally coming to her senses. They had Ethan to thank for that.

Val could hear her son and nephews hauling tools and scaffolding over from Ethan's construction trailer, which was parked in front of the resort's lodge. She'd been glad when Renee agreed to their brother's suggestion to make this ambitious project a teaching moment for a few of their kids. Nothing like hands-on work to learn some tricks of the trade. And no one better than Ethan, a professional contractor, to provide the guidance. Dave, Val's oldest, had been eager to help. She wasn't sure how much help a twelve-year-old would be, beyond an extra set of hands. But, like so many projects out at Whispering Pines, this was turning into a family affair.

"Ethan, what are we supposed to do with all this old junk?" Dave asked, scanning the interior as he handed his uncle the crowbar he'd sent him out to retrieve.

Ethan shrugged. "Ask your mother."

Val rolled her eyes at her brother but surveyed the items inside the tiny cabin. Her perusal didn't take long.

Robbie, Renee's son, jogged through the door, the wooden screen door slapping behind him. "Sorry, guys, I had trouble finding the dolly in the shed. It was stuck behind some old window screens." He paused. "Man, it *stinks* in here!"

"Yeah, it's been closed up too long," Val agreed, then motioned to the avocado-colored appliances in the kitchen. "That dolly is a great idea. It's probably the only way to get this old fridge out. Your mom said most everything should go to the dump. You saw that big roll-away bin in the parking lot, next to Ethan's trailer, right? Toss the mattress, bed frame, and headboard in there. Same with the kitchen table and chairs. Even this old sofa needs to go, but it'll take at least two of you to get it into the rollaway. It's heavy. Maybe ask your uncle for help with that, okay, boys?"

Dave nodded and wandered over to the fireplace. "Anything you *don't* want to toss?"

"Knowing Renee, she'd feel guilty ditching that fancy dresser—it's in decent shape—but I want *everything* out of this cabin. Ethan, can Dave put the chest of drawers in the back of your pickup for now? Maybe you could drop it off at a thrift store later?"

"I guess," Ethan said, grunting as he stretched to take down the dirty glass globe hanging above the rickety table.

"Got it," Dave replied, disappearing into the back bedroom. "I'll grab the mattress first."

Renee had replaced all the mattresses at the resort except for the one in the Gray Cabin. Val remembered her sister had bought most of them at a hotel liquidation auction when she was first getting the resort back into shape. Since no one had slept in here since Renee had reopened Whispering Pines—at least, no one who was *supposed* to sleep in here—Val suspected she hadn't gotten around to buying a new bed for this cabin yet. She'd need to remind her sister to pick one up soon. It shouldn't take them long to fix up the cabin with so many hands involved.

She watched her son try to maneuver the old, limp mattress outside. Ethan moved to help, but Val stopped him with a hand on his forearm.

"Let him do it."

Ethan sighed. "You need to stop treating me like I'm breakable. I'm fine."

Val hoped he was right, but still . . . Ethan's heart attack in early spring had served as a wake-up call for all of them. They weren't getting any younger—although, as the baby of the family, Val often felt thirty instead of her actual age of forty-three. Except when her four boys ran her ragged. On those days she felt like she was eighty-two.

"I never said you were breakable, bro. But there's no reason we can't let these kids do the heavy lifting." She glanced Ethan's way. Any reminder of his health scare tended to put her brother in a foul mood.

She could relate. Her own scare the previous summer when she'd found a lump in her breast still haunted her, even though it had turned out to be nothing. At least that's what the doctor assured her.

So why do I have to keep going back to have it checked?

Ethan was saying something. Val tucked her nervous thoughts away. She was fine and there was work to do.

"Sorry, what?"

"I said I'm glad Renee is working over at their new house today and leaving us to take care of things here. I know how much she despises this little cabin. Hopefully we can change that."

"And I'm glad Luke took the rest of my boys out fishing so they aren't underfoot today," Val added, grabbing a scruffy-looking broom from the corner. Frayed bristles stuck out at odd angles; its effectiveness would be questionable.

Once Dave and Robbie wrestled the old, bulky dresser out, Val headed back into the now-empty bedroom, Ethan on her heels with his toolbox and crowbar.

"Ever since Jake went ice fishing out here last Christmas, he's been hounding Luke to take the boat out," she continued. "I just hope Luke can keep them all *in* the boat. That water has to be freezing still. We haven't had much warm weather yet."

Ethan snorted and his tools clattered as he set his equipment down next to the back wall. "Yeah, Jake has a way of finding trouble. I thought for a second we were going to lose him down the hole in the ice when Julie snagged that whopper. Maybe he wouldn't have actually *fit* through the hole, but I wasn't taking any chances."

"Jake still talks about that day," Val said, shaking her head as she thought back to that afternoon on the frozen lake. Ethan was right: If there was trouble to be found, her youngest would be the one to find it. And then he'd try to charm his way out of it, often successfully. "I just worry Luke is too easy on the boys . . . especially Jake."

Ethan said nothing, but Val could feel his eyes on her.

She spun to face him. "What? You don't agree?" she challenged, hands on hips.

Ethan shrugged, turning his attention back to the window trim he was attempting to pry off. "Luke handles the boys just fine. They respect him. Just because he doesn't yell constantly doesn't mean he isn't able to discipline them."

"Are you saying I yell too much?"

The crack of breaking wood and a grunt were her brother's only reply.

"Yeah, well, screw you, Ethan. A little yelling never hurt anybody," Val bit out as she began to sweep. She caught his smirk but chose to ignore it.

They worked in silence, the bristles of her broom stirring dust into the air. Ethan sneezed, then sneezed again, finally sliding open the window he was working on. Val knew it was petty of her to enjoy his small measure of discomfort.

But she didn't care. She also knew he was right—she *did* lose her patience with her kids more often than her husband. *Probably more often than I should,* she thought, although she'd never admit that out loud. Who wouldn't lose it sometimes with four boys to keep corralled—five when she included her husband? Some days it took everything she had to keep them all fed, clothed, and relatively safe.

So maybe I'm not the perfect parent, but at least I'm trying, she reminded herself, working the broom more vigorously than necessary. Ethan sneezed again and she couldn't help but smile.

It felt good to be helping Renee out with the cabin. Val was usually stuck in the kitchen, feeding everyone. This was a nice change of pace.

Soon, as the boys filed in and out of the Gray Cabin, all the furniture was gone. Val set her broom aside for a minute to pull the curtains down from two small windows in the front of the cabin. The thread-bare fabric was so thin, her finger poked through one of the panels. She glanced into the bedroom, but the window Ethan was disassembling was bare.

She called to him, "I'm going to burn these in the firepit, like we did a couple years ago when we helped Renee clean up the other cabins. She can't salvage these."

"I'll take any excuse for a bonfire," Ethan said, nodding at her suggestion. He tossed the last bit of trim board from the window onto a pile on the scarred wooden floor and used his crowbar to remove a couple stubborn nails.

Val turned and caught her son checking his phone. They'd finally caved and bought him one a few weeks earlier when he came home with an impressive report card. He was the last of his friends to get a phone of his own—a fact he'd often reminded them of over the last year—but they'd waited because money was tight.

"Dave, put your phone away and clean up that pile of wood for your uncle."

Dave glanced at his mother, slipping the phone into his shorts pocket. He knew better than to argue with that tone.

After the old window trim was cleared away, Ethan helped Robbie wrestle the shabby kitchen cupboards from the walls—despite Val's silent disapproval. She needed to stop worrying about her brother.

The screen door squealed open and slapped shut again.

"Where have you been?" Val asked Dylan, Ethan's youngest, now standing next to Dave.

"Aunt Renee's new house, helping haul boxes of tile in for the bathroom."

Despite being only two years older than Dave, Dylan had six inches and at least thirty pounds on him. Ethan's two boys both played football, just as Ethan had, and Val suspected Dylan might be the biggest kid on his JV team.

Grunts and muted swearing filled the small cabin. The cupboards were apparently giving the guys some trouble. "I think your dad could use some of your muscle, Dylan."

She couldn't help but grin when her nephew flexed his right bicep and gave her a salute before stepping over to help his dad and cousin.

"Gee, thanks, Mom," Dave said, sarcasm dripping from his words. "Muscle Boy steps in and suddenly I'm worthless?"

"Not even a little, bud. Go grab Robbie's dolly out front and bring it in here. Your uncle should have some straps lying around someplace. Once those cupboards are out, the appliances are next."

Between the four guys, the kitchen was emptied of all but the kitchen sink relatively quickly. Val followed behind them, sweeping up old debris that had collected under everything through the years. She cringed when she spied mouse skeletons, but she kept going.

Maybe we should be wearing masks . . .

Alone now, Val continued to work her way around the kitchen and living room with her broom, dumping her dust pan into the industrial-sized garbage bin sitting where the kitchen table had been. Despite the dust, things already looked brighter, lighter.

She needed to ask Ethan whether or not the tub and toilet should be replaced. That would be a big job. She could hear him talking to the boys through the open windows, explaining where they would need to start with fixing the leaky roof.

It didn't take long for Val to work her way back to the half-swept bedroom with her broom. *This room still gives me the creeps,* she thought, remembering all those crazy things that had happened with Renee's daughter. She hoped the old ghosts would be eradicated once Ethan had the stained back wall replaced and everything freshened up.

"There's no such thing as ghosts," Val whispered to herself, not for the first time. They'd spent summers at Whispering Pines as kids, and retelling old ghost stories around the bonfire had been a favorite pastime. As the youngest of four kids, she'd been teased mercilessly about her fear of ghosts and had learned a long time ago to keep her thoughts to herself. No one needed to *know* she was still a tiny bit afraid of the dark.

A thud came from above, making her jump. Ethan's lessons must have progressed from outside on the grass up onto the roof.

She got back to work as footsteps creaked above her. She needed to finish sweeping and then run over to the lodge to pull lunch together for everyone. Maybe Ethan would let her rip out the old paneling in the bedroom this afternoon. That would be fun. She opened the door to the cabin's only closet, relieved to find it empty. She pulled a string hanging above her head and there was a click, but no light. Glancing up, she could see a light bulb. It probably burned out long ago.

She resumed sweeping, moving deeper into the closet, until her broom smacked against the back wall, catching on something.

"Crap." Her voice echoed in the closet. She couldn't pull the broom loose.

Dropping to her knees, she shone her phone's flashlight beam into the dark corners to see what the bristles had snagged on. The lower back portion of the closet wall looked different, like an extra wooden panel had been screwed over the base of the wall. She pulled harder at the broom handle. It took a few tugs, but the broom finally came loose. She slid it behind her, the handle rattling across the wooden floor.

She could see a small gap between the bottom of the panel and the floor. Curious, she lay down on her side, her head resting on the floor as she angled the flashlight beam to see if there was anything behind the panel. Probably plumbing or electrical stuff. Or nothing. Her light glinted off something; it looked like metal. She should probably leave the wall alone and keep cleaning, but now she was curious. There was barely enough room for her to wiggle her fingers through the sliver of space under the bottom of the panel.

Good thing I haven't bothered with a manicure lately, she thought. Today's activities would have trashed fancy nails. Who was she kidding? She hadn't treated herself to a manicure since their girls' weekend in Minneapolis well over a year ago. Pampering wasn't high on her list of activities—she had neither the time nor the money for that type of thing.

She set her phone aside and tugged at the corner of the board as best she could, but it barely moved. She got back up on her knees for better leverage. It looked like the panel was held in place with nails and not screws. She yanked again, putting more muscle behind it this time. The unmistakable screech of nails pulling out of wood filled the tiny alcove. More tugs and the panel eventually came off in her hands. She angled her body to set the panel carefully out of the way, the exposed nails pointing down.

"I feel like a treasure hunter," she uttered aloud, sitting down on the closet floor to get a better look at what the panel had concealed.

Her eyes widened.

There, standing on end and tucked between wooden studs, was a greenish metal box. Val reached out with her free hand to touch the dented metal. As her fingers brushed the cold surface, her mind struggled with a vague memory. She pushed her phone into her pocket and felt around in the near-dark, wrapping her fingers around the back edge of her find.

More footsteps creaked above her. Goosebumps climbed her arms.

The box was wedged in tight and it took two hands to dislodge it. When she finally broke it free of its hiding spot, a dense cobweb clung to the metal surface, stretching as Val stood with the box in her hands. She lifted the container as high as she could in order to break the stubborn strands of sticky web, using her tennis shoe to scrape off the offensive mess, praying any spiders were long gone.

Taking the box over to the back window for better light, Val could hear things rattling around inside. She fingered the padlock, her mind flying back to that first summer vacation at Whispering Pines with her family.

How could we have forgotten about this?

Another creak overhead snapped her back to the present. A grin spread across her face and she hurried out of the bedroom, the old tackle box banging against her leg. She burst out the screen door and skipped down the wooden steps two at a time.

"Hey, Ethan, look what I found!"

CHAPTER TWO

GIFT OF INTRIGUE

"What are you screaming about now, Val?" Ethan shot down at her from where he stood near the edge of the roof. "What the hell's wrong?"

Val spun, laughing up at her brother's irritated glare. The hot June sun glowed behind him, blinding her. She tried to shield her eyes with her free hand and hold the battered box high with the other, the surprising weight of her find forcing a grunt out of her.

"Sorry. Didn't mean to scare you. Recognize this?"

Ethan tilted his head to see what she was holding in his direction. She stood on her tiptoes and stretched, trying to give him a better view.

"Don't think so," he replied, shoving the hammer he held into a tool belt he wore low on his hips. He carefully lowered himself to sit on the edge of the small cabin's rooftop, his legs dangling over the edge above her. "Come closer."

Nodding, still grinning expectantly, Val again climbed the stairs. Grabbing the pitted metal stair rail for support, she stretched as far as she could and felt Ethan take hold of the box.

She skipped back down to the grass, feeling like a little girl again, as Ethan inspected the old tackle box. She hadn't thought about that box since she was a kid.

"I'll be damned," Ethan muttered, turning the box over in his hands.

How could we have forgotten about it? she wondered again.

As Val turned, tiny alarm bells rang as she spied her son and two nephews inching their way on their knees toward the edge of the roof, curious what Ethan was looking at.

"You kids be careful up there!"

Ethan glanced over his shoulder and held a hand up to stop them in their tracks. "Careful, guys. I'm not sure the roof can support all our weight on this edge. Tell you what—go climb down. It's time for a break anyhow."

Val jogged around the east corner of the cabin. "I'll hold the ladder!"

Soon, all five of them were gathered in a knot on the dead grass out front. Ethan still held the old metal box in his hands. He tugged at the hefty padlock.

"What is that thing, Dad?" Dylan asked. He stood behind Val, easily looking over the top of her head.

"You kids aren't going to believe this, but I think it's a time capsule your aunt and I put together the very first summer we came out here to Whispering Pines. Renee and Jess, too. I was like twelve or something."

A round of "No way!" and "Let me see!" echoed around the group.

"What are you guys doing?" a deep voice cut through the ruckus.

Val looked up to see Matt, her brother-in-law, and her sister, Renee, coming up the concrete walking path in their direction. "You aren't going to believe what I found, sis."

Renee approached, craning her neck to see.

"I found it in the closet, in the bedroom back there," Val explained, jabbing her thumb over her shoulder at the cabin. She watched Renee's face closely, anxious to see if she'd recognize the box. "By the way, you have paint in your hair."

Renee brushed absently at the top of her head as she reached them. "I'm sure I do. Painting ceilings is hard on the hairdo. Let me have a look." She stepped around her son, Robbie, to get a better look at whatever it was that was causing such a commotion. She paused. "But that closet was empty," she protested, staring down at the tackle box in confusion. "I looked in there myself, more than once."

"I know. *I* thought it was empty too," Val agreed. "But this was hidden in the back."

"What do you mean, *hidden?*"

Ethan and the boys continued to examine the box as Val explained to Renee, and everyone else, how she'd found it tucked behind a board she'd snagged with her broom.

"That is *so* cool, Mom," Dave said. He fought to keep his place beside Ethan as everyone vied to see. "Maybe it's full of money!"

Renee laughed. "We could use a box full of money about now, pal. But it's probably just junk."

"It isn't full of money," Ethan said, handing the locked box to Renee, a delighted grin still spread across his face. "I can't believe you don't recognize this."

"Well, excuse me for having a few too many things on my mind these days," Renee pointed out as she took the box. Val could see the moment recognition dawned on her sister's face.

"How could we have forgotten about this?" she asked, repeating Val's looping thought ever since she'd pulled it out of the back of the closet.

Matt laid a hand on his wife's shoulder. "Renee, do you care to fill the rest of us in on what has you three so excited?"

"Oh, hon, you aren't going to believe this," Renee replied, glancing up at her husband briefly before returning her intent stare to the old box. She turned it over in her hands. Things clunked and rattled around inside. "Back when we were kids, we filled this thing up with stuff. Like a time capsule. It was our first summer out here, and it was nearly time to go home. We were getting bored, so Ethan came up with the idea to put this together."

Val grunted. "Yeah, we were *bored*, Renee, because you'd sliced your leg open on that innertube, and Ethan's friend nearly died in the woods, so we weren't able to do much else."

"Dad, your friend almost died in the woods?" Dylan repeated, staring with concern into the dense thicket of trees and brush behind the cabin.

Ethan rubbed at his jaw, following his son's eyes. "Val exaggerates a bit, but yeah, we ran into some trouble that summer. That's a story for another day."

"That's a hefty padlock," Matt pointed out, reaching around Renee to finger the lock. "Got a bolt cutter around here, Ethan?"

"Probably in my truck."

"Wait, guys. We can't just open this thing up," Val interjected.

Ethan looked down at her in surprise. "Why not?"

Val threw her hands up in exasperation. "Well, for one, Jess would *kill* us if we opened it without her."

Jess, their other sister, would be back out to Whispering Pines later that afternoon.

Renee sighed, handing the box back to Ethan. "She's right, bro. They'll be here tonight for burgers. We better wait. In the meantime, we have lots of work to do over at the house. How are things coming over here?"

Val shrugged, hoping they'd replace that dubious expression on her sister's face by the time they had this little cabin fixed up. "Good, I think. Pretty much everything is out. I was cleaning when I found the box. The guys are getting started on the roof." She turned to the whole group. "Do you want me to show you where I found our old box?"

The boys and men in their group were loud enough in their assent to nearly drown out Renee's hesitant "Not really . . ." that Val thought she heard. The three boys hurried ahead of the adults, bounding up the steps and into the cabin. Ethan held out his hand, inviting Renee to go ahead. Val watched as Matt took Renee's hand and headed inside, gently pulling her behind him. Ethan rolled his eyes for Val's benefit.

"Be nice," she warned, poking him in the stomach as she headed in.

"If you four put the time capsule together when you were kids, why didn't you know where it was stashed?" Matt asked, glancing back at the box Ethan still carried and then around at the empty cabin.

"Wait. That's a great question, Matt," Val said, stopping so suddenly that Ethan ran into her from behind. She looked over her shoulder at her brother. "Did you stash it in that closet before we left that summer?"

Ethan gave Val a nudge to keep her moving. "No. Back then, there was this old guy who helped Celia keep this place up. He offered to hide it for us. That way we could make a game out of finding it later. I bet he didn't think we'd wait *this* long to find his hiding spot!"

Val shrugged as she pushed her way through the group, turning her phone's flashlight on as she did, and crouched down inside the back closet to show everyone where she'd found the box.

Robbie shook his head. "How could you guys forget about something like this?"

Renee smirked at her son. "You forget stuff, bud. It was a long time ago, and we weren't very old when we put it together. Ethan wasn't even a teenager yet. Val was barely out of diapers."

"Cute, sis." Val grimaced as she knelt on the wooden planks, her knees protesting. She probably wouldn't be able to get out of bed the next day. "I was at *least* five, wasn't I? But it was just something we did, Robbie. It was fun at the time, but then that was it."

"Until now," Renee concluded, crouching down next to Val. It was a tight squeeze. "What are the odds you'd find it back here? That board propped outside the closet was over this hole, huh? Guess that's why I never noticed it."

"Yep," Val said, shining her light into the gap in the wall. "Wait . . . you see that? There's an envelope or something on the floor in here."

She gave the envelope a hard shake as she pulled it out. Ugh—more spiderwebs.

"What is it?" one of the boys asked.

Val stood, groaning as her knees popped. "No idea. Should we take it outside?"

"Um, yes," Renee agreed. "It's too tight in here."

Val could feel the discomfort rolling off her sister. They'd managed to empty out the old cabin, but the space still obviously made Renee uncomfortable. Hopefully they'd be able to change that with their planned improvements.

Val led the parade back out onto the lawn. In the sunlight, she could make out the names on the front of the envelope, although the ink was smeared and faded. " 'Ethan, Renee, Jess, and Val,' " she read out loud. "Guys, this looks like *Celia's* handwriting, doesn't it?"

She held the envelope up so her brother and sister could better see the inscription across the front.

"Definitely," Renee said, nodding excitedly, her discomfort seemingly forgotten. "We should probably wait and open the letter when Jess is here, too, don't you think?"

A round of disappointed sighs rose from the boys, but Ethan held up a hand. "Guys, be patient. I'm sure your grandparents will want to see what's in here, too. It'll give you something to look forward to as you're ripping those old shingles off the roof this afternoon. It's going to be a long, hot few hours."

Now it was a round of disappointed groans.

* * *

At five o'clock, Ethan and Val decided they'd done enough on the Gray Cabin for their first day. Jess had called to say they were done at the auction they'd spent the day at and she'd pick up groceries for the barbeque. Val hadn't told her what they'd found, just that they had a surprise for her. Renee had called their parents, George and Lavonne, and invited them as well. They'd get a kick out of seeing what was in the time capsule.

The remodelers gathered in the coolness of the lodge, waiting for everyone else to arrive, making plans for what they hoped to accomplish on the cabin the following day.

"Now it's you guys that *stink!*" Val complained, waving her hand in front of her face as she dug a first-aid kit out of a kitchen drawer and began rummaging for a tweezer. Dylan was complaining about a sliver in his finger.

Renee flung open windows and the back door so fresh air would cut through the thick, unmistakable odor of a day spent doing hard work under an early summer sun.

Val found what she was looking for and directed Dylan to sit on a stool next to the island. She captured his hand, and it wasn't long before he was squirming as she worked to remove the nasty splinter from his left thumb.

"Ouch, Aunt Val, jeez . . . that hurts!" he whined.

"Don't be such a pansy, Dyl," Robbie shot over his shoulder as he dug around in the fridge.

"Robbie, out of the fridge, and Dylan, hold still," Val ordered without looking up. She knew the unmistakable sound of someone rummaging through a refrigerator. Kitchens were always her domain, and they were all used to taking orders from her while in one.

Sighing, Robbie let the fridge door close. Dylan chewed on his lip, quiet now, while Val patched him up. She wrapped a band-aid around her nephew's finger and then stowed the first-aid box back where it belonged. Dave chilled nearby, his elbows resting on the kitchen island, staring with curious eyes at the tackle box now waiting in the middle of the stainless-steel countertop, a bolt cutter beside it.

"Hello, hello," a woman's voice rang out, announcing a new arrival. Jess entered carrying two bottles of soda, and she was followed by a man with a toddler on his hip. Plastic grocery bags threaded around the fingers of his free hand.

Val reached for the soda, discretely checking out her sister's ring finger at the same time. *Nothing.* A part of her wished Luke hadn't mentioned the conversation the guys had around the campfire a couple weeks back during their Memorial Day camping trip. Apparently Jess's boyfriend Seth had announced he planned to ask Jess to marry him. *"Boyfriend" sounds like such a weird term,* Val thought—but she didn't know how else to refer to Seth. They *were* dating, and even though Jess had just turned forty-six in May, she sometimes acted like a teenager around the man. So maybe the juvenile term worked in their case.

They'd all been impatiently waiting for a marriage proposal ever since the camping trip. Everyone except Jess. Val didn't think her sister had any idea Seth was already thinking about that level of commitment. If Jess didn't accept, Val would bop her over the head. Val was convinced Seth was the best thing to happen to her sister in a *very* long time—aside from the little girl he was holding, of course. Despite the unorthodox way little Harper had become Jess's youngest, the child had quickly found a permanent home in all of their hearts.

Val set the soda aside while Renee helped remove the knotted grocery bags from Seth's fingers. Seth set little Harper down on the floor, but the young toddler clung to his leg and began to cry. Caving to her noisy demands, he picked her back up with a sigh.

"Harper sounds just like you, Dylan. Crying like a baby," Robbie joked.

Dave burst out laughing at his cousin's expense.

Val rubbed at the tension building at the base of her skull. She'd had enough of their friendly bickering for the day, and a crying baby added to the mix brought her to her tipping point. "Out! Everybody that isn't going to help pull this meal together, get out of this kitchen right now," she ordered.

"Come on, Seth, Matt, I've got beer in the cooler out back," Ethan suggested, leading the parade of men out the back door.

Jess plucked her tired toddler out of Seth's arms as he passed her.

"Great, I could use a cold one," Robbie replied as he followed Ethan, but his comment earned the teenager scalding looks from both his uncle and his mother. "Kidding, just kidding!"

"Fine, you guys go outside, but you're all on clean-up duty!" Val shouted to their retreating backs, slamming cupboard doors as she started prepping their meal.

"How'd things go around here today?" Jess asked Val and Renee, setting Harper down with a stack of cups to play with. This time the child didn't fuss.

Val wondered when Jess would notice the box sitting in the middle of the island, and if she'd recognize it. Maybe Jess would see Celia's envelope, now tacked to the front of the fridge with a magnet, before she spied the time capsule, currently incognito in the form of a beat-up old tackle box.

"Things went great on our house," Renee jumped in, excitement in her tone. "I'm still hoping we can officially move in before the Fourth of July." She gestured at the paint in her hair, which she hadn't bothered trying to wash out. "We finished painting ceilings today."

Jess grinned at her big sister as she snagged a cold bottle of water out of the fridge. "Nice color."

Val laughed. "I love how you and Matt situated your new house back in the trees. Perfect spot! It'll give you some separation from the resort, plus a beautiful view of the lake."

Val truly was excited for her sister. Ever since reopening Whispering Pines and transitioning to her new career of running the resort, Renee and her two teenage kids had been living in a rundown old duplex on the edge of the property. Jess had moved into the other half of the duplex the previous summer. But ever since Renee had married Matt a year ago, their quarters had been tight—crowded, even—living in such close proximity to family. A shared wall couldn't provide much privacy. Val was actually surprised they were all still speaking.

Renee nodded. "It'll be so nice to have new appliances and no more shag carpet."

"Hey, don't bash the shag carpet," Jess warned. "I'm doing my best to incorporate that *vintage* aspect of the duplex into my decorating theme. The gold shag goes particularly well with the orange-striped wallpaper, don't you think?"

The sisters laughed. Val glanced between Renee and Jess. She knew they'd been doing too much "making do" in recent years. But they both had new, exciting things happening now, despite their struggles. Val was starting to feel like the odd woman out.

Again.

Same house, same kids, same man, same money struggles. Her sisters had both made changes in their careers, moved, and found amazing new men. Not that Val wanted to trade in her home or her man—at least not at the moment.

You've also avoided all the heartache, Val reminded herself. *Besides, I've always been the odd man—or girl—out.*

"Wait, what is that?" Jess asked, her tone snapping Val's attention back to the kitchen. "Why is that filthy old thing sitting in here, on the island. I don't think those cobwebs will go well with dinner."

Val laughed, tore a paper towel off the roll on the counter, and reached for their box. She cleaned the bottom off with a couple quick swipes and tossed the offending mess in the garbage. Setting the box down directly in front of Jess, she waited, hands on her hips.

"Still gross" was all Jess said before she turned away to pull paper plates out of one of the bags Seth had brought in.

"Seriously, Jess? I can't believe you don't recognize that," Renee said, pointing at the box.

Jess set the stack of plates on the end of the island, glancing back at the box. "What's the big deal? It looks like something from that auction Seth dragged me and Harper to today. He felt compelled to quiz me as to the original use of nearly every piece of old junk they sold. I failed miserably. This just looks like a banged-up, old metal box. For fishing, maybe? Hey, Val, wasn't Luke taking the boys out in the boat today? Did they forget this?"

"You failed this quiz miserably, too! I hate to point out the obvious, Jess, but why would an old tackle box be locked with a big padlock like that?" Val teased.

Finally, Val saw recognition dawn on Jess's face. Slowly, Jess picked up the box, turned it over, and ran a finger over the long, narrow dent in the surface. Eventually, Jess said, "Holy crap. Is this what I think it is?"

Renee nodded. She stood next to Val and put an arm around her waist, smiling. "Our baby sister here decided to play Nancy Drew, and she found that thing behind a false wall in the back of the bedroom closet in the Gray Cabin."

"No friggin' way," Jess whispered. She grabbed hold of the hefty lock and tugged. "Let's open this sucker up!"

Val laughed. "That's the plan! But we wanted to wait for Mom and Dad to get here, too, before we cut the lock off. I think they'd get a kick out of seeing what we put in there after all these years. Oh, and there was something else."

Val wriggled away from Renee and went to the fridge, plucking the magnet off the stainless-steel surface. She took down the sealed envelope and handed it to Jess. "Recognize the handwriting?"

Jess stared at the envelope, eyes widening. "Of course. Only Celia could write in cursive like that! Was this with the box?"

Val nodded, but before she could say more, the outside door directly into the kitchen burst open and her husband and three young fishermen descended upon them with complaints of starvation and thirst. Her boys were *always* hungry. At nearly the same time, her parents entered the kitchen from the other direction.

"Did we miss the burgers?" her father asked, hands extended. "Your mother was late getting home from her bridge game."

Food first, then we can open things, Val thought, taking the envelope back from Jess and stowing it and the box on a back counter, out of the way.

They'd already waited almost forty years to open it. Another thirty minutes wouldn't matter.

CHAPTER THREE

GIFT OF CHILDHOOD WISHES

*H*ungry kids and adults alike devoured the burgers and hotdogs in record time. Grilling and paper plates made for quick cleanup. Val ran back into the lodge kitchen to retrieve the old tackle box, Celia's envelope, and the bolt cutter.

She noticed Luke following close behind. "Since you didn't come in with a stringer full of fish earlier, I take it no one caught any keepers?"

Luke grinned. "Actually, the boys caught a few nice ones. They're still in the cooler down by the water."

"You better bring them up here, then, and start cleaning them. You know the rules. You catch 'em, you clean 'em."

Coming up behind her, Luke put his arms around Val's waist and squeezed, then let his right hand sneak upward to brush the bottom of her breast. She swatted at his hand.

"Luke! Knock it off. One of the kids might walk in."

"Relax. No one is going to come near the kitchen when there's food to put away, Val."

Her irritation notched up over both his wandering hands and the truth in his words. She tried to wriggle out of his arms.

"Why don't you like me to touch you anymore?" Luke whispered, still managing to hold Val close as he nuzzled his face against her neck.

Val couldn't help but giggle at the tickle of Luke's breath against her skin. "Luke. I'm serious. Knock it off."

With a sigh, Luke backed away. When Val spun to face him, her arms crossed, the smile she'd heard in his voice had slipped away. "Where have I heard that before?" he asked, though she knew he wasn't expecting an answer. Not that she'd have given one. She was tired of this back and forth, Luke acting like a neglected husband. She didn't have time for his pouting. He got as much of her time and attention as she had left to give.

And right now, people were waiting for her outside.

Ignoring the temptation to remind him of this, she pivoted. "Come back outside with me. I have a surprise for you. I found something today."

Luke shook his head. "Sorry, babe, I promised I'd take the boys back out on the water after we finished eating. Can it wait? The old guy at the bait shop said the fish have been hitting hard at sundown. Didn't you notice how antsy Jake was? He didn't even eat a second hotdog. I need to grab the bug spray or those mosquitoes will eat us alive out there when the sun goes down."

Val bit the inside of her cheek in an attempt to avoid another argument. She was used to Luke putting the boys' desires ahead of her own. Heck, she knew she did the same thing more times than not.

Besides, she and her siblings had put the time capsule together well before Luke entered the picture. And if Luke took three of their four boys back out in the boat, that meant she'd be free to focus on what was inside her discovery instead of worrying whether or not the boys were getting into trouble.

"Fine. Go fish. I'll show you the surprise later."

Luke's smile flashed back. He grabbed her in for a quick kiss, giving her breast a brief squeeze in the process, too fast for her to even bat his hand away this time. Despite her near constant vexation with the man lately, she couldn't help but let out one short bark of laughter. How was it he was able to irritate her and curl her toes at the same time? Despite four kids and years of marriage, he could still charm her with his dimples and his touch.

"Dad!" a young voice yelled through the screen door. "Are we going or what? Does Mom have snacks for us?"

Glancing over his shoulder toward Jake, their youngest, Luke motioned with his head for the boy to come inside. "Come grab the garbage, Jake. Take it out to the big metal dumpster on the north side of the lodge. Be sure to get the lid back on tight, too. Then grab the green can of bug spray out of my truck. We'll go in a minute."

Jake came in, mumbling about having to do everything. *A claim with absolutely no merit.* Luke must have sensed the harsh words on the tip of Val's tongue, holding up a hand in her direction to silence her.

"What did you say?" Luke asked the boy in a stern voice. "Because if that was a complaint, we'll skip the fishing tonight."

Jake paused, hands clasped behind his back, a serious expression on his face. "Nope, not complaining, Dad. Is there anything else?"

Val rolled her eyes. Jake's quick comeback—a bit *too* quick for sincerity—meant he'd still get to fish until dark, just like he'd wanted. Luke *thought* he was in charge, but Val knew their youngest could get pretty much anything he wanted out of his father. Good thing she wasn't such a sucker for the sweet talker.

But then again, maybe she was. Jake was an awful lot like his father.

* * *

"Ethan said you had a surprise for us, Val," her dad, George, said, standing to take the old tackle box out of her full hands. "Is this the surprise?"

"It is, Dad," Val confirmed, setting everything else, except Celia's letter, in the grass—the bolt cutter and two beers people had requested—and sinking into the lawn chair to her father's right. She tucked Celia's envelope under her leg. She was anxious to open their time capsule, but she allowed herself a moment to enjoy the soft breeze and the hum of insects one could only hear at twilight. It had been a strenuous day of work in the Gray Cabin and then feeding the big, hungry crew that was her family. It felt good to get off her feet.

The sun was just starting to sink behind the tall pines in the west, the sky a mixture of gold, orange, and turquoise. George held the box higher to get a better look at it in the fading light. "What is it?"

"You'll see in a minute," Ethan said from his seat across the circle of lawn chairs.

George shook his head. He handed the box back to Val and sat down.

"How about you, Mom?" Renee asked. Lavonne was relaxing next to Ethan, drinking white wine from a plastic margarita glass. "Do *you* know what this is?"

Lavonne squinted at the box in Val's lap, a small, almost secretive smile softening her expression. "Hmm. Perhaps."

"I know *I* didn't tell you or Mom about it," Ethan said. "Celia's friend, that old guy—what was his name?—he helped us find a box to use back then, and he offered to hide it for us. That was our first summer out here as kids, wasn't it?"

George leaned back, crossing his legs, and glanced at each of his four adult children. "What old guy? What's this about my sister Celia? Why am I in the dark here?"

Ignoring the string of questions, Ethan set the bottle of beer he'd been nursing down on the grass and stood, cursing under his breath when it toppled over and the little bit of liquid remaining spilled out. He waved dismissively at the tipped bottle and crossed over to take the box from Val. He then picked up the bolt cutter from where she'd dropped it in the grass moments earlier.

"Someone want to hold this with their foot?" he asked, setting the box down in the middle of their circle.

Dylan popped up to assist. Ethan showed him where to plant his size-twelve foot to anchor the box while he worked to snap the old, heavy-duty padlock. After two failed attempts, the lock finally snapped open and Dylan stepped back.

"Who wants to do the honors?" Ethan asked, glancing at each of his three sisters.

"Why don't you do it, Ethan? Putting together a time capsule that summer was your idea," Renee suggested. Jess and Val nodded their agreement.

"Time capsule, huh?" George said, watching with interest.

Val quickly explained how she'd found the box hidden away in the closet.

Seth, sitting next to Jess, leaned forward. "I've stumbled across a time capsule or two in my day, but never one stowed away in an old tackle box."

It made sense that Seth would be interested in time capsules. He worked in old buildings, salvaging architectural pieces and reselling them. Jess had met the man through his business. Val smiled at the way Seth put his arm across the back of her sister's lawn chair—and wondered for the umpteenth time when he'd get up the nerve to pop the question.

"When you're twelve years old and have no one left to hang out with at the lake except your little sisters, you have to get creative. Find a way to kill the boredom somehow," Ethan said with a smirk.

"Well, your friend wouldn't have had to leave early that summer if you hadn't been so gullible," Renee said, returning Ethan's smirk.

"What do you mean, 'gullible'?" Ethan asked, still standing over the now-unlocked metal box, the bolt cutter in his hand and a perplexed look on his face.

Renee's comment earned her curious glances from around the circle of chairs. Val wasn't sure what her sister meant either, and thought maybe Jess was the only one who looked like she understood Renee's snarky comment.

Renee simply shrugged, feigning an innocent look.

"Whatever," Ethan said, kneeling down beside the box.

Val laughed. She wasn't sure what her sister was talking about, but she couldn't help but think both Renee and Ethan were acting like the children they'd been when they'd filled the box with curiosities back in 1980. Some things would never change.

Ethan flipped back the lid on the box. A white envelope, seal side up, concealed any other contents. Ethan picked it up and flipped it over.

" 'Renee,' " he read, then removed three more envelopes, each with one of their names penned across the front in varying styles of child-like penmanship. "I forgot about these damn letters you made us write to put in here, Renee."

As he stood back up he let out a heavy groan. "Those old shingles did a number on my knees this afternoon. Here." After he'd handed an envelope to each sister, he sank back into his own chair.

Robbie, who'd been poking the logs in the firepit, trying to get a bonfire to light, took three steps toward the now-exposed contents in the box, but Seth stopped him with a hand on the teen's forearm.

"Let them read the letters first, Rob."

"Sorry." Robbie nodded. "I've been dying to see what's in the box since Val showed it to us *hours* ago."

"I remember helping you write that letter, Val," Lavonne said, waving a finger in her direction.

"So much for not telling Mom or Dad about our time capsule," Ethan said, shaking his head.

"What? I was a little kid and needed some help," Val reminded her brother. "She didn't tell Dad. Mom was always good at keeping secrets."

"Always," George tossed in.

Val turned her attention back to Lavonne.

"Mom, I remember sitting with you at that old picnic table between our cabin and Celia's, but I can't remember what I told you to write," Val said, fingering the clumsy letters scrawled on the front of the envelope. It was hard to believe she'd been a year younger than Jake when she'd penned her own name.

Where have the years gone?

"Do you kids want to read the letters out loud?"

Val glanced up at her father. "I don't know, Dad. That might be embarrassing."

"How embarrassing can the words of a four-year-old be?" Jess asked.

"I was *five*, Jess," Val countered.

She carefully inserted her finger under the edge of the seal to open the envelope without tearing the letter inside. She remembered dictating the actual contents of the letter to her mother. She probably could have done it herself—she'd taken to writing fairly quickly—but Val seemed to recall wanting her mom to be part of it, too.

Removing the folded letter, Val smiled at the stationery. It read *Whispering Pines—the perfect family getaway!* across the top. "Look, they even had real stationery back then."

"That was back when people still used snail mail," Dave, who had been sitting quietly in the grass next to Robbie's chair, chimed in knowingly. "No one sends real letters anymore, so Aunt Renee doesn't need stationery."

"Letter writing is a lost art, honey," Lavonne added, winking at her grandson.

"What does it say, Mom?" Dave asked.

"Do I have to read it out loud?"

"Please," he encouraged.

Taking a deep breath, Val sat taller in her lawn chair and began to read.

" 'Hi. If you are reading this now, you have found our time capsule. My big brother and sisters thought it would be fun to put letters in here, to go with some of our favorite things, and maybe we can find them all when we are grown up. Renee said to list things we like to play with, and to watch, and to listen to.' "

Val paused to glance at Renee and then their mother. "Did you have to write it all down verbatim, Mom?"

"Of *course* I did."

With a slight shake of her head, Val continued, curious what she'd asked her mom to write for her so long ago. "Good news, everyone. It's short. Okay, where was I? 'I love my *Boxcar* books. They are about four brothers and sisters that live in an old, deserted railroad car all by themselves in the woods. I can kind of read them, but it is more fun when Renee or Jess read to me. If they are too busy, I like Mom to read it to me.' "

As Val read the words she'd scribed to her mother, she was reminded of how, as a young girl, she'd often felt left out. Her two older sisters were inseparable back then, even though they fought constantly. They had little time for their younger sister, so Val did her best to pretend she didn't care, instead doing things like learning how to bake and cook beside their mother.

Funny how things hadn't changed much in the years since.

She continued reading. " 'Besides books, I like watching cartoons on Saturday morning. *Scooby-Doo* is my favorite, but I like *The Flintstones*, too. I love to bake cookies and make art. Someday maybe I will be a teacher or cook in a fancy restaurant or own a bakery. I haven't quite decided yet.' "

Soft laughter rippled around their circle.

"I'm not surprised you didn't know at five what you wanted to be when you grew up, Val," Jess said. "I'm *forty*-five, and some days I still feel like I don't know."

"Ah, correction—you are forty-*six*, sister. You just had a birthday last month," Renee chimed in.

"Argh . . . thanks for the reminder, sis," Jess said with a sigh, shifting Harper from one shoulder to another. The toddler had fallen asleep as soon as they'd finished eating, tired out.

"Almost done," Val said, pulling everyone's attention back to the contents of her letter. If they didn't read through the letters faster, it would get too dark to see what else was in the box. " 'My favorite toys are my Easy-Bake Oven and my Farrah Fawcett Glamour Center.' "

"What's Farrah Fawcett?" Dave asked as the older people snickered.

"Who, not what," Ethan corrected his nephew. "Farrah was a gorgeous actress, Dave, back when I was your age. Smoking hot. I'd forgotten your mom *used* to like playing with makeup."

"Ha-ha, Ethan," Val said, suddenly hyperaware of her makeup-free face, despite the obsession she used to have over girly things.

Val started to fold up the letter.

"Wait, Val. We were each going to write down one wish for the future," Renee said. "Did you write one at the end of your letter?"

"No, I read you what I wrote," Val lied, stuffing the letter back into the envelope. She caught the confused look her mother gave her over the open time capsule and she shook her head ever so slightly at the older woman. She wasn't obligated to share her childhood ramblings with anyone. "Okay, who's next?"

With attention diverted, Val fingered the envelope in her lap, the final words of her letter ringing in her head.

When I grow up, I want to have a daughter and travel all around the world with her. We'll go to Paris and learn how to make the best spaghetti ever, like in The Aristocats.

She'd forgotten how she used to think it would be fun to travel the world and work with fabulous chefs. She'd always hoped for a daughter someday, someone she could share her love of cooking with, like she had done with her own mom. Was she disappointed none of that had actually come true? She'd never even gotten her own passport, and she was raising a houseful of boys that only cared about *eating* food. Not a single one of them had showed any interest in learning how to *prepare* the food.

Maybe looking back at the hopes and dreams she'd had for herself as a kid wasn't such a good idea after all. It was kind of depressing, if she was being honest.

Renee's voice cut through her thoughts. Her sister was listing all of her favorite things, including her favorite book (*The Secret Garden*), her favorite TV show (*The Love Boat*), and her favorite movie (*The Shining*).

"Why am I not surprised you'd list *Love Boat*, Renee? All you cared about back then was boys," Val chimed in, anxious for a distraction. But her eyes were drawn to the now-deepening shadows in the woods beyond the edge of the resort at the mention of *The Shining*. She'd always hated that classic horror movie. And she'd never really gotten over her fear of the dark.

"Boys, huh?" Matt repeated with a grin. "What were you, like, ten years old? Already chasing boys?"

Renee laughed, angling over to plant a quick kiss on her husband's lips, her lawn chair dipping precariously. Matt righted her chair. "Not chasing, honey, only *dreaming* of them back then. And reading about them. I admit, I used to be a bit obsessed with boys."

They each continued reading the contents of their letters to the group.

Renee's wish to someday marry Shaun Cassidy, a teenage heart-throb of those days, earned a round of groans when Jess started singing his signature song, "Da Doo Ron Ron." Renee covered her ears, complaining that the words would be stuck in her head now for the rest of the night. "How can I remember the words to a song I haven't heard for decades, but I can't ever remember where I put the car keys?"

"Did you know a girl band named The Crystals sang that song first, in the early sixties?" George pointed out. "Your boy Shaun just sang it as a cover."

Renee whipped her head in George's direction, her face shocked. "Dad, how could you *ruin* such a perfect childhood memory for me?" Renee asked in mock disbelief.

"My turn," Ethan said, seemingly unimpressed with his dad's knowledge of old music.

Ethan, who'd been less than thrilled as a kid at the requirement to write a letter for their box, had kept his short and sweet. He'd listed his favorite movie as *The Empire Strikes Back*, TV show as *The Dukes of Hazzard*, and favorite hobbies as skateboarding, baseball, and football.

"Did you list a wish?" George asked.

Ethan snorted. "I was not a *sappy* twelve-year-old, Dad."

"All right, Jess, you're up," Lavonne directed.

Jess pulled out her letter and followed her siblings' example, quickly reading through it.

"Isn't there some controversy right now about that show?" Lavonne asked when Jess's letter talked about her favorite book and TV show, *Little House on the Prairie*.

Jess nodded. "Actually, there is. Some people don't like how life on the prairie and Native Americans were depicted in the book. But that isn't anything new. Lots of classic books come under scrutiny at some point. People's points of view evolve over time, but books are written in pen and ink. I'm not going to let today's debates over the validity of the stories tarnish my childhood memories."

Lavonne nodded, letting the subject drop.

"I hate to admit this," Ethan said, standing once all four letters had been read, "but you were right to suggest the letters, Renee. That was fun—like having a little peek into our much younger selves. But it's getting dark and that wimpy fire Robbie started isn't keeping the mosquitoes away. Let me show you what else is in here. Dylan, come here, I'll hand you the stuff as I take it out."

Dylan rose and came up next to Ethan, glancing into the box curiously.

"I'll pull something out," Ethan said to his sisters, "and if it was yours, claim it."

He plopped down onto the grass and began pulling things out one at a time.

First came a rolled-up piece of paper and a photograph. Renee rose to take them from her nephew. Waving the roll in the air, she explained it was a drawing of Whispering Pines and they could all look at it when they went inside with better light.

"And this is one of my favorite pictures of Aunt Celia," she said. "I want to frame it and put it on our new mantel. None of us would be here if not for Celia."

Murmurs of agreement came from around the circle of lawn chairs. This very place was one of the ways their aunt had changed all their lives: Celia had passed Whispering Pines on to Renee at her death a few years earlier.

Dylan fingered the miniature Rubik's Cube his dad handed to him —the third item Renee had stowed in their box. "I've always wanted to try one of these."

"And here is my stuff," Ethan said, removing a cassette tape and a large stack of baseball cards held together with a rubber band. The band, brittle with age, snapped as he handed the stack to Dylan, and the stack of cards tumbled into a mess at their feet. "Careful, Dylan!"

Dylan, Robbie, and Dave all helped pick up the cards.

"Can we check these out, Dad?" Dylan asked, knowing his cousins would be just as interested as he was to see if there were any hidden gems in the stack.

"When we're done here, guys. Hold on."

"Val, this pet rock has to be yours. And the Barbie?"

Renee laughed. "I remember when you put her in there, Val. We were worried you'd be mad the next day when you couldn't play with your Barbie anymore. And didn't you make a whole *family* of pet rocks during that vacation?"

"I did!" Val laughed. "I was maternal even then. How about Jess? Where's her stuff?"

"Jeez, patience never was your strong suit, was it, little sis?" Ethan sighed, chuckling.

Val shrugged unapologetically. "We still need to read Celia's letter, too."

Ethan pulled out a slim newspaper and a well-used paperback copy of Jess's favorite book. "Jess's stuff was so big it had to go on the bottom."

"Let me see that," George said, reaching for the newspaper.

Jess laughed. "Now I remember! I took that from the bathroom after you were done reading it, Dad."

This was met with groans and laughs. George simply grinned and set the folded newspaper on his lap. "I'll read it inside."

"Just keep it out of the bathroom, dear," Lavonne added. "That thing is nearly an antique now."

Val stood up. "Well, that was fun. Why don't we move this inside before we all get malaria from these mosquitoes? I still want to read Celia's letter, but it's gotten too dark."

"Wait. Sit down, Val. There's one more thing in here."

Val couldn't imagine what was left in the box, but she did as her brother ordered and took her seat again.

Ethan turned to Jess. "What was it you said your wish was, sis?"

Jess threw her hands up in exasperation. "Really, Ethan? You're going to make me repeat myself? Isn't that a tad bit sadistic?"

Ethan just shrugged, waiting for a response.

"Fine, if you're going to be an ass, I'll repeat myself. My letter said my wish was to someday be the editor at a big newspaper, marry a kind, handsome man, and live happily ever after. Obviously, none of that is going to come true since newspapers are fading out of existence and my marriage was a sham. Must you rub it in?"

"Ethan, be nice," Lavonne scolded.

Val couldn't figure out why Ethan seemed to be pestering Jess. She watched as he reached into the box and pulled out something small and dark. He held his hand out, palm up, and now she could see a small, black box resting there. It suddenly dawned on her what Ethan might be up to.

Is that . . . ?

She looked to Renee and saw her face light up as well. Their eyes met, nods were exchanged, and Renee stood up. She walked over to Jess with her arms extended.

"Why don't you let me take Harper. I can run her back to the duplex and lay her down," Renee said, taking the limp child from her sister. Jess's face reflected her obvious confusion, but she handed over the child.

"Seth, I believe this is yours," Ethan said, continuing to hold up the small box.

Seth rose without a word, took the tiny, velvet-covered box from Ethan, and turned back to Jess, his face serious. Val watched, joy replacing her exhaustion after their long day and her own less-than-inspiring trip down memory lane.

If Jess says no, I'm giving up on her.

A soft gasp from her mother—Lavonne had caught on, too. Everyone else was silent around their family circle as Seth sank to one knee.

Jess snapped her mouth shut, her eyes wide open. A tiny smile appeared and Val thought she could see a sheen in her sister's eyes.

Seth held the now-open ring box in the palm of his hand, much as Ethan had done, in front of Jess. With his other hand on her knee, he took a deep breath. "Jess, hon, do you believe in second chances? I can't help with the whole newspaper part, but maybe I could do something about the marriage and the happily ever after."

A tear slid down Jess's cheek. Val dimly heard Harper squirm in Renee's arms. Jess laid her hand on top of Seth's on her knee, a wide smile now lighting up her face.

"I do, Seth. I do believe in second chances. And I'd love to marry you."

Cheers and laughter erupted around their circle.

Jess hadn't even given Seth a chance to ask those four little words.

She is every bit as impatient as I am, Val thought, clapping in delight over her sister's new chance at happiness.

CHAPTER FOUR

GIFT OF A MOTHER'S INSIGHT

"Quick, shut the door before every mosquito in Minnesota gets in here!" Val cried as the whole group piled into the lodge. She was shivering, either from the spring chill in the air, excitement over Seth's proposal, or both. She still clutched two envelopes in her hand—her own letter and Celia's.

"*Brrr*, it got chilly!" Lavonne declared, rubbing her upper arms. "Is there any decaf in here? Are your boys still out in the boat, Val? They need to come in. There isn't a light on that fishing boat. They can't be out in the dark."

"I'm sure they'll be back shortly," Val said, glancing at the time display on the oven clock.

As if on cue, the rest of her crew came bursting through the back door.

"Catch any more tonight?" George asked the cluster of excited boys. Her father loved to fish, but hadn't been able to go along, as the old aluminum fishing boat was already maxed out with Luke and the three boys.

"It *smells* like they caught plenty," Dylan said, waving his hand in front of his nose.

"Caught four big walleye and some other stuff," Jake declared, strutting up to his much taller cousin, hands on his hips. "Bet you couldn't catch that many, Dyl."

Dylan's hands shot out and he caught Jake up under his armpits, swinging him around and tickling him mercilessly. Jake's screeches echoed throughout the large kitchen.

Luke strode in with a large cooler in his arms, grunting as he hoisted it a little higher to set it down on the island. A bit of water sloshed onto the surface despite the closed lid.

"Oh no, you don't," Val declared, grabbing up a roll of paper towels and thrusting them at her husband. "You can't clean those in here."

Luke rolled his shoulders, rubbing at his left one that always gave him trouble. "I know. We'll take care of it over at the old fish-cleaning station out back, but we had to grab the filet knife and some bowls. Is the hose attached yet for fresh water?"

"For God's sake, why didn't you just leave them outside?" Renee asked.

Val caught the look Luke shot in Matt's direction, but this time she kept her mouth shut. Normally Luke wouldn't bring a cooler full of uncleaned fish inside. She wondered if something was up. Or *out* there. Wild animals were not unheard of in Minnesota lake country. Even a bear or two wandered in now and then. As the sheriff in the area, Matt might have warned Luke about a sighting. She'd have to ask one of them later.

"Boys," she jumped in, "grab the electric knife and a filet knife out of that drawer over there. Jake, bring two of those big plastic bowls off that stack under the island."

Jake groaned, claiming near starvation.

"You just ate a couple hours ago. Work first, then snacks," Val ordered. "Come on. You know the rules."

Matt stepped forward and grabbed hold of one of the handles on the cooler. "I'll help. It'll go quicker."

"Thanks, Matt," Val said, patting her newest brother-in-law on the shoulder. She suddenly realized he wouldn't hold that title for long. "Luke, have Matt update you on the latest news. You missed out."

Luke nodded his appreciation to Matt for the assistance and took hold of the other handle to lift the cooler up and off the island, leading his parade of young fishermen back out the door. "Anybody else want to learn how to clean fish, let's go," he threw over his shoulder.

Dave, Robbie, and Dylan followed them out the door. Val suspected they'd had enough adult talk. Fish guts must have sounded more appealing.

As the screen door slammed shut behind the group, Val grabbed Jess's hand to inspect the rock now glittering on her left ring finger. Renee joined her and all three sisters voiced their approval to Seth.

"We wondered what the hell he was waiting for," Val said as she gave Jess a quick hug.

"You knew?" Jess asked, surprised.

"We basically *all* knew except for you. Did you suspect? And by the way, Ethan, how did you get the ring into our old capsule? It was sealed up tight."

Ethan shrugged as he twisted his body in his habitual attempt to loosen up sore back muscles. "Earlier, when you were getting supper ready, I told Seth about the time capsule. We thought it would be fun to slip it inside the capsule if I had a chance. When the baseball cards fell in a mess on the grass, you were all distracted. Abracadabra!" he said, wiggling his fingers in her direction.

"I had no idea," Jess said, beaming.

"Well played, boys, well played," Lavonne complimented Ethan and Seth. "Now, can we maybe go sit upstairs in the library? Aren't you curious about what's in Celia's letter? It's getting late and we have to head home soon."

"Sure," Val agreed, motioning toward the stairs. "Celia's letters never seem to disappoint."

As she climbed the stairs behind her parents, Val thought back to the letter her Aunt Celia had left for her when she died. As she'd read her aunt's final words, it had felt like Celia was still right there in the room with her, reassuring her that life had so much to offer.

Once upstairs, the adults settled into comfortable chairs and sofas scattered around the casual library. Renee flipped on a small space heater to chase away the chill. "It's too late to start the fire up here tonight."

"You sit over here, Val, by this light, and read that letter," Lavonne instructed.

Val did as her mother instructed, settling back into a deep loveseat, crossing her ankles since her feet didn't quite reach the floor. She flipped on the table lamp, pulled out the contents of the envelope, and tilted the paper for a better view. Groaning, she reached for the spare pair of reading glasses someone had left on the end table.

Ethan started to comment, but Val killed his teasing with a glare. *I only need the readers because of the poor light,* she assured herself, hating the fact her near-perfect eyesight wasn't as nearly perfect as it used to be.

Able to make out the elegant handwriting through the glasses, she cleared her throat and began.

" 'Dear Ethan, Renee, Jess, and Val. If you are reading this letter, my fear that Wayne's hiding spot was too difficult was unfounded.' "

Ethan snapped his fingers. "*That* was his name!"

Val paused and looked up, grinning. "I wonder if Celia ever thought we'd be practically living out here as adults when we finally found it!"

"She'd be thrilled you're all here so often these days," George commented. "Keep reading."

Val nodded, then continued. " 'I have no way of knowing when, or even if, you (or someone else) will ever find your time capsule hidden here in the closet of this little cabin. This used to be my favorite cabin at the resort, back when I first started coming here with college friends. Small and cozy, it was perfect for one person, or a couple. But bad things have happened here.' "

Unable to help herself, Val peeked at Renee to gauge her reaction, but Renee's expression was closed off. She went on:

" 'I've been tempted to tear it down. However, I couldn't afford to lose the rental income. Wayne always insisted I was foolish to hate it so, and now I can see he might have been right about this, too, but I couldn't help how I felt. Besides, I never told Wayne the whole truth.' "

"Drum roll, please," Ethan interjected.

Val glanced over the readers at her brother. "Are you going to shut up and let me read this?"

"Sorry, sis. Continue."

" 'He thinks I dislike the cabin because of an old legend that claims the cabin was inadvertently built on top of the grave of a young Indian maiden and her newborn. The story of the ghost boys that Wayne told you around the campfire during your first visit isn't the only tale of ghosts walking this land. Some say they can hear the soft cries of a baby when it rains at night.' "

Val shivered at the thought. While she'd never heard any cries, the tiny cabin had given her the chills more than once. She could only imagine how Renee felt. She took a deep breath, then read on.

" 'I hope the old story has no basis. I personally have never heard a child's cries. No, my aversion to the place stems from an incident with an odd woman that was staying in the cabin when I came back here as an adult. She was the sister to the previous owner. When I took over the resort, she expected to stay on, rent-free. I couldn't afford to allow that, and when I had to eventually have her forcefully removed, she didn't go quietly. It was a nasty scene I'd block from my memory if I could. As the sheriff led her away in handcuffs, she cursed my little cabin. I thought it was all baloney at the time, but I've learned not to be so dismissive of that type of thing.' "

Renee smiled despite her aunt's dark message as Val took a beat to flip over the sheet of stationery. "I'd forgotten how often Celia liked to use the word 'baloney'!"

Jess nodded but said nothing, her expression glum.

"Why so serious?" Val asked, noticing Jess's pursed lips. "I would think as a newly engaged woman you'd be more *bubbly* tonight."

"Oh, I'm plenty bubbly," Jess said, a smile returning as she captured Seth's hand on her knee. He smiled next to her on the couch. "It's just that I had a dream once about a young woman holding a baby, sitting on a beach. *Our* beach, here, at Whispering Pines . . . and the woman was crying. In my dream, I remember worrying about the baby she held. The look on the girl's face was heartbreaking. That was the same night I found pictures of the Gray Cabin in that old resort book I showed some of you last summer."

Renee, seated on the floor across from Jess, pulled her knees up to her chest, wrapping her arms around her shins. "Be quiet, Jess. Don't tease about this. You know I'm already freaked out about that cabin."

"I swear to God, Renee, I'm not kidding. I wish I was."

Silence descended on the room. After another beat, Val continued.

" 'After that, the little cabin no longer gave me joy. I'm convinced her curse made it a magnet for trouble. Couples used to arrive at Whispering Pines, excited to be on vacation, but after spending only one night in the cabin, they'd argue and fight viciously, their trips ruined. Another time, an old man came with a new puppy, and the dog must have gotten into something, because it was found dead on the top of the cabin stairs early one morning.' "

"Jesus," Ethan muttered. "Why is she putting this in a letter to us? We were *kids*. Talk about morbid."

Val was thinking the same thing. Celia wasn't normally a doom-and-gloom type of person. She caught her father's eye, curious what he was thinking about the letter his big sister had left for them.

"Celia was always a practical woman," George reminded them. "Keep reading, Val. There has to be a reason she's sharing this with you kids."

"We were kids when Wayne hid our time capsule, Dad, but you can hardly call us that now," Val reminded him.

Was Celia trying to warn us about the curse?

Her mind flitted back to the incident that she was sure haunted Renee's dreams. Her poor niece . . . Jess couldn't be the only one bothered by nightmares.

Taking a deep breath, Val picked up where she'd left off. " 'It's been nearly thirty years since any of you have visited Whispering Pines. You probably assumed I sold the resort years ago.' "

"Wait—" George held up a hand. "I assumed Celia put that letter in with your time capsule back when her hired man hid it away in the closet. Read that part again, Val."

Val was equally confused. She repeated the passage, then paused again. "She must have slipped it in there much later. More than thirty years later, apparently. So she knew where it was hidden the whole time. She knew it was in a cabin that scared her, and she went anyway. But she would have been in her *eighties* when she did that." Val giggled despite her confusion over the timeline. "Can't you just see her, down on her knees, trying to force this envelope through the tiny gap?"

Lavonne pushed up out of her chair and walked over to the window to the left of the cold fireplace. She crossed her arms over her chest, looking out into the dark spring night beyond.

Her reaction seemed strange to Val. "Mom?"

Glancing back over her shoulder, Lavonne offered a small smile, first to Val then to each of her other grown children, before turning back to the window. "Celia asked *me* to do it."

George sat forward in his chair, resting his forearms on his knees, hands clasped. "What did Celia ask you to do?" he pressed his wife.

With a sigh, Lavonne turned around to face them all. "She'd invited me over for coffee one afternoon. She did that once in a while, and we always had a good visit. Even though Celia was twenty-plus years older than me, I like to think we were close. She surprised me that day, though. She informed me she wasn't getting any younger and she needed to get her affairs in order. 'Just in case' is what she said. She wanted to update some things in her will, get more specific in what she was planning to leave to each of you. She thought I might be able to help her with that." She nodded at the envelope in Val's hands. "And *that*."

Stunned silence followed Lavonne's brief explanation as to how Celia's letter ended up in the tiny closet.

Renee was the first to react. She stood up from her position on the floor, eyeing her mother closely, and plopped down into the empty spot on the loveseat next to Val. "You mean you *knew* Celia was going to leave this place to me? Leave me Whispering Pines? And you didn't think to *warn* me, Mom? You know, give me a little heads-up?"

Val could hear Renee's distress increasing. When she laid a hand on her sister's arm, Renee shrugged it off, still staring intently at their mother.

Lavonne hurried over, kneeling in front of Renee. From her vantage point, Val saw their mother grimace in pain. Lavonne had been battling problems with her knee for months. She took Renee's hands in her own. "I had to respect Celia's wishes, honey. Celia coming to me for input as to what to do with her estate was a surprise . . . and, frankly, an honor. She had ideas, but really wanted to be thoughtful with how she handled things. She could have simply requested everything be sold off after her death and the proceeds divided amongst you all, but she didn't want to do that."

"Why not?" Ethan asked, his tone curious. "That would have been more straightforward. Maybe more equitable, even."

Lavonne shook her head.

Seth stood and helped the older woman up out of her kneeling position. "Here, sit next to Jess," he instructed, helping her sit and then taking her old chair for himself.

Nodding her appreciation to Seth, she glanced back at George, as if trying to decide how to articulate her husband's sister's motives. "You kids know it was never about the money for Celia. She wanted all of you to live your best lives possible. She was convinced that in order to do that, you needed to find work you love *and* find ways to serve other people. It needed to go both ways. Money can't buy happiness. You four all know that. It was how Celia lived her own life."

Val considered her mother's words, trying to ignore the irritation rising in her chest at her mother's preachy tone, the one that always got to her.

"If any of Celia's worldly possessions could help you do those things, she wanted to give you a more direct line than just a wad of cash."

George grunted, shaking his head while a slow smile spread across his face. "I always wondered how Celia was so intuitive in what she gave to each of you. It makes sense that your mother had her hand in things."

"But I don't understand," Renee said, looking between her parents. "You have to admit, leaving me Whispering Pines doesn't appear to be an obvious choice. A single mom working a corporate job in

Minneapolis isn't exactly the ideal candidate to become a resort owner. Ethan would have been the more obvious choice."

"Celia was well aware of all that," Lavonne explained. "But, remember, she was always single, too, and I don't think she ever saw that as a handicap. She loved this place, and never forgot how much you used to love it, too. When you were young, Renee, you used to tell her you wanted to live out here with her. When we met over coffee, she was worried that your career was leaching the joy out of your life and hoped maybe this place could give you some of that joy back, like it had done for her."

Renee considered this for a second before responding. "I guess she wasn't all that far off the mark. What a lucky fluke that I got laid off and was in the hunt for a new career."

"Maybe it was fate, honey," Lavonne replied before turning to face Jess and Ethan. "You two, on the other hand, seemed to already enjoy what you did for a living, but she thought she might be able to enhance things for you. Jess, she appreciated your head for business. The people at the small businesses she was still working with up until her death were like family to her. She thought you might be able to help them keep their doors open."

"And she might have been matchmaking a bit too," Val threw in, winking at Seth. "Even though Jess was still saddled with her loser husband at the time, Celia probably suspected that wasn't going to last much longer."

Jess laughed, unoffended at Val's dig and probably still on an engagement high. "Turns out even Celia knew some of the crap Will was up to before I did. But I doubt she'd have put Seth and me together. I know *I* wouldn't have."

Seth gave a mock gasp, hand on his heart. "And you say that on the same day I propose to you? What is the matter with you, woman?"

Jess grinned over at her new fiancé. "She couldn't have helped but notice how cute you are, Seth, even if she had about forty years on you."

"Make that fifty years, hon," Seth said with an exaggerated wink.

Val laughed. It was a not-so-subtle reminder that *Jess* had some years on him, too. Val was glad to see that fact no longer seemed to bother Jess. *Much.*

"One of Celia's boyfriends, way back when, wasn't even forty yet when she was fifty-five," George offered. "Age was never an issue for her."

Lavonne jumped back in. "And you, Ethan. Celia knew how much you enjoyed running your own construction company. She hated the thought of selling off her investment properties and possibly displacing her long-term tenants. She hoped you would be able to handle the additional work of keeping up the units and at the same time appreciate some extra monthly cash flow."

Ethan sat back in his chair and crossed an ankle over one knee, pulling at his lower lip as he considered his mother's words. "All valid points, although we nearly lost three of her tenants in the fire."

"An unfortunate set of events that none of us could have foreseen," Lavonne replied. "And all's well that ends well."

Val knew her mother would finally get to her next. Given Lavonne's earlier comment around money and how it couldn't buy happiness, she was curious to hear why that was exactly what she'd received as an inheritance from her aunt.

"And that brings us to you, Val. You were the tricky one," Lavonne said.

Val blinked. "Tricky?"

"Yes, honey. Tricky. Let's see. You would have been about how old at the time?" Her mother questioned, looking up toward the ceiling and then down at her fingers, silently counting, before again making eye contact with Val. "Thirty years old—this was back when I sat down with Celia. You were married and David was a baby. You'd been working in a few different fields since getting your degree, but you were planning to stay home to raise your children."

Val's mind traveled back to those days. She'd yet to discover work she enjoyed, and once she became a brand-new mother, her mediocre job held no appeal. Luke promised to help her be home with baby David if that was what she wanted.

"Honestly, Celia felt conflicted. Never having had kids of her own, she admired your stance but couldn't really relate. She suspected the day might come when you'd be ready to go back to work or start something of your own, in addition to raising kids. Neither of us knew what that something might be, though, which is why she left you money. It was so you'd have options."

Val could tell her mother was choosing her words carefully, but the words still stung. They brought up many of the insecurities she'd been feeling lately. Their family had grown from one to four boys through the years, and it was getting hard to make ends meet on Luke's paycheck alone. Had her choice to stay home been selfish?

It wasn't as if she could justify buying an around-the-world plane ticket, as she'd dreamed of as a young child, with the money Celia had left her.

It would have lightened the burden to use her inheritance to fund some of their everyday expenses, but Celia's wish was for Val to use it to start some kind of business of her own when she was ready. Had Celia thought poorly of her, of how she was living her life? Had she viewed her lifestyle as somehow *not enough*?

Old insecurities washed through her, but Val refused to let her family see her distress.

"I get it, Mom. I love having options," she forced out, hoping no one would notice the truth in her eyes behind the reading glasses. "Should I read the rest of this? It's getting late."

"Yes, please do, dear."

Val nodded, once again angling Celia's letter toward the lamp and rereading the beginning of the paragraph.

" 'It's been nearly thirty years since any of you have visited Whispering Pines. You probably assumed I sold the resort years ago. But I could never bring myself to do that. You see, some of the best—and one could even argue the worst—days of my life happened at Whispering Pines. Even though your family stopped coming to the resort, I still found peace there, and I wanted to share it with other families.

" 'When I was a young woman, I promised someone very important to me that if I ever was in the position to protect Whispering Pines, I would. The stars aligned and I found myself in a position to do just that. But I'm not sure how much longer I'll be able to hang on. It's nearly time to pass the torch.' "

Val flipped to another page and glanced around at her family. All were watching her expectantly but George. His eyes were on the unlit fireplace.

" 'I've spent countless hours deciding which of you might love Whispering Pines enough to protect it against those that would raze the resort in the name of progress. The contents of your time capsule intrigue me, and I was tempted to break the seal to see if they might help me decide how I can help each of you. But you were young children when you put your capsule together. The dreams of children give little indication of what they may want later in life. At least, that's what I used to think. But now I realize my dream to spend as much of my time at Whispering Pines was born when I was a young woman, and that dream never left me.

" 'Since I knew opening your time capsule would be wrong, I'm doing the next best thing. Your mother is on her way over here to help me decide how I can best help each of you when the time comes to pass on my worldly possessions. A mother's insight is priceless. My wealth and properties will be but a start for each of you. It'll fall on you to actually use those things to help you live your best lives. No one but you can do those hard things that are often necessary for you to accomplish all you seek.

" 'So why this letter? Because I allowed my love for this tiny cabin to be tainted. I can see now, with the beauty of hindsight, that I was wrong to let such a peaceful little place deteriorate. I wish I would have maintained my favorite cabin and ignored the crazy woman's tirade that awful day. I felt guilty, as she likely had nowhere else to go. I let her anger plant nasty seeds of fear and darkness in my mind.

" 'If, as a family, you are continuing on with my tradition of protecting Whispering Pines, please consider bringing my little cabin back from the brink. It was once a joyful place. I think it could be again. Just like so many of my dreams, it has been buried under layers of silt and dismay. Please make it special again. Instead of being the eyesore of the resort, it could be its brightest gem. It isn't really a bad place. Bless you all. Love, your aunt, Celia.' "

Val returned the glasses to the side table, slowly folded the pages of Celia's letter, and stowed them back inside the envelope, pondering her aunt's words. Did Celia die with unlived dreams still inside her? Her letter seemed to indicate that this was indeed the case. But she was gone now, so they'd probably never know what those dreams used to be.

George stood, holding a hand out to his wife. "Come on, Lavonne. It's late and these kiddos are all tired. Ethan and Val put in a long day doing exactly what Celia hoped for—polishing up the Gray Cabin. And Matt and Renee have been working tirelessly on their new house."

Val followed her father's lead and stood, shaking her foot that had fallen asleep when she'd mindlessly tucked it up underneath her while reading the letter. "And let's not forget Jess and Seth's monumental day!"

Lavonne took George's hand and he pulled her to her feet. "I hope none of you are mad at me for keeping my mouth shut about helping Celia. It wasn't my place to say anything."

"We know that, Mom," Renee assured the older woman as she looped her arm across Lavonne's shoulders. "But I don't understand how this letter got in the closet."

Lavonne shrugged. "How do you think it got in there? Celia had me drive her out here the next day. It was midsummer and hot. We wandered around the resort, visiting with her caretakers, and then she had me slip the letter into the hiding spot. By then, no one was using the old cabin anymore."

"Would you have eventually told us about the hiding spot, Mom?" Ethan asked. "You know, if Val hadn't found it today?"

"Perhaps," Lavonne replied, noncommittal.

"Well," Renee said, squeezing her mother's shoulders, "I guess now we all know that if there's a secret we need kept, you can be trusted with it, Mom!"

CHAPTER FIVE

GIFT OF BICKERING BOYS

*A*fter a long, hot Monday of laundry and shuffling kids between baseball practice, basketball camp, and home again, with a quick trip to the neighborhood pool tossed in, Val was ready to relax over a glass of white wine. Her body was still sore following two full days working on the Gray Cabin. She didn't want to argue with the kids about who should clear the dishes following their quick meal and had to fight the urge to clean up the mess herself. *It would be faster to do it myself, but I'm not raising lazy kids.* At least she was trying not to.

"*Mommm*, I cleared the table last night," nine-year-old Noah whined as he stood in front of an open refrigerator with a bottle of ketchup in his hand. "It's Dave's turn."

"Put that on the third shelf from the top and shut that fridge door, Noah!" Val yelled from across the room, where she struggled to pull the overflowing garbage liner out of the twenty-gallon plastic container. "Dave twisted his ankle at practice, so he gets a pass tonight. Get the dishes in the dishwasher and then take this out."

The boy jammed the condiment into a too-small slot on the appropriate shelf, slammed the fridge door, causing bottles to jangle, and slouched back over to the table. He piled multiple plates on top of each other, pivoted on his heel toward the dishwasher, and bumped into Jake. His little brother was bent over the dog bowl, pouring in kibble. The top dish slid from the stack and hit the floor with a crash, the unrelenting tile busting the old Corelle plate into smithereens.

Val stopped mid swipe in her effort to clean the countertop on the kitchen island with her rag. *One, two, three . . .* She breathed deeply as she fought to grab hold of her temper. Its tail had a nasty whip. She bit her tongue to keep it from snapping.

"Noah, how many times do I have to tell you to be careful? Jake and Logan, get out of here. Now. Take Storm and get out of the kitchen before someone cuts their foot open on this mess. Noah, grab the dustpan and broom and get to work. I'll go get the vacuum."

"Way to go, klutz!" Logan shot over at Noah as he hoisted their sixty-pound golden retriever into his arms. Storm laid her snout on his shoulder, her calm eyes gazing back at Val, as if reminding her owner to be patient with this rowdy group. Val offered up a prayer of thanks for the one other female in this family, even if she was a dog. Despite her reservations about adding a puppy into their already hectic schedule two years earlier, Storm had been a blessing. At least if you didn't count the eight-hundred-dollar vet bill she cost them when she ate Dave's jockstrap.

"Screw you, Logan," Noah zinged back.

Val didn't even bother to reprimand Noah for his sharp tongue. Her middle two boys, just eleven months apart in age, were constantly at each other's throats. She was too exhausted to yell at them, or to ground Noah like she probably should. Besides, if Noah's glares could kill, she'd only have to haul three boys around tomorrow.

"Don't cut yourself," Val ordered as she headed for the basement stairs and the vacuum.

She wished, for the umpteenth time, that she had a beautiful butler's pantry to store the vacuum and the mop in so they'd be close at hand. She'd love to have one like Ethan's. He'd built a pantry into his new kitchen remodel. *Don't I deserve the space as much as Ethan?* After all, she had twice as many boys underfoot as he did.

Skipping down the stairs, she took another deep breath. She needed to quit being so bitchy. She'd been on edge all day, and she knew she'd been taking some of her crap mood out on her kids. It wasn't their fault that the family checking account ran out of money before she'd reached the bottom of her stack of bills this morning. Not unless their very existence counted against them.

Luke gets paid tomorrow. We'll be fine. This month.

Finding the vacuum cleaner, she grabbed hold of the heavy machine and lugged it up the stairs. Her short stature made carrying the awkwardly shaped piece that much harder. *She* should have done the sweeping and sent Noah downstairs.

She dropped it down with a *clank* and a *thud* in the now-empty kitchen. The worst of the shards from the shattered plate were gone, as was the stuffed garbage bag. Noah had apparently used her absence to make his escape.

With a sigh, she vacuumed the cool tiled floor. It sounded like she was sucking up sand as she crisscrossed over the floor, moving chairs as she went. The *nearly* indestructible dishes held up well against rough handling—at least until they were smashed onto tile. Then all bets were off. The old dishware couldn't be chipped, but it could certainly be shattered into a million pieces. After she was done with the vacuum, she got down on her hands and knees with a wet cloth to finish the job. The last thing she needed was another trip to the emergency room.

The back door slammed and heavy boots thudded to the floor as Luke came in. "Sorry I'm late, hon," he hollered, unable to see Val down on the floor on the other side of the island. "Did you save me any food?"

If I lay down here on the floor and keep quiet, is there any chance I can avoid waiting on another male in this house tonight?

Doubtful.

"There's a plate in the fridge for you," she yelled back just as loudly as she peeked over the edge of the countertop at her husband.

He jumped back and grabbed his chest. "Jesus Christ! You scared the shit out of me. I didn't see you down there. What are you doing?"

"Cleaning up a broken plate," she said, grabbing a nearby stool to help hoist herself back onto her feet.

She carried her balled-up rag over to the sink and set it gingerly inside so the shards wouldn't shake out and go down the drain. Noah hadn't thought to replace the liner in the garbage can. She did it now, going through the motions automatically.

"Those old plates never break. They were a wedding gift."

She smirked. "They don't break until a kid drops one on the tile floor. If it hits just right, *bam!*"

"I've always hated those things," he said. "They remind me of my crabby grandma. She had ones just like that. Maybe I should toss the rest onto the tile floor, then we can get new ones."

"You wouldn't dare," she replied, though she was sure he was kidding. Or she hoped he was. He *had* always hated the dishes. "Why so late tonight? Sorry we didn't wait for you. I've had about enough of the boys today and just wanted to get supper behind us."

"Tough day?"

Val shrugged. No one liked a complainer, especially her.

Luke came up behind Val and started to massage her neck and shoulders. She shrugged off his hands, still feeling prickly. She pulled Luke's plate and then a bottle of white wine out of the back of the fridge. There was only one-third of it left, but she'd gladly accepted the partial bottle from Renee when they'd left the resort on Saturday evening. She'd forgotten about it until tonight. Maybe it would settle her. The boys were off somewhere in the house, and Luke would head up to shower once he'd wolfed down his food, standing at the counter. She poured herself a glass, using one of her new wine glasses Jess had given her for her birthday, and took it out to the dining room table where she'd left her laptop and the stack of bills.

She ignored the offending pile of envelopes as she fired up her computer, planning to spend thirty mindless minutes browsing Pinterest for new recipes.

She sipped her wine and relaxed, losing herself amongst the artfully arranged pictures and tempting recipes. She started a new board of fall dishes she'd like to try. The women's retreats Renee and Jess offered at Whispering Pines would start up again in October. Val helped them out with meals, so now was the perfect time to start testing new dishes. Cooler weather and fall foliage would mean long walks for their guests, followed by comfort food. She liked to find old standbys and make them healthier.

After the unseasonal heat and humidity today, sweater season sounded appealing.

Remembering an idea she'd had while waiting for Logan and Noah to finish up with camp earlier, she set her wine aside and opened the cabinet flanking a wall of windows. Her mother had given her all of Celia's old recipe boxes and cookbooks when they'd cleaned out her kitchen two and a half years earlier. As the only one in the family who truly enjoyed cooking, it made sense for Val to take them. But at the time she'd given the recipes little more than a cursory glance before tucking them into the cabinet.

Maybe, instead of making secret boards on Pinterest, she'd start posting pins promoting her cooking at the retreats. Could she rework any of these old classics?

A *thud* from above meant the boys were screwing around in the small TV room, where they often gathered once the sun went down to play video games or watch movies. There was a second *thud*, but no screams—always a good sign.

Turning back to the metal box of recipes, she pulled out a card. She squinted to read it. Damn, she should have kept those reading glasses. The cursive had an odd slant to it, the ink faded in places. Some ingredients she recognized, some she didn't. There weren't precise measurements. But something about the combination intrigued her, and all at once the side dish began to take shape in her mind.

"What are you looking at?" Luke asked, joining her in the dining room. He had changed into a tank and loose-fitting basketball shorts. His hair was damp and tousled from his shower; she caught a whiff of his soap when he dropped a quick kiss on the top of her head before taking the chair next to her.

"Just some old recipes I got from Celia's house."

The unexpected affection and fresh smell caused her eyes to roam over his still-broad shoulders and hard biceps. She knew there was strength there, despite the slight paunch around his middle. Her pulse kicked up a notch as she watched her husband pull another recipe card out of the box, squinting much as she had in an effort to read it. His wavy blond hair was darker than it used to be, shot through with silver around his temples. How long had it been since she'd run her fingers through that hair like she used to?

Spontaneous touching and casual sex had become a fixture of their past. A shout and another *thud* from above reminded her of their present—no privacy and little intimacy.

And why the hell does the gray make him look more distinguished, but it makes me look old? She had to color her hair more often these days to keep from looking like a red-haired skunk.

He stuck the card back into the box and shut the lid, turning his attention instead to the stack of bills she'd been doing her best to ignore since she'd done the depressing math that morning.

She felt her peaceful mood evaporate in a flash.

"Those are bills we can't pay until your paycheck hits our account," she said, hating the bitterness she heard creep into her voice. Luke worked hard and shouldn't have to listen to the resentment she often felt over their financial situation. He wasn't to blame.

Luke's brow furrowed as he studied the clinic bill on top of the stack and the corresponding insurance claim she'd matched up to it earlier. They were still in the messy middle of hitting their annual deductible for the year, meaning the cost of Logan's emergency room visit the month before for a sprained toe would come out of their own pockets—pockets that were currently empty, other than some loose change and dryer lint. At least Luke didn't point out the fact she was the one that insisted they take Logan in, sure his toe was broken.

Not wanting to argue again over the touchy subject of money, Val drained the tiny bit of wine remaining in her glass and stood, taking her empty glass with her. "I'll get the boys started on showers. And I'll remind them to keep them short," she added, remembering that their water bill had been absolutely ridiculous last month.

He nodded absently as he made his way through the rest of the pile, concern etched into the lines fanning out from the corners of his eyes, his mouth set in a hard line.

She placed her empty wine glass in the sink and headed upstairs, straight to the boys' bathroom. She'd scrubbed it the day before, so it didn't look too bad—yet—but a damp towel lay next to the tub and the seat was up on the toilet, leaving the telltale sign that a messy boy had recently visited this room. Scooping the towel off the floor and closing the toilet lid for what had to be the millionth time, she twisted the faucet on the shower, starting the stream. At least someone had taken the initiative to shower without having to be told—but she'd guarantee it wasn't her youngest. Leaving the water running, she headed for the TV room.

"Jake! You need to shower, bud! It's almost bedtime."

She grinned as she heard his automatic response of groans and complaints. The seven-year-old hated slowing down enough to shower, let alone go to bed. He did his best to keep up with his three older brothers and hated it when she carved him out like this. But ticking Jake off instead of another argument with her husband seemed like the better option if she didn't want the evening to be a total bust.

She paused at the doorway, taking in the sight.

The room was dark, shades pulled, while Dave and Logan enjoyed a fierce battle over some game on the screen. How she hated those games they played! But it was a losing battle for her to try to eliminate them altogether. She compromised by limiting their screen time as best she could. Noah was sprawled in the old La-Z-Boy that had been downstairs until its stained upholstery got it relegated up here. Storm was curled at his feet. How she could sleep amongst the chaos was a mystery to Val—and an envy.

Jake was on the floor next to the dog, twisting and turning a Rubik's Cube, his face a study of concentration. Ever since they'd found the keychain-sized Cube in the time capsule, he'd been playing with this larger version, a toy left over from Luke's childhood. Her youngest had been doing all he could to try to solve the puzzle, including going online for pointers.

"Jake, the shower is running for you. If you go take a shower now, without fuss, I'll let you stay up until ten tonight."

Glancing her way, his frown of concentration slipped away, replaced by a thankful smile for the extra thirty minutes.

"Get in there, okay? It's running," she said again, gathering up scattered glasses and an empty candy wrapper. Her mind was already skipping ahead to their schedule for the next morning. It would be another full day of running.

Luke was still bent over the pile of bills when she got back to the kitchen. Opening the dishwasher, she rearranged things to fit the stray glasses she'd brought down. She'd have preferred a second glass of wine, but the bottle stood empty on the island, so she loaded the wine glass, too. She threw a dishwashing pod in and turned the machine on. Not a day went by that she didn't have to run it.

"Jake's in the shower now," she reported.

Luke nodded again, scribbling something on the pad of paper she'd been using earlier that morning.

She eyed her box of old recipes, wishing she could continue to make her way through them instead of having another discussion about finances, but she sensed Luke wanted to talk about it.

Snapping the light off in the kitchen, she crossed over to the dining area. It was really just one big open room now, Luke having taken out the adjoining wall years earlier. Val preferred this layout, but it was still tight when everyone was in here.

Taking her chair again, she glanced at the figures on the paper. "How does it look to you?"

"Shitty," came his curt reply as he set his pencil to the side. "Did you really spend four hundred and eighty dollars on basketball camp and baseball fees this month?"

Did I spend $480 this month? Did he really just say those words out loud?

Outwardly, she tried to keep her face neutral—not something that came naturally. "*I* got them registered for the things *we* decided each of them would do this summer. You know none of it's free. It adds up. Fast."

"Apparently," he conceded. "Sorry. I know that expense isn't all on you."

His tight grin didn't do much to cool her frustration. What she wouldn't give to be able to write out the checks to those sports organizations without having to juggle other expenses to make ends meet. *If only . . .*

But she stopped herself, tired of beating herself up for the decision she'd made—correction, *they'd* made—long ago for her to stay home with the kids.

For the umpteenth time that day, her mother's words about Celia's gift to her sprang to mind. She shook the thoughts away. Not the time.

She reached over and squeezed Luke's hand. He tried. She knew he worked hard. It was just that the company he worked for seemed to be shrinking instead of growing. The bonuses they used to throw Luke's way had dried up. Now they were even threatening to go down to four days a week instead of five. She didn't know what they'd do if that actually happened. They couldn't survive on twenty percent less of a paycheck. At least they hadn't cut benefits. *Yet.*

"Look, I know you don't like this idea, but I think I need to get a second job," Luke said, pushing the pile of bills away and scraping his chair back from the table. He crossed his arms in front of his chest, as if he were bracing for yet another argument on this touchy subject. He'd come home from their Memorial Day camping trip to announce he'd talked to the guys about it and Seth had offered to let him come work some weekends with him.

She wasn't sure what ticked her off more—the fact he'd shared their financial situation with her family, or the idea that she'd be acting as the sole parent of their boys even more often than she already was.

"But that would mean you'd have even less time with the boys."

Luke rubbed the back of his neck, frustration gripping his expression. "What the hell else do you suggest I do, Val? We should have moved for that job when Dave was a baby. I would be making twice as much as I am now."

Val could feel her blood pressure rise. Anytime he brought up that missed opportunity, he'd make it sound like staying had been something she'd insisted on. She hadn't wanted to raise their sons far from her family. He hadn't argued. She'd always interpreted that to mean they'd decided together.

God, I'm tired of these same old arguments.

"And I suppose that's my fault too?" she spat out, her voice rising.

Luke, on the other hand, kept his voice level. "Val, be quiet. The boys don't need to hear this. You know how I hate yelling in the house."

It was the exact wrong thing for him to say to keep her calm.

"Dammit, Luke, I don't want to be a single parent *all* week and *all* weekend while you're off gallivanting around the countryside with Seth, playing around in old buildings."

Luke's eyes narrowed and he leaned toward her, hands on his knees. She'd obviously struck a nerve. He opened his mouth to say something when a fat water droplet plopped onto the yellow notepad he'd been scribbling on. His eyes were drawn upward, and Val followed his lead.

"What the hell?" he uttered.

Val's brain was confused at what her eyes were seeing.

Another droplet hit the paper tablet.

How can it be sprinkling in the dining room?

A drop of water hung suspended from the light fixture above. It was as if everything were in slow motion. The droplet quickly turned into a steady stream. The light bulbs flickered, followed by a *hiss* and a popping sound.

"Shit!" Luke yelled, flinging his chair backward as he sprung to his feet, racing for the stairs.

It can't sprinkle inside the house, Val thought as she stood, still staring at the ceiling, her brain slower to put the pieces together. But then the horror of what might be happening grabbed hold of her brain.

"Shit!" she echoed, automatically snatching her laptop off the dining room table and spinning to follow Luke. But her eye snagged on the old box of Celia's recipes. She grabbed those, too, and bolted across the room, following Luke up the stairs. She could feel her bare feet squish through water, the carpet already wet on the treads. Just as she reached the top step, she heard a crash downstairs.

Suddenly the cost of the boys' summer ball programs was the least of their problems.

CHAPTER SIX

GIFT OF CONTRITION

*U*pstairs, chaos reigned.

Luke was yelling.

Storm was barking.

Dave emerged from the TV room first, the three younger boys gathering in the doorway behind him, eyes confused.

"Val, grab towels! David, get downstairs and flip the main on the fuse box! Now!"

Val stood frozen at the top of the stairs, trying to process what was happening. A huge dark spot on the cream-colored carpet spread outward from the closed bathroom door, ominously seeping down the hallway in both directions—a trail also leading down the stairs, thus the squishing. All she could think about was turning on the shower and then casually heading downstairs, foolishly expecting her youngest to actually listen to her for once and get in the shower.

But showers don't overfill bathtubs!

Luke yanked open the bathroom door. Based on the crash she'd heard, Val half expected to see a gaping hole in the middle of the bathroom floor. But there was no hole. An inch or more of water covered the black-and-white tile, flowing for the door. Val watched in horror as a waterfall sluiced over the edge of the tub. The yellow rubber duck that lived on the far corner of the tub floated toward them, grinning up at Val, skimming across the bathroom floor.

Sliding through the water, Luke gave a vicious twist to the faucet, stemming the flow. Val, still rooted to her spot at the top of the stairs, watched helplessly as he bent over, fishing around in the bottom of the tub.

Then she remembered the stopper—it was loose! When she'd cleaned the bathtub earlier, she'd struggled to keep the drain open. The stopper kept slipping closed on her while she scrubbed. She'd meant to tell Luke it needed to be replaced.

She'd forgotten.

"Val! Help!" Luke screamed again, his arm still plunged deep into the tub.

His words finally sunk in and she bolted past the bathroom door for their bedroom. Setting the laptop and recipe box down on her dresser, safely out of harm's way, she grabbed up a stack of clean towels from their bed. She'd folded the laundry earlier, just before sitting down with the boys to eat.

As she exited their bedroom, the lights in the hallway and bathroom snapped off, sending them into semidarkness. Dave must have gotten to the fuse box. Val didn't know much about electricity, but she knew power and water could be a deadly combination.

She threw a towel at each of their three sons still standing there, dumbfounded. Jake, normally the one who was seldom quiet, had silent tears streaming down his face.

"Noah, Jake, help your father mop this up. Logan, come with me," Val ordered. She needed to see what was happening downstairs. She grabbed his hand on her way back toward the stairs, pulling him with her. They met Dave, limping up the stairs on his bad ankle as they descended.

"What do you want me to do?" her oldest yelled as they skirted around each other.

Val glanced back up the stairs. "I have no idea. Go ask your dad! We're going to check the dining room."

Bounding to the bottom of the stairs, Logan right behind her, Val held her breath, hating to see the damage she feared awaited them. She took two steps into the kitchen and pulled up short, Logan running into her from behind, pushing her into the room a couple more steps.

With dismay, she took in the scene before her. The crash she'd heard earlier hadn't been in the dining room as she'd feared. The section of ceiling above the stove and refrigerator had collapsed, huge chunks of drywall now hanging down precariously. Water still dripped down from various spots in the ceiling. The section of the ceiling over the dining room table bowed ominously, and she watched in horror as the pressure proved to be too much and there was another loud crash. Val stood stock still, feeling helpless as she took in the destruction before her.

Their kitchen and dining area looked like a bomb had gone off.

"Oh my God, Mom, what should we do?" Logan whispered from behind her.

Something crashed into her legs. She stumbled, Storm rushing past her, running farther into the kitchen, barking. It snapped Val into action and she grabbed for the animal.

"Here. Take her outside. Hook her up on her chain in the backyard. Take my phone," Val ordered, snatching it off the kitchen island where she'd left it earlier and thrusting it into her son's hand.

Logan looked down at the phone. "Who should I call?"

Before replying, Val turned back to the horrific scene behind her. She wasn't sure what to do next. She could hear Luke yelling instructions to Dave, Noah, and Jake upstairs. Her husband probably had no idea what awaited him downstairs.

"You better call Uncle Ethan and tell him we have a bit of an emergency and could use his help. Tell him to bring his shop-vac. And call your grandfather. We're going to need lots of hands."

* * *

Once the worst of the water was sopped up with towels and the industrial-sized shop-vac Ethan brought over, George insisted Val bring the boys and Storm over to their house. Darkness was falling fast now and it was harder to see inside the house. They'd been using flashlights and a battery-powered set of spotlights Ethan happened to have in the back of his truck.

"Let's get out of here so Luke and Ethan can try to assess the damages. Maybe things will look better in the morning," George suggested.

Or the bright morning sun will reveal the full extent of the disaster that was my kitchen, Val thought.

Aloud, she conceded. "I suppose that's for the best. We can't hardly stay here without power. Ethan already has his buddy coming over in the morning. He does electrical work for Ethan on his jobs. He'll be able to tell us if it's safe to turn the electricity back on."

George nodded. "And Luke let me know he talked to your insurance agent already, too. They'll send someone by tomorrow. That will give you a better idea of what you're dealing with."

"Would you mind taking the boys home with you now?" Val asked as she started gathering up wet towels. "I just . . . need to talk to Luke for a minute . . . and hang these up outside. Then I'll be over."

"Of course. See you shortly," George said, turning to gather his four grandsons and one anxious granddog.

* * *

After she'd draped nearly every towel they owned over every inch of the large deck off the back of the house, she went to find her husband. They'd barely had time to say two words to each other since The Great Flood, as she'd already dubbed the night's debacle. She could hear male voices upstairs. Heading up, she braced herself for the discussion she knew she had to have with Luke. Would he blame her for this?

Do I blame myself for this?

She ascended slowly, overwhelmed by everything that had transpired. Her eyes and fingertips trailed across the four framed school pictures lining the wall of the staircase. She updated them every year.

Keep things in perspective, she reminded herself. *No one got hurt. But I never should have assumed Jake would follow orders and get in the shower the first time I told him.*

Both men were in the kids' bathroom, the origin of The Great Flood. Her brother was down on his knees inspecting wallboard behind the toilet. Luke stood, watching Ethan, his features slack with what might have been shock. He glanced in Val's direction but didn't meet her eye.

Stopping at the threshold, she leaned against the doorjamb and sighed, watching her brother—more thankful than ever for his contractor skills—as he checked for damage. When he straightened, his expression was inscrutable.

"How bad is it?" she asked. Not that she really wanted to know.

"The water didn't sit, at least up here, but moisture can wreak havoc, even if you get it cleaned up quickly. Thank God you were home."

"This wouldn't have happened if we weren't home," Val bit out, her frustration over her own carelessness growing.

Now Luke did meet her eye. She hated the tears she could feel welling up as he came over and pulled her into a hug, rocking her back and forth.

"I'm so sorry, Luke. This is all my fault."

Luke stepped back, squeezed her shoulders, then dropped his hands. "No. It's not really anyone's fault. Shit happens. Then we deal with it."

"Water *is* destructive . . . but hey, at least it wasn't a fire," Ethan offered, but his attempt at levity fell flat.

Val thought back to the massive damage one of her brother's rental units had suffered before the holidays. That had been a *real* disaster. People had nearly died. And it may have marked the first step toward her brother's heart attack. He was right, of course. It could have been so much worse.

Val nodded. "Dad took the boys home with him. I'll go, too. I don't want them here until we know more. There isn't any more we can do tonight, is there?"

"Nah," Ethan agreed. "It's dark, and you really shouldn't touch much until the insurance adjuster comes in. Why don't we lock up? Things will look better in the morning."

He is just *like Dad,* Val thought, wishing she believed their assurances.

"I'm staying," Luke announced. "I just want to keep an eye on things. You go. Be with the boys. You should maybe come back in the morning so you're here, too, when the adjuster and electrician get here."

"You sure?" Val asked, not liking the idea of him staying in the house.

"I'm sure. Take the dog. She can't be roaming around the house at night, and she'll be looking for the boys."

"Dad already took her too," Val offered weakly.

She headed for their bedroom to grab an overnight bag. If they were out of the house for longer than one night—which, now that she thought about it, was sure to be the case—she'd need more things, but this would suffice for now. She also grabbed a few essentials for each of the boys.

Ethan and Luke were down in the kitchen by the time she was ready to leave.

"I'll walk you out," Ethan said, picking up a tool box he'd brought in earlier. "Luke, keep whatever else you need. I'll just get it back from you later. You gonna be all right here tonight?"

"Yeah . . . I'm just not comfortable leaving."

Ethan went out the back door ahead of Val, holding it open for her to follow.

Turning back to her husband, Val felt another wave of guilt, leaving him standing in the mess that was their kitchen. "I really am sorry, Luke."

"Yeah, hon, I know you are."

* * *

The rhythmic *tick-tock* of the ever-faithful alarm clock of her youth wasn't enough to lull Val to sleep. If anything, its glowing digits were a painful reminder of how long she'd been searching for the oblivion of sleep. The murmur of voices through the wall behind her headboard had quieted. Dave and Logan must have finally drifted off.

Every time she closed her eyes, she'd see that damn rubber duck, grinning up at her as it skimmed across the bathroom floor, reminding her of the destruction she'd caused with her carelessness.

Her finger automatically found the rip in the girlish pink comforter pooled at her waist. She should have opened a window before getting into bed. The room was stuffy, magnifying the scents she'd been too accustomed to as a girl to notice.

Was Luke awake, too, back at their house?

Did he blame her for what had happened hours earlier?

The familiar *squeak* of a loose floorboard in the hallway meant someone else was still up. She listened intently, trying to determine who was wandering the halls, much as she'd done as a child. But now, instead of one of her siblings, it would surely be one of her four boys. Her parents slept downstairs.

The soft sound of footfalls paused, followed by the telltale *creak* of her bedroom door.

"Mom? Mom, are you awake?"

Val automatically scooched over on the bed, holding up the edge of her faded pink comforter in welcome. Young Jake peered at her in the soft glow of moonlight.

"I'm awake," she whispered back.

Deep shadows made it almost impossible for her to make out Jake or the door, but she heard the *swoosh* of it closing followed by the soft *click* of the latch. Bare feet slapped against the hardwood and the mattress shifted as Jake's small body collided with hers. As Val wrapped an arm around the boy, she could feel the wetness of his tears where Jake pressed his face into her armpit.

"Hey, hey, what's wrong, hon?" she cooed, brushing a dark lock of his hair back from his forehead.

"I'm *so* sorry, Mom . . ." Jake whispered, his voice thick. "I didn't listen and now our house is ruined. It's all my fault." Val could hear the heartbreak in his tone, the guilt hanging heavy in his words.

"Oh baby, our house isn't ruined. We'll fix it. I shouldn't have left the water running and gone back downstairs either. I guess we both messed up."

"I should have listened," Jake hissed back, his voice cracking.

Val lay quietly, softly stroking her son's head until his breathing evened out. She felt his body relax as sleep finally came for him. In the darkness, Val accepted the fact that this would be a hard lesson for both of them. She needed to let Jake feel the weight of responsibility, too, even though her natural tendency was to protect him from the pain.

Her old clock made a clicking sound as the hour digit flipped from 2 to 3. An owl hooted in the backyard. With a sigh, she reached over and flicked the annoying clock off, much as she'd done when it had pestered her as a teenager.

The morning would arrive regardless, and she'd deal with the mess they'd created.

CHAPTER SEVEN

GIFT OF SPRING BLOSSOMS

*V*al and Luke spent the next day with an insurance adjuster, Ethan's electrician, and each other, assessing damages and formulating plans to put their house back in order. George and Lavonne kept the boys, and the dog, out of their hair. It felt strange to be in the house, together, without any of the kids around.

Repairing the damages was going to take time. Some of the appliances were damaged and would need to be replaced.

Val called her mother to update her.

"I don't know what I'm going to do without a kitchen, Mom. It could take weeks, even *months*, depending on what we decide to do and how long it takes the insurance to come through. Luke thinks now might be the time to do some of the updates I've mentioned before, but we can't really afford that. Insurance will cover some things, but not *upgrades*."

Lavonne's sigh was staticky over the phone. "Oh, hon, I'm sorry you have such a mess on your hands. You know you are welcome to stay with us as long as you need to. We have plenty of room."

Bedrooms, yes, Val thought, *but how long do Mom and Dad really want to have six extra people in their home? Not to mention a hyper dog.*

"Thank you, Mom. You know we appreciate that. We'll do our best not to inconvenience you for long."

Lavonne scoffed. "Don't be silly, Val. You're family, not an inconvenience. But I am going to have to get some groceries in this place. Those boys of yours sure can eat."

Val laughed, although she knew exactly what her mother meant.

"It's been less than a day, Mom!"

The boys did eat a lot—especially if they were bored, which would happen before too long, staying at their grandparents'.

"Your father is out running them around to their activities right now, so I'm heading to the store. Say, honey, if you'd rather stay at the house with Luke tonight, don't feel like you have to come back here. The boys are fine, and I know you have your hands full over there."

Val was surprised at her mother's offer. But the idea of sleeping in her own bed did hold a certain appeal. As did a quiet house for a change—even if the house was in disarray.

"Really? You wouldn't mind?"

"Not at all. It would be fun! Maybe we could even take them down to the ballpark. My friend Ethel told me her grandson plays a double-header tonight. Could hot dogs and chips at the diamond count for supper?"

Val laughed again—she and her mother both knew the boys would love it.

"Without a doubt. If you're sure you don't mind, I'll take you up on your offer. I think Luke is feeling overwhelmed with everything that's going on. He missed work today, but hates the idea of missing again tomorrow. If we can get more done yet today, it would help him out."

"I wouldn't have offered if it wasn't okay. Stay, get some work done, and then maybe even go grab a bite or something. Just the two of you. When was the last time you two had a night to yourselves?"

If Val were being honest, she couldn't remember.

* * *

Val could read the relief on Luke's face when she shared her updated plans with him. There were things to do and decisions to be made about the house. He needed her.

"The kids will love going to the ballgames tonight. We'd even talked about maybe going, but that was before all this," he said, motioning around at the destruction surrounding them.

"And it'll be a distraction for the boys, too. I talked to Noah this afternoon and he was already whining about being bored over at Mom and Dad's. He said Jake's been unusually quiet. That worries me a little."

Luke snorted. "The boredom?"

"Uh, *no*, complaining that they're bored is nothing new. I'm worried about Jake. He crawled into bed with me late last night. He blames himself for this. I hate to see him so upset."

Luke shrugged, a resigned expression on his face. "Val, he screwed up. He always thinks he can wiggle out of trouble with a little charm and redirection. Life doesn't always work that way, and maybe it's about time he figures that out."

She should have welcomed Luke's sentiment. She'd been pushing him for a long time to be stricter with their youngest. Instead, it rankled her.

"*Now* you decide to actually call Jake out on something? Luke, this is as much my fault as his. Maybe this isn't the time to go all 'tough love' on him." Val hated the sarcasm she allowed to seep into her words.

To her husband's credit, he didn't take the bait. "He needs to learn to listen."

Val watched Luke walk away unruffled. She knew he was right. But this was an expensive lesson for all of them.

* * *

"Luke, hon, I'm starving. We've been at this for hours. I've given up on finding any more hidden treasure," Val joked, waving the broom she'd been cleaning the kitchen floor with into the air. "Do you think we can call it a day and go eat somewhere?"

"Hidden treasure?" Luke repeated, his tone distracted.

"Yeah, treasure. Like I found in the Gray Cabin . . . with my broom," she added, but there was no salvaging the joke. "Never mind."

She glanced at Luke and giggled when she saw the white coating of dust covering his hair. Together they'd pulled down the worst of the damaged sheetrock from the ceiling and hauled it out to a dumpster Ethan had brought by for them to use. Luke grunted as he struggled to push the fridge back into its usual spot. They were going to have to replace it, and had taken the food that had been in there over to Val's folks' house so it wouldn't spoil, but he'd had to move it to do some cleanup.

"What time is it?" he asked once the appliance was back where it belonged.

Val pulled her phone out. "Seven thirty. Geez, no wonder I'm hungry. Why don't we shower and go out?"

He wiggled his eyebrows at her, and she didn't have to be psychic to read his mind.

Laughing, she shook her head; a little chunk of sheetrock fell out of her bangs. "Not gonna happen, big boy."

He stepped toward her. She hustled around the dusty island, out of arm's reach.

"Aw, come on, Val. We never get this place to ourselves."

"Food first," she said, wagging a finger at him.

"And then . . . ?"

"And then we'll strip naked, run around inside the house like crazed coeds, and have sex on the dining room table."

Luke paused midstep, his eyes widening. "Really?"

Val busted out laughing at the hopeful expression on her husband's face. "Probably not. The table is damaged. But . . . hey . . . feed me and then we'll see where it goes."

* * *

Thirty minutes later, Val led the way out the back door and Luke locked it behind them. It had felt good to wash away the sludge of the day and put on a cool, pretty sundress. She'd even slicked on some mascara and spent ten minutes fixing her hair—something she rarely took the time to do anymore. Glancing back at Luke, she smiled. His turquoise polo contrasted nicely with his hair, which looked like warm caramel in the setting sun. He walked around in his baseball hat so often, it was nice to see him without it for a change.

"What?" he asked, squinting at her as he jogged down the stairs.

"You look nice."

He caught her hand and pulled her in for a quick kiss as they walked side by side to his old Ford truck, parked next to their garage in the back. "Well, thank you. So do you, babe."

He opened the door for her and helped her crawl up into his pickup. Her short stature always made it tough to get into the truck, but normally she was left to fend for herself. A little pampering felt nice.

"You think you're going to get lucky tonight, don't you?" she asked, still grinning.

"I figure my luck will turn around one of these days," he joked as he climbed behind the wheel and threw the truck into Reverse. "Where to?"

"Preferably some place where we don't have to order at a front counter or listen to screaming kids. Beyond that, I don't care where we go. You pick."

"You really don't care where we go?" Luke asked, glancing at her as he turned out of their alley and headed north.

She lowered her window to let the fresh spring air in and chase the slightly musty scent of the old vehicle out. Laying her head back, she closed her eyes, relaxing for the first time all day. "As long as it meets those two requirements, I don't care if we eat in freaking Narnia. Surprise me."

Luke chuckled. Val kept her eyes closed. The radio came on and she hummed along with the random song playing on the station he chose, not caring that she didn't know the words. The fresh air felt good on her skin and she inhaled the scent of lilacs mixed with the smell of Luke's bodywash.

She'd missed this. A night out with the guy she'd been crazy about since the first night she'd met him on the dance floor of an old bar while out with a group of work friends. It had been so long ago. These days, he often drove her crazy for other reasons. But either way, the man kept her on her toes. She knew she was lucky to have him.

I need to stop taking him for granted, she reminded herself, feeling the tension she so often carried these days begin to slip away. *God, it feels good to relax.*

* * *

She jerked awake, looking around in confusion. Twilight sparkled like diamonds on water far below. Dust floated in through her open window.

"Oh wow . . . did I fall asleep?"

Glancing over at Luke, she was surprised to see a large, white paper bag on the console between them and two sodas in the cupholders. She eyed the food, skeptical.

"That looks like something you'd order from a counter. And what are we doing out here at the lake?"

Luke opened his door, grabbed one of the sodas and the sack of food, and jumped out of the Ford. "Not only did you fall asleep, you were snoring like a sailor. You might want to wipe that drool off your chin."

Gasping, she wiped at her face. "You rat! I didn't *drool.*"

He let out a belly laugh. "Maybe not, but you did snore. The girl at the drive-thru window giggled when she heard you."

Val started to chew him out but caught herself. *Who cares?* Besides, he was *probably* just teasing.

"We've been stuck inside all day. The thought of sitting in a noisy, crowded restaurant sounded awful. Grab your Coke and follow me."

She did just that, her sandals kicking up dust in the gravel parking lot as she followed Luke toward a picnic area overlooking a wide expanse of water. The parking lot was empty around them. They'd have the sunset to themselves.

He set the bag of food down on the splintery wooden top of a picnic table. She was relieved there wasn't any bird poop on the surface, at least.

"You do know this isn't exactly what I had in mind when I suggested we go out for dinner, don't you? Which, by the way, we haven't done minus the kids for months?"

Luke pulled a wrapped burger out of the sack and handed it to her once she was seated across from him. There was still warmth to the sun; it felt good where it touched her face and bare shoulders. A bird twittered close by, and from somewhere out of sight the unmistakable call of a loon floated on the light breeze.

"I know. But I couldn't resist. Besides, you have to admit, a sunset picnic *is* romantic."

She unfolded a napkin and laid it on top of the old table like a placemat, then set her burger down and unwrapped it. She lifted the top bun off, but there were no pickles to remove.

"Extra ketchup, no pickles," he said, watching her before taking a huge bite out of his own sandwich.

"Now *that's* romantic," she conceded. "A husband who remembers how I take my quarter pounder."

He nodded, taking in the scenery as he ate his meal. She followed his lead, enjoying the deep reds and oranges that spread across the horizon as the sun sank lower.

"I do recall this isn't the *first* time you've brought me here for a picnic at sunset, Luke."

He scrunched up the wrapper from his burger and pulled another out of the bag. "Good memory. We came out here that first summer we were dating. We ate up here, just like we are now, and then we took a path that used to run down to the water over there. If memory serves *me* right, there might have been a bit of skinny-dipping that night."

She sighed, closing her eyes and picturing their younger selves, picking their way down the hillside, slapping mosquitoes as they went. There had been swimming, and a bright yellow moon hanging low on the horizon, dipping into the water like melted butter. That night had been a turning point in their relationship.

And now, here they were, eighteen-or-so-odd years later, married with four boys and a dog and a house in the suburbs. A house that often felt too small to contain their ever-growing boys—and one that was minus a ceiling or two at the moment—but a cozy home to be sure.

She reached across the table and entwined her fingers with Luke's. "This is nice. Thank you."

"Does that mean you want to find that old path and go dip a toe in the water?" he asked, giving her an exaggerated wink.

Laughing, she gathered up their mess and shoved it all in the now-empty bag, then swatted at something that bit her cheek as she walked the trash over to a garbage bin. She had to loosen a tarp strap to open the top, throwing the bag in quickly and letting it slam shut again to cut off the buzz of flies and the stench of whatever else had been tossed inside.

"Ugh. Smells like dirty diapers," she cried, covering her nose as she spun away.

"Damn, that just lost me a couple points in the romance department, didn't it?" Luke came up beside her and caught her elbow. "Come here, I want to show you something."

Val slapped at another bug as it bit her on the shin. "Luke, I'm getting eaten alive. Let's get in the truck."

"Don't be so dramatic," he countered, rolling his eyes. "Where's your sense of adventure? Come on. It'll just take a second and then we'll stop for ice cream on the way home."

The mention of ice cream had her reconsidering. She could spare him a couple more minutes if it would earn her a cone. "Okay. What are you so anxious to show me?"

"Just come over here. I saw them when we drove in. Not sure if they're still there or not," he said, quieter now as he lowered his voice and stepped softly. "I don't want to scare them away if they're still there."

She nodded and played along, and when he stopped and pointed, she looked. Halfway between them and the water were four deer, walking lazily through high grass, eating and playing. One deer was large, three were small, bearing white splotches.

"Triplets?!" she asked in an excited whisper.

Luke nodded, grinning. "I should take a picture for the boys," he whispered back, carefully pulling his phone out of his pocket so as not to scare them off with any sudden movements.

The mother deer swung her head in their direction and Luke froze. They stared at each other for a moment, and then she dropped her head to graze some more, apparently determining they weren't a threat to her babies. He snapped a few shots, and then a short video. One of the babies jumped and pawed at the other two, as if instigating a game of tag. The boys would love the footage.

The crunching of tires behind them disrupted the quiet of the evening. This time when the mother raised her head, she stood still for only a second, and then bolted for the protection of a nearby grove of trees, snorting at her babies to follow. In the blink of an eye, they were gone. Car doors slammed. Shouts and laughter filled the air. The peacefulness of their spot was lost.

They made their way back to Luke's old blue Ford. Val waved to the group of teenagers now tossing a frisbee around near where they'd just finished eating. One girl waved back and a tall, lanky boy shouted, "Nice wheels!"

Luke raised a hand in acknowledgment and again opened Val's door for her, joining her inside the truck a moment later. "God, that used to be us."

Val nodded, watching the group of five as they laughed and played catch, not a care in the world. She'd bet *they* didn't have a huge hole in *their* kitchen ceilings back home.

"What was that you said about ice cream?"

* * *

Val licked a dribble of chocolate off her cone, her fingers already sticky.

"You know, if you close your window, your ice cream wouldn't melt so fast."

She shook her head. "It's a beautiful spring evening and the air smells heavenly. I refuse to close the window."

Luke popped the rounded tip of his sugar cone into his mouth and shook his head. "You are a stubborn woman. But you smell heavenly, too."

Val gave her treat another lick and batted her eyes at her husband. "Aw, shucks, honey, you are so sweet."

"Smartass," Luke shot back, but his grin didn't fade. He seemed to be enjoying their evening of freedom. "Home?"

"Home."

Val admired the fresh lawns and inhaled the scent of blooming crabapple trees. Those with white blossoms shimmered in the dusk, almost ghostly in the twilight. Trees sporting deeper pink blooms were recognizable only by their scent, their flowers fading into the darkness. Which flower color matched her own style these days? The way she'd been feeling, she'd have to pick the deep, dark color. She, too, felt as though she were fading into the background. Even the color she chose to use on her own hair wasn't too far off from that of the dark blossoms.

She sighed, hating to let a sense of melancholy steal in and tarnish the glow of their evening. Yes, they were going home to a mess, but they'd figure out a way to deal with it. Tonight had reminded her how lucky she was to be married to a man like Luke, to be raising a family with him. The frustrations of their daily grind had allowed her to forget that.

Maybe *he* wasn't the problem.

Her five-year-old self's wish came back to her again. Maybe *she* was the one disappointing her younger self.

Their tires crunched as he pulled back into the alley that sliced their block in two. Luke snapped the radio off, allowing the buzz and hum of insects to fill the air. It was such a peaceful evening.

Once inside, they avoided turning on any lights downstairs. The mess would still be there for them in the morning. They didn't need another reminder of it now. Slipping out of her sandals, Val reached behind her in the darkness and found Luke's hand. Although a small beam of light fell across the floor through the small, rectangular window in the back door, she didn't need it to find the stairs. Years in this house allowed her to traverse it in pitch blackness.

She gently tugged Luke toward the stairs. He resisted for a second, and there was the sound of him kicking off his own shoes. They seldom had the chance for uninterrupted intimacy these days. Usually the best they could do was sneak in a few minutes of hurried coupling behind closed doors, desperate to hide the fact that married people really do still enjoy sex once in a while. Or else they were out of sync with their desires. One would have a headache, or be too tired, or simply not in the mood. And they'd reverse the roles at times. It was always something with one or the other.

Tonight wasn't one of those nights.

Tonight they could relax and enjoy each other's bodies, much as they'd enjoyed each other's company throughout the evening.

Luke closed their bedroom door behind them. Val could feel his eyes on her in the dimness. A moon had risen outside, and beams of light crisscrossed over the bed, broken up by the grid in the window. They could leave the curtains open and see a few bright stars twinkling in the spring sky above their home.

Val's white sundress glowed, reminding her of the crabapple trees lining their path home. She reached for the bows on her shoulders, but Luke caught her hands.

"Let me," he whispered, a reminder that this didn't have to be a hurried affair.

She closed her eyes, heard the whisper of fabric as he undid her ties. Her dress slipped down, catching on her hips, and she could feel the breeze sliding through their open bedroom window glide over her bare breasts. Earlier, when she'd dressed for the evening, she'd debated about going braless under her pretty summer dress. Its structure allowed for it, and Luke's reaction told her he'd failed to notice until now. She wriggled her hips just enough to force her dress to fall free to the ground.

There was something incredibly sexy about standing naked in front of Luke. As his hands reached out to caress her breasts—the ones she worried were starting to droop with age and motherhood—she was transported back to another time. A time when it had been just the two of them, facing the world of adulthood and responsibilities nearly alone . . . but not completely.

The rough calluses on his hands abraded her smooth, pale skin, and his breathing shifted. She reached for the hem of his shirt, but he caught her wrists and held her arms back down at her sides. He, too, was enjoying this. Val, normally the one to take the lead as they maneuvered their family through their everyday lives, was enticed at the idea of turning the reins over to him. He'd honed his skills through years of practice with her, a fact she sometimes forgot.

She'd let him remind her now.

* * *

Later, snuggled under the covers, Val breathed in the night air wafting through the open window adjacent to their bed, tasting a hint of rain. Luke snored softly beside her. It had been too long since she'd felt this sated, this relaxed. *Parenting and life's inconveniences have a way of stealing peace from our daily lives,* she thought, stroking the arm of her sleeping husband where it draped across her stomach.

The sense of unrest she'd been feeling for months was suddenly noticeably absent. As she lay there, staring up at the flecks of sparkle barely visible in the texture of their ceiling, she counted her blessings.

Yes, money was tight, and the monotony of her life felt stifling at times, but they were raising four amazing boys together. Dave, nearly a teenager already, was a born leader. He was always quick to help, and Val knew their lives would be more challenging without him. She supposed this was typical for the oldest child. Logan, with his charm and athleticism, reminded her of what she suspected Luke had been like at ten. He liked to push against any boundaries she tried to put up, and he was sure to keep them on their toes in their efforts to help him safely reach adulthood. And then there was Noah, their quiet child—at least when Logan wasn't picking on him. Noah reminded Val of Jess when she was younger. Serious and studious, usually with a book in hand. Noah had devoured the *Harry Potter* series at an amazing pace. Val couldn't wait to see what the world had in store for him—or how he'd change that world.

And that left little Jake. Not that he was quite so little anymore. At seven years old, his mission in life was evolving into the need to keep up with his older brothers. Where Logan pushed the boundaries, Jake simply ignored them half the time. It was as if, as the baby, Jake thought the rules didn't apply to him (and maybe he was right).

She thought back to the weekend, when they'd all read their letters from the time capsule out loud. Dave had been the only one of her children present at the time, but she'd still avoided reading her childhood wish out loud . . . her wish for a daughter. There would be no daughter, but her sons each owned a piece of her heart, and they always would. Besides, she'd finally managed to bring another female into the house, even if it was a dog instead of a child. Storm was good company in this sea of males.

Thoughts of the time capsule led her mind to again consider what she might do with her yet-untouched inheritance from Aunt Celia. There had to be something big she could do, some grand leap she could take to prove to Luke, to her family—to herself, perhaps, most of all—that she was more than just a wife and mother.

What the hell is the matter with me? she thought, the anxiety she'd been fighting flooding back in. *Being a wife and a mother is the most important job anyone can have!*

Luke murmured in his sleep and pulled his arm away, rolling over to face the open window, his back now facing her.

She sighed. *So why isn't it enough for me?*

Maybe she should try volunteering. She remembered when her own mother had done some of that at the local hospital years ago. But Val quickly dismissed the idea. If she didn't have time to carve out for a job, how could she find time to volunteer?

She rolled over, facing the opposite direction from Luke. The cool breeze no longer caressed her face, but she knew she couldn't fall asleep in any other position. Willing herself to put all thoughts out of her mind, she concentrated on her breathing.

Tomorrow would be another full day and she needed some sleep.

* * *

A shrill ring jarred her awake. Disoriented, she reached for her phone on the nightstand. But there was no call. The display read 2:37 a.m. The bed tilted behind her as Luke grabbed for his phone, the awful sound emanating from his, not hers.

Val's sleep-laden mind immediately jumped to a worried state. Had something happened to one of her boys? Was it her mother or father, calling to report something awful?

Luke reached behind him to lay a calming hand on her arm, as if sensing her automatic reaction.

"What is it, Dad? Are you all right?" she heard him ask.

The cobwebs of deep sleep tore away and her concern shifted. Luke's seventy-year-old father lived in North Dakota, six hours away. He'd never call in the middle of the night unless something was terribly wrong.

Val reached for the light on her bedside table, Luke's comforting hand sliding off her as he listened to whatever his father was saying on the other end of the phone.

The silence was deafening. Something bad *had* happened. She could feel it in her bones. In her heart.

"But . . . how? What happened?" Luke replied, his voice holding a note of disbelief.

"What's wrong?" Val hissed, her whispered words echoing around their shadowed bedroom.

Luke shushed her with a sharp wave of his hand. A gust of wind pushed through their open window, the white curtains twisting and dancing. A flicker of light, followed by a low rumble of distant thunder, was her only answer for the space of a heartbeat.

Had something happened to Luke's mom?

"Is anyone there with you now?" Luke asked into the phone, giving Val frustratingly little to go on, but the set of his shoulders and the flat tone of his voice told her something was dreadfully wrong. Luke sagged back against their headboard, still listening, and Val watched as a tear coursed down her husband's cheek. "All right. I'll call them now. And I'll call you back in the morning. Arrangements will have to be made," he responded, his voice cracking on his last word.

Arrangements will have to be made . . .

Luke continued to hold the phone up to his ear. Val couldn't tell whether Luke's dad was still on the other end. Her heart, full such a short time ago when she was counting their blessings, ached now at the sorrow reflected in Luke's eyes as he stared blindly ahead. His hand slowly sunk to his lap.

"My brother's dead."

CHAPTER EIGHT

GIFT OF BROTHERLY LOVE

*V*al let the warmth of the June sun soak into her skin, to her very core, and the chill she'd felt throughout the past week finally started to dissipate. She couldn't help but smile as Dave stood on the end of the dock, screaming at Noah and Logan not to go out any deeper.

"You guys are going to freeze your nuts off!"

Cringing, she glanced around, hoping no one else was within earshot. She didn't approve of his language, but she didn't have the energy to reprimand him. Besides, he wasn't wrong. Even though the sun was warm, the water still bore the remnants of a long, cold winter.

Jess crossed over the sand, smirking as she handed Val a bottle of water, keeping one for herself, before plopping down on the scratchy wool blanket next to her.

"Sorry, there wasn't any beer left in the lodge fridge," she explained, holding her own bottle of water up, the sun glinting off the contents inside.

"Excuse his language."

Jess shrugged. "He gets his potty mouth from his mama."

She's not wrong, either, Val silently agreed. Aloud, she again thanked

Jess for taking Storm while they were out of town for her brother-in-law's funeral.

"Watching your dog was the least we could do. I'm sorry we weren't able to drive over for the funeral, but I was glad Renee and Matt were able to take Mom and Dad over with them."

Val nodded, still staring out at the lake, keeping an eye on her two middle boys while also trying to block the awful scenes from her mind that she'd been part of over the past week. "It's a long drive. I know you'd have come if you could. Luke knows it, too. He appreciated you sending the bouquet."

Jess sighed. "I doubt Luke paid any attention to the funeral flowers. How's he doing? He was polite on the phone, but I couldn't really get a read on him. I can't imagine how it must feel, to lose a brother like that."

Slowly turning the cap of her water bottle, Val considered Jess's question. She was having trouble reading Luke's emotions, too. He'd been swinging between extremes ever since they'd gotten that terrible, middle-of-the-night phone call. Most of the time he was quiet, withdrawn. She'd never seen him so expressionless. Other times, he was livid. Luke's brother's death had been a horrific accident. And, to quote her husband, "utterly unnecessary." There'd been an accident on the family farm. Val knew Alan had been crushed when a piece of equipment fell on him while working in the shop late at night, but she knew little of the details. She shuddered. She didn't *want* to know more. All that mattered was her husband's only brother, his only sibling, was gone. Luke was still reeling from it all, and she didn't know how to help him.

"I wish there was some way to take away his pain," she said, glancing at Jess. "But he won't talk about any of it."

Jess said nothing for a moment, then looked around with some alarm. "Val, where's Jake?"

"He ran back to the van. He wanted to try out his flippers, but he forgot them in the vehicle," she said, nodding toward the front of the resort.

84

Jess visibly relaxed, leaning back on her forearms and looking up into the cloudless sky. "How are Luke's folks coping?"

Val thought back to the heart-wrenching scene at the graveyard following the ceremony at the church. Luke's parents somehow made it through the funeral itself, but when they walked up to the closed casket at the cemetery, his mother had collapsed with grief. Watching her father-in-law half carry, half drag his grief-stricken wife to a chair set up for the mourners would be a sight forever etched in Val's memory.

"Theresa is walking around like a zombie. Not that I blame her," Val finally replied. "No mother should ever have to bury one of her children. And I know KC blames himself. I think he was there when it happened. It was like he aged twenty years, almost before our eyes."

Jess, never one to shy away from silence, only nodded, leaving Val space to continue to process all that had happened. Alan wasn't the first person they'd lost that was roughly their same age. Renee's first husband, Jim, had gotten sick and died nearly fifteen years ago. Death at any age was terrible. Death of someone similar in age to yourself always made a person hyper-aware of one's own mortality.

Renee had survived the death of her husband, and eventually thrived again. Luke and his parents would come back from this, too. At least, that's what Val tried to convince herself of as she thought ahead to future holidays and life events without Alan. Her brother-in-law was a lifelong bachelor. He'd left no wife or kids behind.

Eventually, Jess sat back up. "How did the boys handle things? Had they ever even *been* to a funeral before?"

Val shook her head, a small smile stealing across her face despite the sad memories. "They were surprisingly strong. For once, they didn't fight me when I made them put on dress clothes. All four behaved amazingly well. I was worried. Because you're right. They've never had to face the death of someone in our family before—other than maybe Celia, but they were younger when she died, and they would have thought of her as 'old.'" Val emphasized her words with air quotes. "But Alan was only three years older than their own father. You'd have been proud of them, Jess, the way they stood tall, two on each side of Luke out at the cemetery. When their grandmother got so upset, I saw Jake waver a little, but Dave calmed him down with a strong hand on his shoulder. I think they helped Luke make it through, too."

Just then, Val noticed Logan, standing waist deep next to the dock, slash his arm across the water and send a wall of icy water up on Dave. Dave jumped back, his khaki shorts sporting big wet splotches as he held the phone he'd been fiddling with high into the air.

"Mom's going to kill you if you get my phone wet, and if you *ever* come out of that water, I'm going to beat the crap out of you!" Dave screamed at his brother.

Noah must have found the whole encounter funny, because he joined in on the splashing. Jake wandered down to the water's edge, flippers in hand, watching his three older brothers from a safe distance. "Someone's gonna get it," he said, shaking his head. "And this time it's not gonna be me."

A few years ago, Val might have intervened. But she'd learned that sometimes she just had to let them battle it out amongst themselves. They weren't disturbing anyone else on the beach. It might serve Logan right if Dave knocked him down a couple pegs.

"What's going to happen back at the farm?" Jess asked, seemingly unfazed by her nephews' antics. "I thought you said Luke's dad was pretty much retired and Alan was running things on his own these past couple years?"

Val picked up a four-inch stick not far from her feet and used it to dig a tiny tunnel into the sand next to the blanket. "I'm not really sure," she confessed. "I suspect that might have been one of the topics between Luke and KC during their closed-door discussions. I had to help Theresa with things after the funeral. Extended family and friends kept stopping by, many of them bringing food. She was in no shape to deal with any of it. It was like she'd been functioning on auto-pilot up until the funeral, but after . . . she basically shut down. Some days she wouldn't even come out of their bedroom until nearly noon. I did my best to track everything people brought over, all the cards and memorials, and keep the house semi-presentable. I was able to get most of the thank-you cards written."

"I'm so sorry, Val, that's a lot."

Val sighed, nodding. "It wasn't like I had a choice. And these four monkeys here," she added, motioning at her boys, "they'd had enough. Inside the house, the atmosphere was heavy, depressing. They stayed outside from morning until night, avoiding all the strangers. They did manage to have fun. I couldn't keep them off Alan's four-wheeler and Luke's old dirt bike, once they discovered those in one of the outbuildings."

Jess shuddered. "How terrifying."

"Right?! But I had to bite my tongue. Luke survived growing up on that farm. There were some bumps and bruises, but we got out of there in one piece. Dave did get one nasty gash on his knee, which is what's keeping him out of the water now, but there were no stitches. Maybe I should have taken him in. It'll probably scar."

"Aren't scars part of farm life?"

Val laughed. "That's probably true. Luke has a few."

"So now what?"

Looking quizzically at Jess, Val considered her sister's question. "Again, I'm not sure. I guess we'll take it day by day, see what happens. All I know is that we need to get our house back in shape so we can get out of Mom and Dad's hair. We all miss sleeping in our own beds."

"Ethan and the boys were able to get all but the finishing touches done on the Gray Cabin while you were gone," Jess shared. "Too bad it's only a one-bedroom. You guys could have hung out there this summer until your kitchen is back in commission. The kids would love a summer out here at Whispering Pines."

Val was *glad* the Gray Cabin only had one bedroom. It gave her an excuse to never stay there. Celia's comment about "bad things happening" in the cabin would be forever stuck in her brain.

A shout followed by a splash drew Val's eye back out to the water, where Dave must have finally had enough. A glance at the dock revealed he'd had the good sense to leave his shirt and phone there, out of the water. He was currently chasing Logan down, doing the zombie walk through waist-deep water in his direction. She hoped there was antiseptic in the first-aid kit in the kitchen. He was going to need it for that cut.

* * *

In a valiant effort to get back into their daily summer routine, Val got all four boys delivered to their Thursday morning activities. They'd all missed ball practice and some days of camp while out of town for the funeral. She'd have to start picking them back up around one o'clock. In the meantime, Luke had called, asking to meet her for lunch.

She immediately got a bad feeling about it. A lunch invite from him during the middle of the work week was out of character, but especially today, it being his first day back on the job.

He pulled in next to her as she parked at the restaurant. Slamming the door on her old minivan—the one she'd been driving since boy number two arrived on the scene—she waited for her husband while he finished a phone call inside his truck.

"Hey," he greeted her, reaching for her hand and leading her toward the door of the chain restaurant.

He's still wearing that mask, Val thought, unable to read his expression. Feeling shut out was getting old, though it had only been two weeks since the accident.

Once they were seated and placed their orders, Val decided it was time to push a little.

"To what do I owe this honor of a lunch date, midweek?"

Luke fisted his hands together and laid them on the tabletop, angling his body in her direction but staring out the window. Val glanced outside but saw nothing of interest. Her husband's mind was elsewhere.

"We need to talk."

It was amazing how those four little words, when strung together like that, never failed to kick a person's pulse up a few notches. Val nodded. They obviously needed to talk—she *did* want to know where his head was at these days. She just didn't know where to start the conversation.

"How was work this morning?"

He finally swung his eyes back to look at her. "It was fine. Listen, Val, I've been doing a lot of thinking these past few days."

She bit her lip, making the conscious effort to let him talk. She'd try not to interrupt.

"I'm afraid Dad can't handle things by himself at the farm."

She waited. When he held her eye but said nothing more, she experienced a wave of trepidation.

"Is there someone he can hire to come in and help?" she asked, hoping her practical suggestion would fend off what she feared was coming.

He shook his head slowly, letting his eyes fall to the tabletop. "He needs family right now, not some hired man."

She let that sink in. There *was* no other family—at least not immediate family—other than her husband.

"Do you need to go back to the farm, then, for a week or two? That's all right if you do. I can hold the fort down here for that long. I understand. Your folks need you right now. Your work will probably understand, too."

Luke loosened his fists, turning his palms up toward Val. She had a feeling she wasn't going to like what he was about to say, but habit had her reaching for his hands. As his fingers tightened on hers, she wasn't sure whether he was holding on to gain strength or give support.

"Things at work are slow. This morning my boss called me in first thing to let me know they'd cut our shifts down to three days a week, with a mandatory two-week shutdown in July. And when I'm not working . . . they aren't paying."

He paused, as if to let that sink in before continuing.

Val swallowed—those cuts, she knew, would be too big of a blow to their already precarious finances.

"I've decided I need to go back home for the summer. To help out.

The crops are planted, but there are animals to take care of and plenty of work to be done between now and harvest."

Val wasn't sure she was understanding his thought process. He belonged here, with her. And the boys. They needed him every bit as much as his parents. Slowly, she began to shake her head in disbelief.

"*You've* decided?"

He released her fingers and held up his palms again in defense. "Think about it, Val. We can't live on sixty percent of my regular paycheck. Dad would pay me. He'll pay me more than I would have made working full-time at my regular job. We've discussed it."

Val grasped for something, anything, to keep him from leaving them, even if it was only for the summer. "I thought you were going to do some work with Seth. That would help."

Luke sank back against the cushioned backrest of their booth, resignation in his eyes. "It would help us out financially, but it might not be enough. Besides, Dad doesn't have any other decent options. He needs to decide—*they* need to decide—what they want to do with the farm long-term. But right now there are things that need tending to. Immediately. Val, I can't just leave them in the lurch."

Their waiter brought the food, discreetly slipping a plate in front of each of them. *He can probably sense the tension floating between us,* Val thought, sparing the young man a nod of thanks.

Once he was gone, she said, "But it's okay for you to leave *us* in the lurch?"

"Come on, Val. It's not like that. You have all kinds of support here. Your folks are great. Ethan, your sisters, everyone . . . they'll all help us get through this."

Luke was right about her family. She had plenty of other support. It was one of the reasons they'd never left the area. Maybe they *could* make this work.

"Can we at least get the kitchen fixed up so we can be at home while you're gone?"

Luke sighed, picked at his pile of fries, but didn't eat anything. "I don't think so, hon. I talked to our insurance agent this morning, and our claim isn't even fully processed yet. I need to know what we have to work with for money before I can put the rooms back together."

This just keeps getting better and better.

"We're stuck at Mom and Dad's for the foreseeable future then? I'm sure *that* was not part of my parents' summer plans."

"Jesus, Val—*dying* wasn't exactly part of Alan's plans for the summer, either, so I'm sorry if it's an inconvenience for you, but it's not like we have a lot of options here," Luke spat out, glaring at her.

Pictures of Alan flashed through Val's brain: Alan, laughingly telling them about the time a bull tried to corner a then-teenage Luke in the pen out back. Alan, grinning at her from his place beside Luke at the altar on their wedding day as he stood up for his little brother.

She'd always known she had an ally in Alan. Luke wasn't the only one who lost him in that terrible accident.

Tears welled up in her eyes and a dreadful sense of loss washed through her. Even while sitting *in* the church on that horrific day, half listening as the priest droned on, she'd felt some kind of wall between her and her own grief over Alan's death. Suddenly, that wall was gone, and she realized Alan was truly gone.

And that left Luke to pick up the pieces.

The least she could do was give him the space to try to do that. She could handle things at home. Well, not exactly *at home*, but all this was just temporary.

Wasn't it?

CHAPTER NINE

GIFT OF TEMPTING OFFERS

"*N*oah, Logan, get your butts down here and clean up your breakfast mess, right now!" Val yelled up the stairs of her childhood home, trying to make herself heard over an argument between the boys in the bathroom. Something about the last of the toothpaste and a toothbrush falling—or being thrown—into the toilet bowl.

Hanging her head, she took a deep breath, then another, attempting to force the haze of red to clear from her eyes. Their bickering was driving her nuts, and it was getting worse. Luke had been gone for a week, but it felt like a month.

She tried again. "Noah, are you up there? Grab Logan and get your butts down here!"

The front door opened and Lavonne entered her front living room, newspaper in hand. "For crying out loud, Val, I can hear you yelling all the way outside. What's all the commotion about in here?"

Val sunk down onto the bottom step, defeated. "These boys are going to be the death of me."

Lavonne tossed the paper onto the coffee table and strode over to stand next to Val. "No need for drama, dear. What happened?"

Val opened her mouth to explain, then snapped it shut, realizing it would sound ridiculous. The boys had left their cereal bowls in the kitchen sink instead of putting them in the dishwasher. At least they'd made it to the sink.

"Forget it." She sighed, slid over, and patted the space next to her, inviting her mother to sit. "I'm sorry. My temper is getting the best of me these days. I'm not always such a bitch."

"I hate that word, Val," Lavonne said, her lips pursed. "It's derogatory to women and we should *never* use it."

Not quite able to contain an eyeroll, Val gave a light laugh. "Now who's being dramatic?"

"Touché," Lavonne conceded, sinking down next to Val. "I know it's hard being out of your house. And having Luke gone. Have you talked to him since he left?"

"We try to touch base quickly each evening. He likes to hear what the kids have been up to."

"How is it going at the farm? Are his parents starting to cope with things yet?" Lavonne asked, concern shining in her eyes.

"It doesn't sound like Theresa is doing much better. Luke thinks she might need to go see someone. You know, get some antidepressants or something. KC is *full* of anger. Luke said he wanders around, surly as a snake."

Val sighed again, feeling more ridiculous by the moment. Her own situation with the kids and the house might not be ideal, but poor Luke had it much worse. Here she was, yelling about cereal bowls.

"I wish there was something we could do for KC and Theresa. They are good people. None of this is fair."

Val shook her head. "No, you're right, Mom. None of this is fair. *Death* isn't fair. It isn't fair that Luke has to miss the summer with his boys either."

"And with you," her mother reminded her.

"Well, yeah, with me too," Val acknowledged.

Lavonne put a hand on Val's knee. "Why do you always do that, honey?"

"Do what?"

"You make it all about the boys. You do realize you are an integral part of your family, don't you? And I don't mean as chief laundress and housecleaner. Your husband loves you. And I know he misses you. You need to be careful. You want to keep your marriage strong, too. You can't afford to become one hundred percent consumed with parenting. There is more to life than raising your kids, you know."

Val, seldom speechless, was caught off-guard by her mother's intensity as she delivered what Val took to be a lecture.

"Jeez, I know that, Mom. What crawled up your butt?"

Lavonne squeezed Val's knee and then grabbed hold of the bannister to help pull herself up to standing. Val caught the wince on Lavonne's face when her mother's knee seemed to catch.

"Nothing *crawled up my butt.* And you wonder why your boys are starting to talk trash?"

"No, actually, the origin of their colorful vocabulary isn't really a mystery. But back up a minute. Why the comments about my marriage? My marriage is just fine."

Lavonne crossed her arms over her chest, staring down at her daughter, as if to say she didn't believe a word of it. "Look, Val, just be careful. We all tend to take things for granted for too long sometimes. Take it from me—that can crack the foundation of any relationship, no matter how strong it might have been up until that point."

Val was intrigued. She would have sworn she saw a shadow pass over her mother's eyes. Was she speaking from personal experience?

Hardly. No one had a stronger marriage than her folks.

* * *

"How are things over at Mom and Dad's?" Renee asked as she handed Val a plate out of the cupboard.

Val grimaced, taking the dish and wrapping it in blank newsprint. It was finally moving day for Matt and Renee. Val had brought the boys out to Whispering Pines to help. "Just about how you'd imagine. The boys are sick of not being home. They get bored at Mom and Dad's. They don't have any friends close by, and I know they miss their dad, too."

"I'm sure they do," Renee said, getting down off the step stool and brushing her hands together. "It's a tough situation any way you spin it."

Val waved her hands. "Enough about us. We are all fine—or will be. How about you? Are you *thrilled* to finally be moving into your new house with that hunky husband of yours?"

Renee laughed as she opened and then slammed various cupboard doors, glancing inside each. "You have no idea just *how* excited I am. This shabby duplex has served my needs for the past couple years, but it was always meant to be temporary. Building my dream home, on the edge of Whispering Pines, *with Matt* . . . it still feels so surreal. Pinch me!"

Val reached over and did just that.

Renee screeched and slapped her hand away. "You bitch! I can't believe you actually did that!"

"Don't let Mom hear you say that. She chewed me out for it yesterday."

Rubbing the red mark on her upper arm, Renee shook her head. "Is she driving you nuts yet?"

Val felt a twinge of guilt for opening her big mouth. She shouldn't act so unappreciative. It was incredibly kind of her parents to take her and four young boys *and* a dog in with no warning. While her mother might be driving her a tiny bit nuts, Val didn't need to actually admit that out loud.

"No, Mom's been great. So has Dad. I'm just going a little stir crazy over there. It's nice to come out here. The weather is great today, and the kids can burn off some of their energy. I just hope they don't disturb any of your paying guests."

Renee pulled a tray of silverware out of a drawer and placed it in a handled bag for transportation across the resort. "Everyone here this weekend is pretty chill. We should be fine. I just can't believe I get to sleep in my new bedroom tonight. I bet if we sleep with the windows open, I'll be able to hear the waves from the lake. I never could hear them from back here, the way the duplex is tucked back in this far corner."

Val pinched her again. "Well then, sis, we better get a move on if you need to get your new bedroom set up before dark."

* * *

Val hitched the box of dishes up on her hip and headed out the door toward Renee's new house. She'd been careful not to let it get too heavy so she could carry it to the other side of the resort. This wasn't a box she'd dare trust to any of her kids to carry. Given the horrors that followed the broken Corelle dish, she'd keep the boys away from any and all tableware during the move.

The concrete path took her past the Gray Cabin. She paused, setting the box of dishes down on the side of the path, grimacing as the contents clanked together.

Maybe I should have used more padding.

She marveled as she approached the small structure. It did indeed look much better, just as Jess had promised. Ethan and the boys had brought it back to life. From the outside, all it still needed were a few homey touches and it would be perfect.

Since she'd missed out on much of the work during their week at Luke's family farm, maybe she could help out by getting some bright annuals planted in the new flower box under the cabin's front window. Someone had scraped the peeling white trim and applied a bright red paint to match the other cabins. The new roof looked great, and all the old debris was cleaned away from the siding. She'd thought the gray log siding hideous before, but now that it was cleaned up, it provided the perfect backdrop to the pops of trim color, a brand-new screen door, and fresh black shingles. Throw two white Adirondack chairs in the grassy area out front and it would look as good as the picture in the old book Jess had found that included a few pages on Whispering Pines.

She couldn't wait to see the inside. Strolling up the steps, she let herself in through the unlocked door, now sporting new hardware. The transformation continued inside. The kitchen looked charming with the old upper cabinets out and replaced with open shelving. It was a very small cabin, but it had been spiffed up to look nearly new. Val especially liked the whitewash treatment on the fireplace.

Walking farther back into the cabin, she peeked into the tiny bathroom. Fresh and clean, with new grout and a frame around the old mirror over the vanity. Next, she checked out the back bedroom. The far wall had been redone. New sheetrock had eliminated the water-damaged paneling.

No more imaginary blood stain.

The room still needed a bed, but overall, she approved.

Turning on her heel, she headed back for the door. They still had lots to move for Renee and Matt. But as she reached for the doorknob, she hesitated.

What was that sound?

She stilled, straining to hear it again. But there was nothing out of place. She could hear Jake somewhere nearby, quizzing his cousin Robbie about why he'd picked the smaller of the three bedrooms in their new house.

Shaking her head, she let herself out, carefully closing the door behind her. The old place looked great, shined up like a new penny. Val smiled at the memory of one of Celia's favorite sayings—*shined up like a new penny.* She was sure their aunt would have approved of what they'd done with the old place.

* * *

Val collapsed on Renee's brand-new sofa. She'd lost count of the number of trips she'd made between the new house and the duplex.

"You better not be getting sweat on my new furniture, baby sis," Renee said, handing her a cold beer.

"I don't sweat—I sparkle."

Renee sank into one of the recliners, positioned to face an impressive view of the lake. "Oh yeah, I forgot. Just *Jess* sweats."

Laughing, Val held up her bottle of beer in mock salute as their other sister strode purposefully into the room, still barking orders over her shoulder to someone in the kitchen. Renee was right. Jess's dark hair, partially caught up in a high ponytail, had wet tendrils stuck to her neck.

Jess paused in her tirade to look at her sisters. "What?"

"You look like you just ran a marathon, Jess."

Grabbing the bottle out of Val's hand and swigging half its contents down in one shot before returning it, Jess nodded in agreement. "I know! Maybe I'm having a hot flash. I've never had one before, but I'm wringing wet."

"A menopausal bride. Lucky Seth," Val said, wriggling her eyebrows. "I wasn't actually offering you my beer, you know."

Jess shrugged, knelt down, and collapsed onto her belly, spread-eagle on the pale blue area rug. "And to think we thought moving you from one end of the resort to the other would be a piece of cake."

A scuffle in the kitchen and shouts to hold the door—the men were coming in with another piece of furniture.

"God, I hope that's my bed," Renee muttered, although she didn't move a muscle.

Val suspected none of them would be moving much by tomorrow. They'd be too stiff.

Ethan kicked Jess's outstretched foot as he came through the doorway carrying one end of a brand-new mattress still wrapped in protective plastic. "Get out of the way unless you want to get stepped on, Jess."

Knowing better than to test her big brother, Jess rolled to the side and out of the path leading to the stairs. The mattress kept coming, her fiancé on the other end.

"Tired, hon?" he asked, spying her on the floor. "Come on, ladies, we have another bed to get moved over here if Robbie wants to have somewhere to sleep tonight. Hop to it."

Jess gave him a dismissive wave, but Val noticed how she kept an eye on him until he'd disappeared up the stairs. "Sure glad I can't read that mind of yours, Jess, the way you're watching his cute little behind. You haven't even set a date yet, but I saw you two kissing back at the duplex. Already acting like newlyweds."

Jess sighed, rolling onto her back so she could raise her left hand in the air and admire the sparkle on her ring finger. Val thought this ring suited her sister so much better than the gaudy wedding set she'd sported for years. The man she was marrying would be a better fit, too.

"You're just jealous that I have a sexy guy to share my bed with tonight while you're missing yours. It's about time both Renee and I have a man handy instead of you."

"Ha-ha-ha," Val shot back, although Jess did have a point. Luke and Val had seldom been apart in the years they'd been married. This separation was new for them. Meanwhile, Renee had been a widow for ten years and Jess had been unhappily married for at least that many. And then divorced, but that was more recent.

Yes, she missed Luke. But apart from wishing he were there to help with the boys, she was kind of enjoying a tiny sense of freedom. Their normal routine had been disrupted. That wasn't necessarily a bad thing. If she could sleep in her own bed, and not the one she'd slept in for the first eighteen years of her life, this little hiatus from each other might be welcome. *Absence makes the heart grow fonder and all that.*

Not that she'd voice those things out loud.

She glanced around the sitting room they'd collapsed into, looking to change the subject. "I do love this new furniture, Renee. You didn't feel like bringing over the gold velour couch from the duplex, huh?"

Renee laughed. "No, I think I tolerated that about as long as a woman should have to. I also didn't want to bring any of my old stuff from the house in Minneapolis. Now that we are renting it out, and the people asked if they could rent it furnished, we decided to buy new."

Jess pushed up to a seated position with a groan. "It is great. But it needs something more. Decorations."

Renee finished off her beer, nodding. "I know. I just haven't gotten around to that yet. We'll get settled, get through the Fourth of July, and *then* I'll make time to cozy it up in here. You know how crazy it gets out here for Independence Day."

Val loved to decorate almost as much as she loved to cook. "Can we help?"

"Absolutely. I'll provide wine and pizza, and you two provide your HGTV skills."

Ethan and Seth came pounding back down the stairs.

"Still no movement out of you three, huh?"

"Up yours, Ethan," Renee said. "We're tired. I started packing boxes two hours before you'd even thought about opening your eyes this morning, bro. Hey, where's my husband?"

"We left Matt and Robbie back at the duplex, hauling boxes up out of your basement. They might be heading over here with the first of those," Seth chimed in. He stopped in front of Jess and reached a hand down to her. "Come on, girl, no rest for the wicked."

Val watched him yank Jess up to her feet and steal a kiss before heading back through the kitchen. She rubbed her own eyes before standing.

Okay, maybe I miss Luke more than I thought.

* * *

Later, after George and Lavonne showed up with Chinese food for everyone, Val and Renee headed back to the duplex for one last armful of bedding before calling it a day. Although the sun had nearly set, all the kids were tossing a football around in a large grassy area. Val hoped they weren't getting too bit up. She checked for Jake, not yet entirely comfortable letting her youngest roam unsupervised around the resort. There he was in the middle of the pack.

"Boys, we'll head out in about half an hour," she warned them as she passed.

She didn't mind the groans she earned in reply. That meant they were having fun, and thus would sleep like logs.

"I love that all the cousins have so much fun together. Robbie gets kind of bored out here when none of you are around, even though he's older than all the other boys. He's a big help, mowing lawns and keeping things up for his summer job, but when the work is done, there isn't much to do."

"Yeah . . . it won't be too many more years before they're all scattered, doing their own thing," Val agreed.

They walked along in silence for a stretch.

"You know, Val, I've been thinking. With Luke gone for a couple months . . . would you ever consider moving out here for the rest of the summer?"

Val laughed. As tempting as two months at Whispering Pines sounded, the idea was ridiculous. She said as much to her sister.

Renee stopped Val with a hand on her arm. They were right behind the lodge now, and the motion-sensitive light over the back door flipped on, bathing them in a soft yellow light, the night deepening around them. "But *why* is it ridiculous? Half of the duplex will be empty. I bet Jess will move out, too, as soon as they decide when to get married. Matt and I have already decided we'll remodel both halves of the duplex and start renting them out next summer. But I don't even want to start that big project until late fall, after all our renters are gone. Remodeling the duplex and running our retreats will take up my winter. But that still leaves it open for the rest of this summer."

Val had never considered an extended vacation out here at Whispering Pines at this stage in their lives. They'd spent a week out here a few times, even brought their old camper out and parked it next to the duplex when the cabins were full, but she never would have been able to afford renting a cabin out here for longer. And Renee couldn't afford to let people stay in any of the cabins for free. Their season was too short as it was, and the resort was expensive to maintain.

Val couldn't afford it before, and she couldn't afford it now.

"Forget it, Renee. There's no way I could make it happen. Besides, the boys have busy schedules and it's a forty-five-minute drive out here. We couldn't do that every day."

Renee grunted noncommittally as they resumed their original trek.

Val tried to put the idea out of her mind. While tempting, it wasn't feasible.

* * *

Back at the duplex, together they gathered up the necessary bedding, stripping blankets and comforters off the old beds.

Thinking, Renee said, "I have fresh sheets over at the new house already, but I don't have time to wash the blankets and comforters right now."

"I wouldn't worry about it. As long as we don't drag them on the way over, these should be fine."

Renee stooped to pick up her stack but paused, standing back up to face Val, hands on her hips.

"Why are you being so stubborn? I think this might be the perfect solution to your summer problem. The boys are bored at Mom and Dad's, and you can't go back to your house until Luke has a chance to fix up your kitchen. My half of the duplex will sit empty. Maybe you should ask the boys what *they'd* like to do. Camps and baseball . . . or running wild at the lake for two months?"

When Val didn't respond, Renee pushed on. "Why not? Would it leave any of their teams short? Do any of them love it so much that they intend to use baseball for college scholarships or something?"

Renee was really getting wound up now.

She has a point, Val thought. "Actually," she admitted, "all their baseball teams are pretty full. My boys do lots of sitting during games. And they don't have any sports camps in August, just July. If I pulled them out now, I might even save some money."

"See?! Ask them. Don't just assume they'd prefer a structured summer of mandatory practices."

She *could* ask them. Maybe they would surprise her. But that still left the issue of cost.

"You might be right about the boys. They love it out here. But, Renee, I'm going to be perfectly honest with you. Luke and I . . . things are stretched pretty thin these days. I can't afford to rent from you. I've been insisting on giving Mom and Dad grocery money, but beyond that, we are pretty much living paycheck to paycheck. Except for my money from Celia, of course, but I can't use it to lounge around out here for a couple months."

Renee stared at her as if she'd grown two heads. "Do you think I suggested you stay in the dingy old duplex, which otherwise would sit empty, to make money off of you? For God's sake, Val. That is insulting."

"Oh—" Val stuttered, "I just assumed . . ."

"And you know what they say about assuming, sis. No, there would be no cash exchanged. The duplex will sit empty for the rest of the summer if you don't use it."

"I couldn't stay out here for nothing. That isn't fair to you," Val countered.

Renee took two steps toward Val and rested her hands on her shoulders. "Valerie, Whispering Pines is our *family's* resort. Celia may have signed the deed over to me, but this place is special to all of us. It has been ever since we came here as kids. Opening our time capsule was a great reminder of that. I came here to heal and start a new life. Jess came here to do the same. Maybe now it's your turn, even if it's only for the summer. I've been getting the feeling you're not exactly thrilled with the state of your life these days. Give yourself some space. Stop trying to do so much for those kids all the time, and keep a perfect house for your husband, with perfect meals on the table every day. Shit, Val, you don't exist on this earth just to serve them. They don't want you to do that."

Val felt tears stinging her eyes. "I don't need your pity, Renee."

Renee dropped her hands with a sigh. "You are so damn stubborn! You always have been. I don't *pity* you. I've always *envied* you, in fact. Up until recently, you've seemed so happy with your life. But sometimes we need to shake things up a little."

"I didn't know my *discontent* was so obvious," Val muttered, twisting her wedding ring in frustration.

Renee picked up her pile of bedding and made her way to the door. Val followed her lead, chewing on all Renee had said.

"I'd want to talk to Luke, and the boys, before deciding," she finally said—but, truth be told, now that her sister had planted the idea in her head, she was starting to see the possibilities.

"I wouldn't necessarily call it discontent, Val," Renee said over her shoulder as she carefully descended the steps out front, balancing her stack of linens. "But Mom did say you were kind of bitchy lately."

Val nearly tripped on the top step, and their laughter rang out across the darkened tree tops.

CHAPTER TEN

GIFT OF UNSTRUCTURED TIME

"What do the boys think?" Luke asked later that night when Val called to share Renee's crazy idea with him. "I haven't said anything to them yet. I wanted to talk it over with you first, but I didn't want to wait until your visit this weekend. What do *you* think?"

Luke was quiet for a beat on the other end of the phone. Val could hear a television playing in the background, could picture KC and Theresa, each sitting in their chair, staring at a screen but not really watching. How dismal for Luke. "Well, hon, it's up to you . . . but the boys' coaches are going to be ticked if you pull them out for the summer."

Val had been warming up to the idea of spending the rest of the summer at Whispering Pines ever since Renee tried to convince her it was a good idea. But part of her had been waiting for Luke to squelch the idea all along—and here it was.

"Do we really care what they think?"

"Come on, Val. You know how competitive sports teams can be these days. Especially Logan's team. He probably has the most promise, but if he bails on his team midseason the coach might not let him play next year."

Val sighed, considering. Because what Luke said was true. Luke had never played organized sports as a kid, but his warning was on point: if their boys wanted to play, skipping part of a season would make it tougher.

"That *could* happen," she said. "But would it really be so bad if he went back to playing for a team that doesn't travel all the time? You know, like next summer? Those short trips were getting so expensive . . . I'm not sure we've got our priorities right here, Luke. Push, push, push. More times than not, the boys whine when I tell them it's time to leave for practice, and they don't even get that much playing time during games. Maybe they'd enjoy the rest of the summer off, to play out at the resort. And I wouldn't let them be total bums. They could help out with some yardwork, hauling wood, that kind of thing."

"Well, I guess I won't tell you *no*. This summer is so messed up as it is. Why don't you talk to the boys? See what *they* want to do?"

For some reason, Luke's response grated on Val. She hadn't called to *ask permission*. She was a grown-ass woman. If she wanted to spend two months, for free, out at the family lake resort, they would.

"I will get *input* from the boys, and then *I'll* decide whether or not to take them out to Whispering Pines for the rest of the summer. Kind of like *you* decided to spend your summer at the farm."

Val could hear Theresa yell something to Luke.

"Sorry, Val, sounds like one of the cows got out and is eating Mom's gladiolas. I gotta go take care of it. I'll support whatever you decide. Miss you. Looking forward to seeing you and the boys in a few days."

Click.

Val stared at her silent phone, irritated. Had he even realized she was still mad at him? Would he care if he did?

But Luke was right about one thing: this was a screwed-up summer.

Now she had the chance to make the best of it, and since Luke planned to be back for the weekend, he could help them get settled at the lake.

The boys don't stand a chance of talking me out of it.

* * *

"You kids are going to have a great time," Val heard her father tell one of his grandsons as she hauled a heavy suitcase down her parents' staircase. "Robbie can take you out fishing, and maybe Matt can take you for a hike in the woods. But don't ask your Uncle Ethan to take you. He got into some trouble when he headed off into the woods with a friend as a boy. He wasn't much older than you. He might not make the best guide, but don't tell him I told you that."

Val grinned at the memory, careful not to miss a step. She'd been young when Ethan ran into trouble in the woods. In fact, she was pretty sure it had been the same summer they put their time capsule together. She still didn't know why the boys had gone off into the woods alone. They weren't allowed, and, sure enough, Ethan's friend had gotten hurt—broken his arm or something.

"Just be sure to reiterate they can't go into the woods without an *adult*, Dad," Val said, grunting as she caught the bottom step with a wheel on the heavy suitcase.

"Dave, grab that for your mother. What are you doing, making her haul that big thing down herself?"

"Sorry, Grandpa," Dave said, stepping forward to take the beast of a case from Val and then turning toward his three younger brothers in the kitchen. "You guys need to go up and get your own stuff and bring it down here. Dad will be here with the truck any minute."

Val offered her oldest a thankful smile as he set down the suitcase and rushed upstairs. He'd stepped in earlier, too, when Logan resisted this idea of a Whispering Pines summer. Of her four boys, Logan loved his baseball the most. And as Luke had said earlier, he might have the most to lose if he dropped from his team midseason. Dave had reminded Logan of all their father had lost that summer, and maybe it wasn't such a bad thing to spend more time with each other. Val's eyes had misted over, recognizing, not for the first time, that her eldest had what she thought of as an old soul. Most twelve-year-old boys would want to be anywhere *but* stuck in a cabin with their three younger brothers for the better part of a summer. Dave's words had gone a long way to convince Logan, but he wasn't totally on board yet. Val hoped he wouldn't give her too much sass. Noah and Jake had jumped at the chance for more time out at the resort. Their summer just went from boring to the possibility of endless nights of campfires and days on or near the water.

What more could kids ask for?

A horn blared outside.

"And that would be your father, here to help you get settled at the duplex," Lavonne said, snapping the towel she'd been using to dry dishes at her youngest grandchild.

"Grandma! Watch it," Jake cried, sidestepping her towel and surging in to grab Lavonne's wrists. Lavonne wriggled free and caught him up in a bear hug.

"I'm going to miss you guys," she huffed out, then released the squirming boy. "I won't miss the daily trip to the grocery store, but I'll miss *you*."

"Jake! Come on!" Dave hollered down the steps. "Your suitcase is still sitting up here."

Groaning, Jake gave Lavonne a quick hug before heading upstairs. "Thanks for letting us stay here, Grandma. I'll miss you, too."

Lavonne laid a hand over her heart. "Keep an eye on him. He's a charmer."

Val grinned, giving first her mother and then her father thankful hugs. "I don't know what we'd have done without your generosity these past couple weeks."

"You know you are welcome anytime," George reminded her before striding to the back door to let Luke in.

"You guys ready to roll?" Luke asked, nodding a greeting.

Val didn't recognize the western-style shirt her husband wore. The jeans and boots were nothing new, even in the summer heat, but normally he'd wear a T-shirt in weather like this, topped off with a baseball cap.

"Dad!" Noah yelled as he entered the kitchen with a suitcase and backpack. He dropped both and raced to his father's side. Luke caught him up and swung him around, his face reflecting pure joy—something so often missing from Luke ever since that late-night phone call.

"How are you doing, bud? I've missed you," he said, ruffling Noah's thick, sandy-blond hair.

"I've missed you, too. I wish you could stay with us at Whispering Pines! That would be so cool. We'd catch so many fish!"

Luke put an arm around his son's shoulder and squeezed. "You've got me for a couple days. I'm sure we can get out on the water again once or twice before I have to go back to the farm. That is, unless you're worried that I'll catch more fish than you?"

Noah pushed away from Luke with a laugh, picked up his bags where he'd left them, and headed for the back door and Luke's truck. "You can try, old man, you can try . . ."

Val laughed as Noah's voice trailed away. "I think the gauntlet has been thrown down."

She stepped into Luke's arms, cutting off his smirk with a kiss. Her folks busied themselves while she greeted her husband.

"Thanks for coming to see us this weekend. Your visit turned out to be perfect timing! I appreciate your help getting us moved out to the duplex," Val said, stepping back but keeping a hand on his forearm. "I've got a few things over at the house I'd like to pick up, too, if that's all right."

Luke grinned over the top of her head as his other three boys trundled into the kitchen, arms full. "Hey, guys, good to see you!"

Val stepped to the side to allow for more hugs. It was nice to have all her boys in one place again, even if it was only for a couple days.

Val groaned, covering her head with a pillow. She reached beside her, but the bed was empty. Tossing her pillow aside, she lay still for a moment, willing herself to *enjoy* the bird song weaving through the open window. The musical little thing had woken her up . . . but she supposed it was better than waking up to the screech of an alarm. For a second, she reached into her memory bank to try to remember if any of the kids had an early practice. But as a soft breeze brushed over her, reality returned. They were at Whispering Pines. She had things to do, but nothing on the list resembled a carpool or killing time while waiting for a practice session to wrap up.

Where's Luke?

Swinging her feet out of bed, she glanced at the time. It was only 6:30. Had he decided to take the boys fishing? He hadn't mentioned it.

She threw a robe on over her shorty pajamas and padded toward the stairs in her slippers. She glanced through the open doors of the other two bedrooms. All four boys were still sound asleep, their new rooms already in various states of disarray. And, for a change, she didn't care. They were on vacation.

Sort of.

The scent of coffee floated up to meet her as she skipped down the stairs. Luke must have started a pot. But where was he?

Sure enough, a half-filled pot of coffee waited for her on the counter. In the sink sat an empty cereal bowl that hadn't been there when they'd gone to bed. But her husband wasn't here. Filling her mug with the steaming brew, she glanced out the back door. He was there, sitting on an old lawn chair, staring off toward the trees that lined the back of the yard. The duplex sat in the far corner of the resort, originally used by resort staff. Which, considering all the work she had in mind for the boys, maybe they could be considered "staff" anyway.

She sipped her coffee, watching him, wishing she could see inside his mind. Her husband was normally relaxed—fun, even. He helped keep her slightly more volatile nature grounded. She'd always thought they made a good pair. But ever since his brother's accident, that light had left his eyes. She had noticed flickers of the old Luke over the past two days—always when he interacted with the boys—but not as often as she'd like.

Would time help fill the gaping hole she was sure he felt over the loss of his brother? Or was this the new Luke?

What was it Renee had said? Something about everyone changing over time. She supposed that applied to her husband as well, but still she missed the old Luke.

Then again, she shouldn't judge. Of course she missed Alan, too, but it wasn't the same for her. If she lost Ethan or one of her sisters, she couldn't even imagine how she'd feel.

She took one more sip of coffee and then a deep breath as she pushed through the door. She could smell the aroma of the gently swaying pines and an undertone of earth.

It's peaceful here. This will do him good.

Luke glanced her way and gave her a brief smile before turning back again to stare off into the woods.

"I wish you could stay through the holiday," Val said, pulling a second lawn chair closer to her husband. Metal legs scraped across the pitted concrete of the old patio as she swung the chair around to face the woods. "All the nieces and nephews will be home for the Fourth and the cabins will be full of renters."

Luke sighed. "I'm glad you guys will have fun. But you know I can't stay."

"Are you sure? What's so pressing? Didn't Alan ever take any time away from the farm?"

Luke grunted in response, giving her a quick glance.

They sat in silence. She felt chastised, though he hadn't said a word. Val wrapped her hands around her coffee cup, chilled by both the early morning air and Luke's attitude. Nothing she said seemed to sit well with him.

Eventually, he spoke again. "I'm beginning to realize just how hard Alan had to work to keep the farm. All those years I left him to do it alone . . . well, Dad was there with him, too, but I'd forgotten what it's like. Here I've been thinking we were *so* busy for all these years, working eight or ten hours a day, then chasing the kids around when I'm not at work. What a joke."

" 'What a joke'?" Val repeated slowly, the peacefulness of the morning evaporating. "Are you calling your life with us a *joke*? Because last time I checked, I thought we had it pretty good."

"But don't you see, Val? That's exactly the problem. We *do* have it good. I let myself get all caught up in our life here, and never went back to help at the farm. Once Dad decided to retire, Alan had to do it all himself. He never even had a chance to get married or have kids of his own. All he did was work. And now he's dead."

Luke's synopsis of Alan's life both surprised and saddened her. She didn't agree with her husband, and she suspected Alan wouldn't have appreciated Luke's comments, either. "That was his choice. The marriage-and-family part, I mean. Alan was a great guy. I'm sure he could have married if he'd wanted to. I guess I just thought he enjoyed the bachelor life. He dated through the years."

"He did. But he was never serious about any of them. Except for Kennedy."

She gave him a curious look.

He explained, "He told me once, probably after a night of too much alcohol, that she had been the love of his life. They started dating in high school. It turned out she hated farm life. She couldn't wait to get away. But he never wanted to leave the farm. I think giving up so easily on her was his one big regret in life."

Val took a minute to consider Luke's words. "Luke, babe, you are *not* responsible for the choices Alan made in his life. He was your big brother. I know how much you looked up to him, and he was always good to you, but you can't blame yourself for his choice to stay single. He could have left, too, gone off to college like you did and done something else with his life."

Luke shook his head. "You don't understand, Val. It's not that simple."

"Do you honestly feel like it's your fault he never left the farm?" Val asked. "Luke, this isn't the pioneer days. Farms that remain in families for generations aren't the norm anymore. You know that."

Luke pushed up out of his chair and wandered to the edge of the patio, his back to her. "Val, the farm wasn't the problem. It was the girl. Kennedy broke his heart. And that *was* my fault."

Val wasn't sure she'd heard him right. Who was this Kennedy chick and what did she have to do with Luke? She'd never even heard her name before.

"You lost me."

Luke dumped his dregs of cold coffee onto the lawn before sitting back down next to Val. "Alan was three years ahead of me in school. Kennedy was two years behind Alan, so one year ahead of me."

Val moaned. "Luke, don't tell me it was a case of two brothers fighting over one girl."

"Do you want to be quiet and let me tell the story?" he asked, leaning down to pick up a pinecone near his foot. He chucked it far into the backyard.

"Sorry. Go on."

"It all started the night of Kennedy's senior prom. She'd been dating my brother for over a year at that point. Alan had already been out of high school for a couple years, but he agreed to be her date. She didn't want to miss her prom, and Alan had no intention of letting her go with someone else. Kennedy's best friend needed a date, too. I hadn't asked anyone yet, so Kennedy begged me to ask her friend. We'd double-date, she said. I didn't have a girlfriend at the time or anyone else I wanted to ask, and Alan was fine with the idea. None of his buddies were going. They'd all moved on after high school."

Val tried to picture Luke and Alan, wearing rented tuxes with big-haired girls in gaudy dresses clinging to their arms. She said as much.

Luke laughed at her vivid description. "You got the tux part right, but those girls weren't gaudy. In fact, they were gorgeous."

It was Val's turn to grunt in reply.

Luke continued. "But it didn't take me long to figure out that Kennedy's friend was trouble. We picked her up last, and we'd barely rolled out of her farmstead before she pulled a flask out of the duffle bag she'd brought along. I figured there might be some drinking after we left the dance—there was always a big bonfire down by the river back then—but not before. Hell, Mom and Dad were chaperones! She kept passing the flask around, but I refused. I don't think Kennedy drank much, either. Alan, on the other hand, kept up with my date."

"What was your date's name?"

Luke rubbed his chin. "Hell, I can't even remember now. She

moved to town at the start of that school year and left right after graduation. Suffice it to say we did *not* hit it off that night."

"But something must have happened."

"Yeah, it did. I could tell Alan was uncomfortable, being older than most everybody else that night. Even a couple years feels like ten at that age. I don't know if he was trying to look like a badass, or what. Things went all right at the dance, but then when we stopped over at Kennedy's house to change into different clothes on our way to the bonfire, Alan and Kennedy got in this big shouting match. It was ugly. The tension was thick when we got back in the car. I took the keys from Alan at that point. I figured he'd tipped the flask a few too many times by then. At least he didn't fight me on that."

Val couldn't help but chuckle. "Oh, the drama of high school prom. It's a miracle we all survived."

"Yeah, no kidding. When the boys get older, *do not* push for them to go," Luke said, shaking his head. "Anyhow, we headed to the bonfire. I was ready to ditch all three of them by that point and find my buddies. In fact, I did just that. For a while, at least. At some point, Kennedy's friend took off with some guy. My dear brother passed out in the backseat of his car, leaving Kennedy to wander from group to group. But after that scene at her house, she was miserable. It was their first big fight."

"And let me guess," Val chimed in. "With Alan out of commission, you were the shoulder for Kennedy to cry on."

Luke shrugged. "I guess. We talked. People started taking off, but we sat there until the sun started coming up—sat on old rubber tires, I think. Yeah, I still remember the black mark on the butt of my favorite jeans. It never did come out."

Val thought back to a bonfire she went to in college where they'd burned tires. The black smoke and stench were unforgettable. "So you stepped up and took care of Alan's girl that night, like any decent friend—*or brother*—would do. That sounds admirable to me, and not something you should regret."

"Alan didn't see it that way," Luke countered. "Some of what we talked about that night were our plans after high school. She admitted she wanted to get away, to go to college. She hated everything about small-town life. But she was afraid to talk to Alan about it. She swore to me that she loved him and didn't want to lose him. She was afraid he'd dump her if he found out how different their dreams were for the future. Later, Alan blamed me for planting those ideas in her head."

A window slid open behind them and Jess yelled a morning hello to them from her kitchen on the other side of the duplex.

"Morning, Jess!" Val tossed back, then turned her attention back to Luke. "That doesn't sound fair."

Luke shrugged. "After that night, things were pretty rocky for them. Kennedy did leave for college that next fall. She went to NDSU."

Val raised her eyebrows. "NDSU, as in your alma mater? Let me guess—you ran into her when you went there the following year?"

"Yeah. At first it was great to see a familiar face. But by then her relationship with Alan had fizzled. They'd decided to 'take a break' and 'date other people,'" Luke said, using air quotes to emphasize his points.

"I'm guessing your interpretation of 'other people' might have been different from your brother's?"

He nodded. "She kept pestering me to take her out. Against my better judgment, I finally caved. We went out for about a month. I liked her, she was funny and nice and we had lots in common, but it felt too weird. I broke it off and thought that was the end of it."

Val waited, suspecting he wasn't quite done with the story.

"Word got back to Alan that we'd been seeing each other. He went ballistic. I'd never seen him so mad. It didn't seem to matter to him that he was dating other girls by then. He barely spoke to me for the better part of a year after that. In hindsight, I could see how much I hurt him."

Val set her now-empty mug on the ground and stood, moving to stand behind Luke. She placed her hands on his shoulders and started to work out the kinks. "Hon, you need to quit with this notion that Alan's problems in life were your fault. And that includes his ill-fated love life. If he'd really wanted the girl, he could have gone after her. Won her back."

"But don't you see, Val?" Luke said, reaching up to grab one of her hands. "He was trying to do just that. And then he died."

"What do you mean? All that stuff was decades ago."

He dropped her hand and resumed staring off into the woods. "She came back. Her dad got sick, I guess, and so she came back and she and Alan were just starting to try again. But the accident ended that, too."

Another wave of sympathy and loss flowed through her body.

Alan deserved happiness . . . but he waited too long.

A screen door slapped shut behind them.

"Why so glum out here?" Jess asked, a pot of coffee in her hand. "It's a beautiful summer morning and it's Sunday! I think we should go spend it on the beach."

Luke stood and headed for the house, holding his hand over his cup as he passed Jess. "You two have fun. I've got work to do."

Jess watched him leave, then turned back to Val to refill her cup. "What's got him so uptight?"

Val sighed. "Not what. Who."

CHAPTER ELEVEN

GIFT OF FUN IN THE SUN

*T*hree days later, Val *did* wake to the incessant chirping of her alarm. It wasn't a day to allow herself the luxury of sleeping in—not that she ever managed to stay in bed much past seven. Fumbling for her phone, she silenced the annoying beep as quickly as she could, not wanting to wake anyone else.

Storm stirred near the foot of the bed, her silky head popping up to eye Val expectantly. Val smiled, which of course was invitation enough for the dog to crawl up and curl against her side. The weight of the animal's warm body convinced her to linger a few more minutes.

She mentally reviewed her "to do" list. Today would be their third annual Fourth of July celebration at Whispering Pines. As she stretched and yawned on top of her comfortable bed, she was thankful to be *inside* the duplex this year instead of in their old camper parked out in the yard, which was where they'd spent the last two Fourth of July holidays. The mattress in their camper was basically a four-inch-thick piece of foam, and while the length of it had never bothered *her*, Luke complained that his feet hung off the end.

She felt a twinge of loneliness—she *missed* Luke, now that he was gone. But, given his brooding nature of late, the day would undoubtedly be more fun without him.

And that probably makes me a cold-hearted bitch, she thought, considering the reason Luke wouldn't be hanging out with the rest of the family today.

But she refused to feel guilty. She rolled out of bed and got moving. They had a jam-packed day full of eating and festivities planned. Time to get to it.

She showered and dressed in lightweight capris and the go-to T-shirt she always wore on the Fourth. She ran a quick brush through her hair, cringing at her red shirt in the mirror. The formerly bright cotton was now more of a washed-out salmon. But the American flag emblazoned across the front made it the only patriotic thing she owned. She had to be festive.

"Good Lord, I *am* becoming my mother," she whispered to her own reflection. Lavonne never missed a chance to wear holiday-appropriate apparel.

After completing her minimal morning routine, she headed out of the duplex. Storm tagged along on the stroll over to the lodge, where Val had already started preparing dishes for the day's menu the night before. Early rays of sunlight stole through the tall pine trees flanking their path. The morning air held the dewy freshness that she loved, the kind you missed if you were up much later than the rising sun. No one else was out and about yet, but with the cabins full of renters and most of her family already at the resort, things would be bustling soon.

Inhaling deeply, Val tilted her face up toward the dappled sunlight, feeling grateful. She'd been slogging through her days, feeling stuck in many ways, but today was a day to focus on the good. It was still hard to believe they didn't have to go home at the end of this week. Time here, at this resort, always calmed her. She felt a sense of nostalgia about it that she didn't fully understand. Yes, she'd spent a few summers here as a child, but it went beyond that. There was a history here.

What stories could these old buildings tell of all the travelers who've passed through here? she wondered. Her aunt first came here as a young woman, in the 1940s, and the resort was even older than that.

The nostalgia she always felt at Whispering Pines had given her an idea. Because she loved to cook, she was now usually the one to feed her extended family during their various gatherings instead of her mom. Val was happiest when she was creating in the kitchen. Having a houseful of preteen boys meant they went through lots of food, but the kids didn't appreciate variety.

The night of The Great Flood, she'd been thumbing through one of the old recipe boxes she'd brought home three years earlier when she'd helped her mom and sister clean out Celia's kitchen. She was so glad she'd thought to stow the box out of harm's way when the first *plop* of water fell from the ceiling. She'd only glanced at a few recipes that night, but one card in particular was firmly entrenched in her mind.

When she'd first read the old card for a recipe called piccalilli, her mind conjured up a scene from an old-fashioned summer picnic, the kind she'd imagined Celia would have attended as a child. Most of the ingredients could have been picked from the garden. The pile of vegetables it called for were to be diced, sprinkled with a cup of salt, and then stored overnight in a stone jar. Maybe it was that last part that caught her attention. Stone crocks, once a staple in every kitchen, had become expensive collectibles used for decoration instead of their original, utilitarian purpose. She *had* to give it a try.

What if she dug out a few interesting-looking recipes from the old box and intermixed them, kind of like experiments, with the tried-and-true dishes she wouldn't dare skip for their holiday barbeque? That way, maybe the surprise would slip by the boys and they'd realize they actually *liked* this new food, instead of complaining about her switching things up.

She imagined Celia collecting the sizable assortment of recipes from friends, acquaintances, and family. Most of the cards were varying shades of plain white paper, but a few sported kitschy illustrations of enamel ranges or women wearing aprons over day dresses.

Once the idea to try some of the old recipes took hold, she ran with it. In fact, she'd already picked out ten new recipes to try—mainly salads and desserts. She was confident any dessert she put on the table would disappear; her family never shied away from sweets. The salads were more of a gamble, but she couldn't resist the challenge.

She entered the hushed interior of the lodge kitchen, Storm at her heels. Her sense of wellbeing intensified.

When Renee had hired Ethan to remodel the lodge, she'd allowed Val and Luke to oversee the kitchen overhaul. The budget had been limited, but Val loved the openness of the tweaked layout, the stainless-steel top on the island, and the new appliances that were more than adequate, even if they weren't top of the line.

She pulled her menu out of the pocket of her capris. Hot dogs, brats, and a variety of toppings would provide the main course, surrounded with both her new dishes and old favorites. No one would go hungry, regardless of whether or not they liked any of the new recipes. Her hope, however, was that some would love the additions to their standard holiday menu.

Storm lay down on the cool tile, having already nosed her way around the main floor. Val was sure the young dog suffered in the early July heat, given her heavy coat, and the floor had to be a welcome relief for her. It wasn't hot outside yet, but it would be.

The dog provided a sense of companionship as Val got to work. Digging a huge wooden spoon out of a drawer, she removed the heavy stone lid from the crock she'd filled the night before. She'd originally spied the crock in the old garden shed behind the lodge the previous summer. It was amazing the piece hadn't been damaged or stolen. She pushed the spoon down deep into the salted vegetables, mixing everything again while trying to read the recipe card on the counter next to it.

Unlike some of the recipe cards she'd pulled out for today's party, this one for piccalilli wasn't dated, but Val suspected it had to be one of the older ones. The card was a shade darker than the others, the color reminding her of the driest areas of sand on the beach outside the lodge. The card bore some stains, and was even missing a small chunk out of the bottom center. Val wondered if Celia's mother refer-enced this very card while working in her kitchen, two lifetimes ago.

The thing has a few battle scars—just like the rest of us.

Val chuckled to herself, and then propped her phone up on the island's metal top and started a random playlist. Singing along to "Shallow," she did her best to keep up with Lady Gaga's range, but was afraid she fell woefully short. Not that it mattered. No one was around to complain.

Storm lifted her head and howled.

"Must have been worse than I thought," she admitted, reaching down to pet the critic.

She pulled a plastic bottle of vinegar and a hefty bag of white sugar out of the pantry. This was the part of the recipe she'd worried about. She'd need to drain the vegetables, then "scald" them in a mixture of vinegar and water. Then prepare a dressing by boiling vinegar and sugar together.

Doesn't vinegar stink when you boil it? She supposed she'd find out.

She got to work, grunting as she tipped the heavy crock full of diced cabbage, cucumbers, peppers, onions, and tomatoes on its side to drain the salty water, then she started her work with the vinegar.

"Holy hell, what is that *stench?*" Lavonne cried as she came in through the kitchen door. "Val, it's the Fourth of July, not Easter. It smells like you're dying Easter eggs in here."

Val laughed, having already gotten used to the odor. "Hi to you, too, Mom. I thought I'd try one of the old recipes from Celia's recipe box. Actually, I thought I'd try a bunch of them."

"Bold move," her mother said, picking up the tan-colored card. "If all the dishes smell like this, I better order a bunch of pizzas. What does it mean to 'scald' the vegetables?"

Val shrugged as she dumped the dressing into the crock, stirred the mixture one last time, then placed the heavy cover back on it again. Maybe the smell wouldn't be so strong when she served it outside. "It just means to blanch them, I think."

Lavonne nodded. "Ah, so drop them in boiling water for a sec, then into ice water, like I used to do when I cut corn off the cob to freeze it.

Back when I bothered with stuff like that. What else are we serving today? And how can I help?"

Val picked up the other old recipe cards she'd selected and shuffled through them. She'd already baked the carrot cake and the apple cake the evening before, along with getting the lemon icebox dessert into the freezer. But the salads still had to be made.

Holding up two recipe cards, she turned to Lavonne. "Would you rather make the Asheville salad, or this one, the . . . *lush* salad?"

Scrunching her face up, Lavonne reached for the two cards. "Let me see those. I've never heard of either."

Val waited for the reaction she was sure was coming.

"Ew, these both sound awful!"

Taking the cards back from her mom, she scanned them again. "Come on, where's your sense of adventure? Aren't you the least bit curious what lemon Jell-O, undiluted tomato soup, and stuffed olives taste like? Oh, and don't forget the celery and onion. Doesn't that sound 'luscious'? " Val joked.

"Val, no one is going to eat that. It sounds like a horrific Jell-O dish you'd find at a Lutheran funeral in some dinky little town."

She laughed at her mom's exaggerated reaction. *She might be right. Maybe I shouldn't have picked the strangest ones I could find.* But she still thought it might be fun.

"Don't knock it until you try it. Besides, maybe we'll play our own version of *Fear Factor* to get the kids to taste these. You know, dare them to try something different."

Her mother still looked skeptical. "Yeah. Good luck with that."

* * *

"Mom? Mom! Where are you?!" Jake yelled, crashing through the door into the lodge kitchen.

Val spun toward her youngest, throwing her dishtowel into the sink and rushing over to where he stood. His hands were shaking.

"What?! Are you hurt?" she cried, grabbing his arms and holding them high to get a good look at him. No blood. Good sign.

"Mom, one of my turtles is missing!"

Exhaling, she dropped his arms. Relief surged through her, followed by a wave of frustration. "Bud, you can't do that to me. I thought something was really wrong."

"A missing turtle *is* serious! We have the big race today and now we're short one."

Lavonne snorted behind them, clearly getting a kick out of this.

Val said, "Jake, what am I supposed to do about a missing turtle? I'm busy making enough food to feed a small army today, or at least this big family. Go have one of your brothers help you."

Jake stomped his foot, exasperated. "I can't do that. Mom, it's a contest! Every man for himself. These were *my* turtles! I had three ready to go, just in case."

"Where were you keeping them?" Lavonne asked, coming to stand next to her daughter.

"In Dad's cooler. The lid was on! No *way* one crawled out."

Crossing her arms over her chest, Lavonne looked thoughtfully at her grandson. She wore a serious expression, but Val knew that look in her eye. "Maybe someone was worried you'd win because you had the fastest turtle. Maybe they let him escape. Or maybe they plan to use him themselves. Did you mark your turtles?"

Val did her best to maintain a straight face.

Jake's eyes widened as he stared up at her. "Grandma! Do you think that's what happened? Like stealing secrets, but turtles instead?"

Lavonne relaxed her arms and held her hands up, as if questioning everything. "I don't know, Jake. Could be. But there'll be no way to prove it. You better run back and carefully mark the two turtles you still have. Don't hurt them, though—in fact, you should let them go after the race today. And if you think you need a faster turtle, you've got time," she counseled, checking her watch. "At least four hours. Go. Find an even faster one than the one that got away. Be smarter than whoever stole your turtle."

Jake held her eye, clearly debating the wisdom of her words. He slowly began nodding his head. "I'll show them." He turned back toward the door, but then he stopped and wheeled around, his face scrunched up in disgust. "By the way, Mom, something really stinks in here. I hope that's not supper."

And with that, Jake blew back out the door to find a new, faster turtle.

"You aren't by any chance serving creamed turtle, are you dear?" Lavonne joked, heading back to where she'd been stirring a batch of frosting on the stovetop.

It was Val's turn to scrunch up her nose. "Ew, gross, Mom. No. And no turtle *soup*, either."

* * *

Val observed from the sidelines. After spending her morning in the kitchen, with help from first Lavonne and then others as they meandered in, things were in good shape for a late-afternoon feast. There'd be games set up to keep everyone occupied between now and then, but someone else could deal with organizing those. She'd done enough.

First, the baseball tournament. The grassy expanse between where the cabins stood near the firepit and the walkway marking where the beach began would be the ball field. Since the area was plenty big to set up the bases, but only allowed for a small outfield, it changed to Wiffle ball instead of the real thing. Besides, the lightweight plastic balls and bat were a great equalizer. All ages could play. With over twenty eager players—a combination of family and resort guests—Ethan had his hands full organizing them all. Rebecca, his girlfriend, volunteered to keep score.

Val had been glad to see Rebecca arrive. Their relationship had been anything but stable, but Val's gut told her Rebecca was good for Ethan. So much better than that hard-to-please ex-wife of his.

"Hey, aren't you gonna play, Mom?" Dave yelled to her from where he'd assumed his assigned position on second base.

Shaking her head, Val motioned to the crowd of players Ethan was struggling to deal with, where it seemed there was much debate regarding team assignments. "I think your uncle has more than enough players already. But do you want to be my partner for the cornhole tournament?"

The thumbs-up she received meant Dave hadn't forgotten what happened the year before. The two of them had a title to defend.

Soon, the game was in full swing. Grandpa George was first up to bat, and his easy swing sent the ball lobbing just over Dave's head. Strong-armed Logan rushed behind his brother, scooped up the ball, and threw it as hard as he could to his cousin, Nathan, manning first base. But no matter how hard you throw a Wiffle ball, you aren't going to get much speed. Val grinned at the exasperated look on Logan's face when his grandfather beat the ball to the base.

The game continued, no one at much of an advantage. Young and old alike played. The renters who weren't participating didn't seem to mind the game—this was what you'd expect on the Fourth of July, after all. Matt was pitching, and Renee stepped up to bat, swinging the thick yellow bat around in circles as she settled in the batter's box.

"Let's see what you got there, Mr. Sheriff," Renee teased, winking at her husband.

Matt executed an exaggerated wind-up and whizzed one across the plate into Noah's waiting hands. Renee swung hard enough to spin herself around, but there was no satisfying sound of plastic connecting with plastic. With a grunt, she readjusted her stance and waited for a second pitch. Val watched her grinning son toss the ball back to Matt. Glancing around, she smiled at how much fun all four of her boys seemed to be having. Jake was on deck, standing behind Renee, warming up himself.

Bringing them here was the right decision. This is how summer days should *look.*

Matt wound up again and pitched the ball in, but a gust of wind pushed the ball off course, and it caught his wife in the temple. Everyone froze for a second, and Val could read the *Oh shit!* her brother-in-law mouthed. Renee slowly raised a hand to her head, dropped the bat to the ground, and sprinted in Matt's direction. Matt held his hands up in mock self-defense, laughing as he backed away from the woman barreling toward him. She leapt at him, wrapping her arms around his neck and her legs around his thighs, sending them both in a tumble to the ground. They rolled, twice, with Renee ending up on top, pinning Matt to the ground, before she planted a sloppy, wet kiss on his mouth. Cheers rose from the peanut gallery of chairs rimming the game, and Val heard her nephew Robbie yell out his disgust, "Mother, knock it off! That's gross!"

Matt easily pulled Renee's hands off his shoulders, holding them in his bigger ones. He glanced in his step-son's direction with a huge grin. "Lighten up, Robbie!" Matt tickled Renee under her arms and then rolled her off him, helping her to her feet. He brushed the loose grass from her backside and gave her a playful push back toward home plate.

Val called out teasingly, "Ethan, are you going to allow distractions like that? Where is the sense of order in this game?"

Their playfulness set the tone for the rest of the game—which was probably a good thing, given how competitive this group could get. Rules were lax and everyone had fun. It was a great start to the festivities.

* * *

Despite plans for the turtle race and a beanbag tournament, everyone voted to take an hour to cool off by the water. The temperature had risen to the mid-eighties and people were hot and sweaty, despite the gusty winds that had wreaked havoc with the Wiffle ball game.

Val couldn't remember their beach ever being this crowded with people. Kids were running everywhere, diving in and out of the low waves, and building sand castles on the edge of the water. As her eyes wandered over the beach, the swimming area, and where the woods encroached on a rocky shoreline farther south, she wondered if this was what Celia had envisioned when she'd held on to Whispering Pines for all those years.

She thought back to summers they'd spent here as kids. Their two-week-long visits had never felt long enough. There were bonfires, games, plenty of fights with her siblings (usually because of the games), and swimming. She supposed they'd spent half a dozen summer vacations here.

But as her sisters and brother got more involved with sports and summer jobs, they'd eventually stopped coming. For Val, being the youngest, summers seemed to lose some of their charm after that. She remembered spending time in the kitchen with her mom more out of boredom than any kind of enjoyment. But, thinking back, she supposed that's where her love of cooking had been born. When Renee, Ethan, and Jess would come home after long days of doing their own thing, they'd be starving. They'd try most anything she put in front of them, and if they liked it she'd feel a glow deep inside. Usually they just ignored her, the youngest kid, but not when she fed them. Even if they didn't like something she made, it was still better than being ignored.

Not much has changed, she thought with a sigh. She was still good at feeding them all, but she wasn't sure what else she was good for these days.

She jumped as something icy-cold bumped against her arm.

"You look awfully serious, Val," Rebecca said, tipping her dripping bottle of beer in Val's direction before she took a sip of it. "The weather is great and everyone's enjoying themselves. Why so glum? Missing Luke?"

"Oh, sorry. Yeah, it's too bad he couldn't be here for the party."

Val's reply was automatic, but was it even true? She hadn't been thinking about her absent husband, and hadn't since earlier in the morning when she'd been grateful that he wouldn't be around to argue with or spoil her good mood. He might not be here to bring her down, but apparently he wasn't the only one able to do that. She was doing a fine job of it herself.

She forced a smile onto her face.

Rebecca bent over and pulled a second bottle out of the cooler in the sand, handing it to Val. "Ethan mentioned you and the boys get to spend the rest of the summer out here. You are so lucky."

Val used the towel draped over the arm of her lawn chair to twist the top off her beer. "It wasn't luck that got us here—at least not *good* luck—but I am grateful for the chance to stay out here. It's funny how things work out sometimes."

Nodding, Rebecca grinned at something out in the water. Following her line of sight, Val noticed someone had rolled a big black inner tube out into the water and a bunch of the kids were playing on it.

It brought back warm memories of their first visits out here.

"How are things with you and my brother?" Val asked, suspecting their relatively new relationship wasn't without some struggles. After all, no relationship was ever perfect. Ethan's ex-wife was a difficult woman, and she was still part of his life because of their children.

Rebecca smiled. Before answering, her eyes searched along the shoreline. Her grin widened when she spied Ethan sitting on the end of the dock next to Seth. "Good, I think. We're finding our way through the messy situation with Stacey."

"I'm sure that is tricky. Stacey can be . . . *challenging*." Although *bitchy* would have been a more accurate description.

"She can be. But I think we're all trying to make it work for the sake of the kids."

Val thought of Ethan's three kids. His sons, Drew and Dylan, hadn't struggled too much over the divorce. But Elizabeth, Ethan's oldest, had turned bitter. She was a recent college graduate and was working for him in his business. Val knew Elizabeth had hated Stacey for leaving Ethan, had felt just as deserted as her dad had when her mother up and left with little warning. They'd *all* been surprised. But now, as Val was feeling her own waves of discontent with her own life, maybe she was beginning to understand her ex-sister-in-law better. Not that she'd *ever* bail on her own family, but even she fantasized about a fresh start sometimes.

Screams out on the water pulled her attention out to where the crowd of kids was splashing around on and near the black tube. Something was wrong. She saw Ethan and Seth stand up on the end of the dock, their attention focused on the kids, too. Out of habit, she began counting heads, trying to account for everyone.

Where's Noah?!

She couldn't understand what the kids were yelling. She watched with alarm as Ethan jumped into the water, feet first, and swam in the direction of the tube.

Jumping out of her chair, Val ran down to the water's edge, straining to spot Noah in the water.

Seth ran back up the dock and onto the sand, zigging toward her. "Val, do you know where Noah is?"

"I thought he was out there with the rest of the kids," Val said, pointing, unable to keep the sharp edge of panic out of her voice.

It didn't take long before the rest of her family joined her along the water's edge. She could see Ethan reach the knot of kids, and her apprehension ratcheted up as arms pointed and he turned, swimming farther out into the water.

"Where is he going?!" she cried, but she was afraid she already knew the answer. Noah fancied himself to be a strong swimmer. And he didn't enjoy playing in big groups as much as her other three.

Seth must have reached the same conclusion, because he gave her upper arm a reassuring squeeze before he ran out into the water, heading in the same direction as Ethan.

"Be careful, Seth!" Jess yelled from just behind Val.

Val took one step toward the water, but was stopped by a strong hand on her shoulder.

"Stay here, Val. They'll get him," Matt ordered. His tone was serious. His sheriff's voice. Most people probably obeyed him when he used it.

She shrugged him off and took three more steps before he caught her up around the waist, lifting her feet off the ground and walking backward.

"I mean it, Val, I don't want to have to swim out and save your ass, too. Ethan's already almost to him. Let your brother play hero today."

"I am going to embarrass that kid with the biggest hug he's ever received, and then I'm going to kill him," Val spat out, wriggling out of Matt's grasp. But she stayed, seeing the wisdom of his words. She'd let Ethan bring Noah to her.

Sunlight glittered off the undulating surface of the lake; Val had to shield her eyes to see what was happening. Noah had a skinny arm around Ethan's neck now, and her brother was slowly making progress back toward shore with a long sidestroke.

"What's all the ruckus about down here?" Lavonne asked, trudging through the sand to stand between Renee and Jess.

"Apparently Noah thought he'd try to emulate the long-distance swimmers he watches on YouTube," Val said, never taking her eyes off her son and brother.

"Well, that's a little scary."

"Ya think?"

Lavonne stepped forward and put her arm around Val's waist. "He's fine, honey. It looks like Ethan has things under control. Boys will be boys."

Val wasn't buying it. "He can't just swim way out in this lake. It isn't safe. He could have drowned." She hated how her voice cracked on the last word.

"But he didn't. Besides, Ethan did the same thing when he wasn't much older than Noah."

Now that Noah was in safe hands, Val turned to look at Lavonne. "He did?"

Lavonne motioned toward the lake. "He got into trouble when he went out too far and got a cramp. But that time, there were no adults around. Some kid jumped in and saved him. I wanted to kill him, too, only we realized he'd learned a valuable lesson. After that, Ethan showed a new respect for water."

"Wait, Mom, are you talking about the time Ethan went out after that pink raft?" Renee chimed in, her voice incredulous. "We didn't think you knew about that!"

Lavonne wandered to a nearby lawn chair and sat down, kicking sand out of her sandals. "Please. You kids weren't nearly as sneaky as you thought you were."

A look passed between her sisters. Val couldn't help but wonder what other things they'd done as kids that they'd hoped their mother didn't know about.

"I don't remember Ethan going out after a pink raft," Val said.

"You were too young," Renee said dismissively.

Story of my life.

Letting it go, she turned back to the water, watching as Ethan unwound Noah's death grip from around his neck as soon as they were in shallow-enough water.

"Thanks, Uncle Ethan . . ." Noah's voice was weak as he staggered a step or two sideways, fighting to catch his balance in water that still lapped at his chest. "I might have gotten a little too far out. Sorry about that."

"Best not to try that again, all right, Noah?" Ethan replied, standing to tower over his nephew. "I swam out too far one time when I was Dave's age, and I would have drowned if a stranger hadn't saved me. What would you have done if no one was here to help you?"

Noah's eyes widened and he nodded his head vigorously as he tilted it back and held Ethan's gaze. Val took a measure of pride in Noah's response. Her boy was in trouble, and knew it, but he didn't cower.

And he better not sass me, either.

"Noah Rylie Swanson, get over here," Val demanded, keeping her voice level and low. She held out the towel Jess had handed her and Noah walked into her arms, his thin body shaking with cold and emotion. She wrapped her arms around him and held him close, her eyes pinched shut against the tears of relief that threatened.

"I'm sorry if I scared you, Mom. I didn't mean to."

Val turned away from the water, still holding Noah tight. Beginning the walk back to the lodge, she bent over and whispered in his ear.

"You are just lucky your father isn't here."

CHAPTER TWELVE

GIFT OF CONSEQUENCES

*I*f there was one thing Val had learned as the mother of four boys, it was that you needed to pick your battles. Noah made a stupid mistake, swimming out so far, but she hoped it would be an important lesson for him, like it had been for Ethan when he was a boy.

With the turtle races and beanbag tournament still scheduled before it was time to eat, everyone got out of the water along with Noah.

Once Noah was in dry clothes, Val enlisted his help to dish up servings of the lemon icebox dessert to tide them over until their big meal. She'd used another recipe from Celia's old recipe box. She was confident they'd scarf this one down without complaint. It was hard to screw up lemons, vanilla wafers, and whipped cream.

Val had picked this particular recipe card in part because it bore the name of a woman she remembered. The woman had been one of Aunt Celia's best friends. The card was typewritten, a couple of spelling errors adding to the charm.

Noah helped her stack paper plates piled with the frozen concoction on a large metal cookie sheet. She carried the tray to the beach, not trusting him with it, handing him a paper bag of plastic forks instead.

As expected, the treat pulled the kids in like flies to honey. Her tray was soon empty. She accepted the compliments tossed her way with a smile. She could only hope they'd appreciate some of the wonkier dishes she'd made for later.

Seth finished off his piece with a moan. "Val, that was so good. It reminds me of something my grandma used to feed me."

Val pulled the recipe card out of her pocket. She'd grabbed it at the last minute, figuring Seth would get a kick out of seeing it. "I bet it does taste familiar," she said, handing him the card.

"Oh wow, no wonder," he said, smiling when he read *Ruthie Poole* in the upper righthand corner of the card. "This was Grandma's recipe."

"Really?" Jess asked, coming over to stand next to Seth and look at the card. "That is so cool!"

"Ruthie and Celia were the best of friends," Lavonne said, nodding toward the card in Seth's hand. "There are probably more of those in the box of recipe cards Val brought from Celia's."

Jake, anxious to get on to the turtle race, dropped his now-empty plate and used fork on Val's cookie sheet. "Come on, everybody. We've got turtles just itching to show us what they've got!"

After much debate regarding the size of the circle out of which the turtles would race, Robbie used the skinnier end of the Wiffle bat to mark the circumference in the sand. Then he marked out a much smaller circle inside, earning a thumbs-up from his youngest cousin, Jake, who was so excited for the turtle race that he couldn't stand still.

Jake had scrounged up one more turtle, for a total of three. Each of Val's other boys contributed two more turtles to the cause. Lavonne exchanged a knowing grin with Val as they watched Jake check out his brothers' turtles. They all looked the same to Val, but Jake paid extra attention to one of Logan's turtles. He didn't say anything, but he looked suspiciously at his brother. Val hoped Jake's original third turtle had simply escaped the cooler. Logan better not have taken it.

Rules were established and the racing began. Who would have thought a group of five slow-moving creatures per heat could elicit such wild cheers and encouragement from a crowd of onlookers? When the dust settled, and the heats were done, Jake stood proudly in the middle of the circle, holding the turtle he'd found earlier that morning high into the air in victory.

"You were right, Grandma!" Jake yelled over to Lavonne, his face glowing with pride.

From there they moved off the beach and back to the expanse of grass where they'd played ball earlier. It was time for the beanbag toss.

It was Jess's turn to take charge of a game. "How far apart are these supposed to be?" she asked, as Robbie and Nathan worked to place the set of wooden targets.

"Twenty-seven feet apart, base to base," someone threw out.

"Ethan, do you have a tape measure in your truck?" Jess asked, to which Ethan scoffed.

"I don't think we have to be quite that precise, Jess," he said, instead beginning to walk off the distance with his feet, counting as he placed heel to toe.

Similar to the other games they'd played, old and young could compete in the beanbag toss. No one was at any particular advantage. Dave and Val were once again partners, committed to defending their title. Jess worked to pair everyone else off, and the games began again. The mother-and-son team eliminated Ethan and Rebecca with little trouble, but Seth and Jess proved to be tougher competitors.

"Watch this," Dave said, taking careful aim with the faded blue beanbag in his hand. "I'm knocking that one off."

Despite his warning—or bragging—his bag knocked Seth's through the hole instead of off the board, and they found themselves down by three points. Jess and Seth only needed one more to beat them.

"Come on, Mom, you got this!" Dave coached Val from where he stood next to Seth, watching intently.

I've got this, she thought, eyeing her target.

The one point Jess and Seth needed to beat them was already resting on the platform, Jess having made a nice shot. If she didn't knock her sister off the board, they'd be out. Taking a deep breath, she let the bag fly. The height looked promising, but she motioned with her hands in a futile attempt to magically push it right, already able to tell she was off a hair. If sheer will alone could have tweaked the path of the flying beanbag, they'd have had a chance, but it wasn't to be. Val fell to her knees in a dramatic show of defeat. Smack-talk rained down on her ears—the victors were clearly not the best of sports.

Dave ran over to her side and held a hand out to help her up. "Good try, Mom. We almost had 'em. Maybe next year."

With a grunt, Val stood up straight, raising her hands in a high five to Dave. Just knowing he'd still pick her as his partner in the future meant more to Val than beating Jess. *Almost.*

The loss was well timed, since she needed to get the food set out. With help from Lavonne and Renee, as well as Elizabeth, Ethan's daughter, and a few of the older kids, two long picnic tables covered in a wider variety of dishes than usual were soon set out and ready for folks to fill their plates.

"You really outdid yourself this year, Val. This is impressive," Renee said, grinning as she took in the spread. "I'm not sure even this hungry crew will be able to eat all of this."

It took mere minutes before the annoying buzz of flies descended. Val signaled to Lavonne and then nodded in appreciation when her mother stuck her fingers up to her mouth and split the air with her signature *Come and get it!* whistle.

"Come on, guys, you're going to have to take a break from cornhole to come eat!" Val yelled. "If you don't, the flies will get it all."

Not needing to be told twice, kids crowded into a haphazard line to fill their plates.

"Ah, Mom, what is some of this stuff?" Logan asked, turning his nose up at a couple of Val's experiments.

"Try it—you might like it," she suggested, although she'd tasted the lush salad her mother had nearly gagged on earlier. Lavonne had been right. No one was likely to want to try the lemon Jell-O mixed with tomato soup, onions, celery, and olives. She suspected the whole lump of *that* would end up in the garbage. Even the flies seemed to be avoiding that particular dish.

"Yeah, no," Logan said, moving on to more familiar dishes.

Val brought up the end of the line, filling her own plate and then flipping a large white sheet over the top of everything. Covering up each individual item would have taken too long. People could dig under the sheet for seconds, but it should keep the flies off the food.

"Oh my God, Val, I remember eating this as a kid," George said, holding up a forkful of the vegetable, sugar, and vinegar concoction. "It's like a trip down memory lane. Isn't it called 'pickled something'?"

"The recipe card said 'piccalilli,'" Val clarified.

"Does it taste better than it smells, dear?" Lavonne asked. "The kitchen still stinks like vinegar."

George laughed, scooping up another forkful from his plate. "It really does. Want some?"

Lavonne waved his offer away. "No, thanks. But eat lots. Val has a whole crock of it yet inside."

"Good," Ethan threw in. "I like it, too. Way to mix it up this year, Val."

"My pleasure, bro."

Different conversations flowed as people enjoyed their holiday meal. Seconds were consumed, and in some cases even thirds. By the time everyone had finished eating, only the lush salad remained nearly untouched.

"You win some, you lose some," Val laughed as she and others began to clear away the mess. She dumped the whole bowl of lush salad in the trash. She wouldn't bother with *that* particular recipe again.

* * *

Val was shooed outside by others demanding they do the dishes as trade for having done little to help prepare the meal, and she wasn't about to argue. The final matches of the cornhole game were in full swing, and with all her work done for the day it was fun to relax and enjoy the camaraderie.

Her watch buzzed, letting her know she had a call coming in, but she'd forgotten her phone in the kitchen. She could see it was Luke calling, but she knew she'd never get to her phone before he hung up. She'd call him back later.

Jess and Seth were still alive in the tournament—which gave her some comfort, since they'd beaten her and Dave out. At least they hadn't lost to a "one-hit wonder." The tournament had come down to its final match: Jess and Seth versus Robbie and George. The lead flipped back and forth, but eventually Jess and Seth came out on top, George accepting defeat more graciously than Robbie.

A low rumble of thunder in the distance surprised Val, although it really shouldn't have. It had been the perfect summer day, hot but with enough wind to keep things bearable. But now the wind carried a taste of rain with it.

"We might not get a bonfire or fireworks in tonight, folks," George declared, eyeing the darkening horizon. "Why don't you boys get the cornhole game put away in the shed. Put the bags inside this bucket—and make sure you cover it so the mice don't chew them up."

Dave and Robbie nodded, then Dave recruited Logan and Noah to help. They each grabbed something and headed toward the shed. George had made the cornhole set the previous summer. The home-made boards were heavy and awkward to carry.

"Jake, bud," Val said, taking the empty bucket from George, "take this and pick up all the beanbags. There should be eight in total. Don't miss any."

"Check these out," Logan said, unwrapping the towel from around a bundle of bottle rockets he'd hidden in an old box in the garden shed.

"Where the hell did you get those?" Robbie asked, taking the bundle from Logan. "You know you can't light these in Minnesota, don't you? Any fireworks that shoot up in the air are illegal."

"What are you, the fireworks police?" Logan asked, taking the bundle back.

"No, but Matt is the *sheriff*. Where'd they come from?" Robbie asked again, glancing around to see who might overhear them. He nearly groaned when he saw Jake making his way toward them in the shed; the kid was walking funny because of the heavy bucket he was carrying, and thankfully looking down in concentration, but he'd be on them any second now. "Don't let Jake see those," he warned Logan. Stepping out of the shadow of the large shed, he held a hand out to his youngest cousin. "Here, let me take those, Jake."

"Thanks," Jake said with a big sigh of relief. "Those suckers are heavy. What are you guys doing?"

"Nothing. Get out of here," Logan ordered from inside the shed.

"Who's gonna make me?" Jake shot back, hands on his hips.

Great, Robbie thought. *If he sees the bottle rockets, he won't keep his mouth shut.*

"No one is going to make you, Jake. Jeez . . . chill," Robbie said, scrambling for some way to get rid of the nosy kid.

"Come on, Jake," Noah said, coming out of the shed to stand beside his little brother. "Grandpa said he brought sparklers, but we won't be able to do them if it rains. Let's go see if we can light 'em now."

Robbie mouthed *Thank you* as Noah led Jake away, then spun back to face Logan again. "What exactly do you think you're going to do with them?" Robbie asked, hurrying back into the shed.

Logan shrugged.

Dave took the bundle from him. "Dude, where'd you get these?"

"I found them in the barn."

"What barn?" Robbie asked.

"At Uncle Alan's."

No one said anything for a minute.

"You stole these from our dead uncle's barn?"

Logan shuffled his feet. "Don't say it like that, Dave. God. I didn't think it was that big of a deal. It's not like our other grandma and grandpa are going to use them out on the farm. They were in a box—in the barn, like I said—with some other fireworks. Remember, Dad said these aren't illegal in North Dakota. My buddy was telling me how him and his brothers had bottle rocket fights last year." He shrugged again. "It sounded wicked."

"And stupid," Robbie threw in—although, he had to admit, it did sound a little wicked. But Matt would kill them if he caught them shooting off bottle rockets, especially if they were shooting them at each other.

Sometimes it sucked that his mom was married to the local sheriff. Matt was cool and all, but there wasn't much room for Robbie to screw up these days without getting in major trouble. Like the *one* time he'd tried a couple pills from a kid at school and his mom found two more in his pocket. Matt had put her in touch with a cop friend in Minneapolis and there had been hell to pay.

Dave pulled one of the rockets out of the packet, holding it up to inspect it. "Have you ever shot one of these, Rob?"

"Nah, but I hear they make a kick-ass sound if you shoot them into the lake." Despite his threats to Logan, he was curious about the rockets.

A crack of thunder sounded. A storm was moving in.

"Okay, so maybe shooting them at each other is a bad idea," Logan conceded. "But I still want to shoot some off. What if we went somewhere nobody could see, like maybe over by the duplex, and timed it so the thunder covers up the noise?"

Robbie felt both Logan and Dave looking to him. As the oldest of the three, he was pretty sure they would do what he said. And he knew what he *should* say . . . but screw it, it was the Fourth of July.

What's the big deal about shooting off a couple of bottle rockets to celebrate Independence Day?

* * *

They decided the backyard at the duplex would be the perfect spot. It was situated at the far northeast corner of the resort, away from the lodge and the adults.

"Did you find something we can shoot these out of or should we just hold 'em when we light them?" Logan asked as he followed Dave out of the dark duplex.

"You are such a dumbass," Dave said without looking back. "Holding them in your hand is nearly as stupid as shooting them at each other. These bottle rockets are *big*. I found an orange juice bottle, but it's plastic and light, so we'll have to fill the bottom with sand. Otherwise it'll tip over. I hope Robbie finds a punk. We can't light these with a lighter unless we want to chance blowing our fingers off. And personally, I'd like to keep all ten of mine."

"What's a punk?" Logan asked, apparently not as nervous as Dave about losing a finger.

"A punk is this long stick thing that you use to light some kinds of fireworks. Safer than matches or a lighter," Dave explained. Glancing at the sky—dark now with pulsing daggers of light streaking across the horizon as the summer thunderstorm rolled in—he was torn. He didn't want to get caught. But he'd never actually gotten to shoot off *real* fireworks before. All but the lame stuff, like sparklers and cones, were illegal here.

Feet pounded up the path toward them. "Come on, guys," Robbie said, bending at the waist to catch his breath. "It's starting to sprinkle. Everybody else went in the lodge. Noah and Jake already lit a couple of sparklers. After his stopped sparking, Jake accidently poked Noah with the end of his sparkler stick." Robbie grimaced. "It was still glow-ing. Now Val's got them both in the kitchen at the lodge, yelling at Jake and trying to do something with the blister on Noah's cheek."

"Oh shit, his cheek?" Dave repeated, his hand coming up to his own face. "Maybe this isn't such a good idea."

"Those two are just clumsy idiots," Logan countered, waving his rockets in the air. "Come on. Just a couple. When are we going to get this chance again?"

Dave could feel Robbie looking at him. If any of his three brothers were idiots, it was Logan. Noah was a steady kid, and Jake . . . Jake was just young. But Logan was different. He wasn't afraid to do anything, and sometimes that got them all in trouble. But, at the same time, he sure did keep life interesting. Dave jumped as thunder cracked above, louder than ever. No one would hear a couple bottle rockets go off.

Dave nodded. "Let's do this."

Robbie followed Dave and Logan into the backyard, muttering about how they were all probably going to regret this.

Val chewed on her lip as she gently applied salve to Noah's cheek, hating the look of the nasty blister that had bloomed on her son's face. *If Luke were here, he could help me keep an eye on this pack of boys of ours.* They were getting on her last nerve.

"Where are your cousins?" Ethan asked his sons, Drew and Dylan.

Val could smell rain through the open window, and the wind blowing in had cooled, but all she could hear were low rumbles and the occasional crack of thunder. No boys.

Dylan shrugged. "They must be gaming over at the duplex. Robbie didn't move his system over to the house yet and Dave said something about a new game."

Val hated it when they sat around playing video games, but it had been a long day outside, and now, with the weather, there weren't many options. She didn't need them stuck in the lodge, bored.

"I want to go see," Jake declared, jumping off the stool he'd been sitting on.

Val shook her head. "No way, kid. It's late and you need to settle. Give your brothers and cousins some space. You and Noah can go into the TV room and watch a movie. I don't need the two of you out roaming around the resort in the dark. Noah, put this in the bathroom, will you? I need to restock it, and the extra supplies are back there."

Noah took the depleted first-aid kit from his mother and left the room without argument.

Jake stomped his foot and Val's temper kicked up another degree. She was already furious with him for sticking Noah in the cheek with his hot sparkler. He was so careless. The rubber duck floated across her mind again. She raised a finger in Jake's direction. "Not one more word. You are already on thin ice. It's either a movie or bed."

"Fine!" Jake muttered through clamped teeth. "Come on, Noah, let's go watch *Star Wars*."

Val turned back to Noah. The sparkler had caught him just below his glasses. She shuddered as she wondered if the stick had actually been deflected by the glasses, and what could have happened if he hadn't been wearing them, which Noah often did while at the resort. "You okay, bud?"

"I'm fine, Mom. Quit fussing. You've been hovering all day," Noah said, climbing off his stool. He didn't have quite as far to jump as Jake had.

"Yeah, well, when one of my dumbass kids nearly drowns, it tends to bring out the motherly instincts in me."

"Pretty sure you aren't supposed to call us that, Mom," Noah said, his voice sounding comically adult.

She caught him up in a quick hug and then gave him a little shove in the direction of the small room at the end of the hall, set up with a television and DVR.

As her two youngest left the room, her nephews, Drew and Dylan, each grabbed a Coke out of the fridge and headed for the other door. Drew called back, "We're gonna go check out Dave's game, leave you adults to play cards or something."

Ethan waved the two on, then walked over to Rebecca, where she'd stood watching the family dynamics play out, and looped an arm around her shoulders.

"Do we exhaust you?" Val asked her with a grin. Rebecca didn't have any kids of her own, and Val couldn't imagine how disconcerting the chaos her kids were wreaking could feel to someone who wasn't a parent.

Laughing, Rebecca shook her head. "I'm still getting used to it, that's for sure. Let's just say my world is more interesting now that this guy and his three kids are part of my life."

Seeing Rebecca's arm come up around her brother's waist, Val felt happy for them both. Ethan's ex-wife had done a number on them all, leaving like she did. But with the value of hindsight, Val suspected Ethan had been unhappy well before Stacey actually left. He looked happy now as he dropped a kiss on the end of Rebecca's nose.

"Anything we can do, sis?" he asked as Val scooped up two bags of chips and a bowl of dip off the island. "Can I take those in for you?"

"Sure," Val agreed, handing the snacks to Ethan and Rebecca. "I'll just grab a few more things and be right behind you."

As they disappeared through the swinging door into the larger dining area beyond, where she suspected the rest of their crew sat talking at the long table, she sank onto one of the stools her boys had vacated. Exhaustion washed over her. It had been a fun, albeit long, day. She wasn't going to last much longer.

Her phone vibrated where it lay on the island, the screen lighting up with a text from Luke. It was late, he said, and he was sorry he'd missed her earlier. He'd call tomorrow.

She didn't mind.

Had he done anything fun today, or had he worked the whole time? What had been so important that he couldn't spend the day with her, with their boys? He'd missed out on so much. But he seemed to have other priorities now.

Val felt a twinge of sadness, remembering when *she* used to be his priority.

* * *

Ffssssttt, whistle, bang!

They'd taken turns, each lighting off one of the bottle rockets, timing them as best they could to go off at the same time thunder rolled a heartbeat behind a flash of lightning. They were only getting the timing right about half the time, but they doubted anyone else could hear, all tucked inside the lodge, talking or something. At least,

Robbie *hoped* no one had heard anything. There'd be hell to pay if they got caught, and as the oldest, he'd be at the top of the list.

"Shit, I think the punk went out," Logan said.

"Tough guy," Dave smirked, shaking his head.

Robbie looked down at Logan, kneeling next to the plastic OJ bottle, now black with soot in the light of his phone. "You can knock off the swearing, cuz."

Logan grinned at him over his shoulder. "Got a lighter so I can light this thing?"

Sighing, Robbie fished the small plastic lighter out of his pocket. He'd snatched it off the picnic table earlier, while his grandfather had been helping Jake and Noah with their sparklers. One minute they were all laughing, the next minute Noah was screaming. Robbie felt guilty for taking advantage of the distraction. At least he'd made sure Noah wasn't seriously hurt before slinking off with the lighter and the spare punk.

He heard the flick of the lighter as Logan spun the spark wheel.

"Hey, what are you guys doing back here?" a voice rang out, causing Robbie to jump.

Then everything went wrong. There was another *ffssstt, whistle, bang!* but this time the streak of light accompanying the lit rocket flew straight across the yard, toward the house, instead of into the stormy sky above. It was accompanied by a blood-curdling scream from Logan, now rolling around on the grass in agony. The *bang!* of the bottle rocket sounded with another scream, this one from one of the voices coming around the corner of the duplex.

"What the hell?!" came the voice again, and Robbie recognized it to be Drew's.

"Oh man, what happened?!" came Dylan's voice.

Dave dropped to the ground next to Logan to see what was wrong with his brother.

Robbie sprinted toward the sound of Drew and Dylan's voices. Weak moonlight broke through the storm clouds and another flash of lightning revealed Drew, sitting on the ground, holding his chest, Dylan bent over him in a panic.

"Oh man, are you okay?" Robbie yelled as he slid on the grass a few feet from his cousins. He dropped to his knees and fumbled with the flashlight on his phone.

The front of Drew's T-shirt sported a black burn mark, a circle nearly as big as a plate. He watched in horror as Drew pulled the shirt up, unsure what they'd see underneath.

"Oh God," Drew cried, stopping before the shirt was out of the way. "It's stuck."

"Shit!" Robbie hissed. "Okay, just sit tight, I'll go get help."

He jumped up but paused when he heard someone yelling and the pounding of feet coming around the side of the duplex. The light above the patio snapped on, bathing Drew, Dylan, and Robbie in a white glow. Ethan came rushing down the steps. Matt and Seth ran up behind them.

"What the hell are you guys doing back here?" Matt's voice boomed out.

Shit.

Robbie should have listened to his gut.

* * *

"He might lose the top half of his index finger," Val sobbed into the phone, feeling overwhelmed.

It had been an excruciating two hours, ever since they'd heard the tell-tale *hiss* and *pop* of bottle rockets. She'd just sat down at the table in the lodge to join in the conversation when they'd heard the strange noise, so out of place.

"What was that?" someone had asked. Everyone quieted.

Thunder rumbled. "It's just the storm," Lavonne offered, but Matt shook his head. He was already getting up out of his chair when there was another *hiss* and *pop*.

"Someone's lighting off fireworks," he said. "Dammit, where are the boys?"

"Over at the duplex," Val said, sighing inwardly. *Now what?* she'd thought. Those boys were truly bent on driving her nuts.

"I'll go check," Matt said, slipping into his sheriff's voice again.

Ethan and Seth rose as well, following Matt out into the night.

And now they were all at the emergency room. How they'd gotten here was a blur, but *why* they were there was crystalline clear.

Drew caught a launched bottle rocket in the chest, and he was in a lot of pain, but the doctor had assured them he'd be good as new in a week or two. There might be scars, but no serious injuries. He'd gotten lucky, despite being in the wrong place at the wrong time.

"How in the hell did they get their hands on *bottle rockets*? And how did *two* of them get hurt?" Luke asked through the phone, his voice taught with worry. "We always lit them off as kids. We never got hurt. Much. I think Alan still used them to scare away the blackbirds."

Val sighed, leaning against the wall in the stark white hallway of the hospital nearest to Whispering Pines. "We haven't pressed them for details yet. The doctor is in with Logan now. They asked me to step out for a minute, so I thought I better call you, let you know what's happening."

"I'll be there in six hours," Luke said, and by the rustling on the phone, Val supposed he was already gathering a few things.

"That isn't necessary, Luke. I've got things under control."

"It sure as hell doesn't sound like that to me."

Click.

She drew in a sharp breath, staring at her now-silent phone.

"That son of a bitch," she whispered.

Lavonne, standing nearby, shook her head, her expression resigned.

"Sorry, you weren't supposed to hear that," Val said, groaning.

Lavonne ignored the swearing. "Was that Luke?"

"Yes, it was *Luke*," Val said, her hand shaking with emotion as she shoved her phone into the pocket of her jacket. "He actually had the *nerve* to imply I was somehow responsible for this."

"Oh, now, honey, I'm sure that's not what he meant. He's scared. He isn't here right now to help, but I'm sure he wishes he were standing right beside you."

Val wasn't so sure. She crossed her arms in front of her chest, as if subconsciously trying to protect her heart.

Lavonne put her arms out, and when Val didn't step into them, Lavonne pulled her in instead, whispering into Val's ear. "Honey, emotions are high right now. Cut Luke some slack."

Val squeezed her eyes shut against the tears that threatened. "But what if he's right? He bailed on us, sure, but I'm obviously a poor excuse of a mother. Noah almost drowned today, then he got poked in the cheek with a hot sparkler . . . and then Logan nearly blows his finger off while shooting his cousin down."

"Well, when you put it *that* way," Lavonne said, sarcasm sneaking in.

Val stepped back from her mother's embrace. "Be quiet, Mom." But her order was softened with a hint of a smile. "I'm serious. It's hard to keep these guys safe. How did you do it? All four of us survived."

Lavonne seemed to consider her answer before responding. "There were plenty of bumps, stitches, and even a broken bone or two along the way for us, too. And your father *really* drove me nuts sometimes. Just like Luke does to you. There were plenty of times I questioned things like you're doing now. But we muddled our way through it and you all lived to see another day. Your boys will survive these days when you aren't at your best. Besides, you can't shoulder the blame for all of this. They made some dumb choices, and now you have to let them live with the consequences."

Val supposed her mom was right. But *damn*, mothering was tough.

CHAPTER THIRTEEN

GIFT OF PRIVACY

*V*al was at the kitchen table, sipping her already-cooled coffee, as the sun began to peek over the horizon. The sound of Luke's key in the lock startled the dog where she lay at Val's feet. She held tight to Storm's collar, stroking her fur in an effort to keep the animal quiet, and to calm her own nerves. She expected a confrontation, given her husband's final harsh comment over the phone.

The front door of the duplex swung open, and all that was forgotten. Luke looked haggard, exhausted from driving all night. He dropped a duffle bag on the floor just inside the door and came straight for her, not bothering to remove his boots. He wrapped her in his arms and bent forward to whisper into her hair.

"I'm so sorry, babe."

"I know," she whispered back, the buttons of his jean jacket pressing into her forehead.

When he was barefoot she only came up to his shoulder, but his boots made their height difference even more pronounced. Her arms slid around his waist and she breathed him in, comforted by his presence. He rocked a little from Storm's antics as she jumped against the back of his legs in greeting.

He sighed and stepped back. "How is he? How's his finger?"

"The good news is he'll keep the tip, as long as it doesn't get infected."

"Thank God," Luke said, his head dropping in relief. "I was so worried. I wasn't even sure if it was his right or his left hand."

"His left. The burn wasn't as deep as they originally thought. Very painful, but hopefully no permanent nerve damage."

"Was he able to get any sleep last night?"

Val nodded. "They gave him something for the pain, but he may suffer more today. I bet I checked on him at least five times between when we got home and when I came downstairs this morning."

"What time did everyone get to bed?"

"Dave came with us to the ER, but Noah and Jake stayed here. They're sleeping next door at Jess's. It was almost eleven when we headed to the ER. We got back here about three."

"Why are you up already?"

Val shrugged, then turned and snatched up her empty coffee cup. She needed more caffeine. "I couldn't sleep. But it's still early. The boys might not be up for hours. Why don't you go catch an hour or two of sleep? I can wake you if Logan needs us."

"Do you want to lay down with me?"

"No. I spent enough hours lying awake in that bed. But you go on up."

Nodding, he strode over to his bag and picked it up. "If you're sure. I could use a shower, and then maybe an hour or two, so I can at least function today."

* * *

Storm rushed over to greet Logan when he came down the stairs two hours later. Val wasn't quick enough to catch her, but at least Logan had the sense to hold his injured hand high in the air so Storm wouldn't accidently bump it in her excitement.

"How does it feel this morning?"

Logan looked up at her from where he was crouched over, petting the dog. "Like it got smashed with a brick."

Val had suspected that would be the case when the meds wore off. She'd give him an over-the-counter painkiller once she got some breakfast into him.

"Have you heard how Drew's doing?" Logan asked as he wandered through the small living room area of the duplex to the kitchen in the back. "I still can't believe that happened last night."

"I haven't heard any updates this morning," Val reported. "Hopefully everyone's still sleeping over there."

Ethan and his family were staying in one of the larger cabins near the edge of the woods for the week. She hoped they'd still be able to enjoy the last couple days of their vacation, despite the accident. It had been a tough year for Ethan. He needed a break.

Logan pulled a chair out, its legs scraping on the faded linoleum. This boy of hers was normally a bundle of energy when he first awoke, always had been, but this morning he was subdued. He slid into the chair, his injured hand resting on the tabletop in front of him.

"I really screwed up, Mom. I'm sorry. Do ya think Drew hates me now? I mean . . . I know he's tough—heck, he's a *quarterback*—but he was pretty shook up at first."

Based on her nephew's attitude after he'd been checked over by the doctors the previous night, Drew was taking it all in stride. Maybe even hoping to come out of this with a scar to show for the whole ordeal. "Not everyone can claim to take a shot to the chest and live to tell about it," Drew had joked, earning himself a cuff in the back of the head from Ethan.

But she didn't need to point this out to Logan quite yet. She wouldn't minimize the seriousness of it all. She poured him a short glass of orange juice, refilled her own coffee, and sat across from him at the table.

"Do you want to explain to me exactly what happened? Where did those bottle rockets come from? You can't buy them around here. They're illegal."

All questions she'd been itching to ask since the accident but she'd deferred until she could talk with Logan alone, when he wasn't scared to death over the pain in his hand and whether or not he'd seriously injured his cousin.

He had trouble meeting her eye.

She tapped the table, pulling his eyes to hers. "Your father is here. He got in this morning. I suggest you talk through this with me before you need to explain yourself to him."

Logan's eyes widened. "Dad's *here*? Why? I'm gonna be fine."

Val pinned him with a look she suspected her own mother used on her when she'd done something stupid as a child. *Hell, Mom still gives me The Look.*

"Do you want to start at the beginning? Who brought the bottle rockets?"

Logan chewed on his lip, fiddling with the metal splint protecting his finger. "I did."

This surprised her. Where would a ten-year-old get his hands on illegal fireworks?

"You did? How? They don't even sell them around here."

Logan fidgeted, looking everywhere but at his mother.

"I'm waiting. You better start explaining."

There was a *thump* upstairs. Storm wandered off to check it out.

"I didn't buy them. I found them in an old box . . . out at the farm."

"At the farm?" Val asked, confused.

Logan nodded. "Yeah, at Alan's farm. We were poking around in the barn. I'm not even sure why I looked in this one cardboard box—it was on the shelf under his workbench. Maybe because it was kind of smashed. It was full of packages of bottle rockets. I remembered my buddy telling me how him and his brother had bottle rocket wars."

Val held a hand out to stop him, horrified. "You shot a rocket at your cousin *on purpose?!*"

"No—no, not on purpose, Mom! Robbie convinced me that would be really stupid."

"Robbie was *right*. Jesus, Logan! What were you thinking?"

Logan raised his bandaged hand as if to concede the point. "I guess it was pretty dumb. I know it was wrong for me to take the fireworks, even if Uncle Alan isn't around to use them himself anymore. Why do you think he had 'em out there in the first place?"

"Your dad said he used to shoot them off to scare away blackbirds."

Logan nodded. "Makes sense, I guess. Look, Mom, I know it was stupid. I shouldn't have taken the rockets, and I shouldn't have talked Dave and Robbie into shooting them off with me last night. Neither of them thought it was a good idea, but I guess I kind of convinced them it would be cool."

Val would talk with the older boys about all of this. By the sounds of things, Logan was the instigator—but Robbie and Dave should have known better.

Logan fidgeted in his chair. "So . . . now what? Am I grounded for the rest of the summer or something? Because that would really suck."

It was a good question. One she'd been mulling over since they'd left the hospital in the wee hours of the morning. She'd known by then that both boys would come out of this relatively unscathed, but the reality was it could have turned out differently.

"I'll need to discuss that with your father," she replied, getting up from the table to get him a light breakfast. "For now, you need to eat, take something to help with the pain, and go shower. You stink like gunpowder. We're going to have to tape a bag over that hand so you don't get it wet."

"So . . . I guess this means no swimming today, then?" he asked, but the obvious lack of effort put into the request told Val he already knew the answer.

* * *

"I'm not so sure that's a good idea, Luke," Val countered as they walked. "What if he gets hurt out there? It's not like you'll be able to keep an eye on him the whole time. And he'll need to go back for a follow-up to have his hand checked."

But she recognized the stubborn set of Luke's jaw and worried his mind was already made up. Luke had hugged Logan when he came downstairs, but he hadn't yet sat him down to talk to him about what he'd done. Val knew Luke's silent treatment would drive Logan nuts. It worked on her every time.

"Listen, I had a long, quiet drive to think about how to handle this. Logan's been pushing boundaries lately, and he's young yet. He's cocky and reckless. This attitude of his is just going to get worse if we don't reign him in. Besides, that little trip to the emergency room last night is going to cost us *and* Ethan a pretty penny. I think we need to make him pay some of that."

Val didn't disagree, but earning money by going back to the farm and working with Luke? *That* gave her pause. She kicked at a pinecone on the path.

Luke had wanted to go over to see Renee and Matt's house, now that they were nearly settled. The path crisscrossing the resort wove in front of the cabin Ethan's crew was staying in. She saw her brother crouched down next to the front door, screwdriver in hand. *Always fixing.* Val caught Luke's hand and tugged him in Ethan's direction.

"What's wrong with the door?" Luke asked, stopping with one foot on the bottom step.

Ethan stood at their approach. "Hey, Luke. It's sticking. When'd you get in?"

"A few hours ago. How's Drew feeling this morning?"

Ethan glanced through the screen door into the hushed interior. "He'll be fine. We'll have to change out his bandage and watch for infection, but it could have been worse. I sent him back to bed after getting some food and ibuprofen into him this morning. He was all concerned because he'd planned to head home today, stay with his mom over at her apartment. He was scheduled to work tomorrow."

"Are you letting him leave? Should he be driving?" Val asked.

Ethan walked over to where his toolbox sat on a low table on the porch. The table wobbled when he threw the lid back and set the screwdriver inside. "I think he's fine to drive. He could maybe call in sick, but he was worried that would leave them short at work, and he doesn't want to do that. Kind of hard to argue with, so I'll let him try."

"And that's why Logan needs to come with me," Luke said, turning to Val. "Our kids need to feel a sense of responsibility, too."

Val noticed Ethan glance between them, but she couldn't tell whether he was still upset about the accident. He'd been so rattled the previous night when they'd found Drew on the ground, in pain. *No surprise.*

Luke cleared his throat, turning back to his brother-in-law. "Look, Ethan, we're really sorry about what happened last night. It was a reckless, boneheaded move, and Drew got caught up in it through no fault of his own. By the time I get done with them, Logan and Dave will think twice before doing something so stupid again."

A slow smile spread across Ethan's face as he sunk down on the top step, eyeing both Luke and Val. "We all know it was stupid, and Drew getting hit was an accident. Punish them if you think it'll help prevent the next stupid thing they'll dream up, but it's not like you were a perfect angel at their age, Luke. You've told me some stories. And I bet they've overheard some of those stories, too."

Luke leaned against the stair railing, his features relaxing. "Now this is *my* fault? The old 'the apple doesn't fall far from the tree' bit?"

Ethan shrugged. "Let's be honest. What ten-year-old doesn't wish he could light off fireworks on the Fourth of July? The fact that they're illegal around here doesn't make it any less appealing. Maybe more so. But I suspect they've already learned a good lesson out of this."

"Yeah, it's amazing how a trip to the ER can take all the fun out of things," Val chimed in.

"Let me know what your bill is for last night," Luke said. "The best lessons are learned when there's a little kick in the ass built in."

"I'm not letting you guys do that," Ethan countered. "I have insurance. You'll have your own medical bills to deal with on this. Not to mention the water-damage fiasco."

"Luke has this *amazing* idea that Logan should go and work at the farm with him to earn some money to help with last night's expenses," Val shared, arms crossed.

Ethan smiled. "I'm guessing from your sarcasm you don't agree, Val?"

"Oh, gee, I don't know, what could possibly go wrong? Logan, turned loose at the farm, Luke too busy to keep an eye on him. Hmm. I think that's what got us in this mess in the first place."

Ethan shot her a quizzical look.

"Oh, did I forget to mention the fact that Logan found the bottle rockets in Alan's stash *at the farm?*"

"Val," Luke said quietly, a clear warning in his voice.

Ethan sighed. "Look, guys, it was a long night and I don't want to get in the middle of your tiff. I had enough of that shit with my ex to last a lifetime. Why don't you two run along and let me fix this door? I'd like to take my girlfriend for a walk in the woods after, no drama."

Ethan stood and turned his back on them. They'd been dismissed. Val was tempted to warn him not to get lost out there again like he'd done when he was a kid, but the pang of envy over her brother's plans for the day overrode the desire to deliver her sarcastic zinger. A romantic walk in the woods sounded sweet. Too bad that type of thing almost *never* happened in their marriage anymore.

Luke nodded and turned from Ethan's porch with a wave. "I'll see you in a couple weeks. We'll be heading out again in a bit."

Val followed her husband as he walked ahead of her.

I miss the days when he walked beside me.

After a tour of Renee and Matt's nearly complete new house—and receiving a profuse apology from Robbie for his part in the previous evening's fiasco—Luke cut their visit short.

"Why the hell are you in such a hurry? You just got here," Val reminded her husband as she rushed to keep up with his long-legged strides back toward the duplex.

"It's a six-hour drive back to the farm, Val, and this little jaunt home wasn't planned. I've got shit to do."

She grabbed his arm, pulling him to a stop. "Luke, this is crazy. I know your folks need your help, but what is so pressing that you can't even give us twenty-four hours of your time?"

Luke sighed, shaking her hand off. "I hate this, Val. I'm getting pulled in every direction. I can't physically be in two places at once. I know you'd like me to be here more, to spend more time with the boys, but I can't. I'd stay if I could, but there's this thing tonight, and I have to be back for it."

"What thing? At the farm?"

Luke shook his head. "It's a benefit. For Alan."

This surprised her. "For Alan? Why didn't you say anything? We could have come for a benefit for your brother."

Luke shrugged. "I guess I forgot to mention it. It came together pretty quickly."

"How could you forget to mention something like that? Who planned it? And why?"

Luke started walking down the path again, this time more slowly so Val didn't have to struggle to keep up. "Kennedy planned it. To help with some of the bills that have started to pile up. He had a high-deductible insurance plan, and they took 'extraordinary efforts' to try to save him, but of course we all know how that turned out."

"Wait. Kennedy? As in Alan's 'one great love'? And your college crush?"

Luke turned to her, met her eye for a beat. "Don't say it like that, Val. It's no big deal. And it's really nice of her to try to help. I can't *not* show up for a fundraiser thrown in my brother's honor. I don't want Mom and Dad to lose the farm because of the medical bills that still need to be paid. They'd turned the farm over to Alan, but it's still *theirs*, you know?"

He was right. He couldn't miss something like that. But she had a pit in her stomach over the fact that this Kennedy woman was helping Luke, that his life looked so different when he was off at the farm versus the *real* life they'd shared for so many years.

For the first time in their marriage, Val felt insecure. They'd had their fair share of ups and downs, but she'd never questioned Luke's loyalty.

Should I question it now?

She pondered the thought as they walked the rest of the way back to the duplex in silence. It didn't take her any longer than that to realize she was being ridiculous. Luke was busting his butt, trying to help pick up the pieces with his parents. She needed to lose her own self-doubts and show some support.

"Would you like us all to come back with you and go to the benefit? We should be there, too," she said again.

Before he could do more than shake his head, the front door of the duplex burst open and Jake came running out. "Oh, hey, Mom and Dad! Grandpa's taking all us kids to that new game place. You know, the one where you can drive racecars around a big track? We left you a note."

The door opened again—without quite as much force this time—and her father and their three oldest walked out. George raised a hand in greeting. "Mind if I borrow these four for a couple hours? I've been wanting to get them over to that new racetrack, but it's been too busy around here until now. I'm taking some of the other kids, too."

"Logan," Luke started to say, his tone stern, but Val stepped in front of him to cut him off.

"Are you sure, Dad? I'm sure they'd love it, but that's a lot of kids to keep track of by yourself."

George rolled his eyes. "I think I can handle it, Val. Besides, I suspect they'll all toe the line today, given the near-disaster a few of them discovered when they misbehaved yesterday."

Jake raised his hands, feigning innocence. "Some of us were inside watching a movie last night!"

Noah gave his little brother a shove. "Yeah, after you stabbed me with your sparkler."

George laid a heavy hand on top of both of the youngest boys' heads. No words were needed.

Val stepped aside, pulling Luke with her, and waved them on. "Go. Have fun. And for God's sake, behave for your grandfather."

"Cool!" Jake shouted, skipping down the first two steps and then hurtling to the grass below. The other three boys followed. Logan's eyes looked dull as he passed her, the usual sparkle and the pep in his step noticeably missing.

"Logan, if you need some more ibuprofen, your grandfather keeps a bottle in his glove compartment. Don't let the pain get away from you!"

* * *

"Why did you do that?" Luke challenged after they'd watched their boys and George disappear down the path to the lodge and parking lot. "You know I have to leave and I wanted to take Logan with me."

She suspected it was more important to have a few minutes alone with Luke, before he left, than it was for them to spend the time arguing about Logan. Luke had his hands full at the farm. He didn't need the added worry of keeping an eye on a ten-year-old, especially one as talented at finding trouble as Logan.

"Come on. Let's go inside and talk."

Not waiting, Val headed up the stairs and into the cool interior of the duplex. All was quiet next door. Jess and Harper must have been either napping or gone. Storm greeted her, then plopped back down on the cool kitchen flooring. The boys must have worn her out.

Luke pulled the door shut and Val recognized the look in his eyes. He was primed for another argument. She was sick of fighting. Sick of missing her husband. Sick of the questions that were cropping up with increasing regularity in the back of her mind about their relationship.

She faced him. "Hon, let me deal with Logan. We need to keep his injury clean, and there will be a couple follow-up appointments to be sure he's healing properly. I'm better equipped to do that here. You can talk to him over the phone about it, and we'll figure out a proper punishment. He may not be able to wash dishes yet, and I don't really want him on the riding lawn mower at his age, but he can vacuum and dust around here with his good hand. Don't worry—by the time I'm done with him, he'll *wish* he was riding around on the tractor with you at the farm."

Luke considered this. She knew he hated it when she manipulated things, as she'd just done, to get her way. Now, with Logan gone for at least two hours, he didn't really have much choice if he wanted to make it back in time for the benefit.

She checked the time. He didn't have two hours, but she bet she could convince him to stay another twenty minutes.

"You do know you drive me crazy, right?" Luke said, kicking his boots off at the door.

Val could hear Storm's tail thumping on the floor at the sound of Luke's voice, but she kept her eyes on her husband as he strode toward her.

On second thought, it wasn't going to take any convincing.

"I know."

"House is pretty quiet," he observed, stopping in front of her, within her personal space but without reaching out to touch her.

"Doesn't happen very often, does it?"

He grinned, then caught her around the waist, pulling her up tight against him. He dipped his head and kissed her. She could still feel the edge of his temper there, the frustration. But intuitively she knew they both needed this, to purge some of the pent-up emotions, more than they needed another argument.

She let him blindly edge her back until she could feel the abrasive fabric of the decades-old couch behind her bare knees. His rough hands traveled up the back of her shirt and expertly flicked the clasp of her bra open. Next, he'd coax her down onto the old sofa. He'd have no qualms about having sex right there, in what was usually a room teaming with people, coming and going. While they likely had a short window of time with the promise of privacy, she'd prefer a more relaxing location.

Tearing her mouth away from his, she grabbed for his hand. "Come on—let's go upstairs," she suggested, doing her best to step out from between Luke and the couch.

He groaned, his one free hand falling to her bottom and pulling her up tighter against him. "What's wrong with the couch?" he asked, bending in to try to kiss her again.

"Nothing," she giggled, "other than the very real likelihood of me being distracted by how scratchy it is, not to mention the slightly less likely possibility of someone walking in on us. Did you lock the door?"

With a sigh, he relaxed his grip. "You're right. Come on."

Keeping her hand in his, he led her toward the stairs, flicking the lock as they passed the door. Storm trotted over, clearly intending to follow them.

"Stay," he ordered, and the dog obeyed, plopping her butt down squarely in front of the door and watching them climb the stairs with her liquid-brown eyes.

At the top of the stairs, Val habitually glanced toward the other two small bedrooms, even though she knew they were alone in the house. But she couldn't help herself—it was such a rare feat.

Inside their bedroom the air was already beginning to feel stuffy, even though it wasn't yet noon. She stepped around her husband's unzipped duffle bag to turn on the small air-conditioning unit in the window as Luke stripped his shirt off. He also reached up and pulled the string on the ceiling fan—something she would have had to stand on the bed to accomplish.

The movement of the air gave instant relief, and she shivered slightly as she gripped the bottom of her shirt and pulled it up over her head. She was suddenly glad she'd opted for her lacey pink bra when she'd dressed earlier that morning instead of her comfortable, albeit slightly discolored, white one she preferred. She could look pretty for her husband.

Her hands hesitated at the waistband of her shorts, always more subconscious of the lower half of her body. She gave this man four sons, and she certainly wasn't unscathed by the process—a fact the sun streaming through the bedroom window would do little to hide.

But Luke wasn't thinking about stretchmarks or old scars. Val felt the familiar spike of her pulse as her husband lay down on their bed and reached a hand out for her. Leaving her shorts on, she went to him. She'd wriggle out of them eventually, but maybe today they'd have the luxury of a bit of relaxed exploration instead of having to rush right to the main event, ever concerned about getting caught.

"What are you smiling about?" Luke asked as she sank down on the bed next to him, her left leg pinning him down.

"Just enjoying the view. And the privacy."

She ran a finger down his bare chest, admiring the strength there, and couldn't help but notice how he was broader now than when they'd first met. Maybe even more so since he'd been working on the farm. Time had been kind to him, at least so far. He'd grown stronger, with none of the softness creeping in that she knew many men their age experienced. Her husband worked a hard, physical job, and it showed.

His arms were slightly more tanned than his shoulders and stomach, but a stark white line ran along the band of his jeans—the jeans he hadn't yet shed. Her meandering finger traced that line, and she smiled when she could see his stomach muscles jump.

"Looks like someone's been working outside without his shirt on."

A low growl rose up from deep in Luke's chest and he caught her hand, rolling on top of her and pulling her into a kiss full of need and desire. It was almost enough to distract her from the image that came unbidden into her relaxed mind.

She conjured up a picture of Luke, hard at work on the farm, stripped to the waist in the heat of the afternoon sun as he went from chore to chore. Alone so much of the time . . . but maybe not. Her imagination traveled on, forming a picture of a woman pulling into the farmstead, stopping by with some excuse or another to see him.

"Where'd you go?" Luke asked, his intense blue eyes staring down at her.

She pulled herself back to her husband, to his heavy body pressing her into the cool sheets. "I'm right here, hon," she said, her hand threading up into his hair and coaxing his lips back to hers.

He belonged to her, to her and their family, and she'd do well to remember that. Their current situation, separating them for weeks at a time, was only temporary. Jealousy was an ugly, insidious emotion that had no place in their relationship.

Doing her best to put all conscious thought out of her mind, Val reached for the snap on his jeans. He'd know how to make her forget about everything but him, even if the reprieve was short-lived.

CHAPTER FOURTEEN

GIFT OF THE BLUE TRUNK

"*S*omeone's unusually chipper this morning," Renee said, grinning at her youngest sister.

Val couldn't help but grin back. "I'm *always* chipper! Especially when I'm sitting here with you in your bright new kitchen."

"Actually, no. I'd seldom describe you as *chipper*. I'm guessing your sunny disposition might have something to do with a quickie with the hubby yesterday? Nice of Dad to take the kids off your hands for an afternoon."

Val considered deflecting with some off-handed comment, but what was the point? Renee would see right through it anyway. Instead she opted for the truth—sprinkled with a bit of snarky, because truth be told, no matter how chipper she felt, she was still feeling ticked off where Luke was concerned. "You know, it's funny how plenty of time apart—not to mention the added benefit of how compatible you tend to become with someone in the bedroom after years of practice—can feel like the best of both worlds. A little 'afternoon delight' followed by a sound night's sleep in an uncrowded bed."

"Ouch! You almost make it sound like a 'friends with benefits' arrangement. You and Luke are more solid than that . . ." Renee's voice trailed off, as if she were unsure, and the grin slipped off her face.

"You guys will get through this summer. You know that, don't you? I'm sure it's hard being apart, and four boys can be tough to parent alone, but we're all here to help until he gets back."

Val considered her sister's words as she let her finger trace the outline of an early-morning ray of sunlight where it fell across the table between them. She didn't think this odd feeling she'd been experiencing was because she was overwhelmed with her temporary single-parent role. That she could handle, at least for a short time. Besides, Renee was right—out here, at Whispering Pines, she *did* have plenty of help.

No, her emotions had more to do with Luke than their boys. Their marriage had been alternating between comfortable sameness and vexing frustration in recent months. She'd welcomed the feelings sparked by their rare evening out together after The Great Flood . . . but then came that awful, late-night phone call.

Val knew that a tragedy, like the sudden, violent loss of a loved one, could change someone. Alan's death had rattled Luke deeply. She felt a vast distance now between her and her husband.

Maybe Luke really *had* changed . . .

But she had to ask herself: How would *she* feel if she lost one of her siblings like that? Renee . . . Jess . . . Ethan. She shuddered, despite the warmth of the morning sunlight streaming through the window.

"It isn't the boys, Renee. It's . . . something deeper." Val struggled to explain. "I feel Luke pulling away. He's got this deep sense of guilt where Alan is concerned, and I'm not sure it's going away anytime soon."

Renee's face registered surprise. "Why would Luke feel *guilty*? I know Alan's death had to come as a huge shock, but it was an accident. There was nothing Luke could have done to prevent that."

Val tilted her coffee mug, gently swirling black flecks of grounds along the bottom, struggling to find the words to explain her fears. "I don't think it's Alan's death that has Luke so upset."

"Then what is it?"

"I think he feels responsible for how Alan ended up living his life.

You know . . . never leaving the farm, never getting married or raising a family."

She could feel Renee's eyes on her, as if her sister were considering whether or not to scoff at Val's assessment of Luke's possible thought process. She could understand that—she herself hadn't believed it when Luke first tried to articulate his feelings to her.

Renee stood with a sigh, gathering their mugs. Voices floated through the open window: one the nonsensical gibberish of a toddler, the other their sister.

"Some people would call bullshit on what you just said, Val. But I've actually experienced some of that guilt myself. When Jim died, I worried that I'd held him back. His life was cut short, and he never got to do so many of the things he'd dreamed of. Did I ever tell you he tried to convince me to move to Alaska with him soon after we got married? It had been this crazy dream of his. One I never could understand. In fact, I wouldn't even agree to a honeymoon there. Instead, I talked him into Florida and Disney World. He never even got to *visit* Alaska."

Renee's head swiveled at the brisk knock on her door, as if she hadn't even heard Jess's approach, lost in thought as she'd been over the loss of her first husband.

Ignoring the knock, Val said, "You and I both know Jim found a lot of happiness with you and the kids, sis. How long did it take you to get over that guilt?"

"I'll let you know when I do," Renee whispered before plastering a grin on her face, shouting "Come in!" and turning to take Harper out of Jess's arms.

Great, Val thought. *Renee is happily remarried now, and she still feels guilty about Jim, more than a decade after he died?* She prayed it wouldn't take Luke that long to get back to his old self. Jake would nearly be out of high school by then and they'd be facing an empty nest.

But Val refused to spend any more of her morning worrying about her husband and the state of their marriage. She jumped up and made her way into Renee's still-stark family room.

"Come on ladies, we have decorating to do."

* * *

The three sisters spent the rest of the morning hanging pictures and adding homey touches to Renee and Matt's new house. Harper proved a challenge to keep track of, and Jess apologized more than once for the distraction. "Lauren finally has a weekend off and is coming home today for a couple days, but she must not have gotten as early a start as she'd hoped. She said she wanted to spend the whole day with her little sister."

Val was glad to hear Lauren would be around for part of the weekend. Jess's college-age daughter hadn't been out to Whispering Pines at all since they'd moved into the duplex for the summer. Her waitressing job didn't leave her with much spare time. Val missed her, and she knew Jess had to be missing her even more.

Renee seemed excited for a different reason. "Does that mean we get to have a whole *girls'* day, then? Ethan and Dad took the other kids out fishing today," she told Jess. "I don't have any renters coming or going today, either, and Matt's on duty. Maybe by tonight I'll finally feel completely settled in."

"I could use a girls' day," Val agreed.

Jess nodded, too, glancing around at what they'd already accomplished while attempting to keep her feisty youngest daughter content, bouncing her on her hip. "It's amazing what a few pictures on the wall and pillows on the sofa can do to bump up the feeling of home. But something is missing in here, Renee . . . I just can't put my finger on it."

"Yeah, I know what you mean. I love the new furniture, but now I wish we'd have opted for a coffee table, too."

Val agreed. "A table in front of the sofa would be nice. And a little more color. A pop of something bright, maybe. This room is beautiful, but it's not quite perfect."

Giving up on the fight with Harper, Jess set the little girl down on the large rug that covered most of the floor. Harper plopped down on her diapered butt, her white eyelet sundress tenting out over her chubby legs, and began pointing to different colors in the rug's pattern. "Red. Yeyo. Boo."

Val squatted down so she was closer to eye level with the child. "Good job, honey. You know your colors!"

Harper grinned back, then pointed at Val's T-shirt. "Boo!"

"That's right, blue! And what color is this?" Val pointed to her jean capris. They were blue, too, but a lighter shade.

"Yeyo!" Harper screamed as she poked at Val's pants and giggled.

"Yeah," Jess said, "most things are either yellow or blue to her these days. She gets red right, but the rest is a crap shoot."

"Actually, she might be right," Val said as she stood back up again.

"Val, your pants are clearly not yellow," Renee pointed out.

"No, that's not what I mean. I mean I think this room needs a shot of color. Blue, maybe. What would you think of using Celia's old blue trunk? The one we played on as kids. You know, the one you guys said is still up in her attic? Didn't you say there was a white christening gown inside it when you opened it last summer? Harper's dress made me think of it."

The suggestion brought a slow smile to Renee's face. "That might look amazing in here. But it's too low to the ground, isn't it?"

Jess shrugged. "Maybe, maybe not. Seth had this cool old trunk in his shop that was about the same size as Celia's old blue one. He built a base for it, on wheels. It looked great. Very vintage chic. He sold it right away."

"Do you think Ethan would let you have it?" Val asked.

"Maybe?" Renee shrugged. "He has his house all put together after the big remodel. I would think if he was going to use it he would have already, but I don't remember seeing it in any of his rooms. Should I call him? Do you think he has cell reception out in the fishing boat?"

"Yes!" Jess and Val said in unison.

The blue trunk was just what this room needed.

Before Renee could dial their brother's number, a knock sounded from the kitchen door.

"Hello?! Anyone home?"

Young Harper squealed in delight at the sound of her sister's voice.

Jess helped the clapping toddler to her feet and followed the waddling child out of the room, throwing her over her shoulder: "And that would be my babysitter, ladies. What was that you said about a girls' day?"

* * *

"I can't believe it's been so long since I've been up here," Val said, following Jess and Renee up the old wooden steps to the attic of what had been Aunt Celia's house. Ethan had inherited the house from Celia, done a major remodel, and moved his family in a few months earlier. But he'd left the attic untouched.

Jess glanced back down in her direction as she reached the top of the stairs and waited for them, hands on her hips, dust motes dancing around her in the weak sunlight. "It's a lot more crowded up here than when we were kids. Ethan moved a bunch of Celia's things up here when he remodeled. I'm glad the windows aren't blocked with junk."

Renee wandered farther into the clutter that was covering nearly every inch of the attic floor. "Ethan said to help ourselves to anything we wanted up here. I think he's been wanting to clean some of this up, maybe get rid of it, but he hasn't had time."

Val scanned the huge upper room that made up the third floor of Ethan's home. "So where's the trunk?"

Jess nodded. "Follow me. It's back over here."

They picked their way around piles of boxes and the occasional discarded chair, even a large dresser.

"There it is!" Val cried out, hustling over to the old wooden chest.

The robin egg blue of the painted wood was marred with countless scratches and a larger gouge or two. She ran her hand over the top, remembering when they'd used it to play restaurant on it as kids.

"Hmm. It's smaller than I remember. Do you think it's too banged up?"

Renee moved a cardboard box from the top and knelt next to the old trunk. "Actually, I think it's perfect. It'll need a base to bump it up in the air a little, but I love the distressed finish."

"I think so, too," Jess agreed. "Check this out." Jess bent down and tugged at the top.

It didn't open.

"Weird. It shouldn't be locked."

"Here, let me see," Val suggested, stepping around the trunk. The old latch had some rust on it. She pushed on the lever and it nearly opened, but one piece caught. Val pried at it, but felt her fingernail give way. "Dammit. I broke my thumbnail."

"We may all need manicures after today," Renee joked.

Jess tried the lid again. This time it opened, a loud creaking sound filling the air as rusted hinges groaned in protest. A slightly musty smell filled the air. Val turned up her nose, but Jess smiled. "It smelled worse the first time we opened it last summer."

Val watched as Jess pulled back the white tissue paper that protected whatever was underneath it, inside the old trunk. A swatch of silk and lace came into view, and Val reached out to gently caress the supple fabric. "Wow, this is that old wedding dress you told us about, isn't it?"

Jess nodded. "It is."

"What are we going to do with the stuff in the trunk?" Renee asked, glancing inside and then around them. "Is there somewhere else to put it? It looks too nice to stuff in a cardboard box."

Jess nodded again. "It probably needs to be stored somewhere safer than the attic, anyhow. Why don't we leave the stuff in the trunk and we'll figure out what to do with it when we get it back to Whispering Pines? Maybe we can finally solve the mystery of whose stuff this was, too."

"Yes," Val agreed. "Let's. I always love a good mystery."

"Can we carry it?" Renee asked, looking dubiously at the trunk.

"Sure," Jess replied. "It can't be that heavy. I bet two of us can carry it if a third person holds the doors."

Val jumped into her director mode; something she did often to keep a house with four young boys semi-organized. "Here—Jess, you grab that end, I've got this end. Let's see if we can get it over to the top of the stairs."

Together, the two women managed to hoist the old trunk high enough to clear the stacks of old boxes, moving slowly, and finally set it down with a grunt at the top of the stairs.

Brushing her hands off, Jess turned to scan the cavernous area. "Do you think there are other things up here we could use?"

Renee looked around. "I bet there is. Ethan said to take a look and don't be shy, take what we want. Do we have time to dig a little? Julie is moving next week and could use a few things."

"She's moving? Where?"

"Yep. They're in an apartment building now, but apparently they're moving into an old house. The rent isn't much more, but each girl will have more space to themselves. And it's closer to campus."

Val thought back to her college days. Similar to her niece, Julie, she'd shared an old house with a bunch of other girls. They'd had the time of their lives. *Oh, to be young again, without all the responsibilities that life brings.* Not that she'd want to be *that* young again. *Would I?*

"Oh wow, check it out!" Jess said from another section of the attic. "I wonder where she ever got *this*."

Val made her way over to whatever it was her sister had found. There, leaning against a tall old desk that she remembered was in the living room when Celia lived in the house, stood an old framed chalkboard. It was as tall as she was and about three feet wide. *The Bird's Nest* was meticulously lettered along the top of the black surface in white paint, a whirling work of art. The words were underlined with an intricate vine that trailed down both sides of the chalkboard.

"Oh, that is so pretty!" Val cooed. "Couldn't you just picture that in a quaint little café somewhere?"

"Take it."

Val looked at Jess in surprise. "Take it? Where would I put it?"

"Duh—your kitchen, dummy. Remember, the one that's all ripped up right now? Work it in somehow."

Tempted, Val tipped the tall board away from the wall, scanning the back of it. The thing had some definite weight to it. It was the real deal, not some coated plywood knockoff. It would need to be screwed into the wall. But Jess's suggestion opened her mind to the possibilities: she could picture it on one particular wall . . . but it would require moving a cabinet. She wasn't sure Luke would go for that.

"Maybe," she whispered, lost in thought. Suddenly, the layout of her tired old kitchen shifted in her mind's eye, taking on a look more similar to the kitchen Ethan had put in just downstairs in this very house. They'd done what they could in the past, within their limited budget, but maybe now was when they should try for a more extreme makeover, since it was getting an overhaul anyhow. "But we probably can't take it today. It wouldn't fit in the back of your vehicle, and this thing is really heavy."

"You're probably right," Jess agreed. "But you should seriously think about using it. It would be a statement piece for sure."

They continued their hunt.

"What kinds of things does Julie need?" Val asked.

Renee considered. "She mentioned dishes and silverware. I guess what they have is really mismatched. Oh, and a vacuum."

"I remember seeing some boxes of dishes when we were digging around up here last summer," Jess said, peeking into boxes as she went along. "But I don't remember where."

They slowly made their way around the boxes, pulling a few things out here and there that they thought would work for Renee, Julie, or even Val now that she was considering doing more in her own kitchen overhaul.

There was a soft *thud*. "Crap," Renee uttered. "What a mess."

Val looked over in her sister's direction and grinned at the tipped box and papers fanned out around her feet. "Have fun cleaning *that* up."

"Couldn't I just pretend I didn't do it and walk away? Let Ethan clean it up down the road?"

"Real mature there, Renee," Jess tossed in their direction from the other side of the room.

With a sigh, Renee sank down within the mess and started gathering papers back into a pile. Val took pity on her and wandered over to help. Knowing Celia, the papers, whatever they were, were in precise order before Renee dumped them.

Sitting down on the other side of the spilled contents, Val picked up a piece of paper, scanning it. "These are medical records."

Renee nodded. "Yep. Celia's records, from the look of things. I bet these could be tossed, probably shredded, at this point. Who would need them again?"

Val supposed her sister was right, although it made her a touch sad. Life was so fleeting, even when one lived to be in their nineties, as Celia had. Once a person is gone, so much of the things that used to matter fade away to irrelevance.

She kept stacking, scanning a few of the papers as she did so. The date on one sheet caught her eye: July 4, 1974. It looked like a detailed invoice from a hospital stay. "Huh. It looks like Celia didn't have much fun on the Fourth of July back in 1974."

Renee looked up, apparently glancing at a few of the papers she was gathering, too. "Why do you say that?"

Val waved the sheet. "It looks like she was in the hospital for something. I wonder what it was?"

"Maybe she gave birth to a baby we never knew about," Renee joked.

Doing the mental math, Val snorted. "Doubtful. She'd have been, like, fifty or so."

Shrugging, Renee tossed the piece of paper she'd been looking at back into the righted cardboard box. "Whatever it was, it couldn't have been too serious. She lived another forty years."

True, Val thought, but she was still curious. She'd ask her mom later.

Jess's voice: "Ta-da!"

"What did you find?" Renee asked, dumping the last of the spilled papers back into the box.

"Looks like a big set of dishes. They're pretty, too. I think I remember eating off these as a kid."

She held a plate out to Renee. Renee nodded as she took it. "I *remember* these! Oh, I think Julie would love them."

Val's phone vibrated. It was a text from their mother. "Mom wants to know if we want to meet for coffee. She must have talked to one of the fishermen." Val laughed, a bit guiltily. "She's wondering why we're having a girls' day without her."

* * *

Lavonne was already waiting for them at a corner table. Val inhaled deeply as they entered the coffee shop, appreciating the welcoming scent of roasted coffee beans. She smiled at the huge chalkboard behind the register, mounted high on the wall and displaying the shop's menu items. It reminded her of the much smaller version they'd found in Celia's attic.

Val quickly stepped to the counter for her order. She needed a strong cup of coffee after their afternoon of digging around, not to mention their morning of decorating. She'd risk the caffeine keeping her awake later.

"What have you ladies been up to without me?" Lavonne asked, grinning expectantly as all three of her daughters took a chair at the table.

"Oh, you know," Val said, "snooping into Celia's private life."

She laughed, sipping what Val knew would be a decaf vanilla latte. It was Lavonne's go-to drink when she treated herself to something at a coffee shop. "That woman led an interesting life. You never know what you might find, digging into it. I take it you mean the stuff up in her attic?"

"Dad told you what we were up to?" Renee asked.

"Sure did. Sounds awful to me. Which is why I waited a bit and *then* suggested coffee. Digging around through that old junk up there didn't hold any appeal for me."

"Seriously, Mom? I loved it," Jess said, frowning at her mother.

"I think Seth's fascination with all things old has infected your brain, honey."

A silly grin stole over Jess's face, and she looked at her ring.

"I think more than just his fascination with *junk* has infected her brain, Mom," Val added, turning to Jess. "We saw the way you nearly drooled over that old wedding dress in the trunk."

Jess feigned indignation. "Oh, I did not *drool*. It's just pretty, that's all."

"You *are* going to be getting married again, one of these days, if you two would ever pick a date," Renee piped up. "Seriously, would you consider actually wearing it for the big day?"

"Oh, I don't know if that's wise," Lavonne said, surprising them all.

"Why the heck not?" Val asked. "We didn't pull it out today, but from the little I could see of it, and the way Jess described it before, it sounds gorgeous. Why shouldn't she wear it if she likes it?"

Lavonne looked surprised at Val's sharp words. "Jeez. Relax, Val. I only meant that maybe Jess isn't considering a 'big, fancy white dress' kind of affair. After all, this won't be her first wedding."

"But it is Seth's first," Renee reminded their mother, adding, "and hopefully his last."

"True," Lavonne conceded. "I'm sorry. I didn't mean to offend. Jess, honey, you plan whatever type of wedding you want."

Jess, normally quite outspoken, looked between her two sisters and her mother, seemingly taken aback by their animated exchange over her yet-unplanned nuptials. "Ah . . . thanks . . . I guess. We'll keep you posted as to how we choose to celebrate our special day."

Conversation drifted to other topics, as it always did when Val was lucky enough to sit down with the three most important women in her life. She let them talk, watching them interact with each other. She felt a pang of regret that she'd never have a daughter of her own to do this with. Maybe she'd luck out and wind up with daughters-in-law she'd enjoy.

"I don't remember that chalkboard," Val heard her mother say, pulling her attention back to the conversation flowing around the table.

"It's so *pretty*," Jess said. "I can just picture it in Val's brand new kitchen."

"I may need to get back to work on my Pinterest boards," Val said. "Give Luke some direction, if he ever gets back here to us."

"Oh, hon, he'll be back before you know it," Lavonne offered in a reassuring tone.

Val glanced at Renee, wondering if her sister had mentioned their morning conversation about her concerns over Luke to either their mother or Jess. *She better keep that stuff to herself.* Looking to steer the conversation into another direction so she could avoid being the recipient of more relationship advice, she asked her mom about Celia's hospital stay she'd discovered within the spilled paperwork in the attic.

Lavonne blinked at the question. "Heavens, I haven't thought about that in years. That must have been back in the seventies."

"What happened? Was it anything serious?" Renee asked, apparently curious herself now.

"It could have been. She had to have a mastectomy."

"What? How did I never know that?" Val asked. She looked to Jess and Renee. "Did either of you know Celia had breast cancer?"

Both shook their heads, looking just as surprised over the news.

She turned back to her mother. "Why didn't you tell us that before?"

Lavonne gave a small shrug, staring at her latte. "It wasn't something Celia liked to talk about. They caught it early and she never had trouble again. If it had been found today, I suspect she'd have had less invasive options to choose from. Back then it was a pretty radical surgery. In fact, I went to stay with her for a few weeks afterward to help."

Val gave a reluctant nod. "Well, I suppose that makes sense, but still . . . Mom, you know the doctors have been watching that spot I found in my breast for almost a year now. Family history is an important factor. I should tell the doctor if my aunt had breast cancer."

"Val . . ." Lavonne frowned. "You didn't make it sound like anything serious. Is it? Did you lie to me so I wouldn't worry?"

"No. No, of course not, Mom, I'm just surprised, that's all. I'm fine. Don't worry." Val scolded herself inwardly. So much for keeping this about Celia.

To Val's relief, Renee piped up, possibly hoping to steer the conversation away from Val's health. "Hey, Mom, do you remember those pretty white dishes Celia used years ago? We found them in a box today and we're going to see if Julie wants them for her new place."

Lavonne was successfully distracted. "When is Julie moving?"

Val gave Renee a grateful smile, which she knew her sister saw. *Us girls need to stick together.*

"Next weekend, actually," Renee replied. "I wish I could go help, but it's hard to be away from the resort for a weekend in the summer."

Val hadn't really considered how tied-down the resort kept Renee during the summer months. She couldn't just pick up and go like the rest of them. Val knew she loved working the resort, but still, it had to be a huge commitment.

"You should go, Renee," Val said. "I'm sure Julie would love to have you. Helping her get settled . . . it sounds fun!"

"Can't. Matt's on duty next weekend and we're all booked."

"Let me help," Val offered. It was the least she could do to repay Renee for letting her and the boys stay at the resort for two months.

Renee opened her mouth, probably to explain why she couldn't accept Val's offer, but then must have reconsidered. "Are you sure?"

"Duh!"

Renee turned to Jess. "Will you be around to help, if needed? If I go, I'd be back at a decent time on Sunday."

Jess shook her head. "Sorry, but Seth and I are heading up north next weekend. This great old building is getting auctioned off a couple hours away. Mom already agreed to watch Harper for us."

Lavonne nodded.

"For God's sake, I think I can handle a day and a half at the resort by myself," Val insisted. "I can call Matt if I have any trouble. Let me do this for you."

Renee hesitated for only a minute more, and then grinned. "I'll call Julie right now and see if that works for her!"

They watched Renee leave the table to call her daughter.

"That was nice of you, honey," Lavonne said, eyeing Val.

"My pleasure. What could go wrong in a day and a half?"

CHAPTER FIFTEEN

GIFT OF SUGAR AND SPICE

*V*al tossed and turned, unable to sleep. The weather was rough, with lots of wind and heavy rain. They'd been under a thunderstorm watch when she'd headed to bed. Poor Storm hated thunder. The dog plastered her warm, trembling body against Val. As the worst of the storm moved on, Val could feel Storm begin to relax, although she still whined at the occasional rumble. Maybe they should invest in one of those weighted vests meant to calm dogs bothered by thunder and lightning. Luke would probably laugh at the idea, call it a scam.

Restless, Val got out of bed and opened the window, hoping fresh, rain-cleansed air might help her relax.

When sleep finally did come, her dreams were fraught with disturbing visions of old hospitals and massive bandages enveloping her chest, as if she'd had the mastectomy instead of Celia. When a grieving Luke appeared in his black suit, worn only for weddings and funerals, she welcomed the nervous bark from Storm that woke her.

The billowing of the curtain, its sheer white fabric undulating softly, gave her a start. Her sleep-deprived mind was playing tricks on her.

Still not a big fan of the dark.

Turning her back on the window, she wrapped her arm around Storm's neck, willing sleep to return.

"Mom?"

She popped an eye open, unsure if she'd heard someone or dozed off, dreaming again.

"Mom?!"

Not dreaming. It was Jake again. "What, honey?"

"I can't sleep. Noah's allergies must be bad again. He's snoring and keeping me awake."

More like you don't like the combination of a thunderstorm and a noisy, dark night any more than I do, Val thought. Jake was like her in so many ways.

"Do you want to come lay down next to Storm? The weather has her a little nervous. She'd probably appreciate it."

Footsteps approached in the darkness, and then the bed dipped.

"Yeah, if you think it'll make her feel better," her youngest whispered from Luke's side of the bed.

Val reached over blindly and rubbed his shoulder. "I think it would."

The next time Val opened her eyes, it was to a cold nose pushing against her hand and warm morning sunshine streaming through the window. Her smartwatch displayed 8:14—the latest she'd slept in a long time. Not that she'd gotten a solid eight hours in by any stretch of the imagination. Glancing over at Jake, she had to grin. He was facing her, still sound asleep, with a small circle of drool wetting the pillow under his head. Swinging her legs off the side of the bed, she motioned for Storm to come. There was no reason to wake her son yet. Their unstructured schedule while out at Whispering Pines had quickly become her favorite aspect of their two-month reprieve from what had become constant rushing between the boys' activities.

Pulling an old sweatshirt off a hanger in the closet, she slipped it on as she followed the dog down the stairs. No movement yet coming from the other boys, either, which was typical. With any luck, she'd get an hour or two to herself before the rest of the house was awake.

The first level of the duplex was quiet as she padded barefoot across the kitchen. She flipped on the coffee maker and then reached around Storm's big body, which was vibrating with excitement over the prospect of being let out. Pulling open the back door, she let the dog run out, then stepped down onto the patio.

The concrete blocks were littered with remnants of the previous night's storm, including puddles of cold rainwater and debris from the trees. A few sticks were down, out on the lawn, where Storm was intermittently nosing around and squatting.

Val breathed deeply of the fresh air. As was so often the case with summer weather in Minnesota, the sky above was a brilliant blue, already unmarred by clouds. Only the evidence left on the ground— and probably the dark circles under her eyes—hinted at the stormy night that had just passed.

The ringing of her cell in the pocket of her sweatshirt cut through the peacefulness of the hour.

"Morning, Luke."

"Hey, good morning. What are you guys doing today?" His voice sounded normal, without the telltale roughness of early morning. He'd been up for a while.

"No set plans. The kids are still in bed. Jake crawled in with me at some point last night. There was rough weather."

Storm was venturing into the trees rimming the backyard, so Val set off after her, shivering as the raindrops or dew still clinging to the grass chilled her bare feet.

"I wish we'd get some rain here," Luke said. "Things are drying up."

"Storm, get over here," Val ordered, holding the phone away from her mouth.

The dog turned to look at her, but went right back to following her nose. Val sighed, walking faster now to catch up with her. Sometimes Storm didn't listen any better than her boys. The last thing she needed was for the golden retriever to take off into the woods.

"What are you doing?"

"Letting the dog out. Hold on a minute."

Holding the phone completely away now, Val slapped her leg with her other hand. "*Storm*, come here. What has you so curious?"

A few more steps and she'd reached the dog's side. Now she could see that Storm was smelling a nasty pile of something. Val grabbed her collar, trying to pull her back. It was something dead, and she didn't want Storm to try eating it. Storm resisted, looking now into the deeper recesses of the woods ahead, a low growl starting deep down, hackles rising.

Val tried to see what the dog was seeing. At first she couldn't make out anything unusual, but then she saw it. A blur of black, far off in the trees. Wait—two blurs, one larger and one smaller.

"Bears," she whispered, her blood going cold.

This time she yanked viciously at Storm's collar, lifting the dog up onto her back legs and spinning her back toward the house. She ran awkwardly back for the door, still holding tight to the dog. The bears were too far away to pose any imminent danger, but Val had no idea how fast the animals could run.

Once Storm, slightly ahead of her, reached the three short stairs leading up to the back door, she released the dog's collar so she could open the door. When they were both safely inside, she shut and locked the door, then fell against it, fighting to catch her breath.

It was then she could hear Luke yelling through the phone, still clutched in her other hand.

"Sorry, Luke! That was crazy," she panted into the phone.

"What the hell, Val?!"

She hurried over to the window above the kitchen sink to peer into the backyard. All was quiet. No sign of any bears.

"I think I just saw my first bear. Or, *bears*."

"How close was it?" Luke asked, his irritation immediately replaced by concern.

Val closed her eyes and took a deep breath. "They were way off in the woods. I think there was one big one and one smaller one. Maybe a mamma and a cub? Do you think I should be worried?"

"Just be sure to let Renee and Matt know. Matt said there's been some sightings in the area, but last time I talked to him about it he said they hadn't had any trouble so far."

Val's mind flashed back to the night Luke had brought a cooler of fish into the lodge. He'd seemed hesitant to leave it outside before they cleaned them. It was the same night they'd opened their time capsule.

"You might have warned me," Val replied.

"None of the sightings had been near Whispering Pines. I didn't want to freak you out. Look, Val, the reality is bears do wander into that area once in a while. Just be smart and keep your eyes open for trouble. Maybe have Matt educate the boys on what to do, and what *not* to do, if one comes in closer."

She supposed he was right. The remoteness of the area was part of its charm, but also potentially dangerous.

"So," she said, changing the subject, "what are you up to today? How did the benefit go?"

"Today we're repairing equipment. Dad will be over soon. The benefit . . . boy, that was crazy."

Val popped a coffee pod into the machine and started the brewing process. "Crazy *good* or crazy *bad*?"

"Good. I was blown away with the support. People came from miles away. People I hadn't seen in probably thirty years."

Val was glad to hear that. His folks had to have appreciated the turnout, too. Though a part of her still wished she and the boys had gone.

"Kennedy did an incredible job on it all. The money will really help with the bills."

Luke's mention of his old friend's name caused a similar reaction within her body as the bear sighting. A sense of dread, however unwarranted, washed through her.

"Well . . . good. I'm glad she was helpful."

Luke paused, as if realizing Val might not appreciate hearing how helpful Kennedy was while she and the boys hadn't been included in any of the benefit planning or the evening itself. "Yeah, hey, well . . ."

Val could see her husband's face in her mind's eye, probably not bothering to hide his eyeroll over her obviously insecure state of mind. She couldn't help but wonder what this other woman's face looked like. Not that she was *the other woman* by any stretch of the imagination.

Was she?

Val took a deep breath.

What is the matter with me?

It wasn't fair for her to question Luke's loyalty. He'd done nothing to deserve any doubt on her part.

"When will we see you again?" she asked, trying hard for a more welcoming tone. "Your last trip was too short."

Luke sounded relieved at the topic change. "Actually, I was thinking it might be fun if you and the boys would drive over on Friday. You know, spend a few days. Maybe a week? Mom and Dad are going to drive out west, go to the musical in Medora, visit some friends. Mom is still really struggling, and I suggested a change of scenery might do them good. I'll be here alone. The county fair will be here, and I thought the boys might get a kick out of that. You know, rickety carnival rides, rigged games, greasy food? All those things every kid should experience at least once."

Val thought back to one of her early dates with Luke. He'd taken her to just such a carnival. They'd wandered around, talked to some of his old friends, and he'd won her a huge teddy bear at one of those "rigged games" he'd just mentioned. The night had been topped off with a stop in the beer gardens and dancing to The Johnny Holm Band, a group that still toured in the area to this day.

Luke was right. The boys would enjoy it (minus that last part). But then she remembered.

"I'm so sorry, hon, that *does* sound fun . . . but we can't."

"Why not?" he asked, the disappointment clear in his voice.

"I promised Renee I'd watch the resort for her this weekend. She wanted to help Julie move into her new place, but there was no one else to take over at Whispering Pines. Matt is on duty, Jess had other plans, so I offered. She's really looking forward to it. Julie has been so busy this summer, Renee has barely seen her. I can't bail on her now."

"Hmm," he said. "It would be the perfect time for the boys to come out here. What if they still came? You could bring them halfway and I could meet you. I'd keep them for a week and then bring them back out to the resort."

"And I'd stay here for the week?"

"Sure. When was the last time you had a week to yourself?" Luke asked.

Since Dave was now twelve, Val suspected twelve years was the right answer. "Can you keep them safe on the farm without me?"

Luke didn't immediately reply, long enough for Val to realize it was an ironic question for her to ask since their kids kept getting hurt under *her* watch.

"I promise I'll keep a close eye on them," Luke finally replied, for which Val was thankful.

Suddenly lots of ideas of what she could do with a week to herself flooded her brain. "Sorry. Of course they'd be fine. And it would be fun for them. Okay. Sure. Let's do it. When and where do you want to meet?"

They were just finishing up the logistics when Val's phone beeped with another call. "Hey, Luke, Mom is calling. I should probably take it. We'll see you on Friday, then? The boys will be excited."

"Sure. See you then. Love ya, babe. Tell your mom hello."

* * *

"Thanks for bringing the boys over," Lavonne said. "It would have taken your father and I forever to clean up the yard, and my knee is bugging me again. His back is bad, too, although he'll never admit it."

Val nodded as she put the last glass on the shelf and closed the cupboard door. She'd emptied the dishwasher while her mom cleared the remnants of their lunch from the table. "The storm must have hit harder here. You have more damage. We only had a few sticks down."

She could hear her father instructing Noah how best to push the wheelbarrow around in the backyard as they all picked up the damage left behind by the storm. Dave and Logan were arguing about how best to break up an especially large branch. Val hoped Logan was being careful with his injured hand, but she didn't want to make a fuss about it or he'd take it as an excuse as to why he shouldn't help.

"Oh, guess what?" Val said, turning her attention back to her mother. "The boys are spending next week at the farm with Luke."

"Really? Why's that?"

Val explained about the carnival and Luke's parents leaving for a few days.

"That's a great idea. Sounds fun for the boys, and I bet you're looking forward to a week to yourself."

Val leaned her hip against the countertop, her eyes roaming around her parent's kitchen. "Honestly, I am. I can't remember the last time I had even a few days to myself."

Lavonne snorted. "Probably the week before David was born."

Laughing, Val nodded. "My exact thought when Luke asked me that same question."

"What will you do?"

"I think I'll hole up in the kitchen at the lodge and play—at least part of the time."

"Play?" her mother questioned.

"Yes, *play*. I had *so* much fun trying just a few of the old recipes from Celia's recipe box for the Fourth of July. There were more I wanted to try, but I didn't have the time. I've been dying to try to make the watermelon pickles." She laughed at her mom's grimace. "Come on, don't you like to take risks? Some of the recipes include ingredients I've never even heard of. It would be fun to research what those are, maybe even revamp some of the recipes to make them easier for people to duplicate, maybe more healthy."

Lavonne shook her head. "Only you, my dear, would consider *that* fun. But there's no denying how good you are in the kitchen."

"We all have our strengths, Mom. Mine is just a bit old-fashioned in this day and age."

Lavonne took a seat at the kitchen table and groaned softly as she rubbed her sore knee. "I don't know about that. People might not cook as much as they used to, but everybody still likes to eat. And there's something special about old family recipes. Eating food you haven't had since you were a kid can give people a thrill. A sense of nostalgia."

"I suppose," Val agreed. That had certainly been some people's reaction on the Fourth.

"You know, I should have you help me with something," Lavonne said, chewing on her lip.

"What's that?"

"When I was a kid, my mom always made the best sugar cookies. They were crisp and delicious. They never had that heavy taste sugar cookies seem to have these days—you know, that underlying taste of lard or something?"

Val sat down across from her mom. "You mean roll-out sugar cookies, like the ones we frost for Christmas?"

"No, not that kind. These were different. Mom would take balls of the dough, dip them in sugar, and then flatten them with the bottom of a juice glass. Then she'd crisscross the tops with a fork. Oh my God, they were the best cookies ever! What I wouldn't give to be able to eat those again . . ."

Val's grandmother had died when Lavonne was a young woman. She wished she'd have had a chance to meet her. "Do you have a copy of the recipe?"

"Kind of . . ." Lavonne made a move to stand.

Val held out a hand to stop her. "Don't get up. Where is it? I'll get it."

With a thankful sigh, Lavonne pointed toward a lower cupboard. Minutes later, Val held the recipe card in her hand.

Lavonne eyed the card from across the table. "I can't tell you how many times I've tried to make sense of that thing and recreate Mom's cookies. There has to be something missing. Or written down wrong."

Val checked the time. "It's only 1:30. Our afternoon is wide open. Should we play with this?" Val could see her mother's enthusiasm over her suggestion, but she wasn't sure she had the necessary ingredients. "We can always send Dad to the store if we need something."

And so their afternoon of experimentation began. Val mixed up a small batch, following the recipe exactly. Just as Lavonne had said about her earlier attempts, the results were disappointing. Even the boys wouldn't eat them. She made another attempt, tweaking a few things. Those cookies showed more promise, but they still weren't great.

"I've never made these kinds of cookies before," Val said. "Let's check a few other recipes online."

Together they poked around on Lavonne's computer. Val made a few more adjustments, taking notes, treating it almost like a lab experiment. When the first cookie sheet came out of the oven, Lavonne reached for a sample, but Val batted her hand away.

"Patience, Mother. Let it cool for a minute."

"If this isn't it, we'll have to try again another day. I need to get supper started."

But Val was optimistic. She wanted nothing more than to give her mom a taste of a favorite from her long-ago childhood. Five minutes later, she watched Lavonne's face as she tasted their latest attempt. Lavonne's eyes grew wide as she chewed.

"Oh my. I think this is it!"

Giggling, Val helped herself to one. She bit in, loving the crispness of the cookie, the lightness of it on her tongue. "These are *good*."

"Better than good!" Lavonne declared, and Val thought her mom might even have a little tear in the corner of her eye.

The back door slammed and Jake and Noah came barreling in. "Got more cookies for us to try? We're starving!"

"Do we ever," Lavonne said, piling a small stack of them onto a napkin and handing them to Noah. "Take these outside so you don't get crumbs all over. Be sure your grandfather gets one."

Once the boys had made their noisy departure from the kitchen, Lavonne popped the rest of her cookie into her mouth. "Be sure you write down *exactly* what you did, Val. I want to make these tomorrow for my bridge club."

Val couldn't help but laugh when a cookie crumb flew from Lavonne's lips; she was so excited to finally have the right recipe for her mother's special cookies. A few unexpected hours in the kitchen, and she'd been able to give her mom a precious gift.

It doesn't get much better than that.

CHAPTER SIXTEEN

GIFT OF WINE AND BUBBLES

"*I* bet *you're* excited to have a week of peace and quiet," Jess said, bouncing Harper on her knee. "When was the last time *that* happened?"

Harper giggled as Molly, Renee's cocker spaniel, ran across the living room with a rawhide bone in her mouth, Storm right on her tail. The bone, nearly a foot long, hung lopsided in the dog's mouth. Plopping down in a square of light on the rug under the window, Molly began to gnaw on one end. Storm sniffed the other end of the bone, nuzzling it with her nose. When Molly didn't pull it away, Val's dog laid down next to her and carefully closed her mouth over the knot at the other end. Soon, they were both chewing on opposite ends of the bone.

"I can't believe Molly shares like that!" Val laughed. "Maybe if my boys were that nice to each other, I wouldn't be so looking forward to this week."

"*I* can't believe you let those dogs run around in here, Renee. In your brand-new house," Jess said, struggling to keep a squirming Harper contained. The toddler eyed the dogs, reaching in their direction.

Renee shrugged. "They're part of the family, too. Heck, Molly's been around longer than Matt. Besides, they won't hurt anything."

"No, but they *shed*."

"Hey, don't bust on our fur babies just because you're not exactly a dog lover, miss," Renee shot back before turning her attention to Val, repeating Jess's question: "How long?"

"Actually, I don't think I've *ever* had a week to myself. Not since before Dave was born. Plus, the boys were excited when I dropped them off with Luke this afternoon. So everybody's happy."

Renee shook her head. "Well, then, it's about damn time. I'm sorry you have to spend the first couple days helping at the resort."

Val shook her head. "I'm not. It was the reason I'm getting a break in the first place."

"Seth is picking us up in the morning," Jess said, holding Harper's hands high in the air and lightly tickling the little girl's tummy, attempting to distract her from the two dogs she'd love to climb over to, and *on* to. They all knew that would be pushing their luck where Molly was concerned. She'd share with another dog, but not a rambunctious kid, too. "Mom's going to watch her, and we'll probably be back later on Sunday evening. When I called her yesterday to reconfirm, she went on and on about some cookies you helped her bake, and how now her bridge friends all have old recipes they want you to help them with, too. What was that all about?"

Val hadn't talked to their mother since she'd left her parents' house a few days earlier. "Not sure. We went over there after that thunderstorm so the boys could help Dad clean up the yard. Mom asked me to fiddle with an old recipe she had from her mom—from our grandmother. Mom said she used to make the best sugar cookies, but hers never turned out like her mom's. We fiddled around with it, made some tweaks, and *voilà*! The third batch was the charm."

Renee laughed. "I've actually heard Mom complain about not being able to figure out that recipe. I bet you made her day! And Dad's. You know how he loves cookies."

Val shrugged. "It was no big deal. But it got me thinking . . . there are a bunch more recipes I wanted to try that I saw in Celia's recipe box when I was planning for the Fourth of July. I think I'm going to play in the kitchen at least part of this coming week."

Groaning, Jess scrunched her face in Val's direction. "You have the luxury of a week to yourself, at a *resort* on a lake in the middle of summer, and you want to spend it *inside*, in the *kitchen*? You are nuts."

Val tossed her hands up. "What can I say? I like to create. It's not like I'll be inside all day. I'll take some nice, contemplative walks, maybe sit on the beach some. Maybe even read a book." Although she doubted that last one would happen. Renee and Jess were the big readers in the family. *Maybe if it's a cookbook.*

"Careful with those walks," Renee warned, her tone taking on an edge of seriousness. "Matt's a little worried about your bear sighting the other morning. Don't venture too far into the woods by yourself, and maybe keep Storm with you."

This was the one thing that had Val a little concerned about watching over the resort. "I'll be careful. And I'll very tactfully warn your guests of the same. With any luck, Yogi Bear will steer clear of here. You are expecting all the cabins to be full by the time everyone gets in, right?"

"Right. Oh, and did I tell you? Matt's friend Ross will be renting the Gray Cabin."

"Ross?" Val asked, the name sounding vaguely familiar.

"Ross, as in, 'cop buddy from Minneapolis' Ross? Matt's best man?" Jess asked, seemingly surprised.

"Yep. Him."

"Does he not have a family?" Val remembered the man now from Renee and Matt's wedding, but she'd not talked to him that weekend other than a quick introduction. "The Gray Cabin's kind of small . . ."

"No. He's a bachelor, never been married, at least that I know of. He and Matt go way back. I think they met at the police academy, if I'm remembering right. He's the one who helped me that time I found pills in Robbie's pocket but I didn't know what they were."

Val shuddered. "That had to have been scary. The thought of the boys getting messed up in any of that crap scares the hell out of me."

"Tell me about it," Renee agreed. "But we got lucky that time."

"I remember thinking he was kind of arrogant at the wedding," Jess chimed in.

Renee blinked. "Really? Ross? Why?"

"I don't know, there was just something about him. I had to dance with him, part of the wedding party and all."

Renee snorted. "You weren't exactly a fan of men back then, Jess. You were in the middle of your split with your hubby, and Seth hadn't swept you off your feet yet. I suspect you weren't thinking very highly of *any* man at that point."

Giving up the battle to keep Harper contained, now that the dogs had lost interest in the bone and Molly had wandered back out to the kitchen, Jess let the toddler down. Val watched her closely as she took quick, albeit slightly unsteady, steps over to Storm. Harper stopped next to Storm, reached down to pet her, and tumbled onto the dog. Storm didn't budge; she looked between Harper, now half on top of her, and Val, panting.

"She's a good dog, isn't she?" Jess commented, watching the two closely.

"I guess living in a house full of young boys from the time you're a puppy will do that," Val agreed. "Renee, anything else I should know about your renters coming in?"

"There will be a bigger group taking the three cabins around the firepit. A family reunion, if I remember right. And then, like, three or four women in the biggest cabin."

"Sounds fun!" Val meant it; she looked forward to playing resort owner in Renee's absence. "Besides, it's not like Matt will be too far away if I have any trouble. When are you leaving again?"

"First thing in the morning. And I should be back sometime Sunday afternoon. I'm dropping Robbie off at a friend's house first, the family he lived with that semester when we first stayed out here."

"It is going to be quiet," Val commented, looking forward to it more than she'd thought she would. "Maybe it'll give me time to figure some things out."

"Oh, that sounds ominous," Jess said. "Harper, don't pull on Storm's tail!"

Val wasn't concerned. "It would take more than that to upset Storm," she assured her sister. "I just meant I need to really think about some things that have been bothering me lately."

"Wait, hold that thought." Renee held up a finger and disappeared into the kitchen, only to return a moment later with three cans of hard seltzer. "That sounds like a comment that needs to be accompanied with some refreshments."

Taking a can, Val held it up to the fading light from the setting sun. "I've been wanting to try these. Are they good?"

Renee flipped on a light. "They are. Now, you were saying?"

But Val wasn't sure what to say. Part of her hang-up lately was her marriage, but she doubted either of her sisters would understand. They'd think any whining about that was unwarranted. Renee's first husband had died, and she and Matt were still practically newlyweds, having just celebrated their first anniversary in June. Jess's first husband had turned out to be a lying, cheating criminal, and now her sister was practically drooling over that engagement ring on her finger every five minutes.

While Val suspected she wouldn't get any sympathy, she decided to share her struggles with them anyway.

As she'd expected, taking them into her confidence earned Val nothing more than an eyeroll out of Jess.

"Sis, you do realize you have nothing to complain about where Luke's concerned, right?" Renee lectured, her expression conveying her disapproval. "The man adores you. You two are solid. Look, I think every relationship goes through ebbs and flows. Sometimes you have to ride out the dips. You aren't thinking of doing anything stupid, are you?"

"Oh for God's sake, Renee. No. I'm not going to *leave* him," Val assured her sibling. "Like you said, we'll get through it. Maybe it's just me . . . though he is nearly impossible to reach these days, since Alan's death. It's like his old life is consuming him back home. Even an old girlfriend has reentered the picture."

"What?" Jess cried. "An old girlfriend of *Luke's*? Why is this the first I'm hearing about an old flame?"

"Technically she was more of *Alan's* girlfriend than Luke's, but I still get this pit in my stomach whenever Luke mentions her name."

"But why would he be talking about her to you, anyway?"

Val shrugged. "Mainly because he had to rush back to the farm the day after Logan and Drew got hurt with those damn bottle rockets. Apparently she'd organized a fundraiser thingy, like a banquet or something, to help pay for the big medical bills from Alan's accident."

Her sisters seemed to consider this before responding. They all sipped at their seltzers for a moment.

Renee was the first to weigh in. "I'm sure you have nothing to worry about where Luke's concerned, Val. Is that all that's bothering you?"

Val paused. Was it?

"No. I mean, things have gotten pretty tight, money-wise, and I need to figure out a way to help. With all the boys in school now, I'll have more time during the school year. Luke won't let me use any of my inheritance from Celia for living expenses, and I can't think of any type of business I really want to use it for. It's bugging the hell out of me."

"Maybe you're trying too hard to come up with something," Jess jumped in. "Luke's right, you shouldn't use it for daily living expenses. Don't worry, something will pop into your head someday. I mean, who would have thought Renee'd end up running this resort? Or that I would be helping out with three different businesses?"

Maybe that's part of the problem . . .

Val sipped her seltzer, looking between Renee and Jess. They seemed to forget her experience in the business world was much more limited than theirs. Just like their lack of understanding in regards to her marriage, they were coming at her struggles around starting something of her own from a whole different perspective. They were so much more like Celia in that respect than she'd ever be. But she doubted they could see that.

"Don't you guys find it odd that Celia just left me money when she left you two and Ethan more specific things? I absolutely don't mean to sound ungrateful, because I'm not at all. She was very generous with all of us. It's just like she seemed to know each of you would take what she left you and run with it. But me . . . it's like she didn't know what to do with me."

Renee frowned. "I don't know, Val, I guess I never thought about it that way. I actually think you might have received the easiest gift. You have way more freedom to do with it whatever you want, whereas me, Ethan, and Jess don't have as much latitude."

"True," Val conceded. "I guess we'll never really know."

"Not without Celia here to tell us," Jess said, standing and scooping Harper off the floor. "But what really matters is that you eventually figure out something kickass to do with the money she left you. Maybe you'll change the world one sugar cookie at a time."

* * *

Chilled from their run back to the duplex in a light drizzle, Val decided to take a bubble bath—not a luxury she normally made time for, but tonight she had nothing but time. She dug candles and matches out of a cupboard. Why stop there? She pulled one of the mismatched wine glasses out of another cupboard and crossed her fingers, hoping Renee might have left a bottle of wine behind. Sure enough, tucked back on a lower shelf in the fridge was an unopened bottle of white.

Finders, keepers, she thought with a giggle.

She thought back to her time with her sisters and the giggle died away. Jess could be such a smartass. Val knew her sister was joking about changing the world one sugar cookie at a time, but something about the offhanded comment stuck with her.

Storm followed her up the stairs and into the bedroom. Grabbing her robe, she headed for the bathroom but scooted the dog out.

"Not tonight, girl. Guard the door if you like, but not even you get to disturb my bath."

She fought the twinge of guilt as she closed the door on Storm, who stared up at her with her soft brown eyes.

She drew the bath, dropping a dollop of rose-scented bubble bath from a half-empty bottle into the swirling water, where it instantly disappeared against the backdrop of the pink tub.

"It's not every day a girl gets to take a bubble bath in a pink bath-tub," she said with a sigh.

She sank into the exquisite warmth of the scented water. Most adults wouldn't fit comfortably in the outdated tub, but Val had plenty of room to stretch out her toes. Sipping wine in the candlelight, she tried to let all thoughts float away. Soft music played from her phone, set a safe distance away on the vanity. Maybe she'd give herself a pedi-cure after her bath, but first she planned to soak until her fingers and toes looked like prunes. She should probably touch up her roots, too. She'd missed her last salon appointment because they'd been in North Dakota.

Stop thinking, she reminded herself, humming along to an old melody streaming through her phone. She drained the rest of her wine, then sank farther into the water.

Almost automatically, her hand slid over the portion of her right breast where she'd found the lump the previous summer. She couldn't feel anything now, and while she was thankful, the fact the doctors were still monitoring the area worried her. She let her hand roam over both of her breasts, seeing clearly in her mind the paperwork for her aunt's hospital stay.

It must have been horrible for Celia to have to endure a mastec-tomy. How had she felt about her body afterward? Celia had never had kids, had never married, but Val knew she'd dated a bit. *Maybe even more than a bit.* Had her life changed after the surgery?

Is that something I'll have to face someday?

Maybe finding a lump was a blessing in disguise. If anything did eventually develop, their ongoing monitoring should catch it early.

Find the blessings in every struggle.

Her hands floated back up to the surface of the water and she felt the tickle of bubbles.

The water slowly cooled. Storm whimpered outside the door. Reality slowly seeped back in. One glance at her fingertips revealed impressive pruning. It was as if she'd aged fifty years while relaxing in the tub, a trick she'd loved since she was a child. Although wrinkles weren't quite as fun now as they'd used to be.

Time marched on. Maybe it was time she quit watching from the sidelines and joined the parade.

CHAPTER SEVENTEEN
GIFT OF SISTERS HELPING SISTERS

*B*y ten the next morning, she moved from the pampering of her luxurious bath the evening before straight into amplified housekeeper mode. Departing guests cycled through the lodge with promises to be back next year, and as they drove away, Val was again thankful for this one-time chance to spend two months at Whispering Pines instead of only a week. She'd make the most of it.

Checking the list Renee had left her, she calculated that she'd have about two hours to turn over the cabins before the new wave of guests arrived. Hopefully no one would be early. Five cabins to clean—not to mention more than twice that many beds to change—meant she'd have to hustle. Good thing she was an expert at cleaning up behind her own bevy of messy boys.

How hard could it be?

She pulled a well-stocked cart out of the storage room in the lodge. It was piled high with fresh linens and held an impressive supply of cleaning products—there was even a place for the vacuum. It reminded her of the carts you'd see cleaners pushing in hotels. Anything less would make the ongoing cleaning duties an impossible act for one person, and Val knew Renee usually did this all by herself every Saturday morning.

"This is the less-than-glamorous part of resort ownership," she joked to herself. "Scrubbing toilets and stripping beds."

But years of practice in her own home proved useful. Plus, she lucked out: none of the cabins had been left in too bad of shape. She had all but one cabin done just one hour into her task.

Pushing her cart across the sidewalk, she approached the Gray Cabin. If she hurried, she could get back to the lodge and bake fresh plates of those special sugar cookies for each cabin before the next week's guests arrived. She knew Renee liked to make that little extra effort, but her sister didn't always get around to it.

Parking her cart in front of the smallest cabin, Val grabbed a garbage bag and the portable tray of cleaners and climbed the stairs. The sun felt good on her shoulders, like a warm hand promising a splendid summer day. Admiring the fresh red trim around the door, she reached for the doorknob, the metal surprisingly cold against her hand. She pushed the door open and entered, a coolness replacing the heat from the sun. She shivered, although she wasn't sure whether it was the temperature of the room or something else.

Unlike the other cabins, this one was a mess. Which surprised her, given the kindly older woman who'd stayed there the previous week. When Val had checked her out earlier, the woman, seventy or so, appeared neat and tidy. This was anything but. She'd have to really hustle now if she wanted to get those cookies baked. With a sigh, she set the towels and bedding on the sofa and basket of cleaning supplies on the kitchen table. She'd tackle the dirty dishes in the sink first.

She shuddered. "Gross."

The woman mustn't have washed a dish all week. The garbage was overflowing; Val had to fling the windows open to freshen the stale air. How could one person leave such a mess? Maybe she had dementia or something.

Or maybe the haunted cabin made her do it, Val thought with a giggle.

She popped one end of her earbuds in and turned on one of her playlists. Music always helped pass the time when she cleaned.

Once she had the kitchen back in order, dishes stacked neatly on the open shelves her brother had recently installed, she tackled the bathroom. Dirty towels littered the floor. She wondered again how one old lady could leave such a mess. She sprayed window cleaner on the mirror and scrubbed at the splotched glass, banishing water spots and what looked like toothpaste, the smell of ammonia tickling her nose. She wished she could open the tiny, frosted-glass window above the small tub to help freshen the air in here, too, but it wasn't the kind that opened.

She paused, pulling her earbud out. What had she heard? Glancing around, she heard it again. A scratching sound. It sent an unwarranted chill down her spine.

This place still gives me the creeps.

The old "You can put lipstick on a pig" expression flashed through her brain. Which was ridiculous. Ethan had gone out of his way to clean up this cabin. Any old juju that had existed here had been chased away.

But where was that scratching sound coming from? She could still hear it; certainly it wasn't her imagination. She spun to face the window. There—it sounded like scratching on the glass. As she watched, something dark flicked in and out of view beyond the milky frost of the glass.

Clutching her racing heart, she laughed to herself. "Nothing more than the rubbing of a tree branch."

She remembered how trees had damaged the roof in the back bedroom, and the recently repaired wall that had been stained where water had leaked inside, unheeded. With any luck she'd be able to reach the offending branch and break it off. Their next renter wouldn't appreciate being woken by the sound of scratching on glass.

Heading back out through the smallish living room and kitchen, she skipped down the stairs, welcoming the warm sunshine on her face. She'd noticed earlier that there was a small stepstool on the cart. Grabbing it, she continued on around the far corner of the cabin.

The log-sided building and towering pines overhead cast long shadows. She advanced more slowly now. Unlike most of the other cabins at the resort, this one was tucked back into the tree line. Overgrowth and a fallen tree obstructed her view. She'd have to remember to suggest to Renee that they clear the area. Anything could be hiding in here. Maybe she could put her boys to work on it, surprise Renee.

Pushing a prickly evergreen bush out of the way, she set her stool up under the bathroom window, next to the maple tree with the offending branch. The stool was her only hope to reach the bare, dead branch high overhead.

"So help me God, if I see a snake in here . . ." she said out loud in an attempt to bolster her own confidence. She placed one tennis-shoed foot on the first rung of the stool. The fact she was completely alone at the resort at the moment tickled her brain.

Unless, of course, Yogi Bear is rambling around out here somewhere, in search of a picnic basket. Not that a bear would be helpful if she fell off her stool.

She stepped onto the stool's highest rung, stretching as far as she could to try to reach the branch. Her fingers barely managed to nudge the branch closer, but finally she was able to wrap them around the pliant stick.

"Hey, are you Val?" a male voice shouted from somewhere near the front of the cabin.

Startled, Val swung her head toward the voice. It threw off her balance and the stepstool wobbled precariously under her. Time slowed as the stool fell away. Her free hand grabbed blindly for the windowsill, but she had too much momentum. The brittle branch offered little resistance, failing to slow her fall.

It was all over in a flash. She gazed up at the sky. Overgrown bushes had cushioned her fall, but now they poked mercilessly into her backside.

"Oh shit, lady, are you okay?!" the voice grew louder as footfalls ran closer.

Am I okay? Val wondered, squeezing her eyes shut and giving herself a second to catch her breath.

"Don't move!" The man's tone shifted from one of shock to something different.

It grated on Val's already shaky grip on things.

"*Don't* tell me what to do!" she shot back, flinging her eyes open and pushing at the broken branch that she'd manage to pull down on top of herself. "You scared the hell out of me!"

The man knelt next to her and dropped a restraining hand on her shoulder, tossing the offending branch off her with his other. "Just wait, lady. Does it feel like anything's broken? Lay still until you're sure you're all right."

Val slapped the hand away and rolled toward the man with a grunt. "The only thing broken is this bush I fell on. It's poking me in my lower back, and unless you want me to get impaled, I suggest you get out of my way."

Now on her hands and knees, she paused to catch her breath; she then leaned back and sat on the heels of her tennis shoes, resting her right hand against her lower spine and twisting to take away the kink.

"Here, let me help you up," the voice demanded, and this time she didn't argue. She took his outstretched hand and he easily brought her to her feet. He didn't release it until he'd helped her through the worst of the underbrush and back to the sparse grass.

"What are you doing back here?"

He didn't bother to say, *Sorry I scared the shit out of you and made you fall,* she noticed.

"What, no apology? I had everything under control before you yelled at me."

The man looked back toward the side of the cabin and the step-stool, now lying over on its side. "Yeah, sure you did."

She took a steadying breath. This had to be a paying customer, and she was supposed to be in charge, not storming around like a petulant child.

For the first time she looked directly at the man's face, partially obscured under a New York Yankees baseball hat. She felt a flicker of recognition. The close-cropped beard was new, but she was relatively sure she'd seen him before, standing next to Matt at his wedding to her sister. Come to think of it, he sounded bossy, too, just like Matt when he was in full cop mode.

"Let me guess. Ross?"

The man nodded slowly. "And you are . . . ?"

"Val. Renee's sister. I think we met briefly at their wedding."

"*That's* why you looked familiar," the man replied. "Yeah, I'm Ross —Matt's buddy from Minneapolis. Look, I'm really sorry I startled you. Are you sure you're okay?"

Feeling silly as the shock of her tumble wore off, she brushed off her backside and headed for the front of the cabin. When she didn't immediately hear his footsteps following her, she glanced back. He was retrieving her stool.

"Thanks."

"Least I can do."

Once they were back in the warm sunshine, Val tucked the ineffective stool back on the cart. "Listen, I'm sorry about all that. Matt's at work and Renee is gone for the day. I offered to watch the resort for them. I was just finishing up here. In fact, this is your cabin for your stay. If you just want to give me a minute, I'm almost done inside. Then you can get settled. We can mess with the paperwork later."

"That would explain why no one but an overly friendly dog served as the welcoming committee when I stopped in at the lodge."

Val grinned. He didn't seem like the type of man that would be put off by a dog. "That would be Storm. She's nice to have around, but useless when it comes to paperwork."

He finally grinned back. "If you're sure you're all right, I'll go grab my stuff."

Turning away, Val headed back up the steps of the Gray Cabin, waving a dismissive hand back at him. "I'm fine. Now go, or I'll forget you're a paying customer and put you to work in here."

* * *

By two o'clock, all expected guests had arrived. Even with the unexpected tumble, Val managed to send them all out of the lodge with a fresh plate of cookies to welcome them. All but Ross. He'd arrived before she'd baked and hadn't stopped back into the lodge yet to do his paperwork. She had a plate ready for him when he did. She'd considered burning his cookies, or maybe lacing them with something nasty, to get him back for the scare, but she didn't think Renee would approve of such a petty move. *Maybe Renee shouldn't have left me in charge, then.* But in the end, pride over her baking skills wouldn't allow it. She'd have to find a different way to pay him back.

The air inside the lodge kitchen was getting sticky. It had to be at least eighty degrees outside. She could have flipped on the small window air-conditioner unit to cool the kitchen, but she preferred to keep the windows and door open. She set up a box fan instead, keeping things bearable.

The work was finally done, and now she could play.

She planned to spend the remainder of her day experimenting in the kitchen, all by herself. Her next project was to try her hand at the watermelon pickles. She'd pickled cucumbers before, and even peapods, but never fruit. The old recipe had caught her eye and she'd been anxious to try it. The problem was, like so many old recipes, the directions were incomplete. She read the card again, planning the steps out in her mind. This one was written out in a green pen, and whoever wrote it had forgotten to list a key ingredient: watermelon.

No wonder people who seldom cook struggle to recreate their grandma's recipes!

While she pondered this, she brought in a case of old canning jars from the shed, scrubbed them in hot, soapy water, and set them out on the island to dry.

Never having actually eaten watermelon pickles—although she'd seen them on display at farmers' markets—she wasn't entirely sure whether to include the rind or just the pink flesh of the fruit. She pulled up a number of online recipes and was surprised to learn the rind was actually the main ingredient. But the jars of pickles she'd admired in the past had been pink in color. She'd use some of the pink flesh along with the rind, she decided. But there was a problem. Since her recipe failed to mention the watermelon specifically, she was disappointed to discover that all the online recipes called for the rind to soak overnight before actually pickling it.

Guess I won't be finishing the pickles today.

"It's not like I'm in a big hurry," she conceded.

Storm raised her head to gaze at her.

"Sorry, girl, did I disturb your nap?"

The dog put her head back down.

Val chuckled. "You sure are lazy when the boys aren't around."

She'd just have to get the rind soaking, find another recipe to try today, then get back to the pickles tomorrow morning. Her whole week was free, she reminded herself, and she was determined to make the most of it. The refrigerator and cupboards were well-stocked with plenty of ingredients for the recipes she'd been excited to try.

Someone rapped on the back door.

"Come in!"

Storm was on her feet in a flash. Val made a move to grab her collar, but when she saw Ross walk in she let the dog go. It wasn't exactly a mature reaction, but hey, he'd caused her to fall off a stool into bushes earlier. If he didn't like a little love from an overly friendly golden retriever, too bad.

"Hey, girl," Ross said, slapping his chest. Storm took him up on the invite, jumping up and placing her big paws squarely on the Budweiser emblem on the front of his faded T-shirt. He buried his face in her fur, catching Val off guard.

"Dog lover?"

"We met earlier, remember? When I first got here," he said. *"Before* I scared the shit out of you over at the cabin."

I should have burned his damn cookies.

But she wasn't really mad. He hadn't meant to scare her. She was sure they'd all get a good laugh over it once the story spread to her family, which she had no doubt it would.

Not that she'd let him off the hook quite that easily. She'd bide her time, wait for the perfect moment for a little payback.

"Why don't we just forget about that little episode," she suggested.

"Pretty quiet in here," the man said, taking hold of Storm's paws and putting the dog back down on all fours. He scratched her behind the ears as he glanced around the large kitchen. "But those look good." He'd spied the plate of cookies and started to pull the plastic wrap off of them, but then he paused, apparently remembering his manners. "May I?"

"Be my guest. They're actually for you. I baked a plate for each cabin. You just arrived *before* check-in time, so I didn't have a chance to put them in your cabin beforehand."

He didn't even notice her jab—or if he did he didn't care. Pulling a crisp, golden sugar cookie out from under the wrap, he devoured half of it in one bite, moaning as the flavor hit his tongue. "Oh my God, these taste like my grandma's. Will you marry me?"

Val couldn't bite back her bark of laughter. "Well, no, seeing as how I'm already married, and that would be illegal. Aren't you a cop or something? But since you just paid me the ultimate compliment with your reaction, you're forgiven for knocking me on my butt earlier."

His smirk turned into a full-fledged grin just before he finished off the cookie in only his second bite. "I thought you forgave me back at the cabin. You know, I didn't *mean* to scare you."

Crossing her arms over her chest, she regarded him with skeptical eyes. He appeared to be a few years younger than Matt, maybe an inch or two taller, but not as broad in the shoulders as her brother-in-law. He seemed relaxed now, but there'd been a flash, when he'd checked her after her fall, when she'd sensed an intensity to him. *Must be the cop thing.*

"How do you know Matt, my brother-in-law? I remember meeting you briefly at Renee's wedding, but that's about it. Did you two work together or something?"

"Or something," he replied.

His evasiveness was unexpected. She knew he was a police officer in Minneapolis. Renee had told her. It couldn't be an easy job. Maybe he didn't want to think about any of it now, on vacation.

"Sorry he wasn't here to meet you. He thought he'd be back later this afternoon. Oh, that reminds me, I have some paperwork. I'll go grab it. Storm, make sure he doesn't eat *all* the cookies."

She could hear the man talking to her dog—"I thought she said they were for me, huh?"—as she headed down the hallway toward the front office, his voice fading away. It was cooler here, in the dimness. She paused at the wall of photographs, an impressive collection spanning decades. Most were probably previous guests, but there were a few familiar faces.

Val had studied the photos that first summer after Renee took over the resort, but she hadn't given them much thought since. There were shots of her parents when they were much younger, and more of Celia. It was fascinating to see her aunt mature through the years. An older, black-and-white photo showed a group of kids, maybe college age, gathered around a classic black automobile. The vehicle looked too fancy, too stately, to call it a car.

It was Celia's expression in that photograph that beckoned to Val —she could almost hear the laughter, feel the excitement. In other shots, ones where she was a middle-aged woman instead of a fresh-faced young girl, Celia no longer appeared as carefree.

Val wondered, not for the first time, what Celia's life had been like. It would have been so different from her own. She knew her aunt had went to work as soon as she'd graduated from college. Back then, it wasn't uncommon for women to go to college with the sole purpose of finding a husband. But not Celia. George had mentioned money pressures. Apparently her father had died young, and it wouldn't be until later that their mother would remarry and Val's own father, George, and her uncle, Gerry, would be born. Celia never did marry. Instead, she made a career for herself, eventually becoming a wealthy woman in her own right. She'd never relied on a man for support.

The wall was a unique visual summary of portions of her aunt's life, almost like bookends for the middle of her lifespan: college years, when she'd first come to Whispering Pines, then a large gap, then picking up again when Celia came back to the resort later in life, enjoying many years here again.

"Did you get lost?" Ross asked from somewhere behind her.

"Oh! Sorry, I'll be right there."

"No rush, but I think your dog needs to go out. Want me to take her?"

"If you're sure you don't mind," Val replied, somewhat surprised. "But you need to watch her. She can't be trusted on her own."

"Got it," he called from the kitchen, and then there was the faint slamming of the door.

She found the paperwork and was back in the kitchen before he and Storm returned.

"What do you think of the cabin?" she asked. "Do you remember what it looked like before, when you were here for the wedding?"

Ross took the pen she offered him and scribbled his name on the bottom, next to where she pointed. "Vaguely. But I thought it looked lots older, rundown. Isn't that where Renee's daughter ran into some trouble? When I talked to Matt about maybe coming for a visit, he said he had the perfect 'haunted' little cabin for me. What's the story there? It looks much better now. What did he mean by *haunted*?"

"My brother, Ethan, and some of the kids gave it a facelift this spring. I think they did a great job with it. There's a history to the place for sure, but I wouldn't say it's haunted."

Or would I?

Ross grunted. "I hope you're right. I deal with enough freaks on the job. I don't want to have to deal with any *dead* freaks while on vacation."

Val grinned at the immensely immature thought that flitted through her brain. Maybe she could do something to scare him while he was staying in the cabin. Make this tough, big-city cop lose a little sleep over the possibility of things that go bump in the night.

Payback, perhaps?

CHAPTER EIGHTEEN

GIFT OF A NIGHT OUT

*A*fter a few more hours of experimenting in the kitchen, Val realized she needed to stretch her legs and enjoy some sunshine and fresh air. Even *she* couldn't spend all her time indoors on a beautiful Saturday afternoon.

Most of the resort guests relaxed in front of their cabins and on the beach, and a few even sat around a low fire in the firepit, laughing and roasting hotdogs. Val waved as she meandered by, keeping an eye out for anything that might need addressing. While this "being in charge" business had been easy up to this point, she felt a sense of responsibility for every little thing happening at the resort in Renee's absence. Was this how Renee always felt as she went about her days? As if she were *on call?* Val would be glad when Renee got back on Sunday afternoon. Then she could really relax and enjoy her days of peace and quiet. She'd sleep in, make plans for her kitchen back home, and continue to play in the lodge kitchen—things she wished she could do every day but there never seemed to be enough time.

The pathway took her by each cabin. As she approached the Gray Cabin, all looked quiet. Sunlight glittered off a window and bright flowers exploded from the window box she'd planted for Renee. They'd brought the old place back to life.

The screen door pushed open and Ross came out, still in his Budweiser T-shirt but now wearing shorts and running shoes. He jogged down the stairs in her direction.

"Hey, I was just going to head out on a run," he said, stopping in front of her. "Want to come? Show me where to go around here?" Val's face must have reflected what she thought of *that* idea. Ross jogged backward a couple of steps, a wide grin on his face. "Let me guess. Not a runner?"

"Do I look like a runner?" Val asked, looking down at herself and back up at hm.

He shrugged. "Maybe. How about your dog? Does Storm want to go?"

Storm wasn't hard to read. She looked much more interested in the idea. "She'd probably love it, but I can't guarantee she'll cooperate with you."

"She did fine earlier. Would you mind?"

Val glanced down at Storm and could tell the dog was full of pent-up energy. "Why not? You two go have fun. When you get back, you'll find me right over here on this swing, contemplating the meaning of life."

"Well, please, if you figure that out, will you let me know what it is when we get back? The answer to that age-old question still eludes me."

"If I receive any bolts of infinite wisdom, I'll be sure to share." Sarcasm dripped from her words. He laughed, and she pointed off to the right. "There's an old footpath through the trees that butt up against the lake on that side of the resort. You can get to a neighboring resort that way. It doesn't get a lot of use, but it might be more interesting than running on the paths through the resort or on the gravel road leading out to the main highway. Stay on it and you shouldn't get lost."

"Good to know. Thanks," he said with a quick salute and then a slap of his leg. "Come on, girl, let's go explore the woods!"

Val watched as he set out on a jog in the direction she'd pointed,

Storm bouncing along beside him. As they disappeared from sight, she realized she should have warned him about possible bear sightings in the area, but he was gone. And besides, it was late afternoon; bears might be more likely to wander into a populated area when it was quiet, like her early-morning sighting, or even once it was dark out. She'd warn him when he brought Storm back.

Crossing over to the swinging bench that had been here at the resort as long as she could remember—even back when they'd been kids—she gave it a little push. It seemed solid enough. Its construction was self-contained, a wooden structure above with strong chains suspending the long bench, all of it built on a wooden platform. She picked up a nearby twig and used it to scoop cobwebs off the one arm, then settled on the bench.

The wood and chains both gave a comfortable creak; it was a sound she'd always associate with her childhood, with their early days spent at Whispering Pines. When she pushed off the wooden platform with her right foot, the squeaking took on a relaxed rhythm. Her mind wandered, unencumbered. Shrieks of laughter from kids playing on the beach took her back in time to afternoons spent catching minnows in the crystal-clear water and building sand castles on the beach. They'd been lucky to spend time here as kids. She'd been quite young back then, and only remembered snippets, but they were happy memories.

Once the boys got back, she'd be sure they enjoyed some of the same experiences. They'd already had a fun couple of weeks, with more to come.

Pushing off again, she wondered what they were up to at the farm. Jake was probably hanging out by the chickens, making a game out of gathering their eggs for Luke's mother. Noah was probably quizzing Luke about all things farm-related, from the crops to the equipment to the different animals. That kid's brain never seemed to stop. Logan and Dave might be tossing a baseball or football around, roughhousing. There'd be plenty of room and, as long as they kept it outside, nothing to break.

Would spending time with their kids snap Luke out of this funk he seemed to be in these days? Val hoped so. She missed her old husband . . . the one that didn't seem to be carrying such a burden. And if she were being honest, she was already missing the boys, even though she'd only dropped them off with Luke a day ago.

Would they miss her?

An image flooded into her mind of the boys racing on Alan's four-wheeler and the old dirt bike again. She hated knowing Luke was probably letting them ride all over the farm on them . . . it made her think of a story her brother shared about an old friend getting badly hurt on one. In fact, it had been Rebecca's first husband. They'd all been friends back in college. Ethan hadn't even known about the accident, and his friend's subsequent death, until recently.

She'd have to remember to warn the boys to be extra careful when she called them later.

But then something else occurred to her. Something they often fought over. She was doing it again. She was being overprotective, falling into the trap of thinking she was the only one who could keep their kids safe. That obviously wasn't true, given the mess they'd had over the Fourth, first with Noah's trouble out on the lake and then the sparklers and bottle rockets.

They were trying their best. That would have to be enough.

She allowed her mind to wander down another path: Celia's recipes. Her afternoon had flown by while she'd experimented with different recipes in the kitchen. Growing up, she'd loved playing in the kitchen beside her mom. The youngest of her siblings, she often felt ignored by them. Even today, she knew she didn't have as close of a relationship with Renee and Jess as they did with each other. It used to bother her. Now she accepted it for what it was. The extra time at the resort was helping.

On the flip side, she appreciated all the time she'd spent with her mom. While parents never wanted you to suspect they had favorites, Val secretly felt like Lavonne's. The other three interacted more with George. She supposed it was typical family dynamics. What wasn't quite so typical was that they all remained close. No outcasts or black sheep. Even after all these years, everyone still seemed to like each other.

It was what she wanted for her own kids.

She needed to try harder where Luke was concerned. They'd been drifting about lately, but if she allowed that to continue, to drift further, her dream of a close-knit family for her own kids would be lost. She hoped it was still what Luke wanted, too. She did have a tiny seed of doubt, deep in her gut. She'd never experienced that in their marriage before, but it was there now. And it was growing.

It wasn't just Luke. She'd been questioning things, too. She wanted more out of life. She just needed to figure out what that looked like. She'd use the next few days to try to do just that.

The crunch of tires on gravel pulled her out of her thoughts. Matt must be back from work. Good. She'd been feeling oddly responsible for his buddy, Ross. She pulled her feet up onto the bench and waited. He'd walk by here on the way back to their house.

She didn't have to wait long. Matt rounded the corner of the lodge, heading in her direction, and she waved a hand in greeting.

"Hey, how'd it go?" He glanced around, taking note of the knots of people by the firepit and the beach enjoying a warm late afternoon. "Looks busy. Any trouble?"

"No trouble at all. Morning was busy. I didn't realize how much work it is to turn the cabins over between guests. I have a new respect for Renee."

Matt laughed. "No kidding. But she loves it. She still says how much better it is than sitting in an office. It was nice of you to help out today, though, so she could go help Julie change apartments. I just talked to her, and they've got the old place cleaned out and they're making their last transfer to the new apartment now—or house, I guess it is. It sounds like they're having fun, but she was tired."

Val was glad to hear the move was going well. She wasn't looking forward to those years ahead of her and Luke with their boys.

"Your buddy got in, too."

Matt nodded, motioning toward the lodge parking lot. "I saw his truck out front. What time did he get in?"

Smirking, Val noted it was early, *before* she had his cabin ready.

"Why doesn't that surprise me? He's always been like that. For all of his irritating qualities, of which there are many, tardiness isn't one of them."

"How long have you guys been friends? You worked together at some point, right?"

Matt opened his mouth to reply but was cut off by energetic barking.

"Speak of the devil," Val noted as Storm bounded toward them, followed by Ross. He looked like they'd run hard, and he wasn't nearly as energetic as Storm.

Matt turned to Ross as his friend slowed to a walk, sweat soaking his shirt. Ross pulled the bottom of his shirt up and wiped his face, still winded. Based on her glimpse of a flat stomach and a ripple of muscle, the guy would likely run every day this week. A body like that took work to maintain. Maybe he'd take Storm again.

"I'd hug you," Ross greeted Matt with a smirk, "but I'm guessing you're not up for that."

"Smartass," Matt shot back.

Val pushed up off her comfortable seat on the swing, intending to slip away as the two men kicked off Ross's visit, but Matt laid a hand on her shoulder.

"You've met my sister-in-law, Val, then? Again, I mean. You probably met at the wedding."

"I did indeed. I asked her to marry me the minute I tasted one of her cookies, but so far she hasn't taken me up on the offer. I'll let you know when she does."

Matt laughed out loud. "Oh, this little one would tear you to shreds, Ross. And then, when she tired of that, Luke would step in."

"Luke?"

"Yes, you know," Val said, "that pesky husband I mentioned when you proposed?"

"Ah. Yes." Ross laughed, bending down to stroke Storm's head.

Val frowned at her dog, practically sitting on the man's feet, hanging close after their run. *Traitor.*

"Never mind Ross. He's always a pain," Matt said, turning his back on his old friend to face Val. "We're going to go meet up with old Sheriff Thompson for steaks and beer tonight. Join us? My treat to thank you for holding down the fort today."

Val opened her mouth with a nearly automatic *no*, but then thought better of it. Matt was fun, and, admittedly, Ross was, too; she could already tell these two men would be a kick to hang out with at a bar. She also knew the man they were meeting, credited him for saving her niece during that awful episode in the Gray Cabin a while back.

A night out was something she seldom got to do anymore.

Why not? I'm going to get sick of my own company as it is this week.

"You know what? I think I'll take you up on that offer, Matt. As long as you think things will be okay here at the resort. What time are you leaving?"

Matt glanced at his watch. "Everything should be fine. Renee has my number posted in the cabins, underneath hers, so guests can call if they have any trouble. Should we say twenty minutes? Does that work for you two?"

Ross nodded then jogged off toward his cabin. "Make it fifteen. I need a beer!"

Val had to dive for Storm's collar to keep her dog from following her new friend. "Come on, girl, you're coming with me."

Matt sent her a text to meet them in the parking lot. He'd drive. She'd opted for a simple summer dress in bright turquoise. Many of the local restaurants and bars sat on the water. She hoped they'd sit at a table on an outside patio. She couldn't find her flat sandals that matched her dress, so she had to settle for ones with a slightly higher heel than she'd have preferred. She knew she'd catch flack if she kept them waiting and cut into their beer time.

Both men were already at Matt's pickup when she got to the lot. Ross motioned for her to climb in the front seat and he'd get in the back, but she declined. She was the third wheel tonight. She stepped up on the running board and into the backseat. But he got points for thinking of it in the first place. As she'd hoped, Matt pulled into a busy parking lot outside of a large, log-sided bar along the shore of a nearby lake.

"This looks nice," she commented. "Have you been here before?"

"Nope," Matt answered, slamming his door and coming around the front of his truck to stand by Ross and Val. "Thompson suggested it."

"He's the guy who retired and you took over for him as sheriff, right?" Ross asked. "I think I met him at the wedding, too."

"Right. Let's see if he's here yet."

They followed Matt into the restaurant, and then through doors in the back, leading out to a large patio that butted out over the water. Most of the tables were filled; Val recognized the old sheriff sitting at one in the corner. He smiled when he saw the trio approach.

"What a pleasant surprise to see you with these two, Val," the older man greeted her, a hand extended in her direction. She took it and then bent in to give him a hug, noticing for the first time that he was in a wheelchair.

Val straightened but left her hand in his for an extra beat. "Sheriff Thompson, it's so good to see you. Matt said you'd be here and then something about treating for steak and beer, so . . . here I am. I couldn't pass all that up."

As she took her seat, and the men said their hellos, Val hoped the shock she'd felt over the older man's appearance didn't show on her face. He'd visibly aged in the year since she'd last seen him. She'd known of his heart condition—it was the reason he'd brought Matt in to replace him in the first place—but his pallor still unnerved her.

"Tell me, what's everyone been up to over there at Whispering Pines? Where's Renee tonight?" the older man asked.

Matt held up one finger when a waiter interrupted to take their drink order. "Want anything harder than that water you're drinking, Thompson?"

"Want? Yes. Allowed? No. I'll have to stick with the water, but you three better get started on that beer."

After Matt, Ross, and Val ordered, Matt turned back to him. "How've you been doing, Thompson? I'm surprised to see your ass in a wheelchair."

Val cringed. She'd had the same reaction, but wouldn't have come right out and asked. "Jeez, don't hold back, Matt."

He looked at her and shrugged.

I'm tagging along on a guy's night out, Val reminded herself. Probably not going to be much small talk.

"It's fine, Val. I don't mind," Thompson jumped in, slapping his palms on the arms of his wheelchair. "The old ticker's wearing out faster than I'd hoped. Can't be helped. I'm just glad we brought you in when we did, Matt. Should have done it sooner. Might have been able to spend more time down south, like I'd hoped. But I'd have missed the work. Still do. Retired life is damn boring after wearing a star on my chest for a few decades."

Matt nodded. "I get it. I tried civilian life for a year or two, but I missed the action, too."

"Shit, you two should come play cop with me over in Minneapolis," Ross said. "You'd get plenty of action, but it's downright soul-sucking these days."

Val glanced at Ross, caught the haunted expression in his eyes, the hard set of his jaw. This conversation was heading down a path where she'd best talk less and listen more. She couldn't imagine what Ross— or Matt and the old sheriff, for that matter—faced on the job. They'd seen the worst of humanity on a regular basis. What would that do to a person's perception of the world?

Glancing at each one of them individually, she realized how thankful she was for all they'd sacrificed to keep the rest of them safe. Raising her newly arrived glass of beer, she said as much. "Men and women who do what you do help keep evil at bay. Thank you."

Thompson followed suit, holding his glass of water high, its ice jangling in his unsteady hand. "Here, here. Although it's a young man's game these days."

"Getting to be a bit much even for us younger guys," Ross tossed in.

Val was starting to wonder if Ross's trip to Whispering Pines was for more than just a vacation. But who was she to ask?

Matt nodded, and Val thought she noticed a look pass between her brother-in-law and his friend, but then Matt turned his attention back to Thompson. "You asked about Whispering Pines and my gorgeous, yet absent, wife."

Val snorted at his offhanded compliment of her sister.

"What? She is!" he said, winking at Val. "And feel free to tell her I said that. Things are busy as ever out at the resort. Renee does a good job keeping the cabins rented out in the summer. This weekend Val here agreed to help out so Renee could go help Julie move."

Thompson nodded. He'd remember Julie. The troubles she had been having with her ex-boyfriend that first year Renee ran Whispering Pines were what ultimately led to Matt taking over when Thompson retired.

"Renee's even renting out that old cabin where we had the trouble with that young man," Matt reported. "You remember, don't you?"

"It's my ticker that's giving me trouble, Matt, not my brain. Of course I remember that damn cabin. It was the sight of my final courageous act as sheriff. Damn near killed me."

Val shuddered, taking a sip of her beer. It was a night she'd rather forget.

Ross turned to Matt. "Which cabin are you talking about? The one I'm staying in?"

Matt nodded. "Yep, the haunted one. But since you aren't scared of anything, I figured it wouldn't be a problem."

"Great," Ross said in an exaggerated moan, but Val doubted his concern was real.

"That old cabin did seem like a magnet for trouble, though," Thompson said. "That first summer Renee was at the resort wasn't the first time we'd responded to calls centered around it."

"Do you believe the rumors, then?" she asked him. "You know, that say it's haunted or something?"

He considered her question before responding. "I can't say whether or not *haunting* is a real thing, but I have no doubt some places have a kind of feeling to them, a heaviness if you will, where bad things of the past seem to linger."

"Well, let's hope the work Ethan did on the cabin helped banish the bad. We don't want to scare my poor buddy here." Matt clapped a hand on Ross's back. "He might have nightmares."

Ross flashed a middle finger at Matt just as the waiter came back to take their food order.

After that, the conversation moved away from the Gray Cabin.

"You probably didn't know we built a new house out at the resort," Matt shared. "We just got moved in a few weeks ago."

"And they were kind enough to let me and my boys stay in the old duplex for part of the summer, so we're spending some extra time out there this year," Val added.

"How are your boys?" Thompson asked. "If memory serves, you have a few."

Val laughed. "Four, actually. They're currently enjoying a week with their father on the farm where he grew up. It's Luke's turn to keep them in line. They tend to be a bit *reckless*."

"Just a bit," Matt added, one side of his mouth turning up.

"I'm sorry, I didn't know you and your husband split up. I remember Luke. Decent fellow."

She wasn't sure she'd heard him right. "What makes you think we're split up? Luke is back home this summer, helping his parents. His big brother was killed in a farming accident, and there's no one else to take care of things yet."

"Well, damn. Look at me. The old fart puts his foot in his mouth again. When you said Luke had them for a week, and you're here with these two gentlemen tonight, well, I . . ." His voice trailed off, embarrassed.

"Don't worry, I stick my foot in my mouth all the time," Val assured the older man. "But, no, Luke is still saddled with me. It's a weird summer. Hopefully he can get things figured out back home so this doesn't go on too long."

Val felt a surge of guilt, sitting here, enjoying herself, after everything Luke had been through lately. Hopefully he was having fun at the carnival with the boys. She'd call to check on them and see what else they were up to when they got back to the resort.

"Hey, I have a question for you, Thompson." Matt said. Val was thankful for the diversion in the conversation. "I'm curious about the spot where we built our new house out at Whispering Pines. It's in the northwest corner, back in the trees. It's a great spot, gives us some privacy, but there were remnants of a much older foundation there when we first discovered the spot. Once they started digging for our basement, they found a few other things. Obviously there used to be a small building there of some kind. I was wondering if it was a cabin and what happened to it. You've been around here a long time. Would you happen to know anything about it?"

"Matter of fact, I might," Thompson replied, his eyes taking on a faraway look, as if picturing something in his mind. "I was just a kid. Grew up about twenty miles from here. There was a summer storm. A bad one. People died. Tornadoes hit the area, and some of the resorts around the lake took a direct hit."

"Someone died in a tornado at *Whispering Pines?*" Val asked, shocked.

Her question pulled Thompson's attention back from his memories to their table. "No. Not that I recall. The deaths were in a tiny town north of here. Nothing left there now. But Celia told me once that they lost some cabins at the resort. It would have been before she owned the resort, too. I think the cabins around the firepit were all built after that storm. A lot of places had to rebuild. My guess is that's what happened to whatever building used to stand where your new house is now."

"Hmm," Matt said, thoughtful. "Makes me glad we decided to incur the extra expense to put in a basement. You just never know about the weather around here. The duplex has a basement, but none of the other buildings do at Whispering Pines."

"And Robbie appreciates having a whole lower level to himself," Val pointed out.

"True. Makes it more likely he'll visit once in a while after he heads off to college after this last year of high school."

"How is Robbie doing?" Ross asked. "Staying out of trouble?"

The comment reminded Val that Ross had helped Renee out when she'd been terrified her son might be getting into trouble with drugs. It was shortly after her sister first met Matt.

Conversation continued to flow around the table as the four of them enjoyed perfectly grilled steaks. It eventually worked its way back around to shop talk.

"I was in law enforcement my whole life," Thompson declared, eyeing Ross across the table. "But never in a place like Minneapolis. I imagine it's a whole different level of insanity, trying to keep a lid on things over there. Do you enjoy the work?"

Ross took a sip of his beer. It had to be lukewarm by now. No one had opted for refills when their waiter offered. "Honestly, no. I used to. Used to feel like at least some days I made a difference. Not feeling that anymore."

Thompson gave a knowing nod. "Went through some of that myself over the years. But let me assure you, you *do* make a difference."

Ross shrugged. Val thought she could read something akin to resignation on his face. She wondered why. What could he have seen? Did she even want to know?

"I hit that wall when I was working out east," Matt said. "Years ago. The day came when I just couldn't do it anymore. The good stopped outweighing the bad and I had to get out. At least for a while. Until I found myself working again in Fiji. If you've reached *that* point, bud, move on."

"If only it were that simple," Ross said quietly.

Val barely knew the man, but anyone could recognize the pain reflecting in his eyes as he uttered that simple statement. The words had a weight to them, a hopelessness, that made her suddenly want to find a way to help Matt's friend. Because, while they'd only just met earlier that day, she couldn't deny that she already felt some kind of connection with him.

She thought of her own husband then. Of the challenges he was facing back at the farm. And of everything her siblings had endured in recent years. Life was certainly messy, but together they always seemed to find a way to survive and move forward.

CHAPTER NINETEEN

GIFT OF ABANDONMENT

*R*enee called Val early the following afternoon. "I'm home! Are you in the lodge?"

"I was, but I had to run back to the duplex to switch laundry loads. You sound a little staticky, but that's probably because I'm in the basement. Did you get Julie settled?"

"I did. I feel about a hundred and ten years old today. It hurt to roll out of bed this morning, and it wasn't like I got much sleep, sharing a full-size mattress with a daughter who still kicks like a mule in her sleep."

"Maybe that'll help keep the boys out of her bed," Val teased, to which Renee moaned out loud.

"Joke now, while your boys are young, but it's not so funny when they're off at college."

"Sorry. You're right. Cheap shot. What are you doing now? Is Matt home? Did you bring Robbie back with you?"

Val heard rustling through the phone and then the slamming of a cupboard door.

"Matt left me a note. He's out fishing with Ross. I did bring Robbie home, but he went straight downstairs. He slept most of the drive back. I suspect they were up most of the night, doing God knows what."

"Oh, to be young again . . ." Val sighed. "That summer before senior year was so fun. Remember when I worked for the chef at that ritzy country club? I would have hated to wait tables out there—the members all acted so *entitled*—but I learned a lot in the kitchen. Then, after hours, we'd sneak into the pool late at night or go skinny-dipping in the water hazard on the back nine."

Renee snorted. "I didn't know about the 'swimming naked' part. What if your kids did that? You'd have a heart attack. Anyhow, I'm feeling like anything *but* a teenager today. I think I feel even stiffer now after driving in the car for so long. That's why I called. Want to go for a walk?"

"Yes! That actually sounds perfect. It's so nice out today. Meet you by the lodge in five?"

"Make it four."

Click.

Val ran upstairs to change into something cooler. She quickly smeared sunscreen on and stopped in the kitchen for bug spray, stepping out onto the back patio to apply it. Minnesota summers were beautiful, but the mosquitoes could be vicious.

Renee was already waiting for her at the lodge.

"You got over here pretty quickly for a stiff old lady," Val teased. She was happy to see Renee, but she was equally happy to hint at their five-year age difference any chance she could.

"*You'd* feel like a stiff old lady, too, if you'd spent yesterday trudging up and down three flights of stairs, hauling armloads of hanging clothes. Do you have any idea how many clothes kids have these days?"

Assuming Renee didn't expect an answer, Val put a hand on her own waist and twisted. She was stiff, too, thanks to her tumble off a stepstool and into the bushes, but she'd keep that tidbit to herself. "Where do you want to go?"

Renee shrugged. "I'm up for an adventure. Let's go hiking in the woods."

Val straightened, a sense of unease filling her. "The woods . . . as in, 'off the beaten path' and 'watch out for Yogi Bear' woods?"

Laughing, Renee nodded. "That's exactly what I mean. What, are you chicken?"

"No. Just smart. You do remember what Matt said about bears in the area, right?"

"Val, don't forget I run this resort. Of course I haven't forgotten about bears. In fact, I talked to Matt about it just last night. It's my job to do what I can to keep our renters safe. He said the Department of Natural resources had actually been tracking a black bear and her cub closely over the last few weeks. Probably the same set you saw that morning. She was tagged at some point with a monitor. The good news is she's moved on, headed back north, and there haven't been any other sightings around here. Besides, I have this cool little air horn on my keychain that Matt insisted I carry with me." She winked. "Just in case."

Val let her eyes travel along the edge of the woods, still skeptical. She remembered how sheer terror flooded her body when her mind finally comprehended what she was seeing far off in the trees. The idea of walking *into* those trees seemed ill-advised.

"Come on. It'll be fun! We'll be fine," Renee said, sounding much more confident than Val felt.

Somewhat grudgingly, she fell into step next to her sister as she headed off across the lawn for the edge of the woods. "Is there a path or something we can take?"

"Kind of. Last summer, Matt and I used to head off into the woods quite often. He likes to hike. Says it helps keep him in shape for the job but isn't boring, like going to the gym."

Val nodded. That part she understood. She remembered Ross going for a run the previous day. Probably for much the same reason.

"I worried about getting lost out here," Renee continued as they entered the slightly cooler atmosphere inside the tree line. "You know, like Ethan back in the day? So my brilliant husband thought to put up some of these." Renee walked over to a nearby tree and reached out to touch a small red reflector, mounted waist-high on the trunk. "That way, if we'd get turned around out here, we'd be able to find our way back."

"That is rather brilliant," Val conceded. She paused, looking high above them at the massive pines partially blocking out the sunlight. Trees stretched in and around them as far as she could see. The ground underfoot wasn't as overgrown as she would have expected. She took a deep breath, the air rich with the scent of pine and dirt. "It's peaceful. Like there's no one around for miles, even though the resort is right back there."

"I thought you might enjoy this. Come on. Let's stretch our legs. Mine are finally starting to feel like they're loosening up."

They walked on, mostly in silence, one or the other of them pointing things out as they walked.

"I wonder if this was how Ethan and his buddy felt, walking around in here that day," Renee said, her tone holding a hint of wonder.

"I never actually heard the story of how they got lost. But Ethan has never lived it down."

Renee, walking slightly ahead of Val, glanced back at her. "That's right. I forgot we didn't tell you what really happened. You were too young. You'd have ratted us out."

"What do you mean? You weren't with them, were you?"

"No. It was the first summer we came out here. Ethan wasn't happy about the trip to Whispering Pines—he had to miss a baseball tournament, I think. Anyway, there was another kid here, about Ethan's age. His name was . . . Brandon? Kind of quiet. Cute, too, I thought. Him and Ethan started hanging out."

Val nodded. "That was the summer of our time capsule!"

"Yep. And the summer we first heard about the two little ghost boys that rumor has it haunt Whispering Pines." She gave Val a considering look. "Do you remember that?"

"Oh yeah. I definitely remember that," Val assured her sister. She remembered sitting around a bonfire, late one evening, listening to Aunt Celia's friend, Wayne, tell ghost stories. Val was still convinced that was when the dark started to creep her out so badly. A fear she'd never truly outgrown. "That story seems to keep coming up. What were their names again?"

Renee stumbled, probably on a root, but she managed to catch herself. "Albert and Arthur."

"That was it! How could I forget? They were fixtures in my nightmares for *years*. I stayed in the car when Luke and the boys wanted to explore caves during our trip to South Dakota. There was no way I was stepping foot in a cave after dreaming about how those little boys supposedly died in one way back when."

Laughing, Renee nodded. "Ethan probably isn't big on caves, either, I bet—not that he'd ever admit it."

"Why do I have the impression you did something? I know that laugh."

"If I tell you, do you promise not to tell Ethan? Or Jess either, actually. She and I swore we'd never tell anyone."

"You've got me curious. I promise."

They'd reached a natural clearing in the trees. Renee stopped, turning back to face Val. "Remember the part of the story Celia's friend, Wayne, told us about the charcoal?"

"Sure. Even back then I wasn't sure whether or not to believe him. It seemed too farfetched."

"Jess and I thought it would be funny if we played a trick on Ethan and his new friend. We snuck out super early one morning and made a trail of those little square charcoal briquettes." Renee grinned. "Across the grass from the firepit to the woods and as far into the trees as we could before we ran out."

"Seriously?"

"Yep. We thought that was the craziest part of the legend. Wayne had told us the ghosts would sometimes do that as a way to find their way back home again. So they wouldn't get lost in the woods. He even claimed to have seen it with his own eyes. We wanted to see if Ethan and Brandon would think the ghost boys did it."

"No way," Val said, shocked that her sisters would think of something like that. "That's *brilliant*."

"We thought so, too . . . at least until Ethan and his buddy didn't make it home on time. They followed the line of charcoal into the woods, just like we'd hoped they would, but they didn't come back. We got worried. None of us were allowed to go into the woods without an adult, and if something happened to them, we'd be in deep shit."

"Typical," Val laughed. "You were more worried about getting in trouble yourselves than about Ethan."

Renee spread her hands in defense. "We were ten and eight."

"What happened?"

"Believe it or not, Ethan and the other kid actually did find the cave they were looking for, the one where those two little boys apparently died. Celia used to swear that part of the old ghost story was true, that the twin brothers *did* die out here from something. So Brandon stood on top of some fallen trees or brush or something that had covered up the cave, and his weight busted through. He fell in, broke his leg, and Ethan had to run back for help."

"Oh my God! The kid ended up okay, right?"

"Of course. But Jess and I were pretty freaked out."

"Did anyone ever know you and Jess did that?"

Renee shook her head. "No. Mom almost caught us. When we snuck back into the cabin, the sun was coming up, and we were trying to scrub the black crap from the charcoal off our hands. Our fingernails were black with it. Needless to say, she was a little suspicious about us washing our hands at the kitchen sink like we were, first thing in the morning."

"Oh my God, that's a *great* story. I can't believe you've managed to keep it quiet all this time."

Nodding, Renee started walking again, heading deeper into the woods. "Remember, you promised not to say anything."

Val made a big *X* mark across her chest. "Cross my heart, hope to die, stick a needle in my eye."

They both laughed at the saying they'd grown up using. As they continued on the hike, their conversation meandered to other topics.

"How is Ross?" Renee asked.

"Good, I guess. Seems nice enough."

"That's good. I think he's decent. I know he helped me that time with Robbie, and him and Matt go way back. For some reason, Jess didn't seem to like him when she met him at the wedding. She made some comment about him being a 'player.' That she didn't trust him."

Val snorted. "Of course Jess would say that. She's always suspicious of people at first—especially men. Remember, she was less than fond of Matt when he first came sniffing around."

" 'Sniffing around'?" Renee shot back over her shoulder. "Really? That sounds gross."

"Lighten up. You know what I mean. Think about the timing. That was right when she was going through all the crap with Will, our lovely ex-brother-in-law. Will . . . *he* was a player. I think of that as her skeptical phase. Or her 'I hate all men' phase."

"Lucky for Seth, she eventually got over that."

"True," Val conceded. "But yeah, Ross seems fine. We didn't get off to the best start, but I went out for dinner with the guys last night, and he fit right in. Seems like he needs a break from work. He made a couple comments that made me think he's tired of the whole cop thing."

Renee paused, looked around her, and then angled to their right. Val followed, trusting her big sister wouldn't get them hopelessly lost.

"Why didn't you get off on the right foot?"

"He showed up a little early. I was still working on the Gray Cabin, getting it ready for him, and he scared the shit out of me." Val purposely left out the part about her fall and swearing Ross to secrecy.

"Yeah, well, why doesn't *that* surprise me?"

"What, that Ross was early?"

"No, that it happened at the *Gray Cabin*. Promise me you won't tell Ethan, I know he worked hard to fix it up—hell, you *all* did—but that place still gives me the creeps."

Val nodded. She couldn't disagree. There was still something creepy about it. Like something was lurking, just along the edges of what you could see.

She took another deep breath, letting the heady scent of nature ground her. It felt good to walk, to explore. No need to ruin it by letting her imagination play tricks.

A flash in the trees to their left caught her eye. Sunlight glinted off something.

"What's that?" she asked, stopping to try to get a better look.

Renee stopped. "What's what?"

"Over here," Val said, already changing course. It looked like a beat-up old camper or something.

Way out here?

She could hear Renee crunching along behind her. It *was* an old camper, its roof rounded—the glinting metal that had caught her attention—in stark contrast to the many vertical lines of the trees surrounding it, surrounding them. It was obviously deserted. Its walls were a dull gray color, partially obscured with the encroaching forest.

"It looks like something the Boxcar kids might have lived in," Val said, smiling as she tried to play off her initial fear at seeing it. "How did this get way out here?"

They approached it more slowly now that they were closer. An old, busted-up metal chair lay tangled in tall grass to the right of the door. The skeletal remains of a charcoal grill flanked one corner. There was some kind of clothes line, wire strung between two trees, but even on tiptoes Val wouldn't have been able to reach the wire to hang anything. The trees had probably grown up since the wire was first strung.

"I'm sure this is the trailer Lauren found," Renee said, wandering toward the front of the wreck of a camper.

"What?" The comment barely registered, so intently was Val wondering how the camper had gotten in here in the first place.

Renee approached the door, reaching for it.

"Are you sure you should do that?" Val asked.

"This has to be the camper where Matt found Lauren and Harper," she said, dropping her hand and turning back to face Val. "Remember? Harper's mom, Tiffany, came here to take her? She was strung out on something and she scared the hell out of Lauren when they were out on a walk? Lauren grabbed the baby and ran off into the woods."

Val had of course heard about that horrible day, although she hadn't been out here at the time. *"This* is where they ended up?" She shuddered, feeling a rush of sympathy for Lauren. Those were dark days, when Jess nearly lost Harper to the girl's biological mother. Lauren had to have been terrified out here.

"It has to be. Matt said it was an old Airstream. That's what this is. I checked." She pointed to the front of the camper.

Renee had to be right. How many abandoned Airstream campers could there be in these woods?

"We might as well check out the inside. From out here it's actually kind of cute," Val said. The fact that Matt had likely already checked out the old camper made it seem slightly less ominous.

"I don't think *cute* is the description I'd pick, but I am curious."

Renee again reached for the door's handle. Val watched her grapple with it and tug multiple times before it opened by an inch. One more tug and the door popped open. A flimsy screen door stood between them and the camper's interior. Both sisters peered through the tattered barrier. Val was nervous they might be walking in on a family of raccoons or some other wild animals. A musty smell emerged, temporarily masking the freshness of the forest.

Val waved a hand in front of her face. "Ugh. This sucker's been closed up for a while."

"Almost a year, and who knows how many years before that," Renee agreed. "Shall we?"

This time Val reached for the door, slowly pulling back on the screen.

"Be careful," Renee warned from behind her.

Nodding, she placed first one foot and then the other up into the camper. The floor felt solid enough. She stepped inside, giving Renee room to move in next to her. She wasn't exactly sure what she'd expected, but the interior wasn't as trashed as she'd thought it would be. There was damage, and time had certainly taken its toll, but it wasn't completely gutted or anything that drastic.

"I'd have expected it to be worse in here," Renee said, echoing Val's thoughts.

"Me too," Val agreed, taking in the camper's layout. A narrow galley kitchen ran across the far wall, ending in a partition that probably housed a miniscule bathroom. Their view was blocked by a door hanging from a partially broken hinge. To the right was a couch that probably converted into a bed, and to the left, across from the tiny sink and oven, was a dinette set. Matching upholstery on the benches flanking the table and the couch sported brown and rust and gold strips, their colors likely vivid when new but faded and threadbare now.

They both explored the old unit, peeking carefully into overhead cabinets and into what did indeed turn out to be a tiny, walled-off area with a toilet and shower; they were half afraid a mouse—or something worse—might pounce. But there was nothing but creaking hinges and musty smells.

Val wondered again who might have lived here.

"Is that rain?" Renee asked suddenly.

Listening, Val was afraid her sister was right. "The forecast did have a chance of late-afternoon showers . . . sounds like they might have been right for a change."

A rumble of thunder sounded off in the distance.

"We better get back," Renee suggested. "We don't want to get caught out in the woods in a downpour."

Val knew she was right, but was hesitant to leave. She was still so curious about this little, deserted camper, just sitting out here for who knew how long. A flash of lightning lit up the interior.

"We better hurry!" Renee said, hustling out the door.

As curious as she was about the old camper, Val had no desire to be left behind. Slamming the door behind them, she took off after Renee, laughing and stumbling as the initial warm droplets of rain cooled on her skin. They were going to look like drowned rats by the time they got back to the resort.

Who would leave a camper deserted in the woods? Where did they go?

* * *

She didn't have the answers behind the camper mystery, but that didn't stop her mind from trying to fill in the blanks while she slept. Worn out from their hike, and subsequent dash back to the resort through heavy rain, Val collapsed into bed at nine. It felt decadent to be in bed before the sun had even set. Storm still roamed inside the duplex, not yet ready to settle down.

Val considered calling Luke to see how they'd spent their day, but she didn't really feel like talking. She'd call him in the morning. Instead, she lay on her side of the bed and picked up her tablet from the bedside table. In what was becoming a nightly habit, she scrolled through Pinterest, adding to her kitchen-remodel boards.

She nearly missed it at first, her fingers swiping faster than her mind could absorb. Halting, she backed up the feed, then grinned at a photo of a cheerful scene. A camper—much like the one they'd found in the woods, but sparkling clean—glowed in the light of a pink sunset. The silver exterior shimmered in the soft light of evening, enhanced with miniature white lights strung high along the edge of an aqua-and-white-striped awning; a matching strip of colored paint enhanced the lower third of the camper's exterior, softening its silhouette.

On the ground in front of the camper lay a large, rectangular rug, swirls of pinks, yellows, and turquoise completing the welcoming scene. A white bistro table, flanked by old-fashioned, fancy iron chairs one might have found in a vintage ice-cream shop, beckoned: the perfect spot to enjoy an evening glass of wine or an early morning coffee. Planters lush with bursts of summer flowers rimmed the outer edges of the rug. Val could imagine their fresh scent mingling with that of pine and green grass.

It would be the kind of spot women would choose to gather, to create, to converse, to dream.

A low growl pulled Val out of the scene her imagination had conjured up. "Storm, what's wrong, girl?"

She was surprised to see it was full dark outside. She must have dozed off. The dog was in the upstairs hallway, probably near the top of the stairs, based on the muffled growl. It came again, followed by one sharp bark and then the creaking of steps as the dog ran down the stairs.

With a sigh, Val set her tablet aside and swung her legs out of bed. She shivered as a cool breeze washed over her through her open window, the heat of the day having never returned following the late afternoon storm that had blown through earlier. Aware she was highly visible in the soft glow of her lamp, now that night had fallen, she pulled the curtains closed.

Storm was barking downstairs now, and she worried the sound would travel through the adjoining wall and wake little Harper up. Jess, Seth, and the toddler had returned earlier in the evening, tired and, in Harper's case, cranky after a full weekend.

"Storm, be quiet!" Val whispered harshly as she skipped down the carpeted stairs in the semidarkness. "What has you so riled?"

Knowing Jess was literally just a wall away, her dog's actions didn't scare her the way they might have had she been all alone in the duplex, tucked back in the opposite corner of the resort from Matt and Renee.

She found Storm, her chest rumbling with deep-seated growls, pawing at the area rug just inside the front door, her nose jammed against the small gap along the bottom of the threshold.

"What's wrong, girl? Is there something on the porch?" Val whispered, more softly now, her words meant only for her dog's ears. Storm's body jumped when she laid a calming hand on her back, as if the animal hadn't noticed her approach.

For a brief millisecond, Val considered opening the door, until sanity returned. *Yeah, I'm not that brave,* she thought, her nerves stretched taut at Storm's odd behavior.

It was probably just a small animal or something, rustling around in the dark, scared away now by Storm's warning.

The dog backed away from the door, visibly relaxing. She licked Val's hand, and Val could feel the dog's tail swishing against her bare legs.

"Come on, girl, let's get a drink of water and go back to bed. I'm tired."

* * *

Carnival music cloaks the sea of humanity strolling by. Bright lights drown out the stars hiding above in a soft black sky, punctuated with fits and bursts of glowing fireworks. The sharp tang of fried onions and mini-donuts bombards her nostrils, as does the cacophony of voices and occasional shouts of laughter, all mingling together to assault her senses.

In the center of the hodgepodge of food trucks is a rounded, silver camper, the bottom third an aqua blue. The crisp awning is gone, a gaudy, blinking sign in its place, competing for the attention of the fair-goers. As Val watches from the other side of the aisle, her view frequently obstructed by a passerby, she sees herself, leaning out of a high window in the camper, serving cookies wrapped in napkins and sweating glasses of lemonade. Despite the chaos all around, she's smiling as she serves customers, enjoying the hustle and bustle.

There's a break in the steady stream of people flowing between her and the food truck, so she steps toward it, anxious to talk with her happier self through the window. With each step, the lights around her begin to fade . . . the music quiets ever so slowly until the only sounds around her are night sounds . . . forest sounds. The wind rustles through the trees overhead. Something scurries in the under-brush nearby. Flashing carnival lights are replaced by beams of moon-light, washing over muted silver. The window slides shut, ever so slowly, silently.

Glancing cautiously around her, she feels an utter aloneness. Not scared exactly, but aware, as if knowing there is something she's miss-ing, something just beyond the edge of her consciousness that she needs to find.

No light shines out of the dilapidated camper, but she becomes aware of soft strains of music. A tune she somehow recognizes. She begins to hum along, her feet bringing her ever so slowly to the single step below the door to the camper.

Her body is blocking the moonbeams and so it is too dark to see her own hand as it reaches for the handle she knows is there. Her fingers curl around smooth metal and she twists, a grating sensation emanating up her arm, as though a lifetime has passed since the handle has been turned.

Why is she so inexplicably drawn deeper into the darkness?

What waits for her beyond the edge of knowing?

Now the handle turns smoothly, all resistance gone, and a beam of light illuminates the edge of the door as she pulls it open. The light envelops her as she steps up and into the bright interior; she has to squint her eyes against it. The warm scent of vanilla, with an undercurrent of tangy tomato, tickles her nose and she can see herself standing and talking with a group of three women crowded around the tiny dinette table, waving a small card of some kind in her hand.

A hand touches her shoulder and she spins in alarm, the glow of light now coming from the porch light of her own front door.

"What are you doing out here, Val?" Seth asked, his voice shockingly loud, jarring her senses.

She felt cool wood under her bare feet and something darted against her temple. She waved it frantically away, awareness dawning. The porch light was like a flame, drawing in night moths and other buzzing, darting insects.

"Val, are you okay? Why are you out here? Did you let Storm out?" Seth asked, concern etched on his face.

That must be it. The dog must have had to go out.

"Storm, where are you girl?" she yelled, her shoulders relaxing in relief as the dog came into view on the grass below. She could see now that it was raining softly, beyond the protective cover of the porch roof. "Yes. Yeah, Storm had to go out. I'm sorry if I woke you, Seth," Val apologized, looking up at her sister's fiancé.

He gave her an odd look, as if he weren't entirely sure he believed her. His eyes shifted to Storm as she skipped up the steps and nuzzled his bare knees, always happy to be petted. He bent slightly to scratch the top of the dog's head, still looking confused. "If you're sure everything is all right, I'll let you get back inside, then."

Despite her own confusion over finding herself out on the front porch of the duplex in the middle of the night, she smiled as he swatted at a mosquito that landed on his cheek. "Get inside. I'm perfectly fine. Sorry if we were a little loud. Get inside before we get eaten alive out here. Tell Jess I'm sorry if I woke her."

Seth nodded, letting himself back into the other half of the duplex, darkness rushing back in as he flipped off the outside light flanking their door. Val quickly shooed Storm inside then closed the door behind them, twisting the lock and leaning her back against the now-closed door.

"Why were we outside, girl?" Val whispered to the dog, although Storm was already trotting up the stairs, presumably back to bed.

CHAPTER TWENTY

GIFT OF STRONG BACKS AND WILLING
HANDS

"Tell me you have coffee in here," Ross moaned as he let himself in through the back door, straight into the lodge kitchen.

"Good morning to you, too," Val replied as she bent to remove another recipe experiment from the oven.

"What is that heavenly smell, besides the coffee beans?" he asked, coming over to investigate.

Val glanced at him. "Don't take this the wrong way, but you look like shit this morning."

"I feel like it, too. Thus the need for coffee—*and* whatever sugar-laced delicacy you've created there, if you're open to sharing."

Val hoped she didn't look as worn out as Ross. She'd struggled to fall back asleep the night before, after the incident with Storm. Eventually she'd given up and made her way over to play in the kitchen.

"Let it cool for a few minutes and then I'll cut you off a big hunk. God knows I don't need to eat all of this myself."

"It's not something you made for a special occasion, then?"

Shaking her head, Val pulled two cups down from a cupboard. The coffeemaker sputtered out its final drips and she removed the pot and poured them each a cup. "No. My mission this week is to try as many of the recipes as I can from that."

Ross pulled the metal recipe box closer and thumbed through the cards. "These look old. Is this where you found the recipe for those sugar cookies you baked on Saturday?"

"No, that was Mom's recipe. Actually, her mother's recipe. I helped her fill in some missing pieces. She was frustrated that her cookies never tasted as good as her mom's, but we figured out why." She tossed some potholders onto the island top. "Why so haggard this morning?"

"Just one of those nights. Couldn't sleep," he said, flipping the lid closed on the recipe box and rubbing the back of his neck. "Must have been the full moon."

"It was full? I didn't notice with the rain. But maybe that explains it."

"Explains what?" Ross asked, squinting at her over the rim of his coffee cup as he took a sip of the steaming brew.

"I had trouble sleeping, too. Or, rather, staying in my bed, asleep. I think I may have walked in my sleep for the first time ever last night." Truth be told, she was still shaken up by it.

"Really? I did a lot of that as a kid. I used to get up in the middle of the night and jump in the shower. No idea why. It used to drive my folks nuts. It took breaking my arm in a grade school football game for me to quit."

Val smiled. "Sorry, I don't see how a broken arm cures sleep-walking."

Ross helped himself to more coffee. "Guess it was my subconscious making the connection that I couldn't shower with my cast unless my arm was wrapped. The late-night, sleep-fogged showers stopped after that. What do you suppose was behind *your* zombie-like escapade last night, if you've never walked in your sleep before? Which, by the way, maybe you have and didn't know it."

She shrugged, sighing. "I should know better than to play around on Pinterest before I try to go to sleep at night. Gets my mind racing. Yesterday, I went for a hike through the woods with Renee after she got back from helping Julie move. We found an old camper. I have no idea how someone got it out there in the first place. It's actually kind of cool. Very *vintage*. Matt had run across it before and told Renee it was out there, but she'd never seen it with her own eyes, either."

"Is 'vintage' code for 'mouse-ridden and mold-infested'?"

Val laughed. "We were only inside it for a few minutes, but it didn't look to be in that bad of shape. Outdated, filthy, and any soft surfaces have been ruined over time, but I didn't see any nests or droppings."

"And let me guess . . . you were looking at refurbished campers on Pinterest?"

Val held her hand over the coffee cake and decided it was cool enough to cut. She fished a knife out of a drawer and ran its blade around the edges of the cake pan, then cut a generous helping of the cake, set it on a napkin, and handed it to Ross.

"Actually, it didn't start out that way. We're fixing up our kitchen at home, compliments of a tub that overflowed on our second floor, sending chunks of the ceiling into my kitchen sink. I was poking around online, looking at kitchen remodel ideas. A camper remodel popped up, I clicked on it, and down the rabbit hole I went."

"Scrolling Pinterest before falling asleep doesn't seem like the catalyst for your first-ever sleepwalking episode," Ross pointed out, nodding his thanks for the slice. He took a bite, not bothering with a fork, and chewed slowly. "You, my friend, know your way around the kitchen."

"Good?"

Val cut herself a smaller piece, sampled it, and knew immediately she'd have to make it again after the boys got back. Based on her short conversation with Luke earlier that morning, the boys were having fun at the farm, but she also knew her husband wasn't much of a cook. She suspected they might be subsisting on mac and cheese and hotdogs.

"This works," Val acknowledged, holding up what remained of her piece of coffee cake. "A racing mind was my likely culprit for a poor night's sleep. What was yours?"

Ross looked sheepish as he finished off his coffee cake, crumbled the napkin, and tossed it into a nearby garbage can. "Promise you won't laugh?"

"No."

"Then I'm not going to tell you."

Val laughed. "Come on, I'm teasing. Here's me with my serious face. Not even a smile or grin. Did something go bump in the night in the light of a full moon?"

She struggled, with minimal success, to keep a straight face.

"Fine. Laugh if you must, but I kept thinking I was hearing something. Like an animal crying off in the distance. Creepy as hell. At one point I even went outside and wandered around the resort, but I couldn't find anything. Cop instinct, I suppose."

"Did you by any chance walk by the duplex at some point?"

"I guess," he said, a curious look on his face. "Why? It was late. I'm sure you were all sleeping."

"Because at one point, Storm went a little crazy, barking and pawing at the front door. I thought maybe an animal was up on the porch or something."

"What time was that?"

Val shrugged. "I'm not sure. Maybe midnight? I dozed off with the light still on and she woke me."

"Sorry . . . that was probably me, then. But I stayed on the paths. The ground was pretty wet, muddy in spots from yesterday's weather."

"I bet she heard you. Did the walk help?"

Ross sighed. "Not really. Everything was quiet outside, which was no surprise since it was drizzly. No one by the firepit. Cabins were dark. I went back to bed, and at some point the noise started up again. I'm thinking there's a cat nearby with kittens or something."

"Or something," Val muttered, her mind going to the old stories about the Gray Cabin. The same cabin Ross was staying in.

"Do you think it was something other than cats?"

"Well . . . maybe our stories about the cabin being haunted freaked you out a little more than you care to admit. Or maybe there's some truth to the stories."

Ross snorted. He drained the last of his coffee and set the cup in the sink. "Val, I'm a cop in Minneapolis. I've seen some of the worst of humanity. I'm not scared of a little ghost story."

"Who said anything about humans?" she teased, trying to lighten the mood as much for her own piece of mind as his. A part of her would probably always believe the stories about the cabin. There was just a . . . *feel* to it that she couldn't ignore.

"Tell you what—want to come with me now, in the daylight, and look around? See if we can find anything?"

"What could we possibly find?"

He shrugged. "I don't know. The kittens, maybe? Val, I didn't imagine it. I don't think I can take a second sleepless night. I'm supposed to be getting some R&R, not roaming around the resort late at night because I can't sleep."

Something else occurred to Val. "Any chance something else is bothering you, making it hard to sleep? I know you've got a really challenging job. I got the sense you might be tired of it all."

He crossed his arms over his chest, giving her an unreadable look. "Why would you jump to that conclusion?"

It had been a stab in the dark, probably a bit too personal, too, but she'd already said it, so she pressed forward. "It must have been some-thing you said at dinner the other night. You know, when you and Matt and Sheriff Thompson were talking shop? It was like there was an undercurrent around the table. Something you didn't say out loud —at least in front of me."

"I really don't want to talk about it," Ross replied, relaxing his arms but hitching up one side of the waistband of his cargo shorts. It was an unconscious movement Val had noticed Matt make, too, as if in uniform and bothered by the weight of a handgun. "I came here to get away from having to talk about it. But I swear I was hearing *something* last night, and it wasn't in my head."

Taking pity on him, Val let the subject of some mysterious, work-related trauma drop. Glancing out the window, she could see it was shaping up to be a beautiful morning outside. She'd been in the kitchen since dawn. "All right, let's do it."

"Do what?"

"Go find those kittens of yours."

* * *

The soft warmth of the bonfire on her face and chilled glass of wine in her hand was the perfect end to the third day of what she'd secretly dubbed her Week of Freedom. Val had relished in the unstructured hours. No meals to prep or schedules to keep. No disasters to constantly avoid. It was a nice change of pace.

It had been a perfect day, even if they didn't find anything that would explain the noises Ross was sure he'd heard.

She gazed into the blue and orange haze of the deepest parts of the fire, thinking back to ghost stories told around childhood bonfires.

Laughter erupted around her, pulling her back to Matt and Renee's new front yard, where they were all relaxing around their own firepit.

"It was a great idea to build this one over here," Jess was saying, "even if Renee had some mishaps with the skidsteer. Then you can leave the bigger firepit for your guests."

Renee nodded. "Sitting around the fire is one of my favorite things to do on summer evenings, but I never want to intrude on our guests' time. Once in a while we'll join them, but only if they invite us. Thanks to my dear husband, now we can have our own bonfires any night we choose."

"Anything for you, dear," Matt said from across the fire, raising his bottle of beer to her.

Val caught the wink he sent in her sister's direction and felt a quick pang of something. Matt and Renee seemed to seldom bicker. Or, if they did, it was behind closed doors. She supposed part of it was the fact they'd only been married for a year. She missed those days with Luke. Now it seemed all she and Luke did was argue. It was exhausting.

She sipped her wine, kicking herself for letting her thoughts go down that path again. Tonight wasn't a night to brood. "Renee, did you tell Matt we found the old camper in the woods?"

"I did! And to be honest, I've been thinking about it all day."

"Me too," Val admitted. "I even started a new Pinterest board of refurbished campers similar to that one."

"Eventually, I'm sure, it'll completely deteriorate. It seems like such a waste . . . just abandoned out there."

Val nodded in agreement. "Do you know that some people are fixing them up into these cute little units, and then using them kind of like home offices, or little bakeries, or whatever? The possibilities are *endless.*"

"Wait, are you guys talking about that old camper in the woods where Lauren hid Harper from her crazy mother?" Jess asked, obviously intrigued.

"That's the one," Renee confirmed. "Val and I went for a walk when I got home yesterday afternoon and came across it. What a dream it would be to fix that old thing up, to put it to good use, instead of letting it rot in the woods. Once I started thinking about it, I could barely sleep last night."

"Maybe that's why I found Val out on the porch in the middle of the night, totally out of it," Seth teased from his seat next to Matt. "You have to admit, that was a little freaky, Val."

"It *was* freaky! I don't know what got into me. The camper, I guess. I dreamed about it, too."

Ross, sitting on the other side of Matt, had been quiet up until this point. "Could you pull it out of the woods and save it? You know, fix it up and do something like you're talking about with it. Or is it too far gone? You keep talking about it, Val. Maybe it wouldn't be impossible."

"Oh, I don't think there'd be any way to get it out," Val said, although she'd been secretly wondering the same thing.

"But what if you could?" Renee asked. "Would you ever want to try?"

Would I? she wondered. She had to admit, the idea held plenty of appeal. She'd never want to set up at a county fair as a food vendor, like she'd dreamed about the night before, but it could be used for other things.

"Let's pretend for a minute that we were able to get it out," Val reasoned. "I'm sure it would cost money to fix it up. *Then* what could we do with it? Besides, it's kinda yours, Renee. It's sitting on your property."

Renee waved that notion away. "I don't have any use for it. You can have it if you want it. Do you really think you could use it for something?"

"I know!" Jess said, jumping back in. "Fix it up all girly, park it in your backyard at home, and that could be your escape when there's just too much testosterone in the house."

"Hey there, no male bashing," Seth ordered, but the smile on his face told the sisters that he wasn't actually offended.

Jess laughed. "I'm not. Val just has more than her fair share of males running around, big and little. Don't you think she deserves a quiet place?"

Val held up a hand to curb her sister's enthusiasm. "As wonderful as all that sounds, parking it in our backyard at home isn't an option. Our yard isn't that big. Remember, Luke already has a camper and he has to store it in a buddy's storage building. Besides, there's no physical way to get it out of there. I bet it's been there for a few decades at *least*."

Matt, the only one in the party who knew the property as well as Renee, spoke up. "You know, there is a service road not too far from where that old thing is sitting. Maybe pulling it out isn't completely out of the question."

His words hung in the air, the possibility intriguing.

"I'm not very good at sitting around doing nothing," Ross said, leaning forward in his lawn chair, his eyes gazing into the dark woods behind them. "Maybe we should go take a look tomorrow, Matt. You're off, right? You all have me curious about this old thing."

"I'd be up for it," Matt said with a shrug. "What do you think, Val? How serious are you about that old hunk of junk?"

More serious than I care to admit, she thought, but she hated to get her hopes up. Aloud, she tried to reign in her excitement. "What do we have to lose? Maybe we could go back out there in the morning. If there's no possible way to get the camper out, I'll forget we ever found it. If there is a way, I think there just might be something I could do with it . . ."

Jess echoed the words forming in Val's mind perfectly when she said, "If you were Celia, you'd find a way to make a business out of it."

* * *

Despite their late night around the fire, Val was up with the sun again. She was just too excited to sleep. After deciding to check out the old camper in the morning, the evening's conversation had flowed to other topics, but Val hadn't stopped considering different possibilities —*if* they were able to somehow get it back to the resort.

Was she crazy? Would *Luke* think she was crazy? She'd been tempted to call him to discuss it, but then decided to wait to see whether there was even anything to talk about. If there was no way to get the camper out of the woods, or if they did but it was too far gone to save, she'd have to forget about it.

Unless Seth could help me hunt for another one if this one doesn't work out. After all, he saves old things for a living.

Five of them trekked back to the old campsite that morning.

Ross let out a low whistle as the silver silhouette came into view through the trees. "You weren't kidding when you said it was socked in here," he said, sending a questioning look Val's way.

He thinks I'm nuts, she thought. *He's probably right.*

Once they reached the old camper, Matt and Seth dropped to their knees to peer under the front of it. They were pointing, pulling on various parts of the camper's undercarriage, and debating options. Renee and Ross headed inside, scoping things out from that vantage point.

Val stayed back and took it all in. She'd already convinced herself she could deal with whatever challenges the inside presented. It was the removal that had her most concerned.

Matt straightened, glancing up at her as he sat back on his heels. "It doesn't look too bad under here. At least what I can see so far. It would need new tires before it could be moved, but maybe it's possible."

Seth stood and walked quietly back to the other end of the camper. Val held her breath, curious to hear his thoughts, too.

A bird squawked off to her right. She turned, glancing toward the sound. A flash of red darted upward, through the canopy of green leaves. As her eyes struggled to keep up with the movement, she spotted a red bird perched on the bough of a majestic pine, gazing down, its eyes seeming to dart between her and the dilapidated silver camper. It was a cardinal. She couldn't remember ever seeing a real cardinal in nature before. The bird squawked again, looking right at her. Val had the uncanny feeling it was speaking directly to her.

"Val! Come here!" Seth's voice cut through her musings.

"Sorry, coming!" she replied, hustling around to where he stood pointing at something. "What?"

He again knelt down, motioning for her to do the same.

"See these branches here? This tree has grown up under the camper. Look how it's growing up through the floor back here. We'll likely need to pull some of it out to have any hope of moving the camper."

Disappointment flooded through her veins. "Crap. Is that a deal breaker?"

"No," Seth said with a slight laugh. "Just complicates things." He stood back up and held out a hand to help her do the same. He brushed the debris off his palms by rubbing them on the thighs of his jeans. "I just want you to know that if we can get this out of here, it's going to take some time—and some money—to make it usable again. You good with that?"

She saw the challenge in his eyes. She sensed he thought it could be done, but he didn't want her to be naïve about what it would take.

"I'm good with that," she confirmed, and she would have sworn she heard the cardinal squawk for a third time, but when she glanced up all she saw was a flash of red and it was gone.

Seth watched her, as if waiting for something.

"What?"

He slapped a hand against the scuffed, curved rear section of the camper. "I think we can get this baby out of here. Should we call your big brother, ask him to pick you up a set of tires, and get out here with his three-quarter-ton truck?"

"What if he's busy?"

"He's his own boss. You've got all the rest of us here. Now. Call Ethan and let's get this show on the road."

* * *

Nothing is ever as easy as one hopes it will be, of course, but after hours of debate, sketching out a plan, clearing away brush while waiting for help, plenty of sweat, and even a little blood, the old Airstream found a new, albeit temporary, home next to the duplex.

"Rome might not have been built in a day, but thanks to all of you amazing people, this little beauty only needed a day to get a new lease on life," Val proclaimed through the open door of the camper. She ignored the musty smell wafting out around her and the unmistakable tilt that hadn't been there when she'd first stepped into the camper. Something may have twisted as they'd forced the old girl out of its tangled resting spot, but hopefully none of the damage was permanent. "I still can't believe we got it out of there."

She hopped down to the grass, skipped over to Matt, and gave him a hug of thanks. She did the same with every single person in the group; they'd all played a part in this crazy day.

"Hell, Val, I don't know if I've ever seen you this excited about anything," Matt laughed. "You do realize today was probably the easy part, right? It's going to take lots of work, not to mention some cash, to make this baby usable again."

She waved away his concerns. He was right, of course—she had lots of work ahead of her. But she was enthralled with the possibilities. "Good thing it's only Tuesday night, then! I have three more full days to myself before Luke brings the boys back. I think I'll keep this to myself for now." She grinned. "Surprise them all on Saturday."

Jess laughed, having joined them outside with Harper as Ethan had backed the dilapidated old camper into the yard. "They'll be surprised, all right. They're probably expecting to come back to a very lonely wife and mother with a huge meal ready to welcome them home. Somehow I don't think that's what they'll find on Saturday."

"Oh, you're right about that," Val agreed, not feeling even a hint of remorse over the prospect. "But hey, I've got this from here. Thanks again, everybody, for all your help. Now, go. It's getting late. If you need me between now and the weekend, you'll know where to find me."

* * *

Despite her confidence, it didn't take Val long to realize she'd continue to need *some* help. She spent Wednesday ripping out anything that didn't appear to be salvageable. Jess assured her she didn't mind the expanding pile of rubbish next to the old camper. Ethan would bring by a large rollaway—much as he had when they'd redone the Gray Cabin—on Saturday.

Renee popped in and gave her an hour of her time. Jess had left early in the day to drop Harper at daycare and head to a full day of meetings at her company's home office. Normally she worked from home, but she had to go in once or twice a month. Matt was working and Ross didn't seem to be around.

Despite her aching muscles and the fading light, Val was determined to at least try to pull the old refrigerator out by herself. She was convinced it was the epicenter of the musty smell. The interior hadn't been emptied out whenever the last person who'd lived in the camper left for places unknown. The old jars' and containers' contents had long ago solidified or liquified, depending on their original state. The fridge was empty now, and Val didn't think it would be that hard to pull out the small appliance. It reminded Val of a fridge in their college apartment, no more than three feet tall. If it turned out to be too heavy, she'd find someone to help her with it tomorrow. But for now, she was determined to try to pull it out by herself. A strip of metal ran along both the top and bottom, screws anchoring it in place. She'd used an old drill Ethan had left with her to remove all the screws.

Donning her work gloves, she wrapped her fingers around the top and bottom edges of the fridge and gave it a shake to see if it was loose. It wriggled out an inch. She pulled again, harder this time. A noise came from behind the unit, like the sound of air rushing out of a hose when a pressure valve is released. She might only be able to pull it part of the way out before having to cut wires or pipes or something so that it could be removed completely.

Earlier in the day she'd brought in a stepstool—the same one she'd fallen from when Ross had surprised her earlier in the week. Now she moved it under the refrigerator, hoping she could rest the unit on it if need be. She checked to make sure she had both a screwdriver and a snipper in her pocket, then pulled at the unit again.

It slid out easier than she'd expected, falling forward with the force of gravity. She grabbed for it in an effort to keep it from slamming to the camper floor. The stool fell away, ineffective. She bore the weight of the small fridge, holding it at a crazy angle. Now she could see behind it.

She froze with horror.

There, in what must have been a gap between the camper wall and the appliance, was an undulating mass.

The hiss wasn't air.

It was snakes.

She fell back in shock, letting go of the fridge in her panic. It only fell a little farther, still-attached wires holding it suspended. Val tripped over the cursed stepstool and fell backward onto the floor. Her head hit the bench that provided seating at the dinette, the ruined cushion tossed earlier in the day so that now there was nothing between the back of her head and the plywood of the bench.

She barely even felt the impact, her eyes still glued to the horrifying nest of snakes. She felt frozen in place. An ear-piercing scream filled the camper. She squeezed her eyes shut. The screaming didn't quit, and it took her panicking brain a second to realize the screams were coming out of her mouth.

The door of the camper flew open and someone rushed in. Strong hands physically lifted her up off the ground.

"What the hell, Val?!"

Her befuddled mind couldn't follow what was happening, but she recognized Ross's voice. "Snakes," she whispered, attempting to warn him.

"Oh God, your head is bleeding," he said.

She finally opened her eyes and met Ross's concerned gaze. "What happened?"

He kept one hand on her shoulder but used his other to try to see where the blood was coming from, gently tilting her head forward and moving her hair out of the way.

She shook her head vigorously, another wave of pain nearly buckling her knees. Ross caught her again, finally looking in the direction she pointed.

He looked as shocked as she'd been, but luckily he didn't go down. He took an involuntary step or two back, maintaining his composure. Finally, he drew her back with a steady hand toward the door. "Come on, they're just garter snakes. They can't hurt us."

His words registered, but Val didn't care what *kind* of snakes they were—they were still *snakes*.

She let him lead her outside onto the grass. She reached a hand out and slammed the camper door shut, trapping the reptiles inside. She nearly sank down onto the grass, but he kept two strong arms on her shoulders, not allowing her to collapse. He walked her over to the steps of the duplex before letting her sit.

"I need to check your head," he said. "Stay put."

Matt's friend disappeared into Val's side of the duplex. She vaguely heard him greet Storm, who'd been inside the better part of the day because Val didn't want her in the camper while she was basically deconstructing it. What good thinking that turned out to be.

A minute later he was back with a wet dishtowel and a bottle of water. He'd snapped the porch light on, as the sun was beginning to set. She took the bottle of water from him, drank a small sip, and then worked to catch her breath. Again, he made her tilt her head forward, and a strong beam of light teased along her peripheral vision. He must have pulled his phone out.

"I'm afraid you might need a few stitches to close this up, Val."

She pushed his hand away. "No way. This was supposed to be a week free of emergency rooms. No boys around means no injuries."

"Sorry. I know when someone needs to at least be looked at by a doctor. *That* needs to be checked."

The water bottle she'd been holding slipped from her fingers and rolled down the pitted sidewalk. Leaning over, she lay her throbbing head on her bent knees. She wasn't sure what horrified her more: snakes, or another trip to the ER.

CHAPTER TWENTY-ONE

GIFT OF SUPPORT

*S*he'd lucked out. Ross was right about her needing stitches, but at least she hadn't given herself a concussion. The doctor on call recognized her from their previous visit for the boys' firework-induced injuries. Val could read the skepticism in his eyes when she promised not to be back again this summer. She'd keep her fingers crossed that there'd be no more injuries.

Ross had called Matt on their way to the hospital and asked him to take care of the snakes. Having a sheriff for a brother-in-law certainly had its perks. Matt had connections and, despite the late hour, brought in a professional to help remove any and all traces of unwanted critters from inside the camper. The pest control van pulled away from Whispering Pines just as Ross and Val returned.

"That was a gnarly nest you uncovered in there, Val," Matt said, meeting them on the path next to the lodge. "But we got it taken care of. How's the head?"

Val winced. "Other than having the mother of all headaches right now, it'll be fine. Are you sure you got all the snakes out?"

"I'm sure," he replied. "There's nothing to worry about. The fridge is out now, as are the old oven and stovetop. My buddy checked everything and fumigated in there. You'll want to stay out until noon or so tomorrow and then open it all up to air out."

Val worried the snakes would haunt her dreams, but at least they were gone in her reality. She turned to Ross. "Thanks again for helping me with this," she said, motioning to the back of her own head. "Sorry I was such a klutz."

"Val, that's, like, the hundredth time you've thanked me. Don't worry about it. Want me to walk you back to your duplex? I wouldn't want you to trip and fall again."

She caught his teasing tone. "Cute. No, I'm fine. I don't need anyone to walk me home."

"I got this," Matt said to Ross, looking right over Val's head at his friend. "Why don't you go grab a couple beers and I'll stop by shortly."

"Can't argue with that. Take care, Val," Ross said, heading in the direction of the Gray Cabin.

"Night, Ross," she said, turning in the opposite direction, toward the duplex. "Matt, seriously, I'm fine. You don't need to walk me home."

"Shut up, Val. Of course I have to make sure you get home all right. I'd never hear the end of it from Renee if I didn't."

"True," she laughed, then grimaced in pain. Her sister would be looking out for her. "Thank you."

"You got a lot done in that old thing today, all things considered," Matt said, kicking a stick off the pathway as they walked.

Long shadows stretched across the path and Val realized she was glad he'd insisted on walking her home.

"I did get lots done—thanks, in part, to you. I'm still not sure what I'm going to do with the camper, but I know I'll figure it out. Thank goodness Ross came to my rescue today. I was sorry he had to waste his vacation time running me to the hospital."

Matt laughed. "He actually got the better end of that deal. If he'd have stuck around here, I would have made him help me get those snakes out."

Something she was trying her best not to think about.

Matt continued, "By the way, thanks for hanging out with Ross. He needs someone to talk to, to hang out with, while I've been at work this week. I know it helps."

Val glanced toward Matt but couldn't see his face in the shadows. "Helps? What do you mean?"

Matt paused, and Val suspected he was weighing his response. If there was something going on with Ross, maybe it wasn't something Matt felt free to share.

"I'm sorry," she said before he could reply. "Pretend I didn't ask that. It's none of my business."

"Actually, maybe it would help if you knew. He's struggling. Ross is one of those guys who puts too much of himself into the job. And I get it. But it can consume you if you aren't careful. Happened to me, too, years ago, before I ended up in Fiji where I met your sister. I had to get out for a while. That's where Ross is at right now. Trying to decide whether or not to leave the force. After a couple decades, it's incredibly tough to walk away. But staying can tear your soul out."

Val could only imagine what horrors Ross had seen on the job during a twenty-year career. She had no doubt he was good at what he did, based on their interactions over the past week. She said as much.

"Yeah, he's good. But something happened a few months back, something with some kids and a prostitution ring. Things went south, and he blames himself. One of the reasons he came here this week was to do some soul searching. Make some decisions. I've tried to talk to him, but I'm not sure I've been much help. Maybe you can try. He might open up to you."

They'd reached the stairs to the duplex. Storm, having heard them coming, was barking inside. Matt hustled up the stairs and opened the door to let the dog come out and join them.

"Thanks—she'll wake Harper with all that noise," Val said, petting the now-quiet dog. "I'm happy to try to talk to Ross, but I'm not sure how much help I'll be, Matt. I know nothing about being a cop. We have virtually nothing in common."

Matt leaned against the stair railing, stuck his thumbs in his jeans pockets, and peered up into the starlit sky. "Maybe that's what he needs: a completely neutral party. I've seen how he opens up to you. He doesn't do that with everybody, you know. Hell, he seldom does it with *anyone*, myself included. I don't think Jess liked him at all at our wedding. But, for whatever reason, he seems to like you."

Truth be told, Val had found Ross easy to talk to, had enjoyed their visits, and especially appreciated how he'd saved her from her own clumsiness—not once, but twice—and how he'd so quickly thought to bring Matt in to help with the snakes.

"If the opportunity presents itself," she said, "I promise I'll try to talk to him."

Matt nodded and stepped down off the porch. He gave her half a hug, putting an arm around her shoulder, while he snapped his fingers for Storm to come back from her exploration of the pile of debris hulking in the shadows next to the duplex. The dog responded immediately. "By the way, I heard you make a killer coffee cake. Remember those snakes I helped vacate from your new toy? Make me one of those and we'll call it even."

"Fair enough," Val replied, attempting a smile but grimacing again as another wave of pain shot through the back of her skull.

Matt turned her toward her front door. "Enough. Go get some rest, and if you have any trouble during the night, or the pain gets worse, get Jess or call us. Got it?"

"Got it, boss man. Hopefully neither of us will have nightmares about snakes tonight."

Matt laughed. "Hopefully."

* * *

Luke and the boys were due back around noon on Saturday. Val spent part of Thursday morning in the lodge kitchen baking more coffee cake. Ibuprofen muffled the ache at the back of her skull. She wrapped one fresh loaf in a clean linen towel and delivered it to Renee and Matt. Debt number one, paid. She took a second loaf over to the Gray Cabin, intending to repay Ross for the previous day, too.

She wasn't sure if he was in; all was quiet.

She knocked on the door but couldn't hear any noises inside. She hated to leave the treat out here, and she had no intention of going inside, uninvited, to leave it on the table. Debating what to do, she rapped her knuckles on the glass window in the top center of the door. That did it. Footsteps approached and the door swung inward.

Ross stood there, shirtless, in loose shorts, his hair tousled as if he'd just climbed out of bed.

Val felt a stab of something in the pit of her stomach. She fought to mask her surprise, burying the thought of her completely unexpected reaction at the sight of his bare chest deep into her brain, where she'd do her best to forget it ever happened.

"Oh. Val. I thought you were Matt. Sorry. Come in. I had another rough night. Guess I slept later than normal this morning. What time is it?" he asked, striding over to scoop up a discarded T-shirt and pulling it over his bare chest.

"No, I'm sorry. It never occurred to me you might still be sleeping. It's nearly eleven. I'm really sorry. You're on vacation and can sleep whenever you want," she said, afraid she was starting to ramble. For the first time since Ross's arrival at Whispering Pines, she felt uncomfortable talking to him. "I just dropped by to give you this coffee cake. I know you liked it when I made it the first time, and I wanted to thank you again for your help yesterday."

When he started to protest, she raised a hand, palm facing him, adding, "And I promise I'll stop thanking you if you accept it."

He chuckled. "In that case, I'll gladly accept." He took the loaf she'd offered and set it on the table. "Are you going to work in the camper again today? And by the way, how's the old noggin feeling?"

"I have a headache yet this morning, but it's getting better. And yes, I still have plenty I want to do in the camper before Luke and the boys get back. To be honest, I'm a little freaked out about going in there after yesterday, but I can't let that dissuade me. Matt told me to get it opened back up to air it out, and then I can keep going with things."

"Sounds good," Ross said. He unwrapped the coffee cake and began to search the kitchen drawers for a knife. Val pointed to the correct one. "Want some?"

She shook her head. "That's one of three. I already had a slice. Stop over later, if you're bored, and I'll put you to work on something."

"And give up the chance to sit out on the end of the dock and catch absolutely nothing again today? We'll see."

Val laughed, then let herself out the door and into the warm sunshine. As she walked back toward the duplex and the old camper, she realized this morning might have been the first time she'd been inside the Gray Cabin and hadn't had to fight off a shiver of apprehension.

She thought back to the progress she'd made the previous day on the Airstream, making plans for what else she wanted to accomplish on it before Luke and the boys got back. She worried that unless she got it looking better before her husband laid eyes on it, he'd think she'd lost her mind taking on a project like this.

Maybe she had. But she didn't want to hear him put a voice to her own fears.

She shuddered when she noticed the old fridge, now on its side in the grass, but she took purposeful steps over to the door of the camper and tugged it open. A faint chemical odor hit her; she covered her nose and mouth with her shirt for a second while the fumes dissipated. She scanned what she could see of the cabin's interior from the doorway, then made herself step inside. She refused to think about what might still be lurking out of sight, despite Matt's assurances. Instead she quickly opened every single window in the camper and the vent in the bathroom.

What needed to be done next? Her hand grazed over the surface of the cabinets. They felt solid, even though their dark stain looked dreary and dated. Unlike more modern campers, usually fitted with lots of pressed wood and laminate, these cabinets were constructed out of actual hardwood.

"They don't make 'em like this anymore," she declared, deciding the cabinets would stay. She'd seal and paint them—white, or maybe aqua—and give the interior a whole different feel. Luke would hate the idea, but this wasn't Luke's project. He never had to step foot inside it if he didn't want to. For the first time in many, many years, she could do exactly what she wanted in a space. No need to compromise or be practical or neutral in here.

She didn't yet know what she'd use the camper for, but she knew she'd need it to be full of creative energy.

The cupboards would stay, but the dinette would have to go. In its place she'd love to put a vintage metal table with a colorful, inlaid top. She crouched down to try to determine how best to remove the built-in seats and old metal support that jutted up out of the floor, bare now after she tossed its tabletop outside.

Her stomach rolled at the dark stain of blood smeared on one corner of the bench. Her blood.

Yep, that sealed it. It all had to go.

She retrieved a pair of goggles from the basin of the kitchen sink and got to work. Sometimes brute force was your only option, and Val reveled in the feel of splintering wood when she swung a sledgehammer against the old seat base. She kept at it until both bases had joined the pile outside, ignoring the ache at the base of her skull.

Next, Val got to work on the table base, searching the bag of drill bits for the right size.

"Knock, knock."

"Hey, hello again," Val said over her shoulder. "Didn't catch anything?"

"Not even a bite. Only gave it an hour today. I could hear your racket from all the way out there, thought I'd see if I could be more productive helping you than sitting on the dock."

Val pushed her eye protection up so the goggles sat on top of her head like sunglasses. She was sure she looked a fright—not that it mattered; this was hard work.

"Ross, you're supposed to be on vacation. You know, taking time to sit and relax and contemplate the future."

He eyed her skeptically, then picked up a screwdriver from the counter and knelt down to begin removing the splintered pieces of wood from the wall of the cabin—all that was left of the benches. Then he said, "Matt told you, didn't he?"

Val considered denying it, but Ross deserved better than that. If she could be of any help to him, she needed to play it straight. "He mentioned you were considering a career change when he walked me home last night."

Ross nodded but said nothing, grunting instead as he threw his weight into trying to break the old rusted screws loose. Moisture must have leaked through the large window above, causing damage over the years.

"Do you want to talk about it?" Val prodded.

"Not especially."

This must be the same resistance Matt was getting. "Are you sure? Because if anyone can relate to not knowing what they want to do with the rest of their life, it's me."

This surprised Ross. "Really? You seem to have things pretty much figured out. Spending the summer at the lake, kids, a husband. What's there to figure out?"

"You failed to mention what I do for a living in that little list of things I have figured out," Val pointed out.

"Hey, you're a mom. I get it. That's a big responsibility, and a ton of work. I grew up with two sisters. I know how hard my mom had to work to keep our house going, all of us fed, and all the other crap that moms always seem to handle."

Val rolled her eyes. "Oh yeah, I have a PHD in housekeeping and childrearing."

Ross sat down on the littered floor of the camper. He'd removed one section of splintered wood completely. "I take it from your tone that you'd maybe like to add something else to your résumé? You want to do more?"

Val dropped the drill she'd been struggling with, assuming the same position as Ross but leaning her back against one of the cupboards so that she was facing him. It made her nervous to sit so close to where the snakes had made their home, but it was a tight space. "Yes. I need more. I need something that's all mine. Not to mention something that brings in some money—raising four boys is expensive. But it's more than that. It's for *me*. Something that's just for me. Does that make any sense at all? Do you think I'm a terrible mom for not being satisfied with taking care of my kids?"

"Course not. Your kids will grow up. And if all you're left with is a husband and dissatisfaction with your life, you could lose the husband, too. I don't mean any disrespect, but I've seen it before. Even gone on calls where a wife was ready to beat her husband senseless with a vacuum cleaner because she was so unhappy."

Val picked up a splinter of wood the size of a playing card and winged it in Ross's direction. "Now you're just full of it."

"Okay, maybe not a *vacuum* cleaner, but you get the point."

Grinning, Val stretched out her legs and crossed her ankles, looking around the partially gutted interior of the camper. "I get the point. We all need to figure out what makes us happy, and we can't rely on anyone else—our families included—to do it for us. Maybe the inside of this dump is a metaphor for my life right now. It's time I rip out the old, tired pieces and figure out how to liven things up."

Ross nodded, his eyes seeming to lock on an area above and to her left—the place where the den of snakes had been found. "And maybe I'm tired of walking into a snake pit most days on the job."

Val fought the urge to scurry away from the cupboard. *They're gone,* she reminded herself. "I can't imagine doing what you've done for so many years. But there have to be things that have kept you going. Maybe the same things that are making it hard for you to walk away?"

Ross lowered his eyes to meet hers. "I see what you did there. Pretty smooth. You brought this little session full circle, back to me and my baggage."

Val lifted one shoulder and returned his smile. "Friends help friends figure this crap out."

He seemed to consider that, then released a deep sigh, as if he'd reached some type of decision. "There are some rewards to the work, obviously. The people we help every day. But it takes a lot out of you, too. I used to be better at refilling my tank at the end of the day. Not so much anymore, and too often it feels like I'm running on empty.

And when I'm not in a good place, people can get hurt. People *have* gotten hurt."

"Do you want to talk about that piece of it?"

Ross shook his head, picking at a scrape in the battered linoleum. "No. Suffice it to say, the dark is starting to take over the light . . . and I'm not sure how much longer I can stomach it."

His words opened up a tiny crack in Val's heart. She barely knew this man, but he'd allowed her a glimpse into his own psyche. She felt ill-equipped to give him advice. "I'm sorry, Ross. I'm no expert in any of this, and probably of little help to you. But no one should live in the darkness. You're no good to anyone there, especially yourself."

Val watched a shadow sweep over the floor and walls of the camper, a cloud passing in front of the sun. Ross noticed it, too, and smirked at her. "Damn, girl, you're good. And probably right. I guess I came here knowing I need to make a change. But not much else sounds appealing. I'm not sure I want to get out of law enforcement altogether. It's really all I know. I could never work behind a desk. You know what I think is part of my problem?"

"No. What?"

"I worry I'd miss the excitement. Cops can be adrenaline junkies, and I'm sure I'm guilty of that, too, to some degree. Anyhow, now you know my secret. I've been lying in bed at night, playing *What if?* games and listening for the creepy sound of a kittens or a baby crying." He rubbed a hand over his eyes and down his face. "It's exhausting."

"I'm sorry, Ross," Val offered, wishing there was some way she could help him figure things out.

With a heavy sigh, Ross straightened his legs, fitting them around hers in the tight space. "What are you sorry for?"

She thought. "For not having the answers."

He shrugged. "Sometimes a guy just needs someone to listen."

The camper door swung outward and Val and Ross looked up in surprise.

Lavonne's face reflected confusion, and Val chose to interpret her perplexed expression to be about the camper, not the man sitting so close to her on the debris-strewn floor.

She put on a smile. "Hey, Mom! Did you come to check out my new digs?"

"I did," Lavonne replied, stepping farther into the messy interior. "I heard talk of some crazy project my youngest had taken on and I needed to come see for myself."

Lavonne scanned the interior, and Val didn't miss it when her eyes rested on Ross more than once.

"Mom, you remember Ross. He was Matt's best man last summer."

As recognition dawned, Lavonne raised a hand in greeting. "Oh, sure, now I do. It took me a minute. How are you, Ross? What brings you to Whispering Pines?"

Val thought she detected an unusual coolness in her mother's tone. But that was ridiculous. *Now I'm just being paranoid.*

"Hello, Mrs. Richter. It's nice to see you again. Matt's been on me to come back for a visit, so I finally took him up on the offer. But, to be honest, I'm not very good at sitting around doing nothing. And since I came alone, and Matt is at work, I thought I'd see if maybe I could help Val out over here. As you can see, she's taken on quite the project," Ross said, motioning around them.

"Whatever are you going to do with this thing, dear? Renee said Ethan, Matt, and Seth helped you pull it out of the woods?"

"And Ross," Val said, nodding. "But as far as exactly what I'm going to do with it, I'm not sure yet. My mind's been racing. Have you ever looked at all the cute campers on Pinterest, ones women have fixed up and run businesses out of?"

Ross held up both hands, one still holding a screwdriver. "It sounds like you two have some things to brainstorm about and I'll just be in the way. Give me a yell, Val, if you find any more nests of snakes you need me to save you from."

"Cute," Val said, giving him a small wave as he stood and stepped around Lavonne, dropped the screwdriver back on the counter, and left through the still-open camper door.

"It was nice to see you again, Mrs. Richter."

"You too, Ross. Enjoy your vacation."

Val moved her drill out of the way and got to her feet so she could give her mother what would be a very brief tour of the small camper. When she straightened back up, she was surprised to find Lavonne staring out the window over the kitchen sink, in the direction Ross would have headed.

"Here, let me show you the rest of it," Val said, pulling Lavonne's attention back to the camper. "Not that there's much more to show."

Walking down the short hallway, Val pointed out the tiny cubicle containing an even tinier toilet. In the back was a platform bed.

"I'll probably remove this bed, too. I'm thinking maybe some chairs back here, or love seats. I don't know for sure. But I'm not thinking of this as a camper anymore, not in a traditional sense. More of a kick-ass office-on-wheels or something. Maybe somewhere for small group cooking classes."

As she peered around them, all Lavonne said was "Hmm."

"Come on, Mom, I know that tone. What? You don't approve? You think I'm nuts?"

Lavonne shook her head. "No, Val. Just hold on. Give me a minute to process this. I need to catch up with you. Walking into this mess was a bit of a shock—and what did that man mean about snakes? But I'm coming around . . . seeing the possibilities. Wouldn't it have been easier to refurbish a slightly newer version, though?"

Val couldn't help but laugh. "Probably, but it's not like I had a selection of abandoned campers to pick from out there in the woods. Besides, there's something about this old girl. Can't you feel it? Yes, she's worse for wear, but to me she's a diamond in the rough. Lots of potential. She has good, solid bones. Sometimes newer isn't as well built."

"Or as seasoned, right?" Lavonne added, grinning.

"Are we still talking about the camper, or are you referring to us?"

Lavonne walked back toward the front of the Airstream. "A bit of both, I suppose."

Val nodded, then went on to explain how she was starting to envision this front portion.

"All great ideas, honey, but you'll need help with some of those things, and it might not be cheap. I thought you were already concerned about money, especially because of your kitchen at home."

"I am. Come on, let's get out of here for a while. I've got fresh lemonade in the fridge and it's getting hot out here. Why don't we take this brainstorming session out to the back patio? I want your input, and I want to start making some notes. Besides, I better update you on the snakes and the stitches."

Lavonne broke into her first real smile since she'd stepped foot inside the camper. "Maybe you aren't quite as crazy as I thought—unless you prove me right with your snake story. This could be fun," she declared, rubbing her palms together and following Val out onto the grass. "But don't tell me you've been back to the emergency room again!"

CHAPTER TWENTY-TWO

GIFT OF RETURNING FAVORS

"Where did you find all the snakes?" Jake asked excitedly as he rushed around the interior of Val's camper. "Are there still some in here?"

"I hope not!" Val laughed, unable to suppress a shudder. She gently touched the back of her head and felt the stitches she'd have to go back in to get removed the following week. The cut didn't hurt much anymore, but the mental scars were still fresh.

"This place is awesome, Mom!" Jake insisted, his enthusiasm boosting her resolve again after the lackluster reaction she'd received from her husband. "Can we sleep in here sometime?"

Val grabbed her youngest's arm before he could step into the bathroom. "Careful—Uncle Ethan helped me pull the toilet out of there and we need to strengthen the floor. Good thing no one actually sat on the toilet. They might have fallen through to the grass underneath."

This brought a wave of laughter out of Jake. She'd missed him. She'd missed all of them. But with their return came the all-too-familiar doubts.

She'd managed to keep the camper a secret from Luke until they'd pulled into Whispering Pines earlier that morning. He'd acted glad to see her, and she'd honestly felt the same. She'd walked him back to the duplex, pulling him by the hand, anxious and nervous to gauge his reaction.

When he first saw it, he'd laughed. But the next words out of his mouth killed her joy.

"Who the hell is stupid enough to try to save that old piece of crap? Seth? Did someone force him to take it off their hands or something? Good luck bringing that back to a point where its anything more than junk."

Her heart had stopped. *I knew it! I* knew *he'd throw cold water on everything.*

"It's not Seth's," she said quietly.

"Really? Did Ethan take this on, then? I know he had fun on our camping trip over Memorial Day, but this is ridiculous. Is he wanting to fix up an old camper so he can take his kids out?"

Val remembered taking a deep breath, squaring her shoulders, and preparing for the battle she'd known was coming. "It's *my* camper."

"Yeah, right," he'd said, walking around the dilapidated Airstream. He kicked one of the new tires, grunted, then pushed against what Val already knew to be a soft spot that would need some fixing around the original piping used to empty the tanks. "You aren't *that* stupid."

She'd gasped. She'd suspected he wouldn't like the idea, but she hadn't thought he'd be downright cruel about it.

"I'm serious, Luke," she replied, fighting to keep her tone steady. She didn't want this to dissolve into a massive fight. "Fixing this up is my idea. I want to do something with it."

He swung around to face her. "Knock it off, Val. That isn't even funny. Seriously, whose is this?"

She'd stepped closer to him then, taken both of his hands in hers, and held their knotted fists up to her chest. "Luke. Listen to me. This is *my* camper. It was out in the woods and Renee said I could have it. Ethan and the others helped me pull it out of the woods and back here. I'm going to use some of my inheritance from Celia to fix it up. It's an Airstream. It does have *some* value, even if it doesn't look like it right now. You know I've been searching for some type of business I can start. This is the first step. I know it might seem crazy, but you need to have some faith in me."

She remembered how Luke had searched her face, the realization that she was indeed serious finally dawning in his incredulous eyes.

"You used to like surprises," Val gently reminded him, keeping her voice soft. She didn't want to argue. "I can make this work."

She watched as the fight ebbed out of him. A hint of a smile stole over his expression. "And I thought keeping the boys out of trouble at the farm this weekend was exhausting. Now I see where they get their imagination. I can't see it, Val. But, knowing you, you'll do your best to prove me wrong."

He'd issued the challenge. She *was* determined to prove to him she was right to look past the grunge and chase the possibilities.

"If you leave this bed back here, we can sleep in here tonight," Jake said, pulling Val's mind back to the present. Jake's enthusiasm was starting to make up for Luke's lack of the same.

"Tell you what, Jake—maybe when I have this all done, you and your brothers can camp in here with sleeping bags. But that bed is coming out. I have lots of work to do in here before I'd feel comfortable letting you sleep inside. But we'll get there. Do you want to help me?"

"Sure, Mom! What do you need me to do?"

The two of them got to work. By late afternoon, Val was dirty and exhausted, but together, her and Jake, they'd made more progress.

"We better go see about making dinner," Val said, giving Jake a high five and then turning him toward the door. "We did good today, kiddo. Thanks for your help. And guess what?"

He spun back around. "What?"

Val laughed when she looked at his dirt-streaked face. "Since you helped me so much today, and your brothers took off to play in the lake instead, they get to go find two wheelbarrows and start hauling all of this junk to the dumpster out front. You, on the other hand, are free to go do whatever you've missed doing since you've been at the farm. Then you can eat and shower."

"Yes!" Jake cried, pumping his fist in the air. "Can I go tell them?"

"That probably isn't a good idea. I'll tell them. And if I hear you smart off to them about having to help while you play, you'll join them. Got it?"

"I guess," Jake conceded.

* * *

It felt good to sit down to a meal, just the six of them. There hadn't been many family dinners lately.

"What did you guys eat at Grandma and Grandpa Swanson's house?"

Dave coughed. "Let's just say I've had enough pizza and mac and cheese for a while."

"Hey, I told you to help cook something if you wanted variety," Luke tossed in, unconcerned. "There was work to be done."

"I did like that chicken alfredo we had last night," Noah added, and saw Jake vigorously nod in agreement. "You should make that sometime, Mom."

"I can do that, but your dad's going to have to give me his recipe." Val glanced toward her husband. "Since when do you know how to make pasta that doesn't come straight out of a box?"

But Noah cut in: "Oh, no, Dad didn't make it. His friend Kennedy brought it over."

Val could feel the blood rush to her cheeks, feel the burn of her temper rising. What was *Kennedy* doing around *her* boys?

"Kennedy, huh? Isn't she an old friend of your father's?"

Noah shrugged. "Don't know. I thought Dad said she used to be Uncle Alan's girlfriend. She sure is pretty."

Her heart sped faster.

"Pretty?!" Jake repeated, his voice high with surprise. "Noah, she's *old.*"

Val looked around the crowded table, noting the expressions on everyone's faces. Logan was nodding, but she wasn't sure which description he thought was accurate. Dave rolled his eyes, as if to say he thought his three younger brothers were a pain. Luke didn't meet her eyes, instead focusing on scraping the last of his mashed potatoes off his plate.

She'd discuss this topic with him later, when the kids weren't around. "Thanks for getting all that old junk hauled out front while I made supper, boys. I appreciate it."

"I don't get what you're going to do with that old thing, Mom," Logan said.

"You and me both, son," Luke added.

Val's enjoyment over their family dinner dimming, she kneaded the crumpled napkin in her left hand. She hated the idea of that woman coming around the farm, around *her* family, even more than she hated Luke transferring his lack of enthusiasm about her camper to their kids. She sipped her ice water, attempting to maintain her composure. She'd prove them all wrong about the camper, but she was less sure where she stood on the other matter.

"Boys," she began, pointedly trying to ignore Luke's comment. "This is one example where I don't have all the answers. But I've been wanting to start some kind of business, and this might just be a place to start. You've gotta trust me."

"Can I have more potatoes?" Logan asked.

"Logan, what do you say?" Jake demanded.

Val caught Luke's eye, and she couldn't help but grin. This was normal. *This* was what family dinner was supposed to feel like. At least for their family.

"*Pleeeeease*—and if you lip off to me again, I'll beat you to a pulp, twerp," Logan hissed at Jake.

"Boys," Val warned, realizing it was the first time in years that she hadn't uttered that single word, using that tone, in a whole week. But she didn't want to fight with any of them. She wanted to enjoy having them home.

Well, not exactly home, *but with me*, she thought, settling back into her mom mode.

* * *

Val showered off the grunge she was sure covered her from the top of her head to the tips of her toes. The boys had disappeared into their bedrooms and Luke was planted in front of the television. She joined him in the small living room, but the episode he was watching couldn't hold her attention.

"I made this great coffee cake while you and the boys were gone this week," she said.

Luke glanced her way distractedly. He was stretched out on the old couch, crossed ankles resting on the armrest opposite his head. He looked settled in for the evening. "You gonna make us some?"

Val shrugged. "I could. But the oven in here is a little wonky. The new one in the lodge works much better."

Luke grunted, his attention already back on his program.

With a sigh, Val decided she might as well head over to the lodge and whip up another batch of her coffee cake. She wasn't tired, but a night in front of the television held no appeal. "I think I'll go do some baking over at the lodge. Do you mind?"

"No. Go ahead," Luke said. He didn't spare her another glance. "Coffee cake sounds good."

She wasn't entirely sure he was even listening to her. Grabbing her phone off the end table and keys to the lodge off a hook by the door, she paused at the base of the stairs and hollered up to the kids, letting them know where she was going. A muffled reply—*someone* at least heard her.

She let herself out, cutting off the voices from Luke's show as she closed the door. The air still felt hot and sticky despite the setting sun. As she picked her way along the shadowed path toward the lodge, mosquitoes hummed around her and she heard a shout of laughter from the general direction of the guest cabins. Storm had stayed home with the boys. Val missed the dog's presence. But the shadows didn't worry her.

The air inside the lodge felt lighter, the oppressive humidity kept at bay. Val quickly snapped on the lights and lost herself in the comfort of baking.

Once she'd placed two pans of coffee cake in the oven, she dug back into Celia's recipe box, anxious to try her hand at more. She was in her element and lost all track of time, and so jumped when her phone rang. She'd propped it up on the island earlier, soft music keeping her company. Shutting the pantry door, she glanced at her watch as she turned back toward the sound.

11:45? Luke was probably calling to check on her.

But as she reached for the phone, she was surprised to see it was Renee instead of her husband.

"What's wrong?" she said automatically. No need for greetings. Her sister wouldn't call at this hour to chat.

"Let me talk to Luke. He isn't picking up his phone."

"Luke isn't here."

Renee paused for a beat. "What do you mean, he isn't there?"

Val reached behind her for a stool, her feet suddenly aching from the long day. "Well, I mean, he's *here*, but I'm actually over at the lodge doing some baking. He's back at the duplex. He must have fallen asleep."

"Oh, got it. I'll be right there."

Click.

Val stared at her phone, not sure if Renee meant she was coming to the lodge or the duplex. The timer on the oven told her the coffee cake would need to come out in fifteen minutes. She didn't dare leave it.

She didn't have to wait long. There was a pounding on the back door. She'd locked the door behind her when she'd arrived. She might not have been afraid of the shadows on her solo walk over, but it was now full-on dark, and she wasn't *that* brave.

"Come on, Val, open up!" Renee hissed through the door.

"What's going on?" she asked as she swung the door open. Renee's hair was caught up in a messy knot on the top of her head and her face was scrubbed clean of makeup, sure signs she'd been ready to turn in for the night. "Is something wrong?"

"I'm sorry, Val, but I need to borrow Luke."

"What? Why? Did something happen? Oh God, is Matt all right?"

Val had no idea how Renee dealt with what she suspected would be near-constant worry, being married to a man that did what Matt did for a living. If it were her, she'd always be one step from assuming the worst.

"Yes, he's all right, at least until he gets home. *Then* I'm going to kill him. He's out at the bar."

Val recognized that tone: Renee wasn't worried—she was *mad*. She tried her best not to grin, but she failed miserably.

"It's not funny, Val. Matt is the *sheriff*, for God's sake! At least he was smart enough to call for a ride, but he warned me I probably shouldn't come alone. He was actually slurring his words."

"Let me guess. He and Ross went out?"

Renee nodded, her jaw clamped shut.

"Maybe he had a stroke," Val offered, still grinning, then took a step back in self-preservation when Renee shot her a death glare.

"You are *not* helping. Yes, he's out with *Ross*. Apparently they've had too much to drink, and now Ross is out on the dance floor making an ass of himself or something. Matt's exact quote was 'Bring Luke or Seth.' Sorry to steal your husband away, but I need him. I hated to call Seth and maybe wake Harper. Your boys sleep through most anything."

"As you can see, we're not exactly spending a romantic evening together," Val said, motioning around at the lodge kitchen. "Take Luke. I'm sure he'll help. You don't want them to get impatient and jump in the truck to drive home. I'd go get Luke, but I don't want the coffee cake to burn. Wait—I'll call Dave! He always answers his phone, and he probably isn't asleep yet. He'll get Luke for you. Maybe you can have some coffee cake before you go, calm your nerves. It's almost ready."

It felt like it took forever for them to get back to the resort.

She imagined Matt and Ross hanging out at some bar, drinking beer and discussing old cases. Matt would have been trying to get Ross to open up. Ross probably hadn't wanted to, and instead drank too much and skirted the issue. She couldn't help but wonder what he was doing that he was making an ass of himself on the dance floor, and smiled at the picture her mind conjured up. As long as it wasn't *her* man acting the fool, she could see the humor in it.

She considered going back to their duplex but knew she'd never be able to fall asleep until they were all home. Jess had texted her earlier wondering if something was wrong; she must have heard Luke leave. After assuring Jess everything was fine—unless Renee made good on her threats against Matt—she propped her phone on the island again and considered cutting off another piece of fresh coffee cake.

No stress eating, she reminded herself. If she was going to have to compete with this Kennedy chick for her husband's affections, she should probably do something about the twenty extra pounds she'd put on in the last few years.

Noah had said the woman was pretty. *Was* she? Val picked her phone back up—she decided to occupy her time with a little investigating instead of eating. Maybe she could find a picture of the woman. She couldn't remember her last name, though it wasn't like "Kennedy" was terribly common.

She couldn't find anything on Facebook, which wasn't really surprising with so little to go on. Luke wasn't on any of the social media platforms, so it wasn't like she could just look up his friends. Maybe there'd been postings about the fundraising benefit Kennedy had helped organize for Alan.

That tactic proved more fruitful, and it wasn't long until she found a photo from the small-town newspaper highlighting the benefit. Luke's parents stared back at the camera, forced smiles and haunted eyes, their pain over the soul-crushing reason for the benefit evident. Luke was on the other side of his mom, a supporting arm around her shoulders.

She studied her husband's face, his somber expression. He'd changed little in the years since she'd met him. His tawny hair was still thick, with just enough wave that he always looked windblown. There was some silver now, mixed in at the temples, but you couldn't see that in the picture. His complexion, with much of his work done outdoors, was perpetually ruddy. But it was those eyes that still got to her: a piercing blue, made all the more vivid by the contrast with his skin. It was never hard to read Luke's mood. You only had to look into his eyes. Dave and Jake inherited those same eyes from their father, while Logan had her green eyes and Noah's were brown, though they'd never been sure where in the family tree the brown came from.

Standing on her father-in-law's left, according to the caption listing names below the photo, was Kennedy.

Val wasn't sure what she'd expected, but she suddenly wished she hadn't gone digging. The woman in the picture was tall, willowy, and blond. She was also model-pretty.

Everything I'm not, Val thought.

No wonder her boys thought she was attractive. The lady was absolutely *gorgeous*—a fact Luke had failed to point out. But the second that thought entered her mind, she knew it wasn't fair. What would she have expected Luke to do? Provide a point-by-point comparison? Of course not.

Val reached up and fluffed her own shoulder-length hair, which was longer than she normally wore it. She'd used a home coloring kit to freshen up her red tint and mask the gray starting to sneak in. Their unexpected relocation to Whispering Pines for the summer months meant it had been a while since her last salon visit. The kit was a poor substitute for her stylist.

She kept staring at Kennedy. The woman was nearly as tall as Luke's dad. This would put her only a few inches shorter than Luke—unlike her own height of barely five feet, putting the top of her head well below Luke's chin.

She closed the browser, her feelings jumbled. Why had she looked? Now she felt even more inferior to this woman from Luke's past than she had before. She wasn't stupid; she knew sometimes old loves could hold a special appeal, especially during tumultuous times.

Which was exactly what Luke had been facing lately.

Frustrated, she yanked open the fridge and eyed a single bottle of hard cider. She popped the top then sat down on a stool to wait. As she sipped the tart beverage, she debated how best to handle the situation with Kennedy. Should she confront Luke? Demand to know what, if anything, was going on? Or should she take a whole different approach? Should she pull her husband upstairs when he got back and make him forget about any other woman? That might work . . . at least for a while.

She hated herself for doubting him. Her rational mind knew there were no black-and-white indicators that he'd done anything wrong. It was just her gut. Taking another pull from the bottle, she decided not to touch the subject of Kennedy tonight. Luke was helping Renee right now, had done so without an ounce of resistance. He was a good man. She needed to remember that.

Finally, she heard vehicles. Rushing from the kitchen in the back of the lodge toward the front entrance, Val snapped lights on along the way. The wall of photos caught her eye and she wondered, not for the first time, what stories they could tell. Tonight might turn out to be another story to add to the list.

Twisting the deadbolt on the heavy front door, she pulled it open just as Matt's pickup and Renee's Toyota pulled into the parking lot. Dust, stirred up by their tires, still hung in the humid night air as Renee climbed out of her SUV, the interior light revealing to Val that her sister had driven back alone. She watched, curious, as Renee hustled over to the truck and opened the rear door on the driver's side. Matt was in the passenger's side upfront, Luke in the driver's seat, so the hunched figure in the back had to be Ross. Renee grunted as she caught his weight when the door was no longer there to support him.

Val chewed on her lip, fighting back the urge to laugh as Luke slammed his door and swung back to help Renee with Ross. Matt let himself out on his side, apparently in better shape than his partner in crime. He came around the front bumper of his pickup, massaging his jaw. He spared a glance back toward the others, but must have decided they had things under control.

"Tell me you've got a bag of frozen peas in there, Val," he said as he approached her, but he didn't wait for an answer before brushing past to go inside. She caught a glimpse of a split lip and the dark smudge of a bruise across Matt's lower jawline in the glow from the light flanking the front door. She shook her head in disbelief, whispering under her breath.

"Idiots."

* * *

Five minutes later, Luke was plugging in the coffee pot, Matt was leaning into a far corner, holding a bag of frozen peas against his jaw, and Ross was sitting on one of the stools at the island, slumped over, his face hidden in his folded arms.

"So what happened to you guys?" Val asked. She cringed again at the sight of Matt's injuries when he lowered the bag of vegetables to answer her. "Ouch! That's gonna sting for a while."

"No kidding," Matt replied, covering his chin with the peas again. "This isn't bad, though. *He* took the brunt of it."

"I noticed." Val looked toward Ross. He wasn't moving. She wondered if he'd passed out.

The ringing of a phone interrupted them. Luke sighed, pulling his phone out of his jeans. "It's Dave," he said, glancing at Val. Renee was busy at the sink, wringing out a wet dishtowel, while Val watched her husband talk with their eldest. Her pulse picked up as she heard Luke's words: "How the hell did *that* happen?" She waited expectantly, impatient for Luke to give her some indication as to what was happening now, back at the duplex. He sounded mad, not panicked, so it couldn't be too serious.

It never ends.

With a sigh, Luke shoved his phone back into his pocket. "If you guys don't need me for anything else tonight, I'll leave the two of you in the more-than-capable hands of these two ladies." He looked at Val. "Apparently Dave let Storm out and she managed to sniff out a skunk."

"Is she hurt?" Val asked, her heart jumping into her throat at the prospect. Even Ross raised his head to try to focus on what Luke was saying. He wouldn't want anything to happen to his running partner.

"No, luckily. But Dave said she got sprayed. So I need to go deal with that. Do we have any hydrogen peroxide over there?"

"Yeah, in the upstairs bathroom vanity. Do you need me to come help?"

"Nah. I've had to do this before, growing up on the farm. The boys can help me." Luke looked between Matt and Ross, who had returned to his slumped-over position on the island. "Renee might need some help yet."

Luke turned to leave.

"Hey, Luke," Matt said, stopping him at the door. "Thanks, buddy. I owe you."

Luke gave Matt half a grin. "You'd do the same for me."

And he was gone.

Val was confident Luke could take care of their pet, so she turned back to her brother-in-law and her new friend, repeating her earlier line of questioning. "What happened? A rowdy boys' night out, Matt? That's not really your style."

Renee set the cold dishtowel on the island next to Ross and then poured two cups of coffee, handed one to her husband, and offered one to Val. "Do you want a cup?"

Val accepted the hot brew, so Renee went back to the cupboard and pulled down another mug, filling one for herself. Ross probably needed the coffee more than any of them, but his head was still cradled in his arms.

Renee turned back to face Val. "I might have judged Matt too quickly. He'd had a few beers, so he didn't want to drive, but that wasn't why he was slurring his words. *That* came curtesy an uppercut to the jaw."

Val's eyes swung to her brother-in-law in alarm. "Did you lose any teeth?"

"Don't think so. If I do, I'm sending him the dental bill," he said, jabbing a thumb in Ross's direction.

"*He* hit you?" Val asked. She was struggling to reconcile the image of Ross she'd compiled in her mind over the past week with the one slumped over the island now, wreaking of alcohol after having apparently slammed his fist into his friend's face.

But Matt shook his head, then groaned at the effort. "No. He didn't hit me. But he did pick a hell of a fight with two guys who were much bigger and *much* drunker than we were. Well, drunker than *I* was, at least. Ross had plenty to drink."

A flicker of movement caught Val's eye. Ross was slowly lifting his middle finger in Matt's direction. Matt grinned, then moaned again.

"I can hear you, you know," Ross said, pushing up until he was sitting upright.

Val gasped. One side of his face looked like a slab of steak gone bad; it was a mottled mixture of deep reds and purples, his eye swollen completely shut. She hurried over and picked up the cloth, motioning for him to take it. "Didn't your mother teach you not to pick fights with boys twice your size? That's one of the first lessons I taught my four."

Ross grunted and accepted the dish rag, fixing his one good eye on her. "Sorry you have to see me like this."

Matt ambled over and pulled out a second stool, dropping onto it with a sigh. "We've gotten banged up at work before, but never at a bar. At least not to this degree."

"Sorry, bud. That was my fault," Ross acknowledged.

Renee set her coffee down and walked over to stand close to Ross, bending down slightly to look into his eyes.

The man leaned back on the stool, wobbling a bit. "What the hell, Renee?"

Renee straightened and walked back to her mug. "I don't think you should be alone tonight. I already know what you would say if I were to suggest you go in to get checked for a concussion, but I refuse to let you go back to your cabin alone and fall asleep."

Ross snorted, but Matt nodded and said, "I agree, hon, but we don't have a bed in the spare room. I suppose we could wake up Robbie and have him sleep on the couch."

Ross sat up straighter on his stool. "Bullshit. I'm not letting you kick the kid out of his bed. I'm fine."

Matt squinted in Ross's direction, seeming to look closer at him this time. "No. Not fine. Renee, I'll just sleep on the couch, then, over at Ross's cabin. That way I can hold his sorry-ass head over the toilet if he has to puke."

Val couldn't help but grin at the picture Matt's words evoked in her head. "I'm sorry, guys. There would be a bed in your spare room if we weren't using all your extras in the duplex right now."

Matt waved off her comment. "Do you two want to help me get him settled over there? I need to run back to the house and change real quick. *Someone* spilled a beer on me."

Ross moaned again, causing Val to chuckle. She felt bad about the condition of his banged-up face, but it did sound like he'd brought on some of this himself.

"Are you sure you're okay, hon?" Renee asked, walking over to stand behind Matt. She wrapped her arms around his waist and set her chin on his shoulder, keeping one eye on their possibly concussed guest.

Matt patted her hand. "I'll be fine."

Renee's nose wrinkled. "Then go. And you might want to take a shower, too. You stink like the floor of an old tavern."

Val gathered up their coffee mugs, unplugged the pot, and covered up the loaves of coffee cake with a fresh towel. She doubted either Matt or Ross would be able to chew even soft bread given the condition of their faces. She'd come back and get the cake in the morning to feed her family. "Let's go, then. It's late and I think we could all use some sleep."

Matt helped Ross off the stool, keeping a supporting arm around him as the four of them slowly made their way out of the lodge and back to the Gray Cabin. None of the other guests were lingering around the firepit. Not surprising, given the hour.

Once inside the Gray Cabin, Matt waited outside the bathroom for Ross, then helped the man into the bedroom. In the meantime, Val offered to help Renee make up the couch.

"There's pillows and a couple blankets in the closet where you found the time capsule. Grab them for me, would you?" Renee asked.

Val headed back to the bedroom, glancing toward the bed. She thought Ross might already be asleep, even though a bedside lamp glowed. He'd come out of the bathroom earlier wearing shorts and a tank, but hadn't had the stamina to shower as Matt had just left to do.

She jumped at the sound of his voice.

"This is embarrassing," he said, the bed squeaking as he rolled to face her. "I don't normally do this type of thing."

Val nodded, continuing on into the closet and reaching high to pull the bedding off the top shelf. Stepping back out with her arms now full, she turned back toward Ross. "Hey, we all screw up sometimes. Don't worry about it."

Ross shifted again, lying flat on his back, an arm draped over his forehead as he stared at the ceiling. "I suppose I'll have the mother of all hangovers in the morning."

Val suspected he was right. "Why don't I grab you a bottle of water and a couple aspirin? Then I better go check on Luke and Storm."

He didn't reply, so she took the bedding out to Renee and got a bottle of water out of the fridge. On her way back to the bedroom with the water, she stopped next to the couch as Renee set it up for the night. "Do you want to text Matt and have him bring something for Ross to take for the pain?"

"We already talked about it. He's bringing something."

"Perfect."

Val entered the quiet bedroom. Ross hadn't moved. "Here's some water. Light on or off? Matt will be back in a sec. He's bringing you something to take to try to help with that inevitable headache you're facing."

"Just leave the light on, then. Thanks, Val. And thank your husband for me, will you?"

CHAPTER TWENTY-THREE

GIFT OF CAUTION

*D*espite the late night, Val woke at her usual time. She wasn't sure which was the culprit: habit, or Luke's snoring. Her husband had just gotten to bed when she'd returned to the duplex the night before. A slight undercurrent of skunk smell still lingered in the air, but Luke assured her he'd done his best. He'd made a bed in the basement for Storm, not confident enough to let her sleep with the boys or in their room yet. Even if she was still a little smelly, Val felt a bit bad for her: the basement had a cement floor and held little other than the washer and dryer.

She climbed gingerly out of bed, trying not to wake Luke. She rescued Storm from the basement and they headed outside. Her plan was to walk over to the lodge to retrieve the coffee cake to feed her hungry crew when they'd eventually wake up.

The humidity of the previous night had evaporated and the light breeze smelled of fresh pine and bacon. Luke must have done a good job with the dog. Val couldn't detect the telltale odor anymore.

The slamming of a screen door caught her attention. Matt stood on the top step of the Gray Cabin drinking a bottle of water. Storm heard him, too, bolting in his direction. Val followed.

"How are you feeling this morning?" she asked, eyeing Matt

closely. The side of his cheek was still discolored, but she thought his eyes looked clear.

Matt downed the remainder of his water before answering, crumpling the now-empty bottle.

"For God's sake, can you keep it down out there?" a disembodied voice croaked from behind the screen door.

Grinning, Matt jabbed a thumb over his shoulder. "Better than my old friend in there. He's paying the price this morning."

He looked like he had more to say, but he paused, pulling a lit-up phone out of his pocket. She waited as he read the screen.

"Duty calls," he said, holding up the phone. "That was dispatch. I'm going to have to run. One of my deputies needs backup."

Despite the urgency in his tone, Matt lingered.

"What? Don't you have to go?" Val prodded.

Matt looked over his shoulder into the dark interior behind him. "Yeah, I do . . . but he's still in rough shape. I thought I'd run over to the lodge and brew some coffee for us. He doesn't have any food in here, either."

The sound of retching reached their ears. Storm rushed up the stairs, stopping next to Matt, whining softly as she peered inside.

"On second thought, maybe it's too soon for coffee."

Val suspected Matt was right about that. Good thing she was a mom of four and well past the point of being squeamish when someone was sick. "Is he decent in there?"

Matt snorted. "Describe *decent*."

"For God's sake, Matt. Is the man naked?"

"Of course he's not *naked*."

Val stepped forward onto the stairs, motioning toward the smashed water bottle in Matt's hand. "Give me that. I'll go see to him. You need to go. He'll live. Can't say the same for whoever is on the other end of that call for help you just received."

"You sure?" Matt asked, wavering.

"I'm sure. Luke and the boys aren't even up yet. I can spare a few minutes to help a friend. Besides, I owe him."

Relief washed over Matt's features. "Thanks, Val. Tell Ross I should be back late afternoon, when my shift is done. Sorry to have to run like this."

Val grabbed him by the wrist and pulled him down the stairs. "Go!" Matt finally did as he was told, jogging the rest of the way.

She watched him go and then glanced down at Storm when the dog bumped against her thigh. A moan came from inside. With a sigh, Val pulled Storm back to allow her enough room to open the screen door. They both entered, Storm at a much faster clip.

Ross sat on the couch, bare-chested but holding the tank he'd had on when she'd left the previous evening. His eyes were closed. He looked like he'd collapsed there, arms and legs splayed. He jumped when Storm skidded to a stop in front of him, bumping her wet nose against his knees. One eye popped open, and he groaned at the sight of the dog. Val couldn't tell if he was actually looking at Storm, at least with both eyes, because his right one seemed to still be swelled shut.

She caught only a glimpse of his chest before forcing her attention back to his battered face, but the glance was enough to cause two simultaneous reactions. The first was dismay at the bruising there— black and blue, with a wider ring of greenish-yellow spreading down the left side. Were some of his ribs broken?

The other thought was how different he looked from Luke. Where Luke's chest was broad and sprinkled with the same tawny-colored hair as what was on his head, Ross was narrower and sleeker, still strong but in a different way.

She felt a surge of shame at even noticing. The only reason she was there was to make sure he didn't suffer any side effects from the beating he'd taken.

"Do you suppose the other guy looks as bad as you?" she asked.

Ross jumped, as if he hadn't noticed her standing just inside the door. "With any luck. The prick deserved everything he got. *Pricks*, I should say. His buddy jumped right in to the whole mess." He peeked one eye at her, then motioned helplessly toward the bathroom. "Please tell me you didn't hear that."

Val couldn't help but grin. "Sorry, I heard. Matt had to run, by the way—duty called, literally. But don't worry. I'm tough. A little puke doesn't bother me. I'd never survive as a mom to my brood if it did. Do you feel like you got run over with a truck? Because you *look* like it."

Not meeting her eyes, Ross pulled the shirt on, focusing instead on Storm. He rubbed the dog's head as he slowly stood and shuffled to the tiny kitchen, pulling open the freezer and rummaging around in it. "Damn, thought I had some frozen fish in here."

"Fish for breakfast?" Val asked, incredulous.

He looked at her like she'd grown horns. "Are you trying to make me puke again? No, not to eat. My eye is killing me."

Val sighed. "Here, let me make you a bag of ice. You do have ice, don't you?"

Ross shrugged. "Yeah, but no baggies."

Val dug in the cupboards, found a bread bag with only one hotdog bun inside, and used the bag to make an ice pack. Then she rounded up three ibuprofen from the toiletry bag he directed her to and suggested he go back to bed, promising to come check on him again in a few hours.

He winced as he brought the bag of ice up against his face. "No. You will not come back and check on me. At this point, it's evident I'll live, and without any serious injuries to anything but my pride."

"But you were just sick to your stomach. That could indicate a brain injury."

Ross laughed, and then groaned in misery at the pain it caused. "All it means is I was an idiot last night. I drank too much, didn't eat much of my burger basket, and then pushed my luck until someone bigger beat the crap out of me. I'm hungover and I've got a mother of a shiner, that's all. Now go home. I appreciate your help, but don't you have a husband and kids waiting at home for you?"

"I saw those ribs," she countered, pointing at his tank top. "Are you sure you didn't break one? Or two?"

Ross used his free hand to pull up his shirt. It reminded Val of the other time she saw him do that, after his run on the first day of his visit. He shook his head in surprise, as if seeing it for the first time. Given the pain in his head, maybe he hadn't even noticed the injury to his ribs yet. "Don't think so. It would hurt to breathe. Right now, breathing feels like about the only thing I can do that doesn't cause me pain."

"Take my advice and go lay down. I'll come back around lunchtime with some food and coffee. If you're any worse, I'm taking you in. If you can start to function like a human being again, I'll leave you to recover in peace. Deal?"

"Deal," he agreed, although he didn't sound happy about it.

* * *

After a quick stop in the lodge kitchen to grab the coffee cake, she headed back to their side of the duplex. Inside, she found Luke in the kitchen with Jake and Noah, cooking scrambled eggs and talking fishing.

"Morning, hon," Luke greeted her, his tone cheerful as he took the two loaves out of Val's hands. "These will go great with the eggs. Are Matt and Ross out moving around yet this morning? Bet they're feeling tough."

"I think they're both on the mend." Val kept her reply vague as she nodded discreetly in the boys' direction.

Noah drained his glass of orange juice and then turned to Val. "Why? What happened to Uncle Matt? And who's Ross?"

Val looked to Luke, not exactly sure how much to share about the men's drunken brawl.

"Ross is a friend of your uncle's," Luke said. "And your mother's. He's staying at the resort. Last night, Matt and Ross went out. There was some kind of misunderstanding, some punches got thrown, and they both have a few nasty bumps and bruises to show for it."

That works, Val thought, hoping the boys would leave it at that.

"You mean Uncle Matt got in a *bar* fight last night? How cool is that?!" Jake shouted, fidgeting in his chair. "Were there broken bottles and everything? Did the cops come?"

"Jake, getting in a fight is *not* cool," Val reprimanded. "Your Uncle Matt and his friend *are* cops, so they should have known better. We're just grateful your uncle got everyone calmed down enough to walk away, but now they both have some healing to do."

Noah shrugged, his attention already diverted by Storm, who was nuzzling her food bowl toward him. Jake, however, was still pondering the story. Val could see he was processing. "Sounds to me," he said, his tone very serious, "like somebody made some bad choices last night."

Val couldn't help but laugh. "That they did, Jake. And they aren't proud of it, either. But enough about that. Do you boys have plans for today? You aren't leaving today, are you, Luke?"

"No, I'm planning to stay for another day or two. I talked to Dad this morning and he's doing all right without me. We were just talking about what we might do when you came in. Got any ideas?"

Val nodded, suggesting the waterski show she'd heard about that was supposed to be at a nearby lake that afternoon.

"I've always wanted to try to waterski," Jake said, clearly excited.

"Sorry, hon. It's not somewhere you go to learn to waterski. It's actually some people that are already really good at it, and they put on a show we can watch."

He paused, considering this. "Hmm. I guess that would be fun, too. But could we maybe at least go swimming? Is there a fun beach there, too?"

"Probably. What do you think, babe?" she said, turning to her husband. "Want to spend the day with me and the boys, bumming around in lake country?'

Luke held her eye for an extra beat before replying. "That sounds like fun. And long overdue. Boys, run upstairs and wake your brothers up. Tell them to get dressed. We should leave soon—it's already ten."

Both Noah and Jake did as they were told, dropping their breakfast dishes in the sink as they left.

Val sensed trouble behind that look, but she was tired of arguing. She just wanted to spend a beautiful summer day with her family. "Thanks for agreeing to this, Luke. I think a family day is exactly what we need."

Luke scraped bits of egg out of the pan into the garbage and added it to the growing pile in the sink. He turned to face Val, arms crossed. "I agree. We haven't had much of that this summer. But before the boys come back down, I think we should talk about what happened last night. What was *that* all about?"

"What do you mean?"

"Ross couldn't stop talking about you last night in the pickup on the way back to the resort. I couldn't understand everything he was saying, he mumbled a lot, but I think the guy has a crush on you."

This shocked her.

"He doesn't have a *crush* on me, Luke. Come on. You sound like a jealous teenager."

She thought back to earlier that morning, at her own guilt over the thoughts she had as she'd compared Ross to Luke.

"I'm serious, Val. Guys can sense these things. And I'm not too thrilled about it."

Val felt a flash of rage, but she needed to keep things civil. All four boys were upstairs.

"Look, Ross is a friend and he's going through a tough time right now. I doubt he usually drinks like that, as a rule, but I honestly don't know that for sure. Matt trusts him, and we both know Matt is a good judge of character."

But Luke wouldn't let it go. "I think he wants to be more than friends."

This ticked her off even more. "Luke, I've never, *ever* given you a reason not to trust me. Besides, is any of this really any different from you and your old friend Kennedy?"

He kept his gaze steady on hers, but said nothing.

"Oh, wait—yes, it *is* different, because I've never been anything other than a friend with Ross. You can't say the same about Kennedy. Yet you expect me to trust you, right?"

One nod was all she got.

"Then we understand each other," Val said. "Now, can we put this petty jealousy aside and enjoy a beautiful summer day with our kids?"

After a pause, Luke took three steps toward her and pulled her into his strong arms, holding her close. She started to wriggle free but paused herself, realizing that might cause more arguments and ruin the day. He held her for just a minute and then stepped away. "We can try" was all he said before turning away and following Jake and Noah up the stairs.

Left standing alone in an empty kitchen with a sink full of dirty dishes, Val couldn't help but feel conflicted about the day stretching before her. Would it be a fun day, a day to heal? Or would it be filled with an undercurrent of tension?

For the sake of the kids, she was hoping for fun.

She called Renee and asked her to check on Ross at noon, and to take him some lunch. She felt a pinch of guilt at sending someone in her place after promising Ross she'd be back, but set those feelings aside. She wouldn't give Luke any reason to doubt her intentions.

* * *

By the time they returned to Whispering Pines, the sun was starting to set. All six of them were tired, sunburned, and full of pizza and nachos. By most accounts, the perfect summer Saturday.

Val was sure the boys had enjoyed themselves. None of them had ever waterskied before, but Logan and Jake were already planning to see if Renee had any old skis lying around somewhere. When Luke tried to tell them that the resort fishing boat's motor wasn't big enough to pull a skier, they chose not to believe him.

Dave had been more interested in the girls wandering the beach in bikinis than the water skiers.

Noah was intrigued by the specialized boats used in the show. They had inboard motors, tow arches spanning the width of the boats, and platforms off the back that made it easier for people to get in and out of the water. The kid was already researching brands, options, and costs, as if buying one was in their future.

Val scoffed at the notion, reminding him they couldn't afford a jet ski, let alone a huge, specialized ski boat.

Luke took offense at her comment, as if it were a personal attack on his ability to provide for the family—which of course was not how she'd meant it.

When had they lost their ability to communicate? She was beginning to worry more and more that their marriage might actually be in trouble. Most anything either of them did drove the other one nuts.

After running all four boys through the shower and sending them to bed, Val and Luke followed suit. Luke seemed to doze off immediately, so Val tried to read a few pages of a book. Unable to concentrate, she tossed the book back down on the nightstand and turned off the light. When Luke reached for her, she didn't resist.

They came together, much as they always did, being careful to be as quiet as possible. Val tried to think back to their early days as a couple, when they didn't have to have nearly silent sex to hide it from the kids. Those days of spontaneity were long gone. It seemed their days of feeling at ease around each other were gone, too.

She missed them.

* * *

"Where's Luke today?" Lavonne asked as she pulled chunks of raw hamburger from the pile and used her hands to mold patties. "Did he head back to the farm already?"

Val shook her head as she stirred a pot full of baked beans, simmering on the large stove in the lodge kitchen. "These smell terrific, Mom. Thanks for bringing them. I sometimes forget what a great cook you are. No, Luke hasn't left yet. Tomorrow. He wanted to go spend a few hours working on the kitchen at home. He said he'll be back here in time to eat."

"Good. I'd hoped we'd get to see him. Say, I've been curious about his reaction to the camper. Does he see the possibilities?"

Val beat the wooden spoon on the edge of the heavy pan harder than necessary and looked down in disgust when juice spattered the front of her lightweight blouse. "How do you *think* he reacted, Mom?"

Lavonne gave Val a steady look, her hands continuing to methodically mold one patty after another. "I don't know, Val. That's why I asked."

"*He* thinks I'm being ridiculous. He didn't even believe it was mine at first. He assumed it was Seth's, and then Ethan's. When I asked him this morning if he wanted to help me work on it today, he refused. Said he had '*real* work' to do over at the house."

Val dabbed at the front of her shirt, hearing her mother's sigh. She braced herself.

"He might come around," Lavonne said, and left it at that, saying nothing more as she covered the tray of hamburgers and placed it in the fridge.

No lecture? Val thought, glancing toward her mom. She'd half expected Lavonne to tell her she probably shouldn't have taken on the camper project without talking to Luke first.

Maybe I should have. Mom probably wouldn't have done something like that without talking to Dad first.

"Has your sister said anything more to you about picking a date for their wedding?" Lavonne asked, surprising Val further with the change in topic.

"No, why? Did she say something to you?"

Her mom's question reminded Val that she'd paid little attention to Jess lately. She'd been so wrapped up in her own work on the camper, and worries over Luke, that she'd kind of forgotten about Jess and her pending wedding.

"She just asked me if we had any plans in late August. But she didn't say why. I'm not sure why else she would ask that, if not to start to make some plans."

"Mom, it's already almost the end of July. Do you think they'd do something that soon?"

Lavonne reached into a low cupboard under the island and pulled out a large pitcher. "Lemons?"

Val pointed to the fridge, then pulled out a cutting board, knife, and reamer. Years spent preparing meals in the kitchen with her mom allowed them to do some tasks with few words. Lavonne rolled the lemons across the island toward her, and Val scooped them up and sliced them each in half.

"I think Jess and Seth just want to be married. I get the impression a simple ceremony would be enough for them. Initially, Jess thought Seth would want a big, fancy wedding, but now I'm not thinking that's the case. She does seem interested in maybe wearing that old dress she found in Celia's attic, though."

"Mom, earlier you said you thought that was a bad idea. We don't know who it belonged to."

"Does it matter? We might never know who, if anyone, ever wore it before, but I don't see why Jess shouldn't wear it for her own wedding, if that's what she wants. I'm entitled to change my mind, you know."

"You are," Val said, nodding. She took one of the lemon halves and pushed the pulp side down onto the reamer, twisting it from side to side. She loved homemade lemonade and was glad Lavonne had thought to make it. "I think that would be great, actually. Maybe a simple beach wedding at sunset? We should ask her later at dinner. I wonder if the dress fits her."

"I have no idea," Lavonne said, handing Val another lemon half. "But let's suggest it."

Val nodded, finished up with the lemons, then licked her fingers, puckering at the bite of the juice. "God, that's sour."

Lavonne set the canister of sugar next to Val. "Time to sweeten things up."

"With another wedding?" Val asked, suspecting Lavonne wasn't only talking about lemonade.

Her mother grinned, holding out a clean wooden spoon to her. "Love and marriage can sometimes feel a little sour, and you have to add in a little sugar to sweeten things back up."

"And is that your not-so-subtle marriage advice for the day, Mom?"

"I don't know what you're talking about," Lavonne declared, wiping her hands on a dishtowel and walking toward the door. "Why would you ever take advice from me?"

Stirring the lemonade, Val watched her mom walk out of the kitchen, leaving her to her own thoughts. Something she'd had more time to do lately. She wasn't at all sure the extra reflection time was doing her much good.

* * *

"I can't believe we ran out of hamburgers," Lavonne said later, when they were cleaning up after a lively afternoon and early evening of fun.

Val laughed. "That's what happens when the kids spend hours swimming and playing outside."

Renee and Jess came through the door, both carrying an armful of dishes and leftover food.

"Why is it that the dessert is always gone but there are leftover salads?" Renee asked, setting down a half-eaten bowl of garden salad. "I didn't even get a brownie."

"You don't really expect an answer to that question, do you?"

The four of them worked in silence, cleaning up the mess.

"Just once," Jess said, "I think we need to make the guys clean up."

"Next time," Lavonne agreed. "Matt and his friend, Ross, get a pass until they're healed. They still look pretty sore."

Renee rolled her eyes. "I think *Ross* is still pretty sore. He's moving like his ribs are bugging him. Matt, on the other hand, might be working it just a little."

"Yeah, Ross's chest looked really bruised the morning after the fight," Val said, stacking leftover buns back into a bag.

It took her a second to notice the silence around her. Renee, Jess, and Lavonne were all staring at her, strange looks on their faces.

"What?"

Then she realized what she'd said. *Damn.*

"Just how far did you take your nursing duties?" Renee asked, a teasing note in her voice.

Jess just looked confused. Lavonne's expression was harder to read.

"What are you two talking about?" Jess asked.

"Oh, nothing," Val said, handing her the ingredients for s'more's. "Take these out to the kids, will you?"

Jess took the stack of graham crackers, chocolate bars, and marshmallows from Val but set them down on the island. "Oh, no, you don't. I'm not that easily distracted. Why were you nursing Ross? I mean, obviously someone beat him up, but where do *you* fit into the equation?"

Sighing, Val crossed her arms and leaned against the island. "Ask Renee. It was her idea."

Renee shrugged. "As you already know, Matt and Ross ran into some trouble at the bar the other night. Matt said some drunk guy was hassling the waitress, who was clearly twenty years younger and not at all interested. Before he could do anything about it, Ross stepped in. Told the guy to knock it off, getting in his face, shoving. Matt said it was out of character for Ross. Almost like Ross was looking for trouble—even though telling the guy to knock it off *was* the right thing to do. To quote Matt, Ross 'wasn't quite as diplomatic as usual.' Things dissolved pretty quickly, and you can tell from looking at them now that they didn't escape unscathed."

"Were you out with them?" Jess asked, looking at Val.

Val laughed. "Not *that* night."

"I'm not following. Where does the nursing come in?"

Renee sighed. "Both Ross and Matt took some pretty tough hits to the face and head. Neither was willing to go get checked. Stubborn mules. But I was still worried and hated the thought of Ross being alone in the Gray Cabin. What if he had a head injury or something? Matt stayed with him, and when he had to run to work in the morning, Val gave Ross a hand for a bit."

"I didn't do much," Val insisted. "But the guy did help me out when I banged my head in the camper. He ran me to the ER, even, insisting I needed stitches—and he was right. I just wanted to return the favor."

Jess nodded. "Right. The snake episode. So, baby sister, back to Renee's initial comment. Just how far did you take your nursing duties if you saw Ross's bare chest? How did the rest of him look? Pretty good, would be my guess."

Val glared at both of her sisters. "You two need to shut the hell up. If Luke hears you, he'll be pissed again. He wasn't too happy about Ross in the first place."

Renee grinned, but she let the subject drop. "Come on, Jess. Let's take these out to the kids."

Val watched them both prance out the back door. They were obviously pleased with their successful attempt to rile her up. She tossed the bag of buns onto the counter, then carried the ketchup and mustard over to the fridge, pulled open the door, and tried to force them into the already-full shelves, frustration fueling her actions. When she finally found a slot for both bottles, she spun around—

Only to find her mother watching her with steady eyes.

"Not you, too."

"Honey, ignore them. You know they're only teasing. But you do need to be careful. Relationships are more fragile than you think. Sometimes one bad decision can ruin everything."

Val opened her mouth to protest—she'd done nothing wrong—but Lavonne held up a silencing hand.

"Just be careful," her mother repeated, then turned and left the room.

The heat of embarrassment she'd felt over her sisters' teasing faded away with her mother's solemn warning. As much as she hated to admit it, her mother was right.

CHAPTER TWENTY-FOUR

GIFT OF COOL WATERS

A bead of sweat rolled down Val's back. The white shield covering her nose and mouth, plus the safety goggles she wore (both at Ethan's insistence), made it feel twenty degrees hotter inside the camper than the eighty-degree temperature outside. The air was hazy with dust from the vibrating sander she ran up and down the wall of cabinets. She still didn't understand why she couldn't just paint them, but she trusted that Ethan knew what he was talking about.

She'd been up with the dawn, and her husband. He'd left, needing to get back to the farm to meet with a lawyer and insurance adjuster. The business of death could be painfully long when it involved a family farming operation.

Luke wasn't planning to come back until the third week in August, when their new cupboards for their kitchen were due to be delivered. Just in time, too: he'd promised to have their house ready in time for Val and the boys to move home before the start of their school year.

She planned to be done with camper renovations by then, too. Renee and Jess would start holding their women's retreats at Whispering Pines in October, as usual. They'd loved the idea of utilizing

Val's camper this year. No one was quite sure yet what that would look like, but it was a start. And it gave her a timeline.

Kneeling down, she moved the sander over the lowest cabinets. She'd decided to paint them white. It would brighten things up considerably and provide a versatile backdrop. Tomorrow she planned to drive to town to pick up the paint and supplies. She'd arranged to have the old flooring ripped out and new flooring put in while she was gone.

A touch on her back made her drop the sander in surprise. Whipping her head around, she was surprised to see Ross standing there, holding two bottles of water. Val turned off the tool, still vibrating against the floor, and stood. She removed her mask and pushed the safety goggles to the top of her head.

"Sorry. I yelled your name but you mustn't have heard me."

"I hope one of those is for me," she said, pointing to the bottles.

He handed one to her, nodding. "It's getting hot out, and I could hear you working in here. Damn, it's *hotter* in here! Anyway, I thought I'd stop and say goodbye. I'm taking off this afternoon."

"Already?" Val asked, disappointed. "I thought you were staying through the end of this week."

"That was my original plan. But my supervisor called. He needs me back tomorrow for a meeting with IA."

"Internal Affairs?" Val asked. "That sounds . . . ominous."

"Not really. Pretty standard stuff any time we hit a rough patch in a case. That happened shortly before I headed here for vacation. In fact, things got ugly. Bad enough for me to finally take Matt up on his offer to come back to Whispering Pines for a visit. I needed a break. I guess reality is rearing its head again now."

"Let's talk outside," she suggested. "I'm roasting in here."

Ross looked around at the progress she'd made. "I don't have to leave for an hour or two. Need any help before I go?"

Shaking her head, she dropped her mask and goggles on the counter. "I need a break. Fresh air sounds better."

Ross followed her out onto the grass. A light breeze felt wonderful after the dusty confines of the Airstream. She opened the water bottle and took a long drink. "What I wouldn't give to go jump in that lake right now to cool off."

"What's stopping you?"

She hadn't really been serious, but he did have a point. She laughed. "These jeans would get awfully heavy if I torpedoed off the end of the dock in them."

He shrugged, grinning. "Put your suit on. Or shorts, at least. Take a break while it's the hottest part of the day and go back in there later if you have to."

"It *is* tempting . . ."

"Go," he ordered, pointing toward the duplex. "I'll wait. I'm getting hot just looking at you."

Why not? she thought. When she'd decided to come to Whispering Pines with the boys for the summer, she hadn't intended to work the whole time. Her kids had gone down to the dock hours ago. Maybe she should join them.

She was inside the duplex, upstairs, and back outside in a matter of minutes, now in much cooler shorts and a tank. There was no way she was wearing her swimming suit in front of Ross. Storm trotted along beside her.

"You were right—this is *much* better. Why don't we walk down by the water? The boys are swimming down there. Storm was ready to get outside, too."

Ross nodded and fell in step next to her, the dog on his other side.

"Val, I wanted to be sure to thank you before I left today. Getting to know you made this trip a whole lot more fun. That brother-in-law of yours is a busy man, but you helped me stay occupied when he was at work."

Val smiled up at him as they walked. "Honestly, you made the last couple weeks more fun for me, too. Always willing to try my experiments in the kitchen, helped us pull the camper out of the woods, even hauled me to the ER."

Ross chuckled. "And you made sure I lived to see another day after my less-than-brilliant altercation at the bar."

They walked along in silence then, both lost in their own thoughts.

Storm wove back and forth from side to side on the path, her nose leading the way.

"Did you make any decisions about whether or not you're going to make a career change when you get back?" Val asked.

He nodded. "I think I'll finish out the year, but start putting some feelers out. I want to make a change, but I'm not sure yet if that means leaving law enforcement altogether or just mixing it up, kind of like Matt did by going somewhere smaller, slower paced."

They'd reached the edge of the sand leading down to the beach. Her four boys were making a racket, playing on the big black inner-tube. Robbie was on it as well, as were a couple other kids Val didn't recognize. She was glad to see Dave had made Jake wear a lifejacket, and that Noah was sticking close to the rest of them this time. Those two always seem to get into trouble around water.

Val paused, kicking off her sandals. "I think Matt enjoys his job now. There are tough days, just like anywhere, but he never complains. Not like old Sheriff Thompson. That guy was more than ready to retire by the time Matt came along."

"Matt was in the right place at the right time," Ross pointed out. "It seldom works out that well."

"True. He never would have even met Thompson if not for Julie's psycho ex-boyfriend. It's funny how things work out. Be sure Matt keeps me posted on what you decide."

Ross nodded distractedly. He was scanning the beach and checking the water. Always on guard. Always watching for trouble. "Why don't you give me your number so I can keep in touch? I'd love to see pictures of your camper when you get it finished."

Val debated, knowing it might not be a good idea. She remembered Luke's anger; she remembered her mother's warning. But she also considered Ross a friend. He was a close friend to Matt, had helped Renee out when she was in a bind—even before she was married to Matt—and had helped Val, too. He was her friend. Nothing more. She pulled her phone out, asked him for his number, and sent him a text so he'd have hers. No need to make it awkward.

"Let's go sit out on the end of the dock," Val suggested. "I'd love to get my feet wet."

Storm nuzzled the back of her leg. The dog carried a big stick in her mouth.

"You want to play, do you girl?"

She trudged barefoot across the sand, kicking up little plumes in her wake, holding Storm's stick high. Ross walked beside her, grinning at the dog's growing excitement.

"Hey, Mom! Did you bring snacks?" Jake yelled from the tube when he saw her.

She laughed, shaking her head. Jake's disappointment was evident, even from shore.

"Hey, I've eaten some of your snacks. I understand why he's disappointed," Ross pointed out as he stepped up onto the weathered wood of the dock.

Val stepped ahead of him, wound up, and whipped the stick out into the water as far as she could. Storm bolted, making an impressive leap off the end of the dock. The dog seemed to stay suspended for an inordinate amount of time before splashing through the surface of the water, disappearing. The kids in the water clapped and hooted their approval over the dog's acrobatics. When Storm didn't surface, Ross walked quickly to the end of the dock, stopping beside Val. He fidgeted, clearly concerned.

"Wait for it," Val said, raising one hand.

"Hasn't it been too long? Maybe she caught a foot on something."

But Val kept her hand out. She could feel the tension coiling in Ross, knew he was seconds from going in after the dog. While that would be entertaining, it was completely unnecessary.

An eddy swirled in front of them. At first, just the end of a stick popped up, but then Storm surfaced, stick held proudly between her strong jaws. Another round of cheers erupted from the kids.

"You weren't even worried, were you?" Ross asked, incredulous. "I can't believe she can stay under that long."

"Watch," she said, laughing. "She'll want to do it twenty more times, too."

Val crouched down and sat, her feet dangling over the end. She had to scoot as far forward as possible in order to reach the water. Ross stayed standing, watching Storm swim to shore and then race back up the dock in their direction. The dog swerved around him at the last minute. Val could see the dog was out of control and braced herself for the possible impact, but Storm's momentum was too much. One minute she was enjoying Storm's antics, and the next the water was closing in, rushing over the top of her head.

She wasn't scared. The water was deep here, and as she sank down, she could feel the temperature gradient—much colder down around her feet and ankles. Then she felt the tickle of the reeds and, finally, the muck of the clay bottom. Bright sunlight flickered down from above. All was silent . . . peaceful. She let herself go, if only for a moment.

Something brushed against her lower leg, something fast and slick, the sensation out of place and disconcerting. She kicked hard toward the surface, her head bumping against Storm's midsection. The dog's body held her down when she'd expected to reach air, causing her to gulp in a mouthful of lake water.

Strong hands gripped her flailing wrists and she felt herself being lifted bodily up and out of the water, sputtering and gasping for air. The water sluiced off her as Ross hauled her up and over the end of the dock, twisting her so she wouldn't scrape her belly or legs on the way up.

She landed on her side, dazed but unhurt. Rolling onto her back, she stared up into the brilliant blue sky, the sun a hot yellow.

"Val, are you okay?" Ross asked, kneeling over her, his face blocking out the vivid orb of the sun.

Squinting up at him, she imagined how ridiculous she looked, lying there like a drowned rat. Nodding, she sat up, pushing her streaming hair back out of her eyes. She shivered with the shock and chill, reached for where she'd felt that fast, slick thing. "Something hit my leg down there."

"What do you mean?" Ross took her leg in his hands to inspect it, causing her to tip backward nearly onto her back again.

She pulled her leg away, looked at it herself, but saw nothing. "It must have been a big fish. Eww," she cried, shaking her leg as if dislodging something nasty from it.

Ross laughed.

Looking around, she drew in an alarmed breath. "Where's Storm?"

Ross pointed toward the beach behind them, to the left. "Right there. She's fine."

Sure enough, there was Storm, sitting in the warm sunshine as if she didn't have a care in the world, her stick at her feet.

"Oh no!" Val cried, remembering her phone had been in the pocket of her shorts. It wasn't there anymore. "My phone fell out in the water."

"Do you want me to go down and try to find it?"

Val fell back again, this time throwing her arm over her eyes to shield them from the sun. "It's probably not worth it. It'll be water-logged by now."

Ross stood up and slipped over the edge, into the water, despite Val's words. He surfaced empty-handed twice, gulped air, and tried again. The third time was the charm. He set the dripping phone next to her, gripped the edge of the dock, and with a mighty thrust came to a rest sitting next to her. She quickly scooped up her phone before another wave of water could hit it.

"Matt might have to update you as to what I decide to do after all," Ross joked. "Your phone might be TKO."

Val sighed, waving a reassuring hand in the direction of her kids when they yelled over to make sure she was all right, and then grinned up at Ross. "At least I'm not hot anymore."

* * *

"I like what you've done with the place," Lavonne offered, a touch of sarcasm in her voice as she wandered the inside of Val's partially renovated camper. "Instead of putting a built-in couch back in this area, what if you left it open like this and set a rectangular table in this direction, one that could sit six or eight?"

300

Pausing her broom in midsweep, Val considered her mom's suggestion. "You don't think it's necessary to have somewhere comfortable to sit?"

"It depends on what you want to do in here, of course, but I keep thinking you'll land on small group classes or one-on-ones, teaching cooking. Healthy eating, maybe?"

"Hmm . . . I *have* done talks on that at some of the retreats. Healthy eating, I mean. People have seemed very interested. Lots of questions, and I always go over my allotted time. Drives Jess nuts!"

Lavonne laughed. "That's our Jess. Doesn't like to be thrown off schedule. Ever!"

"I wonder what ever happened to the dining room table from Celia's? Ethan isn't using it. That would be perfect in here."

"Maybe that's in the attic, too?"

Val shook her head. "I didn't see it. Though I suppose it could have been covered with boxes—I wasn't looking for it when we were up there earlier this summer."

Lavonne stood in the spot where the table might go, gazing at the holes in the bank of cabinets where the old appliances used to be. "It's too bad you couldn't put full-size appliances in here, though, if you're teaching cooking."

Val leaned on her broom, considering. "Yeah . . . I don't think that's realistic. But what if this space were used for discussions, maybe simple demonstrations on a stove top, and more involved tasks were done in the lodge kitchen? There's plenty of space in there, and nicer appliances."

"You're thinking you'll leave the camper parked out here, then, at Whispering Pines?"

Val nodded. "At least for now. But I also think it would be fun to travel with it. I mean, it's an *Airsteam*, after all!"

"Where would you go?"

"I could maybe take it to different events in the area. I could even take it to farmers' markets sometimes. I want to make the outside eye-catching, too. How fun would that be?"

Lavonne beamed. "Extremely."

"Do it with me, then?" Val suggested, meeting and holding her mother's eye.

"Do what with you?"

"Why don't we partner on some things? You know, kind of like Renee and Jess do with the retreats."

Initially, Val had assumed any type of business she set up would be a solo venture. But she liked the idea of teaming up with her mom— the way they used to when Val was growing up. Even recently they'd partnered well, working to figure out the necessary tweaks to the sugar cookie recipe, and then Lavonne had helped spread the word about Val's talent to her friends.

"I *do* think that would be fun . . ." Lavonne paused, finally shaking her head. "But I don't have much to offer. Our time in the kitchen resulted in the student exceeding the skill of the teacher a long time ago."

Val laughed. "That's bull. Maybe my *interest* exceeded yours, but not my skill. Besides, didn't some of your volunteer work at the hospital involve working with a nutritionist?"

"It did, but that was years ago. Things have changed dramatically since then."

Val grabbed a dustpan and got back to her sweeping. "I'm not interested in teaching about the latest fads. I want to give people a solid foundation they can build on. I love the idea of helping people tweak some of their favorite recipes to make them healthier."

Val dumped a panful of debris into the large, industrial-sized garbage tub her brother had loaned her and turned back to Lavonne. "I think people want to get out of the habit of eating out so much, both for health and financial reasons, but it can be hard when life is always moving so fast. You and I know how to do that. We could help teach others how."

Lavonne still seemed hesitant. "You'd really want me involved in your business?"

Val nodded, smiling. "If you're interested. What do you think?"

Finally, her mom returned her smile. "I think it would be fun!" But she paused. "Though I don't want to work all the time. I am used to the retired life, you know."

Laughing, Val set the broom and dustpan against the cabinet wall. Her excitement ratcheted up at the prospect of including her mom in her fledgling business ideas. "I'm not looking to work you to the bone, Mom. But I do think it would be fun to build something together, whatever that ends up looking like. Are you in?"

Lavonne's eyes roamed the interior of the camper. Val thought she could see a twinkle there, one that had dimmed in recent years. "I'm *in*."

Val gave a celebratory fist pump.

"You looked just like Jake when you did that," Lavonne joked, but then she sighed, her expression turning serious. "I'm in on one condition, though. You need to take the lead. I'll help where I can, but this still needs to be your deal. Your creation. When we disagree on something—and Lord knows we will—you need to have the final say. But I've got your back."

Val smiled at her mom from across the half-gutted camper. "Mom, you've always had my back."

* * *

By the time Luke was due back three weeks later, the interior of Val's camper was completely renovated. The old, split linoleum was gone, soft spots in the floor shored up, and new tile, more durable and easier to clean, had been installed. The walls and cabinets were painted a fresh white, giving the illusion of a much roomier interior. Newer, better quality appliances were installed, along with a bigger sink and faucet. George had indeed found Celia's old farmhouse-style table in the basement of her old house, the one Ethan now owned and lived in, and her brother was happy to have Val take it. A coat of white chalk paint, along with strategically placed distressing, would provide the perfect working surface. Bright pillows, curtains, and kitchen towels added inviting splashes of color. Three cabinet doors had been removed, and open shelving held a variety of pastel-colored bowls and serving dishes. The inside was fixed up, but not the exterior. Val was researching what it would take to clean it up. The original surface had probably gleamed like a mirror when new, but those days were far in the past. Videos showing how to polish it warned of hours, maybe even days, of work. There wouldn't be time to work on the camper over the next week. Luke was coming back, and they'd planned to get their kitchen fixed up. Val and the boys would need to move home soon. School would start the Tuesday after Labor Day.

She looked at the Airstream's exterior and thought, *Might be a great project for next summer.*

Val again met her husband in the parking lot when he pulled into Whispering Pines. There was so much she wanted to show him with the camper. She could only hope he'd be more enthusiastic about it this time, now that the inside was in great shape.

"Hey, hon," he greeted her as he stepped down out of a tall, black Chevrolet pickup, the sides covered in dust and dirt.

"Where's the Ford?"

"At the farm. The alternator was giving me trouble and I'm waiting for a part. Dad suggested I drive Alan's truck. It needs to be driven once in a while. Hard on them to sit."

Val met him in the gravel, sliding her arms around his waist and resting her cheek on his chest. He hugged her back, taking a deep breath, as if inhaling her scent.

"I missed you. And the boys. Where are they?"

"Probably hiding from me. Afraid I'll put 'em to work," she replied, her words muffled against his shirt.

"Well, they sure as hell know *I'll* find something productive for them to do. They can't just play all summer."

She didn't like the bitter note in his voice. All she could do was hope it would fade with time, and her old Luke would reemerge. Her heart squeezed at how he must have felt, driving for hours in his dead brother's truck. Could he still feel Alan's presence there, imagine his hands on the steering wheel? It was a good reminder for her to be patient with him. It would take however long it would take.

"I'm glad you're back. Anything new with your folks? Or the farm?"

Luke squeezed her tight, dropped a kiss on her forehead, and stepped back. "Just lots to do," he said, his voice resigned. "But I'll stay for the week. We need to get our house back in order. Life has to return to *some* kind of normal at some point, right?"

"It will, babe. I'm just glad to have you home. Do you want to see what I've been up to?"

He dropped the tailgate and pulled his duffle bag out of the back, throwing it over his shoulder. Then he went to the cab and motioned inside. "Grab that, will you?"

A covered container sat on the backseat. "Treats?"

He nodded. "Compliments of Mom. She sent caramel rolls. She wasn't up for making them for the boys when they were there, but she had a good day yesterday."

Val could almost taste the mouthwatering caramel she knew her mother-in-law was capable of making. "I don't suppose she sent her recipe, too?"

Luke laughed. It sounded like music to Val's ears. "I said she was having a good day, not that she'd turned over a new leaf. You know she'll never share that with you, don't you? She always says it's the one thing she can make that's better than yours, and she won't give that up."

"I had to ask. Come on. The boys are actually back at the duplex waiting for you."

"Not hiding from us, then?"

"Not yet." Val took Luke's hand. "They missed you, too."

* * *

After an early lunch of homemade caramel rolls, Luke suggested they all head over to their house for the afternoon. He wanted to check on the cupboard delivery and make a game plan for the coming week.

"That's fine, but I want to show you what I've done in my camper first," Val said.

"Yeah, Dad, you should see it. Mom did some cool stuff in there," Noah chimed in as he shoved one of the plates he'd just dried into the cupboard. There was an ominous sound of scraping pottery.

"If you chip up your Aunt Renee's dishes, you're going to have to mow the grass out here for the next ten years, mister," she warned.

Noah snorted. "Mom, these dishes aren't worth as much as I'd charge to make one pass over the yard in the back." Though, seeing the look in his mother's eyes, he was careful in placing the next dish.

"That old thing didn't look any different to me when we walked in a bit ago," Luke said.

Val turned back to her husband. "We've been busy inside. I wanted that part done before we have to head back home for school."

Jake shook dish soap off his hands, making a mess of the window above the sink. "Don't say the s-word, Mom! Can't we just stay out here at Whispering Pines forever? This summer was so *fun*! Maybe you could homeschool us."

"I know what we could do!" Noah jumped in. "Use your camper as a classroom! We could sleep in every day, do a couple hours out there until lunchtime, and then fish the rest of the day."

Val didn't realize she'd given birth to comedians. "I'd give that one week before I'm sent up the river for ten to twenty when your bodies disappear."

"Huh?" Jake said. Her attempt at humor had gone right over her youngest's head.

"That's a little dark, even for you, Val," Luke said, biting back a grin.

"They would be dark days if I attempted to homeschool *this* crew. None of us have the temperament for that. Boys, finish up in here. Jake, wipe that window off, too. I'll show your dad the camper and then we'll head home for the afternoon."

Val walked out, Luke right behind her.

Once outside, they could hear Dave and Logan talking in the back-yard. Luke had sent them back there with a shovel and a bucket after lunch, saying that it was their job to clean up after Storm at home and they could do the same thing here.

"You've made some progress, huh?" Luke said, pulling open the door to the camper. He let out a low whistle as he stepped inside.

Val followed him, pulling the door shut behind her. "So? Do you like it?"

Luke nodded, walking through to the back, his cowboy boots clicking on the new flooring. "I'm impressed. The paint brightens it up." He ran a hand down the front of the new refrigerator and across the digital panel on the new stove. "Nice. A little *spendy*, I bet."

Val shrugged. She'd only used a small portion of her money from Celia. Besides, he'd been wanting her to put it toward something special, and in Val's mind, this camper met that criteria. She refused to get in an argument with him over it. She couldn't tell from his tone whether or not he was trying to pick a fight.

"Wait. There's no bed in here anymore. What are you planning to do with this thing, if not camp?"

Val sighed, exasperated. "I told you camping was never my intent. I'm laying out the framework for a business, but it's still really early. I've decided to get Mom involved, too, in some way or another."

She could read the surprise on her husband's face. "Your *mom*? Why? She's been happily retired for years. Why would she want to do that?"

"Why not? She has time on her hands. I know she gets bored at times. When I suggested it, you should have seen how her face lit up."

"You've already talked to her about it?" Luke asked, his voice flat.

"Sure. I wanted her input. What's the big deal?"

"No big deal." But still the flat voice. "You've done a nice job in here. I'll be interested to hear what you're planning when you're ready to tell me," Luke said, walking to the door. "Let's go. We've got lots to do at home."

Tears stung her eyes as she watched Luke walk back across the side yard. Part of her was crushed at his lack of enthusiasm toward all she'd accomplished over the past month. But another part of her was starting to think there was something else behind Luke's crappy attitude. For some reason, their date night earlier in the summer sprang to mind. She missed that Luke. The fun Luke, the one who acted, at times, every bit as immature as their boys. But also the one who took her seriously and encouraged her to try new things.

She was starting to wonder if her patience would last long enough to allow her to find that man again.

* * *

It felt odd to walk back into their home after being gone for so long. It wasn't just the torn-up kitchen, either—the house itself felt empty. Hopefully that would change once they filled it with life again. The boys certainly did their part to bring the noise level back up to pre–Great Flood levels.

The atmosphere remained tense between Val and Luke. He had to feel it, too.

Weeks earlier, he'd decided to upgrade their cupboards, since they'd had to do so much repair work and tear into things anyhow. She'd been pleasantly surprised at the news. Luke had to have known how much a beautiful, functioning kitchen would mean to her. But now he was muttering comments as he worked about what a dumb idea this had been and how he shouldn't have wasted the money.

Yep, something is definitely up.

The new cupboards were due to be delivered later in the week. They needed to get the old set out, and Luke made everyone help. The boys did as they were told, no longer making so much noise; they seemed to sense their father's foul mood.

Finally, only one cabinet remained. Dave held one end, Logan the other, with Luke in the middle, unscrewing it from the wall. When the last screw let loose, the cabinet slid down the wall two extra inches and Logan lost his grip. Val, across the room and sweeping up years of gunk that had accumulated under a different bank of cabinets, gasped as the section the guys were working on tipped toward Logan.

Luke dropped his drill with a clatter, grabbed hold of the cabinet, and was able to help steady it before it fell on top of Logan, but not before the corner pushed against the large window overlooking the backyard. The sound of cracking glass reverberated through the kitchen.

She'd always doubted that window would survive her boys' many games of baseball in the backyard, but she'd never thought it would be broken from the *inside*. She braced herself for the inevitable outburst of anger from Luke, but it never came. There were grunts as they wrestled the heavy cabinet down to the floor and then out the back door to the garage, but no cussing this time.

"Wow," Jake said, walking over to the window and touching the spiderwebbed glass with his fingertips. "I can't believe Dad didn't totally lose it."

"Don't touch that, Jake!" Val yelled, setting her broom against the wall and rushing to his side, snatching his hand back. "The whole window could still come down."

She was every bit as surprised as Jake that Luke hadn't just lost his shit, but she didn't acknowledge her son's comment out loud. The tirade may still come. Even though it had been an accident, and no one's fault, the window would be expensive to replace.

Luke came back into the kitchen alone, visibly defeated.

"Where are Logan and Dave?" she asked, concerned.

"Restacking the cabinets in the garage so there's room for the new ones when they get delivered." Luke didn't meet her eyes. Instead of the anger she'd expected out of her husband, she saw despair.

"Jake," she said, "go help your brothers. And find Noah. He can help, too. He disappeared into the bathroom a while ago."

Jake glanced between his parents, then quietly left the room with a nod, yelling for Noah once he was away from the kitchen.

"That's going to be damn expensive," Luke said, looking at the busted window.

As if on cue, there was a cracking sound and the damage finally proved to be too much for the glass. A large chunk split off and fell, shattering into the sink, only jagged shards of glass remaining in the window frame.

A giggle escaped Val's lips before she could catch it, and her fingers pressed against her mouth in horror over her ill-timed response. Her eyes met and held Luke's. "Shazam?"

A smile played around the corners of his mouth and he held his arms out to her. She slipped into his embrace with a sigh, shaking her head against his chest, his T-shirt damp with sweat.

"What a mess," she grumbled.

His arms held her, but his touch was light, as if he were weak, exhausted. "I think we may have bitten off more than we can chew in here, hon."

"It's beginning to look that way, isn't it?"

They stayed like that for a space of time, offering each other the support they'd both been withholding lately. A second bit of glass broke off, its crash ending their peaceful moment. Luke stepped back with a sigh.

"Why don't you order pizza for the boys? You and I should get cleaned up. Let's go grab dinner somewhere."

Val gave him a sly look. "As in . . . a real, actual date?"

But Luke didn't pick up on her offer at levity.

"There's something we need to discuss, Val."

CHAPTER TWENTY-FIVE

GIFT OF NEW FRIENDSHIPS

*S*he'd showered and changed quickly, her husband's cryptic words wiping away her initial excitement about an evening out with him for the first time in two months. They took their seats at a nearby chain restaurant. The booths were spacious, giving them a modicum of privacy.

Val ordered a chicken salad, worried her nervous stomach wouldn't be able to handle anything heavy. Luke ordered steak. Apparently *his* stomach was fine.

Possible scenarios had been playing through her head, none of which boded well for their family. She was tired of the *what-ifs*, and caught Luke's hand from across the table as he fiddled with the coaster under his glass.

"Luke, what's going on? You have me really worried."

Somewhere between the busy intersection down the street and the restaurant parking lot, she'd convinced herself he was leaving her. Breaking up their family to shack up with Kennedy. Could she survive such a thing? How would it affect the boys?

Luke squeezed her fingers and left his hand limply wrapped around hers. With his other he took a sip of water, perhaps stalling.

Finally, he met her eyes. She braced for the words she'd convinced herself were coming. Her heart was already cracking, like the window pane had, and just like that window, if he said the words she worried might come, it could likely shatter into a million pieces. Despite the fact Luke had been driving her nuts all summer, she still loved him. Loved their history, the family they'd created, the home they'd built.

But those dreaded words didn't come. What he said was different, but still upsetting.

"I got a phone call from my boss. The company closed for good last week. I don't have a job to come back to this fall."

Despite the gravity of his words, relief surged through her. This *was* bad news, but it could have been so much worse. She pulled her hand back and ran it through her hair, still damp underneath from her shower. "Oh . . . thank God."

He looked at her as if she'd lost her mind. "I tell you I'm unemployed and you're *happy* about it?"

Val shook her head vigorously. "Of course not, I'm not happy you lost your job, it's just . . . I thought . . . I was worried you were going to say you were leaving me."

It was Luke's turn to shake his head. "What the hell goes on in that brain of yours? I can't even pretend to understand you these days. After all this time, all we've been through, you think I'd *leave* you? Why?"

"Shh," Val said, a finger over her lips. "Keep it down. Please. You're right, that was stupid of me. It's just that things have been so strained between us this summer, ever since . . . you know . . ."

Her voice trailed off as she blindly traced a scratch in the tabletop with her fingernail, her brain starting to consider the implications of what Luke had actually wanted to talk to her about.

"You'll just have to find a different job when you get back home after harvest. And I can pick up something part-time, too, if it takes you a while to find one or it doesn't pay as much. I don't have to do anything more with my business right now. That can wait until we get back on our feet. New businesses always take time to build. And we could always fall back on Celia's money if we had to."

Their server slid their meals in front of them and slipped away. Neither touched their food immediately.

"What if we tried something totally different?" Luke held a hand out to her again. She gave him hers, a natural reflex born out of years together. "I've been thinking a lot about this," he began. "Believe me, I have plenty of time to think when I'm on the farm. Lots of solitary work."

Before he even said the words, she could already feel resistance building in her gut. She suddenly knew what was coming.

"It might make sense for us to *move* to the farm. Start over. The boys would thrive there. Plenty of open space for them to run."

Val pulled her hand back, saying nothing as he pleaded his case. Instead, she picked up her fork and toyed with a chunk of chicken in her salad. Her brain—the one he claimed to seldom understand—was zinging, organizing rebuttals to his proposal to totally uproot their family. She let him talk on, expounding on the merits of the idea, but she'd stopped listening. When he eventually talked himself out, having run through the laundry list of reasons why this was their best option, he fell silent. He picked up a fork and knife, slicing off a hunk of steak. She continued to pick at her salad, her appetite gone.

The weight of the silence grew. She let it.

He chewed the steak, then picked a green bean off the tabletop that had fallen from his plate. Finally, he set his fork down.

"I'm guessing, based on your lack of response, that you aren't thrilled with the idea."

Val pushed her plate away, her food basically untouched. "Luke, moving to the farm would totally upend our life. It would mean different schools for the boys, a whole different lifestyle. They wouldn't have the opportunities they have here. They'd have to leave all their friends."

He held up a hand. "They've been away from all their friends this summer and they've done just fine."

"But that was temporary. They're getting anxious to get back and see everyone, to get back to their routine. We'd have to sell the house."

He only nodded, watching her. He'd apparently thought through all of these things already, arriving at the conclusion that they could make this work.

Val was nowhere near reaching the same conclusion. *Miles* from it. Everything in her railed against the idea. She decided to cut to the chase.

"Luke, you've never, *ever* had any desire to live on your family farm. Even as a kid, you wanted out. You wanted a different lifestyle. Hell, the only reason we ever went back there was to see your brother. Spend a little time with your folks. But the farm itself? It never pulled you back."

Luke shrugged. "Maybe it's grown on me."

"*Grown* on you?! No way. I don't believe it. Do you want to know what I think?" she asked, then rushed on without giving him an opportunity to jump in. "I think you're feeling guilty. Guilty because you think Alan never accomplished what he wanted to in life, and now you have to pay some type of twisted penance for it. And on that I call bullshit. Alan was a grown man, doing exactly what he wanted to do. It isn't your job to swoop in and save the family farm. You don't belong there. *We* don't belong there."

"That's where you're wrong, Val. I think that might be *exactly* where I belong."

His conviction left her speechless.

She tossed her napkin on top of the salad she'd barely touched and stood, grabbing her purse. She looked at him, gritting her teeth, doing her best to control her temper that was threatening to flare out of control. "We keep this between us for now. Got it? Not a word about this to the kids until we decide, *as a couple*, what we do."

He picked up his silverware again. "Wait in the truck. I'll give you a few minutes to think through this. You'll see I'm right."

Once again, tears threatened as Luke began to eat his dinner despite everything. She turned her back on him, head held high, and sought the quiet refuge of the truck. Of Alan's truck.

* * *

"And that was that?" Jess asked, her face incredulous in the glow of the bonfire. "You didn't discuss it any more after you left the restaurant?"

"We barely talked about anything after that. I'm sure the boys know something is up. But I made Luke swear to keep his mouth shut for now."

Val had needed to talk to her sisters, requesting this evening with the two of them. She'd been stewing over Luke's proposal for six days and was glad to have Renee and Jess to herself now. Seth was over at the duplex with Harper. Robbie was entertaining Val's boys at his house, playing video games. Matt was at work. Luke was back at his precious farm—instead of at their house, finishing their kitchen, like he'd promised.

Renee stood and topped off all their wine glasses again. Setting the now-empty bottle of wine on the grass, she sank back down into her chair, careful not to spill her glass. "Val, I get that the idea of moving away from everything you know can be scary. Moving here, to the resort, and taking it over? Two of the scariest decisions I ever had to make. But it turned out to be the best thing for me and the kids. Granted, it was hard for Robbie, changing schools so late in high school, but it worked. Julie loved helping me get the resort business going again. Have you thought this through? Are you sure Luke's idea is really so terrible?"

Val sipped her wine, swirling the tart liquid on her tongue, doing her best to give Renee's words consideration instead of lashing out at her sister for not automatically choosing her side. "The big difference between Whispering Pines and the farm, Renee, is you always loved it here. That was never the case for Luke. The idea of farming never held any appeal for him. At least that's what he always told me."

"Good point," Renee conceded.

"What would running the farm mean financially for your family?" Jess asked.

Val groaned—that was Jess, always the most business-minded of the family. She slid down in her lawn chair and dropped her head back to stare up at the velvety black sky above. It was a clear night.

Vast swaths of stars high above made her feel small, diminutive. Was she thinking small, letting the fear of change hold them back? She gave more thought to Jess's question.

"Long term, I don't know what it would mean. The only additional thing Luke shared with me on the topic after we left the restaurant was that he'd been talking to his parents about it and, surprise, they supported the idea. That probably means we could at least make some kind of living off the farm. Theresa and RC wouldn't want their grandsons to starve."

A log cracked deep within the firepit, sending up a rush of sparks that floated on the air. Val sat up, feeling the heat from the flames on her cheeks.

"Now you're being melodramatic," Jess pointed out.

"So what if I am?" Val shot back.

This was all so damn frustrating. She hated the idea of moving away from everything she knew to try to build a different life, out in the middle of nowhere, far from her family and friends. Luke was making the six-hour drive on a regular basis this summer, but she knew that wouldn't last if they actually *moved* out there. She'd be lucky if she saw her sisters, her brother, and her parents more than once or twice a year. But there was so much more to it than that.

"I'm scared," she admitted, looking between her sisters. "You've both done this over the past few years. You basically started over. Wasn't that *hard*? I mean, it's not like we're still in our twenties, with our whole lives ahead of us."

Jess snorted. "Hard? It was scary as shit, Val. But it's not like either of us really had much of a choice. You, on the other hand, probably do have more options. I see why you're concerned with Luke's plan. In all the years you two have been together, I've never heard him talk about the farm. It seems like his brother's death has really messed him up. It probably wouldn't be that hard for him to find a different job around here. He's a hard worker. He's fun."

"Not so fun lately," Val pointed out.

Renee waved her hand as if to banish Val's words. "Give the guy a break, Val. It's been a tough summer for him."

"I know it has, but you should try living with that. Not that I've really had to lately. The days when he's here are . . . I don't know . . . *tense*. I feel guilty saying it, but it's so much better when he isn't here."

"Do you think you two are going through *more* than a rough patch?" Renee asked, swirling her wine, the firelight reflecting off the glass. "This isn't like you."

"I'm beginning to wonder," Val said.

The slamming of car doors caught their attention.

"Maybe that's him now. Coming back to sweep his dear wife off her feet, to assure you that everything will work out," Jess teased.

"Yeah, like that's ever going to happen," Val said, draining her wine glass. "Do you have another bottle in the house?"

Renee shook her head. "Unfortunately, no. Matt might pick one up for us on his way home if I asked. He should be getting off anytime now."

"Now how would that look, me going into the liquor store to buy a bottle of wine in my uniform? Besides, I had to hustle if I wanted to get back before *he* arrived," Matt said, emerging out of the darkness into the ring of light cast by the bonfire. He wasn't alone.

"Hey, honey, I didn't realize that could be you in the parking lot already," Renee said, holding a hand out to her husband. Spying the man behind him, she looked surprised. "Ross? What are you doing back here?"

He nodded a hello to the three sisters then shot Matt a look. "You didn't tell them yet?"

Val was as surprised as Renee to see Ross walk up; her pulse kicked up a notch. When she'd said goodbye to him at the end of his time at the resort, she hadn't known if she'd ever see him again. She'd felt like she'd made a new friend, someone with a fresh set of eyes and perspective. She had been sad to see him go.

It had to be the wine making her heart beat faster now. She was a happily married woman.

That wasn't entirely true. *Usually* she was perfectly happy. Not at the moment, but usually.

"Tell us what?" Jess asked.

Matt moved to stand behind Renee, his hands resting on her shoulders. "I thought I'd wait until I got home instead of over the phone. I'm afraid I have some sad news."

Renee reached up and gripped Matt's hand, panic in her eyes. "It's not Julie, is it?!"

"Of course not! God, woman, why do you even think like that?" Matt said, rubbing her shoulders.

Renee just shrugged, relief flooding her expression.

Val understood, and knew Jess did, too; she remembered Luke saying nearly the same thing to her. *Why is it such a mystery to men that a woman's primary concern is for her kids? Do men and women ever truly understand each other?*

Matt was saying, "I received a call this morning shortly after I got to the office. I hate to tell you this, but Sheriff Thompson passed away last night."

Val felt a wave of shock and sadness course through her. She'd enjoyed their recent dinner together and hated the idea that the kind old man was gone. She looked to Ross. "Is that why you came back?"

He nodded. "Matt called me after he got word. I wanted to come. He was a great guy. Us old cops have to stick together."

She understood. She'd felt a kinship with the man, too, and she wasn't even in law enforcement.

Renee looked up at her husband. "Was it his heart?"

"It was," Matt confirmed, taking a seat on a hewn log flanking one part of their new firepit. "I hate that he didn't get more time to enjoy retirement. It hasn't even been two years yet."

"He would have had even less time if you hadn't taken over for him when you did," Renee pointed out. "Who knows, maybe he would have still been working, even."

The fire continued to snap and crackle as each of them thought back to the man who'd helped Renee out when she first came to Whispering Pines.

"He told me once that he used to come out here on calls when Celia ran the resort," Renee shared. "Now I wish I'd have asked him more about that. It would have been fun to hear some of that history."

"Hon, is the Gray Cabin open?" Matt asked.

Val glanced between her sister and Ross, guessing he was the reason Matt was asking.

"Not tonight. But the guests I have in there now are leaving tomorrow. Then it will be free. It isn't as booked up as my other cabins, since I didn't know for sure until the end of June or so that I'd be able to rent it out this summer. Ross, why don't you just stay in one of the bedrooms in the lodge tonight? We can get you back into your cabin later tomorrow."

"How do you like that? I have a cabin," he said, winking at Renee.

"And I'll only charge you twenty percent more since it's short notice," Renee teased. After a pause, her smile fell away. "It was nice of you to come. Sheriff Thompson was a special guy."

"He was a special guy," Ross confirmed. "But I don't want to cause you any extra work, Renee. I could stay at a hotel tonight, if that would be easier."

"Don't be ridiculous. It's no work at all. We don't use the bedrooms much in the summer, but they're all made up. We use them more in the fall and winter, for our retreats. The cabins aren't winterized, so those aren't an option too far into October."

Matt excused himself to go change out of his uniform.

"I'll come with you," Renee said. "Val had just asked about a second bottle of wine when you two pulled up, and given the news I think I have the perfect one."

"Wait," Val said, stopping Renee as she stood to follow Matt. "You said you didn't have any more wine."

Renee grinned. "I did say that, didn't I? Technically there *is* a special bottle of wine in my basement. It's the bottle Sheriff Thompson gave us for our wedding. I was saving it for something special. I think raising a glass to him among friends tonight would be the perfect occasion. Besides, if we don't use it for this, one of my snoopy sisters—or worse, children—are going to crack it open and drink it sometime when I'm not around, not knowing how special it is."

Val smiled. "Perfect."

* * *

Once Renee and Matt returned with the wine and two additional glasses, the cork was pulled and glasses filled.

"I'll start," Matt offered, holding his wine glass high. "To Pete Thompson, a man of integrity and grit. I have him to thank for suggesting I make a life here when he saw that a certain new resort owner had captured my interest."

"Here, here!" Renee laughed, raising her glass as well.

"I don't think I've ever heard his first name before." Jess grinned. "The poor guy was always Sheriff Thompson."

"*Almost* always," Val said, raising a finger. "But thanks to Matt, he had a little time when he didn't have to pin a star to his chest."

Jess stood up. "To a man who helped keep things safe at Whispering Pines, both during Celia's time and ours. Our family owes him many thanks."

Renee joined her. "I don't want to even imagine what might have happened to Julie that first Halloween here at the resort if not for that man. If he wouldn't have ignored all of his doctor's orders and went in search of my daughter on a hunch . . . I shudder to even think about what Lincoln might have done to her. I bet Sheriff Thompson did that often. Putting others ahead of himself without a second thought."

"A trait that makes for one of the best kinds of cops," Matt added, again tipping his glass to his old friend.

The women sat, and Ross stood. "I first met the sheriff at your wedding, Matt. We shared a beer together, and he talked to me about some of the lessons he learned over a lifespan of trying to help others. While he loved his work, he said he wished there were more programs to help keep kids out of trouble in the first place. Too often, troubled kids grow to be troubled adults, with bigger struggles and more heartache. Those words have stuck with me, and thanks to Pete, last week I finally took the leap I've been considering for years. I quit the force and enrolled in some classes to help me learn how to counsel and work with youth. And my time here this summer with all of you, at Whispering Pines, has inspired me to do some of that counseling outside, in nature. I don't know what that'll look like yet, but I owe it all to Pete Thompson for planting the seed."

"I'll be damned," Matt said, nodding in approval at his old friend. "You finally did it. I'm thrilled for you, bud—and I hope to partner with you on some of that in the future."

"Maybe you could even do some of that out of here, Ross," Renee offered, pointing in the general direction of the lodge. "Our retreats help women during the off-season, but there are plenty of weekends that are open. I have no idea what all you're considering, but keep us in mind when you're doing your planning. After that scare you helped me with, when Robbie got those pills at school, I learned an important lesson. Even the best kids can fall down a slippery slope. All of us should be doing something to help prevent that."

Val watched her family and new friend discussing the merits of Ross's new idea, spurred on by Sheriff Thompson's words of wisdom. She'd been curious what, if anything, had happened when Ross went back to work. The decision he'd shared as part of his toast to their friend felt right. Important. She realized it was her turn to raise a toast to the friend they'd all lost, and she stood.

"I didn't get to know Sheriff Thompson quite as well as some of you," she began, motioning around the circle with her glass, "but two encounters with him will forever change me. The first was the night he saved Julie. He took a chance that night, acted on a hunch, ignored any fear he must have felt, and saved my niece." She smiled at Renee. "I'm sure it was a regular occurrence for him, but for me, it was an important reminder of how bravery can change everything. And more recently, when I tagged along for an evening out with him, I realized how quickly new friendships can be born. So here is to being open to the beauty of new relationships. I'm thankful I got to know him better before it was too late."

Val raised her glass high, glanced at the star-filled sky above, and hoped the kind old man she'd shared an evening with not so long ago was at peace, no longer frustrated by the restrictions of his failing body.

As she sat back down, Ross raised his glass ever so slightly in her direction, and his smile reminded her that not all of her newest friends were gone too soon.

CHAPTER TWENTY-SIX

GIFT OF A WARNING

*A*fter they'd polished off the last of Renee's special bottle of wine, Val rounded up her boys from their video game competition with Robbie and took them back to their duplex. By the time they'd all showered, eaten late-night snacks, and finally gone to bed, it was nearly midnight.

As silence slowly descended around her, she couldn't help but think of Sheriff Thompson. How was his wife feeling tonight? Val didn't think they'd ever had kids, so she must feel so alone.

Val was thankful to have suffered so few losses in her life up to this point. She was thankful to have both parents, and while losing Celia still gave her heart a pang, the woman had lived into her nineties. Her passing hadn't been a surprise.

There's nothing like the finality of death to remind us of the importance of living every day to the fullest during our short time here, she thought, not quite ready to laugh at herself for repeating such an overused message. It was used often because it was valid. *Why does it take the pain of loss to remind us to get the most out of life?*

Her mind kept whirling and slipping into melancholy thoughts. She couldn't seem to go more than a day anymore without pausing to wonder if this was it. Did others feel this way?

began to pull together a large dish of lasagna, thinking she'd run it over to Sheriff Thompson's wife in the afternoon. She didn't know of a better way to help deal with the trauma of death, but she could do food.

She was sprinkling cheese over the top layer of pasta when Ross returned, fully clothed, his hair damp. He must have showered.

"Ready for that cup of coffee?" she offered, careful to keep her tone light and neutral. Her plan was to pretend their earlier exchange had never happened.

He gave her an odd look, as if trying to read her thoughts, and then walked purposefully over to the cupboard that held the mugs. "Yes, but I can get it myself. You've moved on from cookies to casserole? That seems a little heavy for seven in the morning."

She smiled, brushed her hands off, and then reached for a roll of tinfoil. "I thought I'd take this over to the sheriff's house."

He nodded. "Ah, yes. The age-old, slightly morbid practice of plying a dead man's family with food."

Laughing, she tore off a generous sheet and wrapped the top of the pan. "It isn't morbid. She'll likely have a houseful of people, and the last thing she'll want to think about at a time like this is how to feed everyone."

He carried his mug of coffee around to the other side of the island and took a seat. She couldn't help but notice it was a careful distance from her. He sighed as he took his first sip. "I know. You're right. I guess all the death I've witnessed through the years has made me cynical. I'm afraid none of our ingrained customs can take away the pain."

"I'm sure that's true, but maybe it can help a little."

She deposited the prepared lasagna pan into the fridge, then checked the timer on the stove. The air was filling with the comforting scent of vanilla.

"Why don't you tell me what happened when you got back to Minneapolis? How did it go when you gave notice? When will you be officially done? Do you plan to get started with this new mission of yours right away?"

He took another drink of his coffee, watching her over the rim of his cup. As he set it down, he shook his head. "All of that can wait. Val, I can tell you're upset about something. You said you needed a friend. Come on. Pour yourself some coffee, sit your butt down, and tell me what's going on. Then we'll gorge on those delicious cookies of yours, get your boys fed, and I'll go for a run. We can talk about my plans another time."

"Are you sure you want me to take you up on that offer? I have to warn you—there could be tears." She played it off as teasing, but part of her wasn't entirely sure she wanted to discuss any of this with Ross. He had proven to be a good listener in the past, though, and he might be less apt to judge her than her mother or sisters would.

But he looked at her sincerely. "I'll pretend not to be bothered by a few tears."

She paused. "I'm not sure where to begin."

"How 'bout what's bothering you the most right now?"

She snorted. "I'd have to flip a coin."

He shook his head slowly. "You're not as big of a mess as you seem to think. Val, I feel like I've gotten to know you some this summer. You keep your kids—and let's not forget that means *four boys*—in line with love and a fair amount of patience. You're a whiz in the kitchen and can feed big crews of people in a snap, probably with one hand tied behind your back. You worked your ass off fixing up that old camper you rescued from the woods. Not to mention, on top of it all, Storm worships you. In my opinion, dogs are the best judges of character."

Val felt a flush of appreciation for his kind words. Maybe she wasn't a *total* hot mess.

"Luke wants us to pick up and move to the farm—to his family farm—back in North Dakota."

"And you think that's a bad idea?"

She nodded, running her fingers through her hair in frustration. "It's a *terrible* idea. He's never had any desire to live on that farm."

"Are you worried about moving the boys?"

"Sure, but there's more to it than that. He claims it's the most practical solution. The company where he works closed its doors for good this summer. He's out of a job."

Ross considered her words. "Has he looked for something else?"

"No." She sighed. "I don't think so."

"You don't think so?"

"We . . . haven't discussed that part. But I'm concerned it might be about more than the job."

He nodded, encouraging her to go on.

"Well . . . he's spent some time with an old girlfriend since he's been back. And part of me thinks . . . what if that's the real reason? My boys even met her when they were out there a few weeks ago."

"Val, if your husband was having an affair with another woman, I doubt he'd parade her in front of your boys. Men and women *can* be just friends, you know. Look at us. No one would suspect us of having an affair."

She looked away, no longer able to meet his eyes. She didn't want them to, but his words stung. Of course Ross would never think of her in that way. She was a boring, unemployed, frumpy mother of four—exactly why she was worried her husband might stray.

The scream of the oven timer cut through the air and Val climbed off her stool. Trying to talk to Ross about problems in her marriage had been a mistake. He'd never even been married. Plus, he could never relate to her overwhelming sense of inadequacy. The man had confidence to spare.

She grabbed a potholder out of the drawer, flicked off the timer, and dropped the oven door, her motions automatic. As she reached in to pull out the first pan, the back of her hand grazed another, unprotected by the skimpy potholder.

"Shit!" she cried, pulling her hand back, the stabbing pain across her knuckles blinding. She shook her injured hand, tears leaking out of the corners of her eyes.

Ross was beside her in a flash, grabbing her near the elbow of her injured arm, his other hand on the small of her back. He pushed her quickly to the sink and forced her burn under a cool stream of water. The water turned colder, masking the sting, but her heart still stung.

The tears she'd warned him of flowed freely now. She managed to stay silent, but he must have felt the quaking of her shoulders, of her body.

"Hey, hey, it'll be all right," he soothed. His hand on her back began to make small, comforting circles.

Her stomach jumped at the contact. Blindly, she turned to face him, leaning into his chest, seeking comfort. He let go of her wrist, wrapping both his arms around her, swaying softly back and forth. His chin rested on top of her head. She took a deep breath in an effort to calm herself, but his scent only caused her nerve endings to jump. His arms tightened ever so slightly and his head tilted, his lips pressing into her hair.

Her senses were on high alert. She could hear the streaming faucet behind her, feel the extra heat pulsing out of the open oven door, and smell the heady mixture of freshly baked bread and clean man. Her wet hand was probably soaking his back.

Angling her head back, their eyes locked, barely inches from each other, his piercing gaze so much more intense than usual, drilling into hers as though trying to understand what she wanted, where this was going. She let her eyes wander over his face, pausing at his mouth.

What would it feel like to kiss him? Did she dare?

"Smells like something's burning in here!" a voice cut through the haze. The two of them leapt apart. Ross spun away, putting three steps between them as Val reached to shut off the faucet.

Val prayed her mother hadn't noticed her near-kiss with Ross in that split second, but the flabbergasted look on Lavonne's face said otherwise.

"I'll go grab the first-aid kit I saw in the bathroom for that burn," Ross improvised, disappearing through the door her mother had just come through.

Chickenshit, Val thought, dismayed.

She waited for the inevitable wave of guilt and shame to hit as her mother stared at her. Her mind grappled for a reasonable explanation she could offer up, an excuse she would believe. But what was the point? There was no excuse for something like this. Surprisingly, the wave of guilt hadn't hit yet either, although that may still come. Val would do her soul-searching later, when she was alone. But first, she needed to deal with this situation.

"I burned my hand," Val offered, gazing at the vicious red welt that ran across the back of her knuckles before holding it up for her mother to see.

She watched Lavonne inhale deeply, her eyes flicking between Val's injured hand, the open oven door, and the door Ross had made a quick exit through moments earlier.

"That's what happens when you play with fire," she finally said.

Val cowered under her intense stare. Her mother was obviously upset, but Val couldn't tell if she was angry or just extremely disappointed in her. Nor did she know which one would be worse. How could she even begin to explain her behavior to her mother? She didn't understand it herself. In all the years she'd been married to Luke, she'd never even been tempted by another man. It wasn't that she didn't notice them; she could admire them as well as any other woman. She'd just never felt any kind of pull to get close to anyone other than Luke.

Until Ross.

She was a mess and she didn't know what to do about it.

"I'm sorry about that, Mom."

Lavonne regarded her with solemn eyes. "Sorry I saw it, or sorry it happened? Because there is an enormous difference between the two."

Val didn't know how to honestly answer her mother's question.

Lavonne crossed her arms. "Do you think he's coming back with that first-aid kit?"

Despite the tension hanging in the air, Val felt the corner of her mouth tick up. "Not likely."

Lavonne pulled a clean dishcloth out of a drawer and filled it with ice cubes. "Sit down and put this on the burn. I have to talk to you about something."

The last thing Val wanted to do was discuss what just happened with her mother. She was a grown woman, not a kid needing to explain herself.

"I don't want to discuss it," Val declared, setting the wrapped bundle of ice on the island and resting her knuckles against it, palm up. "I have no idea how that just happened. One minute he was helping me with my hand, and the next I was crying and . . . I don't know, I guess we got caught up in the moment. It was stupid, I know. By the way, your whole 'playing with fire' inuendo wasn't real subtle."

Lavonne busied herself pulling the two cookie pans out of the oven, finally shutting the oven door. She helped herself to a bottle of water, stepped to the window to look outside, then took the stool Val had sat on earlier. Finally she said, "I'm worried about you, Val. You've been out of sorts for the past few months. Maybe even longer. You seem unmoored, lost. Do you want to talk about what's going on? And I don't mean what just happened. I think the problem goes much deeper than that."

"Why would you say that, Mom? I'm fine. Sure, it's been a tough summer, but things will get back to normal when we move back home and the kids are back in school."

"Will they?" Lavonne prodded. "Come on, Val. You were struggling well before things got topsy-turvy this summer. What's going on in that head of yours?"

Her mother was right, but Val was surprised she'd even noticed. She thought she'd hid her discontentment well from the rest of the world. Maybe not from her sisters, but everyone else. "I'm not sure, Mom. It's like I don't know *what* would make me feel better. I could blame all of this on Luke, but that wouldn't be fair. He's part of the problem, but I'm not sure there's anything specific he could do that would make me feel better. Other than drop this ridiculous notion he has of moving all of us to the farm."

Her mother seemed unfazed by Val's comment about the farm. Renee or Jess must have already shared this new dilemma with her. "It could be hormonal," she suggested. "You know, perimenopause."

Val couldn't help but roll her eyes. "Sure, let's blame it on the hormones."

"Look, honey, I'm worried about you. What I witnessed when I walked in here could totally derail your life. You do realize that, don't you?"

"Mom. Stop. It was a mistake. It won't happen again."

"Yeah, I've heard *that* before."

Val looked at her, confused. "What do you mean?"

Lavonne knotted her fingers together on top of the island, rubbing her thumbs together. Val recognized the nervous gesture her mother often made when something was weighing on her mind. She waited, curious.

"I said it myself."

"You said what?" Val asked, watching as her mother transitioned to full-blown hand wringing.

"*I* failed to heed the warning signs once, when I was much younger, and I nearly imploded my marriage."

"Mom, what are you talking about?" Val whispered, but she was starting to have an idea, and she was pretty sure she didn't want to hear whatever her mother was planning to say next.

Lavonne laid her palms flat on the island top, took a fortifying breath, and locked her eyes on something just over Val's left shoulder, as if she were unable to look at her when she shared her next words. "Honey, I'd never planned to tell you any of this. There was no need. But given what I just saw between you and Ross, and with how dissatisfied you've been lately, I feel like I have to. I want to save you from some of the pain I suffered. Some of the pain your dad felt."

Val shook her head and covered her ears with her hands. She didn't care how juvenile she looked or how much her burn stung. She didn't want the ideal picture of her parents' marriage she'd always carried in her mind to be shattered into a million pieces.

Lavonne looked at her. "Val, knock it off. I need you to listen to me, and I need you to promise to keep this between us."

Lowering her hands, Val instead crossed her arms in front of her chest, gripping her elbows. What choice did she have but to listen? She'd screwed up, *big time*, and this was her penance.

"Do you remember when I told you Celia suffered from breast cancer and had to have a mastectomy years ago?"

Val nodded. It wasn't something she was likely to forget, given her own struggles over a lump in her breast and the way the doctors were keeping an eye on her.

"It was summertime, and Celia wanted to come here to recuperate. To Whispering Pines. But she needed help, and your father volunteered me."

"When was this? Was I young?"

"You actually weren't even born yet. Ethan was about six, so Renee would have been four and Jess only two."

Forgetting that she wasn't likely to enjoy her mother's *whole* story, she was drawn in. "Dad volunteered to have you come here and help Celia while he stayed home with three little kids? Jess is a pain in the ass now—I can't imagine what a handful she had to have been in her terrible twos."

Lavonne laughed. "You have no idea. But to answer your question: yes, your Dad did exactly that. You see, I'd been really down. I was probably depressed, but that wasn't something that was so readily accepted back then. He thought it would be good for me to get away, to rest. Celia needed help, but you know how your aunt was. It wasn't like she was going to be too much trouble. It would be a three-week vacation for me, with a little bit of nursing care thrown in."

"You weren't working then?"

"No. Not outside our home, at least. Inside our home . . . that was a different story. But I don't have to tell you that, do I?"

Val knew exactly what her mother was referring to—the never-ending, often mind-numbing work of raising little kids and keeping a house while her husband escaped to go to work every day.

"Your father arranged to have Letty come in to watch the kids while he was at work."

Grinning, Val could only imagine how her jittery Aunt Letty, the childless wife of her dad's brother, would have done with three very active little kids.

"Exactly," Lavonne said, smiling. "Things were covered at home, and I desperately needed some alone time. I left my kids in Letty's semi-capable hands and came here, intending to do everything I could to find myself again. I hope that doesn't sound too woo-woo."

"No, not at all. Did it work?"

"Yes . . . and no."

Val braced herself for what she'd feared was coming.

"God, I never wanted to tell you any of this. I'm still ashamed. But I might as well get to the point. I met someone here. And just like you, I thought I'd found a new friend. Well, I had, but I wasn't careful. Looking back, I'd say I was even reckless."

"Part of me wants to ask what happened. But the other part of me really doesn't want to hear this," Val admitted, readjusting her towel-wrapped ice with her good hand and easing her injured one back down onto the chilly surface.

"I'll save you the torrid details, but suffice it to say my flirtation didn't end with a kiss."

Despite having anticipated such a terrible secret, it still hurt like hell to hear her say the words out loud. "You mentioned how hard it was on Dad. You got caught?"

Lavonne exhaled, causing the wispy white hair on her forehead to flutter. "Not exactly. I got swept up in the excitement of it, but we were very discreet. I was staying in what we now call the Gray Cabin. It ended up being two of the most thrilling yet heartbreaking weeks of my entire life."

"Did Celia know? How did Dad find out if no one caught you?" Val was struggling to wrap her head around her mother's recount of a nearly unbelievable love affair—if it *was* love.

"Initially, no one was the wiser. Celia was a very astute woman, but she was spending much of her time in bed, recuperating. If she had any suspicions, she kept them to herself. She was no prude. As my husband's sister, she never would have condoned me actually sleeping with someone, but she wouldn't have thought anything of some innocent flirtation. She had plenty of experience with men."

"Celia could date whoever she wanted to. *She* was never a married woman," Val shot back, hating the judgment that so clearly came through in her own words. *Like I'm one to talk.*

"You're right. She never married. And I hope she never had relations with a married man. But that's neither here nor there. This wasn't Celia's mistake. It was mine."

The self-loathing in her mother's voice nearly broke her heart. She waited, not wanting to push.

"It was a confusing time for me, to say the least. I still loved your father, but things had been strained between us for some time. I can see now that I probably suffered from postpartum depression through the years. It isn't an excuse, just part of my makeup. Anyhow, the time came when I had to go home. By then, I think I realized what I had with the other man—a summer romance, nothing more. It was completely inappropriate, but it wasn't like I fell into a deep, undeniable love for him. Later, I'd come to think of him as a stand-in to recapture what I felt I'd lost somewhere along the way."

Val couldn't help but think of Ross as her mother spoke. Was she destined to repeat the sins of her mother? Was she using Ross to provide a patch, likely temporary, over the holes in her heart? She hated to think that.

"How did Dad find out?"

Lavonne shrugged. "He didn't. Not right away. We went home, and I tried to pretend it never happened. But Val, it ate away at me. Every single day. I finally had to tell him."

"Oh my God. How awful. Poor Dad."

Lavonne was silent, giving Val time to process things.

"He obviously forgave you. That was all a really long time ago. How did you make it through together and get to the other side of the heartache?"

"Time, dear girl, time. And patience. With each other. It was by far the most difficult challenge we'd ever faced. We did weather the storm, and eventually I even found my way back to happy, but it took lots of work—including no more turning to people outside of our marriage vows. I also got some counseling. It was never easy, but it was worth it."

Val wasn't sure if she'd ever look at her mother in the same light again. She could barely believe any of it. The fact she'd nearly kissed

Ross earlier paled in comparison. Or did it? While things hadn't gone nearly as far as the scenario her mother had just shared, she still might have allowed it to happen if they wouldn't have been interrupted. Hell, she'd even initiated it.

The door from the inner hallway swung open and Ross reentered the kitchen, first-aid kit in hand. "I'm sorry that took so long. I got a telephone call from work. Is your hand all right?" he asked Val, not looking in Lavonne's direction.

"It'll be fine. The ice helped. Mom can help put some salve and gauze over it. Thanks, Ross."

He nodded, set the box in the middle of the island, and made a beeline for the back door, stopping just long enough to say, "I'll see you at the prayer service tonight. I'm off to get that run in now."

Val watched him go, feeling a touch of respect for him. It took guts to come back into the kitchen after what had happened.

"It's quicksand, baby," Lavonne warned Val, catching her eye. "Learn from my mistake so you don't have to live through the same pain that I did."

I'll try, Val thought.

She gave her mother a watery smile, quickly brushing away the single tear that escaped down her cheek. Val wasn't sure whether the tear was sympathy for the pain her parents had endured, or if it was for the pain she herself was feeling over the shattered illusion of her parent's supposedly perfect marriage.

She should have known better. *Perfection is always an illusion.*

CHAPTER TWENTY-SEVEN

GIFT OF SELF ASSURANCE

*T*he air felt close inside the church despite the peaceful sound of birdsong floating in through open windows. Someone thought to prop open the heavy front door. Val fanned herself with a funeral pamphlet as they waited for Sheriff Thompson's service to begin.

She'd arrived at the church alone, leaving her boys at the duplex to start packing. She planned to slip away at the conclusion of the service. Their summer at Whispering Pines was quickly winding down. She hated for the boys to be on their own for too long. They had a tendency to find trouble when left to their own devices.

Jess bumped her elbow and handed her a tissue. Smiling at the gesture, Val took it, suspecting her sister was worried she'd get teary-eyed again. She'd surprised herself at the prayer service the night before—she didn't normally cry in public—but it had been an emotion-packed day.

She could see Ross in the pew ahead of hers, where he'd joined Renee's family. She'd been careful to steer clear of him since their encounter in the kitchen. What might have happened if her mom hadn't walked in? The question, along with her mother's shocking confession, haunted her.

The pews were littered with men and women in uniforms from different branches of law enforcement. They'd come to pay their respects to a fallen comrade. There was a kinship here, born of the noble, often dangerous, profession they shared. Val knew Matt and Ross would feel it, too, as they stood proudly in their dress uniforms. She felt like an outsider looking in.

Unlike the previous evening, she remained stoic throughout the eulogy and the haunting strains of familiar hymns. After the solemn exit from the church into the midmorning sunshine, Val declined Renee's invitation to sit with them at the luncheon, driving back to the resort instead. The time had come to talk with her kids about Luke's desire to move to North Dakota.

No one was near the lodge when she arrived at Whispering Pines. As she walked up the sidewalk to the duplex they'd called home for the better part of the summer, she smiled at the evidence of her family's presence. Storm's leash snaked down the staircase, draping over a baseball bat someone had dropped near the bottom step. Jake's bicycle was propped against the bushes lining the front of the porch (leaving the bike outside in their neighborhood would be unwise, but no one bothered it here). A blue hoodie was draped over the porch railing.

It was nearly time to head home. Where had the summer gone? They needed to purchase school supplies and try on jeans, and she worried both would be picked over in the stores by now. The fresh air and sunshine of Whispering Pines had helped add inches to the boys' height, especially Logan's. But such was the life of a parent—keeping kids clothed and properly fed.

Spending the summer at the resort had been an unexpected blessing. It had left her rested and confident to take on all that the new school year promised.

While attending the funeral earlier, she'd found herself contemplating both the brevity of life and the finality of death, and she'd made a decision. Even though she'd asked Luke not to say anything to the boys about the possibility of moving to the farm, she'd realized they deserved to have a chance to weigh in on the subject. The sheriff's funeral brought back memories of her brother-in-law, but not just of his untimely death. Alan had been a good man, and despite Luke's concerns, she believed he'd enjoyed his life on the farm. Was she robbing her boys of the possibility of a similar lifestyle? She'd talk to them about it today.

Voices floated out through the screen door, reminding her of the noisy little birds outside of the church earlier. *This* was her life: her boys. She tiptoed up the porch steps, pausing at the top to watch them. Her three oldest were sitting on the old couch, looking at something on Dave's phone. Jake was standing nearby, facing them with hands on his hips. No one noticed her on the porch.

"It says here that you can't assume kittens have been abandoned by their mother unless she's been gone for at least ten hours," Dave was saying, reading from his phone. "Jake, the mom cat is probably off hunting for food or something."

"But what if the bear got her? Remember Mom and Uncle Matt told us to be careful and keep an eye out because there was a bear around here earlier this summer? I think we should bring both kittens inside to keep them safe just in case."

Logan shook his head. "No way, bud. We need to wait to see if the mother comes back. You can't even touch them. Otherwise, she might desert them, even if they're too young to survive without her."

Kittens? A memory tickled her mind. Had her kids discovered the source of the crying Ross heard while staying in the Gray Cabin?

"And remember, we have to leave tomorrow," Noah pointed out. "Do you really think Mom's going to let you bring two tiny kittens home with us?"

Logan snorted. "No way in hell."

Val stepped forward, purposely making enough noise to draw their attention. "What are you four up to in here?"

Four sets of wide eyes stared up at her.

"You guys look like you got caught with your hand in the cookie jar. Did I hear something about kittens?"

Dave tossed his phone onto the coffee table, facedown, then crossed his arms over his chest. "Jake found them. I told him there was no way you'd let him mess with kittens," he said, a confident look crossing his face.

"Actually, I believe I heard *Logan* tell him that, and I don't appreciate the language, kid," Val replied, shooting a meaningful look in Logan's direction. She turned to her youngest. "Jake, where did you find them? Were they by the Gray Cabin?"

Jake nodded, surprised. "Did you already know they were there? Why didn't you tell us? They are *so* cute, but I'm worried about them. I think they need a home."

"Ross said he thought he heard something crying at night when he was staying there, but when we looked we couldn't find anything."

"Well, we were playing hide-and-seek when you were gone, and I found them," Jake proclaimed, pride lighting up his face.

"Where, exactly?"

"In a hollowed-out log behind the Gray Cabin," Jake declared, but then his expression faltered, realizing he might have shared too much.

"Jake, I've told you at least a hundred times to stay out of the woods! You shouldn't be going behind the cabin!"

He crossed over to his mother and put both hands on her shoulders. It wasn't as much of a stretch for him as it had been at the beginning of the summer. "Mom, it's okay. I stayed super close to the building. It doesn't *technically* turn into the woods until at least twenty feet back from the cabin."

Val mimicked his gesture, placing her hands on his shoulders, his arms trapped between hers. "Jake, you totally made that up. Stay away from the trees and stay away from the kittens. Period. Understand?"

"But *Mom*, what if the bear ate the mamma? We can't just leave them there!"

The fear and anguish on his face were real. She softened.

"Why don't we eat lunch first? There's something else I need to talk to you boys about. Then, when Ross or Matt gets back from the funeral, I'll go check on the cats with them. They probably deal with abandoned animals at work. They'll know what to do. Deal?"

Jake dropped his hands. "Deal."

"But I'm telling you right now, we are *not* going home with a kitten," she declared, hoping he realized she wouldn't budge on that important point. "Okay, everybody, go wash your hands and I'll get lunch on the table."

A few minutes later, the five of them sat around the small table. Storm roamed around their feet, excited about the food.

"I'm not ready to go home yet, but it will be nice to have a bigger table again," Val said, dishing salad out for everyone. "Hopefully we'll be able to use the dining room before too long."

Dave grabbed for the ranch dressing before anyone else could. The bottle was nearly empty and none of them liked lettuce without ranch. "What did you want to talk to us about, Mom? Don't say shopping. We can wear shorts in September. Who cares if our jeans don't fit anymore?"

Val popped a grape into her mouth, considering where to start. "No, bud. It's something more important than that. It has to do with your dad."

"He's okay, isn't he?" Noah asked, worry creeping into the boy's eyes. Clearly the idea of a funeral was still heavy on his mind.

"Of course. Your dad is fine. But something has come up, and I wanted to get all of your opinions on it before your father and I make the final decision."

The ranch dressing reached Jake, but no matter how hard he squeezed the bottle, nothing but droplets sprayed over his salad. "You jerk," he muttered under his breath, shooting a dirty look at Dave.

"Jake, I need you to pay attention. This is important," Val scolded. "You see, guys, your dad had planned to come home after he harvests Alan's crops this fall. He'd go back to his old job. They were holding a spot for him. But his boss called with some bad news."

"They didn't keep his spot?" Logan asked.

"Not exactly. It turns out there isn't a spot to save. The business folded over the summer. There isn't a job to go back to."

"What does 'folded' mean?" Jake asked.

"It means they went out of business," Dave said. He looked at Val. "So now what?"

"Well, that's the main thing I wanted to talk to you guys about.

Your dad and I are discussing whether or not we should consider moving to the farm."

Val hoped that was a diplomatic way to broach the subject. She still hated the idea, but she also realized it wouldn't be fair to sway the boys' opinions by offering her own.

Logan froze with a forkful of warmed-up hotdish halfway to his mouth. "What? You can't be serious."

"I'm afraid so," Val confirmed, then wondered if that was letting her own opinion on the topic creep in, despite her intentions.

"That's crazy," he said, dropping the food back onto his plate uneaten. "I start practice with the team again next week. It's going to be hard to get caught up after being gone for two months. But I know we're gonna have a great year. If we have to move, I'll lose my spot on the team."

"You'll lose more than that," Dave added.

"I didn't like the farm, Mom," Noah offered, pushing his half-eaten plate of food away. "My allergies were terrible and it was boring. We'd have to start over at a different school."

And kids are already back in class over there, Val thought. Unlike Minnesota, the North Dakota schools started before Labor Day. She hated the idea that if they moved, the kids would be starting after everyone else.

"I bet I could bring one of the kittens to the farm," Jake said. "I don't think it would be that bad. Living at the farm, I mean."

Dave pushed his chair back from the table and tossed a half a sandwich to Storm. "It would be *worse* than bad. We'd have to leave all our friends."

"David, don't feed the dog from the table, honey," Val said, sparing him the sharp edge of her tongue, given how despondent he seemed at her news. Val covered her plate with her napkin, wondering if all of these ruined dinners were helping trim her waistline yet. With a sigh, she studied each of her sons' faces. "So, for now, it sounds like three of you are less than thrilled with the idea and one of you thinks it could work."

"What do *you* think, Mom?" Logan asked, searching her face.

"I have some reservations," Val replied, being as honest as she could without undercutting Luke. "Why don't you all think about it some more? I know this probably comes as a shock. I'm going to wander over to see if either Matt or Ross are back to help with this kitten situation. And then I might go for a walk by myself. We all have lots to think about. Please clean up the kitchen. I'll report back on the kittens after a while."

* * *

Val didn't spot any vehicles belonging to Ross or her family in the lodge parking lot. They mustn't be back yet, which was a relief. She was nervous to see Ross, to have a conversation with him, although she knew she'd need to soon.

Guests relaxed outside and on the beach, but the sturdy old dock stood empty, beckoning her.

She hadn't thought to change out of her black sundress, but the lightweight gauze of the skirt was loose and cool. Wide straps on the top left her shoulders and arms bare. She wouldn't get too hot, but she might burn. Not that she would complain. Soon the weather would cool and she'd miss the warm caress of the sun on her skin.

Taking a seat on the end of the dock, she hiked her filmy skirt up around her thighs and dipped a toe into the lake. She remembered the last time she'd sat here, when Storm had knocked her into the water and Ross had plucked her out with little effort.

I'm such a sucker for displays of heroism, she thought with a grin.

It was time to start making some important decisions. She'd had weeks to consider what was next for her, what might be best for her family. Some things were within her control. For everything else, she'd do her best to stop obsessing.

She was done relying on her husband to provide all of the financial support for their family. Her Aunt Celia had given her a gift. She knew her aunt had expected her to use the money to start some kind of business. Celia had been an astute business woman, and she never let anything hold her back. It was time for Val to adopt the same mindset.

When she first received Celia's gift, Luke had been adamant that Val not use any of the money for their ongoing living expenses, and she'd agreed. Maybe it was a point of pride for him. It didn't matter. But it was time for a reality check. If Val *ever* wanted to start a business of her own, she was going to have to be more open-minded about how she would use her inheritance. As she saw it, there were only two options: delay starting something indefinitely because of their current, very real money problems, *or* use a portion of her gift from Celia to cover living costs so that she'd have the breathing room necessary to get started on a business of her very own. The first option had become unacceptable. She was done waiting.

Why had it taken her more than two years to figure this piece out? As Val sat on the very same dock where she suspected Celia used to sit, making plans of her own through the years, she hoped her aunt would approve. She would have had no idea what it takes to raise a family of four boys, but she would have approved of Val's new, no-matter-what attitude.

Val wouldn't be moving to North Dakota. She was staying, and she would build her business with her mother's help. Her gut told her it would be the wrong move for the kids, too. Could they make it work with lots of effort? Perhaps. But the cons outweighed the pros. They'd stay.

She truly hoped she could convince her husband not to move. But if Luke still insisted on going, he'd go without the five of them. His choice, not hers. She hoped it wouldn't come to that, but what Luke ultimately decided was outside of her control.

She thought about the story her mother had grudgingly shared about her long-ago summer fling and the regrets she'd felt ever since. Val did have a moment of panic while lying in bed the previous night, going over and over the story in her head, still struggling to believe the truth behind such an integral piece of the puzzle that was her parents' marriage. The panic had set in when she'd done the math, recalling the date on the medical paperwork they'd stumbled on for

Celia in her old attic. Her mother's affair had taken place the summer before she was born.

Was it possible that George wasn't even her biological father? The idea horrified her. While it was true that she'd always felt closer to her mother, whereas her siblings were tighter with George, she loved both of her parents deeply.

As she'd lain there in the dark, her squirrel brain had even jumped to Celia. Did Celia know more than she'd let on to Lavonne? Had she ever questioned if Val truly was her niece by blood? Was that why she'd given her cash instead of a resort, or rental properties, or three existing businesses?

Again, when Val took a step back and considered her options, she could only see two: trust that her mother would have told her if George wasn't her biological father and forget about the notion . . . or push the issue, possibly find out a truth that would hurt all of them, and rock the foundation of the very family that meant the world to her.

By the time sleep found her, she'd already decided to trust her mother. To do anything else could come at too high a cost.

Today, with the warm sun bouncing off the surface of the lake, glittering before her eyes, she was confident that her late-night decision had been the right one.

She couldn't even judge her mother for the mistake she'd made so many years ago. Val now understood all too well how Lavonne could have felt lost in her own life, how a person could grasp for a lifeline. Her mother had been wrong to be unfaithful, but Val thought she could understand. Age was teaching her that life, and love, was seldom black and white, never perfect.

Val had her own choices to make, ones she never would have expected just a few short months ago. Luke was different now. Alan's sudden, violent death had changed her husband. Was Val being too impatient with him? Probably. Would they find their way back to each other?

Did he even want that anymore?

She hated to leave it in Luke's hands, but he could be a stubborn man. *Almost as stubborn as me,* she thought, grimacing at the truth. She could only hope that his current obsession with the farm would pass. She also hoped the potential relationship between her husband and another woman was nothing more than her overactive imagination. She had no proof he'd stepped outside of their vows, only a feeling in her gut.

These months apart had taught her that she *could* survive without Luke—even *thrive* without him, if being together meant a lifetime of walking on eggshells and second-guessing their commitment to each other. But she wasn't sure she wanted to go it alone.

She kicked her toes in the water again, eyes drawn outward with the ripples she caused. The lake stretched out in front of her. Trees cupping the lake were cloaked in a mixture of deep-green pine and leaves sporting a hint of fall colors. It was all so expansive, so beautiful.

The haunting call of a loon bounced across the water. The cry reminded her of her dinner date at the lake with Luke, before the phone call that changed everything. She spied the bird, grinning at its black-and-white coloring as it glided across the surface of the water. As she took in the peaceful scene before her, she had an epiphany. Everyone's life is the culmination of individual choices made. In her case, she'd taken pride in always choosing what was best for others. It had felt selfless and admirable. Now she could see how letting her own wellbeing become nothing more than an afterthought had been anything but noble.

Like the solitary loon, she needed to start making choices based on what she needed to do to grow into the kind of person she wanted to be. No one else could make her feel truly happy; not her husband, or her kids, or her sisters, or her mom or dad.

And unless she found a way to feel true contentment, she'd never be the person, the mother, or the wife she wanted to be. She needed to find the joy within herself.

It was time she started including her own needs in the choices she'd make in the future.

The loon gave one more lilting cry, sending shivers down Val's spine, before it lifted effortlessly into the air and glided slowly out of sight.

Val closed her eyes and took a deep breath. For the first time in a long time, her heart, too, felt light, like the graceful loon.

* * *

"May I join you?"

Val jumped but kept her eyes shut. She hadn't heard Ross approach. "Sure," she said, her heart skittering at the sound of his voice. She hated how nervous she felt around him after yesterday.

She gave him a chance to get settled; the wood of the dock creaked as he sat down. A hand brushed against hers, but he didn't leave it there.

Maybe he's nervous, too.

"Aren't you hot, sitting out here in a black dress?"

Glancing at him, she could see he'd changed out of his uniform into cargo shorts and a white Def Leppard tank. "No, not really. The sun feels good."

They sat there quietly. Val decided to let Ross start the conversation, since he'd sought her out. A fish jumped close by, it's silver tail flashing before it again disappeared below the calm surface of the water.

"You were pretty upset yesterday after you burned your hand," Ross finally said. "How is it, by the way?"

Val held up her injured hand for Ross to see. A dark burgundy slash ran across her knuckles, but it no longer hurt. "Guess it was pretty superficial. It doesn't hurt today."

"Good thing we both heal quickly. It's been a summer of bumps and bruises."

She nodded her agreement.

Another span of quiet descended.

"Are you leaving soon?" he finally asked, his eyes trained on something far offshore.

Val nodded. "We'll leave tomorrow morning, whenever I can get my crew loaded. School starts Tuesday, and we have lots to do before the boys climb onto the school bus."

"Hard to believe the summer is winding down. I'll miss your sugar cookies."

Val sighed. She'd miss all of this. Including him.

"And I'll miss having you around to take Storm on runs. I hope to hell she doesn't expect *me* to take up running now that you've spoiled her. Are you leaving soon, too?"

Ross finally looked at her, one corner of his mouth curling up in a smile. "I actually haven't decided yet. Being a short-timer at work gives a guy some flexibility. What are they going to do, fire me?"

Val returned the smile and shrugged. "I'm sure it gives you a sense of freedom you haven't felt in a very long time."

He nodded. "It does, and it feels damn good. Quitting was the right decision. I'm hoping that working with kids, without an intimidating shield of a uniform between us, will be more effective."

Val rested her bare feet on the edge of the dock, covering her legs completely with her full skirt. "I'm happy for you. I know it couldn't have been an easy decision. In fact, that's why I'm sitting out here, soaking up the sunshine and contemplating life, instead of hanging out at the duplex ordering my kids to get their packing done. I have some big decisions to make, too."

He waited, as if giving her space to share her thoughts.

As she spoke, she realized how much she'd come to appreciate being able to talk to him like this. She shared with him what she'd decided to do with part of her inheritance and that she wouldn't be moving to North Dakota.

"You know, Val, you sound different today. Surer of yourself. I like it."

She lifted the hair off the back of her neck, a light breeze cooling her. "I *feel* different."

"We should probably talk about what happened yesterday morning. I thought for a minute there that you were going to kiss me." His voice was more hushed, though no one else was close enough to hear their conversation.

"I thought so, too. Well, I wasn't exactly *thinking*. At least not clearly . . ." Val let her voice trail off, at a loss for words. What could she say? On the one hand, she'd been foolish to start down that path. But a tiny part of her couldn't totally squash the curiosity she still felt. What would it be like to kiss Ross, here, in the warm sunshine on a late summer afternoon?

Discreetly, Ross took her hand, running a finger around the angry red mark. "I'm glad it doesn't hurt anymore."

She felt that pull her mother had warned her about, like quicksand, tugging at her.

Giving his fingers a light squeeze before gently pulling her hand back, she sighed. "Ross, I want you to know that I don't regret getting so close to you that day. I know I *should* regret it, but I don't."

She could feel his eyes on her and turned to meet his gaze.

"I regret wishing we hadn't been interrupted," he finally said, not looking away. "But I don't make it a habit to kiss married women."

Val opened her mouth to protest, but he gave a small shake of his head. "And I know you don't make a habit of kissing anyone other than your husband, either. I get it. I think what we've found here this summer is special, and while it's tempting as hell to push for more, I know that would be wrong right now."

A flush rose to her cheeks that had nothing to do with the bright sunshine. "It certainly is tempting," she agreed. "But you're right. I don't cheat. At least, not before . . ." Her voice trailed off again.

"I'm sorry your mom saw us," Ross added, crossing his ankles and swinging his legs off the end of the dock, his feet dipping into the water with each pass. His actions reminded Val of something Jake would do, but her son would use his feet to splash someone. "Not because I'm embarrassed, but because I'm worried she might judge you. Did you two talk about it?"

"Yeah, we did. And I'm not going to lie—it was a tough conversation. But you'd be amazed at the depth of my mother's ability to understand." Val returned her gaze to the expanse of lake. She had no intention of ever revealing to anyone what her mother had shared with her in confidence. "She won't say anything to anyone."

She could hear a phone vibrating in Ross's pocket, but he ignored it, seeming to be lost in thought. "You can answer that."

"Nah, whoever it is can wait. I'm having a nice conversation with a good friend right now," he said, bumping her shoulder with his. "And by the way, if you weren't married, I'd be *very* interested in more of your cookies. But since you are, I hope we can still be friends. No one else is quite as good at inspiring me to try something new—or calling bullshit when I get too full of myself."

"Someone has to do it," Val laughed, relieved to hear Ross didn't scare off easily. She wanted to be friends with him. She didn't want to lose whatever this was between them. "Listen, Ross, I'm sure you've noticed that Luke and I are having some struggles right now. I don't know where things will end up, but I want to thank you for being here for me this summer, and for not letting me do something reckless that I might regret later."

He nodded. "You're welcome. But since I'm no saint, I'm going to say this one time, and then I'll let the subject drop. If you ever *do* find yourself at a point where you have that part of your life figured out, and it no longer includes a husband, you damn well better call me after you bounce back from the heartache."

"I swear, Ross, you'll be the first person I'll call if that ever happens."

Laughing, he put one arm around her shoulders and gave her an easy hug, then pretended to start to throw her into the lake.

"You wouldn't dare!" She smiled as she shrugged off his arm.

"Actually, I would. But I'll give you a break today since you're all pretty and confident in your black dress. So what do we do now?"

She glanced at her watch. "Do you want to go check on some kittens?"

"You're kidding, right? I was beginning to worry that Renee's cabin really was haunted."

CHAPTER TWENTY-EIGHT

GIFT OF A WELCOMING HOME

*V*al pulled into their driveway in the back alley and turned off the motor. Glancing in the rearview mirror, she saw Jake jerk awake and push the hair out of his eyes. *Add haircuts to the list,* she thought.

Packing the car and driving away from Whispering Pines had felt bittersweet, but as her eyes shifted forward, seeing her home waiting for them, she felt a sense of peace settle over her. Her mind flashed back to the day they'd closed on this house. Poor Luke had tried to carry her across the threshold, but she'd been hugely pregnant with Dave and he'd nearly dropped her. She gave birth one month later. They'd brought each of their four boys home to this house.

Car doors flung open and those same four boys piled out. Storm darted for the grass, squatting in the longish grass, reminding Val their college-aged next-door neighbor she'd paid to keep the lawn mowed was already back in school.

"Dave, can you mow quick, once we have the car unpacked?"

Her eldest, standing next to the front passenger side of the car, looked around and nodded. "Sure, Mom. This'll be a piece of cake after all the grass we helped keep mowed at the resort."

"Thanks, hon." She appreciated his help. She'd need it in the weeks to come. "Come on, everybody, grab an armful so we can get this car unpacked."

She popped the lid on the overstuffed trunk, and for once they all did as they were told, grabbing duffle bags and suitcases. Digging the house keys out of her purse, she followed them up the weed-lined sidewalk. "Logan, after we get everything inside, I need you to deal with these weeds while Dave mows, okay?"

"But, Mom, Tyler is picking me up at three to go lift weights at the school."

She'd known their cooperation wouldn't last. She refused to give him an easy out, though. "Good thing that isn't for another two hours. If you hustle, you can be done in one."

He groaned but nodded as she wove around them to the front of the line, keys in hand. She unlocked the door and made her way inside and then stopped, closing her eyes, as the scent of home enveloped her. Luke must have left the air-conditioner on low. The air was mild, not hot and stuffy as she'd expected, and there was a hint of lemon in the air, the way it smelled once a week when she'd finished dusting. The clean smell never seemed to last long enough, and yet somehow here it was now.

She opened her eyes . . . and gasped.

The kitchen and dining room had still been in a state of disrepair when she'd last left to return to the resort, days after their fight about moving to the farm, and she'd assumed Luke had headed back, too, once she'd left with the boys. But he couldn't have left right away. The rooms before her now looked like they had before The Great Flood, only better. Strikingly so.

The walls, once a tired taupe color, had been painted a warm white to match the new cupboards. Everything looked so much lighter and brighter with sunlight streaming through a new window over the kitchen sink. The backsplash of her dreams graced the space between countertop and cupboards: It was the gleaming subway tile she'd pointed out during a visit to a home-improvement store. She'd known the muted greenish-gray hue would look rich in a kitchen, but Luke had dismissed it as too expensive.

Someone bumped the backs of her legs with a suitcase.

"Mom, you're standing in the way," Noah complained, bumping her again.

"Oh, sorry, guys," she apologized, taking a few more steps into the kitchen to give them all room to come inside. "You aren't going to believe this."

"Wow!" Jake said, dropping something heavy on the floor and coming to stand next to Val, staring at their fresh new kitchen. "Did Dad do this?"

Storm wove around their legs in search of her water bowl. Val nodded. "He must have. Jake, find the dog's bowl and get her some water."

Val followed Storm into the kitchen, her eyes trying to take it all in. She stopped in surprise at a new door at the end of a bank of cupboards. Opening it, she felt tears well in her eyes. A new, slim closet had been added, deep enough to hold the vacuum cleaner and broom, with narrow shelves down one side wall already holding a variety of cleaning supplies. While there hadn't been room for a bigger pantry, Luke had found a way to work in a convenient location for the heavy vacuum she was always lugging up from the basement.

Closing the new closet door, she walked toward the dining room and gasped again. There, mounted to what had been a blank section of wall, was the tall, narrow chalkboard she'd found in Celia's attic. Her fingers reached out to touch the fancy white scrollwork that outlined the old board. She loved how *The Bird's Nest* spanned the very top of it and how the heavy frame, its white paint chipped off in places, provided a pleasing contrast to the simple lines of the nearby cupboards.

But best of all were the words *Welcome Home* added in green chalk. She'd recognize Luke's handwriting anywhere.

"Where'd that come from?" Dave asked, inspecting the vintage chalkboard over Val's shoulder.

"Aunt Celia's attic. I mentioned it to your father—I'd thought it was so cool—but I didn't ask him to work it into the design here. He must have called Ethan about it."

Dave turned slowly, taking it all in. "This looks nice. Dad did a good job."

Val nodded, a hand over her heart. It did look beautiful. Luke had worked hard in here, quietly putting his family's home back in order, and she was touched. The sight of the chalkboard made her wonder if maybe he'd had some help from her family, too.

Tonight she'd be able to feed her kids a real meal around their comfortably large dining room table. Instead of fretting about having to spend the upcoming days putting the kitchen back in order, they'd have time to focus on getting everyone ready for school.

And on Tuesday, when the four boys headed off to class, she would start working on her new business instead of painting or tiling an unfinished kitchen.

More tears fell. This was the best surprise he could have given her.

She'd call him as soon as they had the car unloaded. She wondered if she'd be able to catch him during the middle of the day, or if he'd be working outside, too busy to answer his phone.

Then a less welcome thought wormed its way into her brain: What if he hadn't done all of this for them to enjoy as a family? What if he'd gotten the kitchen put back together with the intent of putting their house on the market? As far as she knew, he hadn't changed his stance on wanting to move their family to the farm.

Hoping she wasn't right, she turned away from the beautiful new rooms, heading back outside to bring more in from her car. She needed to be strong in her resolve to remain in this house. Luke might not have meant for her to enjoy her beautiful new kitchen for long, but she had every intention of staying.

"Have Grandma Theresa and Grandpa KC ever been to our house, Mom?" Jake asked. He drained his tall glass of milk and held it out to her for a refill. His stack of chocolate chip cookies was already gone.

He'd come home *starving* every day during the first two weeks of school. Hot lunches weren't keeping him full.

"Of course they've been here," Val replied, pouring the milk. "But it's been a few years. You were young the last time they drove over."

"Don't they like to come here?"

Val had wondered the same thing, but didn't want to admit she'd never been particularly close to her husband's parents, especially to one of her own kids. "I think it's hard for them to get away from the farm."

Exactly what would happen to us if we moved there, she thought.

"Will they be here for supper?"

Val glanced at the clock display on her brand-new stove. "Your dad said not to expect them that early."

Jake took a long drink of his milk and set the nearly empty glass down, wiping the back of his mouth with his sleeve. "Mom, do you think all three of them are coming to try to convince us to move there? To the farm? Because I think I changed my mind. School is more fun than I thought it'd be. I'm sitting next to two of my friends this year. I don't want to have to change schools. Besides, the only reason I wanted to move there was so I could have a kitten. But since *that* didn't work out, I'm not interested."

Val bit back a smile. The farm probably already had plenty of cats roaming around, but she wasn't about to lose her leverage by admitting as much to Jake.

Jake kept talking a mile a minute. "I'm still worried about those two kitties, you know. Just because you said the mother came back when you were watching them doesn't mean she stayed. The bear still could have ate her after we left. Do you think you could call your friend Russ and ask him if they're okay?"

"Finish your milk and I'll put your glass in the dishwasher," she said, holding her hand out. He handed it to her after he'd drained it completely. "His name is Ross, not Russ, and I'm not sure if he's still at the resort."

"Don't you have his phone number?"

She hesitated, not at all sure it was a good idea to call Ross, but

Jake wasn't likely to drop it. She'd said goodbye to Ross on what felt like good terms, had even exchanged numbers again after her phone was destroyed, but she felt funny calling him a week later.

"Please, Mom? I'm worried about the kitties," Jake said again, his eyes wide. For once, she didn't think he was trying to play her. He *was* worried, even if the "bear" line was a stretch.

"Fine. I'll call him quick. But he might not know anything about the cats if he's already gone home. In the meantime, take your dog out back and play with her. You don't give the pet you have enough attention as it is."

Jake grinned. "Thanks, Mom." Then he slid off his stool and yelled for Storm, grabbing a tennis ball out of a basket by the door.

Damn. Maybe he did *manipulate me a little.*

Val pulled her phone out of her purse and tapped to her contact list. She was curious if Ross was still at Whispering Pines or if he'd left shortly after she had come home. Selecting his name, she placed the call before she could chicken out.

He picked up after the second ring. "Miss me already?"

"Well, it's been over two weeks since someone made me fall off a stool or burn myself. Life's been a little boring, what with no injuries, so I thought I'd call."

He chuckled. "No snakes, either, I bet. Did you get the kids off to school?"

"Sure did. Managed to scrounge up enough school supplies from the nearly empty bins at Target to send them off in semi-decent style. Jeans will have to wait. Good thing it's still warm outside. How about you? Are you still at the resort?"

"I am, but I'm actually leaving in the morning. Renee has other renters coming in tomorrow, so it's time for me to head home."

"That's too bad. Whispering Pines is beautiful in the fall."

"I bet it is. So did you call to chit-chat, or do you need something?"

"Actually, I'm calling because Jake begged me to."

"Ouch," Ross said. "That hurts."

"Oh *stop*." Val pushed off from the counter and wandered into the dining area. "He's worried about the kittens."

Ross groaned. "Don't even get me started on those damn cats."

She laughed at the tortured note in his voice. "Are they still keeping you up at night?"

"Not exactly. It's worse. That sister of yours was worried about them, didn't know what would happen to them come winter, so she made Matt and I get close enough to the mother cat to read her tags. Turns out her owners have the resort down the road from Whispering Pines. They'd been worried sick about her. Apparently, when she was still pregnant, some nasty dog belonging to one of their renters chased her off."

"Did you have to round them up and take them home, then?" Val grinned, imagining Ross and Matt trying to herd a skittish mamma cat and two squirming little fluffballs into a basket. She wondered how many scratches they might have gotten for their trouble.

"Oh, no, *that* would have been too easy."

"Don't tell me something happened to them," Val said, pulling out one of the dining room chairs and sitting down.

"Let's just say I'm not going home *alone* tomorrow."

"What do you mean?"

"I mean your neighbors wanted their cat back, but they insisted they couldn't take the kittens. They were going to drop them off at the Humane Society."

"No! You're kidding! They'd abandon their grand-kittens?" Val asked, surprised.

This gave Ross pause. He didn't say anything for a few seconds, and then he burst out laughing. "Only you would come up with *grand-kittens*, Val!"

She shrugged, although there was no one there to see her. "I mean, they kind of *are*."

"Let's just say these grand-kittens grew on me, and I was worried if they went to a shelter they might not get out of there alive. Some shelters take in too many cats and they can't always adopt them all out."

Val shuddered at the thought of the kittens being euthanized.

"Does that mean you volunteered to keep them both? To take them home with you?"

"I must be out of my frigging mind because, yes, that's what it means. I am *not* a cat person. Hell, I'm a *dog* guy. But here I am, packing up kitty litter and cat toys I bought yesterday. Tomorrow, Smokey and Simba will be riding in a tub on the seat next to me. I hope they don't get car sick. I'll have to take them to see a vet next week."

"Smokey and Simba?"

"Yeah, and don't give me any shit about the names, either. They fit."

Val laughed out loud. She couldn't wait to tell Jake the story of his kittens. Storm started barking and she could hear car doors slamming in the backyard. "You'll be Jake's hero when I tell him, Ross. Send pictures of the kittens when you get them home. He'd love that. But, hey, I'm sorry, I have to go. Tell Matt and Renee hello for me, would you?"

"Will do. Oh God, I think Simba just pooped on the floor. Talk to you later!"

Still laughing, Val made her way to the back door, pulling it open and coming face to face with Luke.

"You seem happy," he said, searching her face. "Does that mean you're still enjoying the kitchen?"

She could feel her smile slip away. It had been nearly a month since she'd seen her husband. They'd talked on the phone two or three times a week, and she'd thanked him profusely for what he'd done in the kitchen, but the rest of their conversations had stayed focused on the boys. It was as if he'd wanted to avoid discussing the idea of relocating their family as much as she did. She had a hunch avoidance wasn't going to be an option this weekend.

They exchanged a chaste kiss and she stepped out of the way to let him inside.

"Where are your parents?" she said, peering out at the backyard. "You're earlier than you said you'd be. I don't have food for them."

"They'll be here in a minute, but don't worry—we ate a late lunch. When we pulled into town Dad needed to stop for gas."

"In case they need to make a quick getaway?" Val teased, relieved he wasn't expecting her to cook. Normally she enjoyed serving guests, but she'd been too busy getting the kids settled in school and brainstorming on her new business plan when they weren't home to worry much about groceries or meal prep. So far, the boys hadn't complained about their simple suppers.

"Cute." Luke smirked. "You *are* going to be nice to them, aren't you?"

"Don't insult me, Luke. I'm always nice."

The grunt he made told her he didn't necessarily agree. He headed upstairs with his suitcase. "I need a shower. I'll be back downstairs in ten minutes."

"Great," Val muttered. That meant she'd get to entertain his parents while he was primping upstairs.

Sure enough, he hadn't been gone two minutes when Storm started another round of barking. Back to the door she went, going outside to meet them.

"Hold on to Storm's collar, Jake," she ordered, afraid Storm might knock Theresa on her butt. The woman had looked so small and frail when Val last saw her.

Most mothers would look frail after burying a son, she reminded herself.

Val held her breath, hoping her in-laws wouldn't look as despondent as they had right after the accident. She feared their broken hearts would never heal, but hopefully they were starting to live some kind of life again.

KC climbed out of his black Suburban, waving a greeting to both Jake and Val. Val's initial reaction was relief over his appearance. Her father-in-law looked like his old self again, other than a slight limp as he made his way around to Theresa's side of their vehicle. He opened the door and helped his wife down.

A white scarf covered Theresa's hair, caught in a knot under her chin. Dark sunglasses obscured most of her face. Luke's mother patted her husband's arm and then turned to Jake, her youngest grandchild, arms extended.

Val bit her lip, hoping Jake would accept his grandmother's hug. He'd been terrified by her reaction at the graveside service for Alan. Jake seemed to hesitate for just a moment, but then he walked awkwardly toward Theresa, trying to keep hold of an excited Storm.

Skipping down the steps to lend a hand, Val reached for Storm's collar, pulling the dog over to where one of her leashes was permanently wrapped around a tree. Once the dog was secured, Val walked back to hug her in-laws. Up close, they both looked as good as she could have hoped. A little tired, and seemingly years older, both of which were understandable following a long drive and three months of hell.

"Come. See the beautiful job Luke did in our kitchen," Val said, taking Theresa's arm. "Jake, help your grandpa with their bags."

"Where is that son of mine?" Theresa asked, matching Val's pace as they walked toward the house.

"He ran up to shower quick, then he'll be down. I'm sorry he wasn't here to meet you."

Theresa waved her free hand dismissively. "Heavens, child, that man has been hovering around me for months. He can take all the time he wants. Besides, it gives us a minute or two to catch up without any extra ears listening or lips flapping."

Val smiled, relieved to hear some spunk back in Theresa's words. She opened the door and let Theresa enter ahead of her.

"Oh my, this is *so* nice," the woman said, a sense of awe in her voice. "How could you ever leave this, dear?"

It took a beat for Val's mind to process what Theresa might have meant. "Actually, I have no intention of leaving this kitchen anytime soon," she declared, careful to keep her tone neutral. She didn't want to upset Luke's mother, but she also didn't want there to be any misunderstandings. "Why don't we sit down and talk? Would you like something to drink?"

"No, I'm fine," the older woman said, walking back to the dining area and taking the chair Val had left pulled out from the table a few minutes earlier, when she'd talked to Ross about the kittens. "Come. Join me. We won't have long for just the two of us to talk."

Val did as she was told, sitting across the table from Theresa, bracing herself. Would the woman try to convince her to listen to Luke? To move the boys to the farm?

"What is this ridiculous notion about the farm that my son and husband are talking about?" the older woman began. "Do you *want* to move there, dear?"

Val felt relief flood through her body. Two little questions were all it took to realize she'd have an ally in Theresa. "Not even a little."

Her mother-in-law nodded. "That's what I thought. I don't know what it is with the men in this family and their obsession with that damn land, that *farm*. I'd have left decades ago if I could have gotten KC to agree to it, but of course he'd never even consider it. It was his daddy's land, after all, and so it has been his duty to keep the farm going."

Val couldn't hide her surprise. She'd always thought living on the farm was what Theresa had wanted.

"Don't look so shocked, dear. We made it work, and it's been a decent life for us, but it is past time for KC and I to move on, to go where the icy grip of winter can't settle in our bones. Did you know we had a condo rented for this coming winter down in Arizona? When we moved off the farm and Alan moved into the old house, our new apartment in a town too tiny for a stoplight in the middle of North Dakota wasn't supposed to be the end for us. It was going to be a new beginning. You should see the stack of travel brochures I've been collecting over the years."

Theresa's eyes glowed with excitement, but Val watched as the enthusiasm died away. "Since we lost Alan, I can hardly get KC to even talk about leaving town. He heads out to the farm at the crack of dawn and I don't see him again until dark. Luke is doing his best to keep things going, but farming has changed so much since he was a kid. He can't do it by himself. Alan worked hard to stay up with all the latest technology. KC paid some attention, but not enough."

This was something Val hadn't even considered. She'd foolishly assumed Luke was stepping into Alan's old role, taking care of business. Theresa's words filled her with shame over her own naïveté and selfishness. "I had no idea," she whispered.

"How could you know?" Theresa said. "You've never lived on a farm. Luke never wanted to."

Val nodded. Her mother-in-law just summarized their dilemma in a few short words. "What should we do now?"

"Honey, if I knew the answer to that, I would have done it years ago. I think the best we can hope for is to find a way to convince these men to let the farm go, but I'm not so sure that's possible."

Their heart-to-heart was interrupted as Luke came down the stairs. "Can I get you something to drink, Mom?" he asked, crossing through the kitchen to stand next to the dining room table.

Theresa patted the table next to her. "I'm not here to have the two of you wait on me. Sit. I was just catching up with your beautiful wife."

Luke glanced between the two women, his expression apprehensive. "Where's Dad?"

Val nodded toward the backyard. "Out back with Jake. Some of the other boys might be home by now, too."

"What's the matter, Luke? Do we scare you?" Theresa asked, eyeing Luke carefully.

"Don't be ridiculous." He sighed as he took the seat. "Why would you two scare me? Just because first you"—he looked pointedly at Theresa and then at Val—"and then you, have been running my life since the day I was born?"

Although all three of them laughed, Luke's comment didn't sit well with Val. Was that what he really thought? Had he been feeling stifled, too? Even before losing Alan?

What a mess.

Conversation turned to lighter topics, like the boys' first weeks back at school and how Luke had enlisted help from Val's brother and father to finish up the kitchen before Val and the boys had come home from their summer at Whispering Pines.

"Of everything in here—and I love it all—the chalkboard was the biggest surprise," Val said. "Thank you."

Luke glanced at the board, and Theresa followed suit. Val had left Luke's *Welcome Home* message there.

"Isn't that cute," her mother-in-law cooed. "Wherever did you find that? It looks old."

"It was in my aunt's attic. We stumbled across it earlier this summer when we were up there to get an old trunk out that my sister, Renee, wanted to use for decoration in her new house."

"I wonder where it came from," Theresa said. "Do you suppose it used to be in a store or something?"

Val shrugged. "I don't know, but in my mind, I've made up a story of it hanging in a quaint bakery many years ago. The offerings of the day would have been listed, along with prices and seasonal drawings."

Grinning, Theresa glanced back at the sign again. "I can picture something like that. Tell me about this old camper you pulled out of the woods. Luke mentioned you plan to use it in some type of cooking business?"

"Oh, yes, my camper! One of my more impulsive moves this summer," Val said. The simple mention of her summer project and the business ideas she'd been working on ever since brought a smile to her face. She went on to tell Theresa about all the hard work she did, with help from others, to bring the vintage unit back to life.

Luke listened, not saying a word. He'd never asked for this much detail, so parts of the story were new for him, too.

Theresa turned to her son. "You see, honey? That right there is what I'm talking about."

"Don't even start, Mom," Luke said, straightening in his chair. Val could almost see the wall coming back up.

"Don't you sass me, Luke. No one should feel an obligation to take something new on unless it makes them feel like that. Excited! Inspired! You need to think about that as you decide what your next career move is going to look like."

Val got the impression this particular topic had been discussed at length between mother and son recently, and that perhaps they were at an impasse.

The door into the kitchen burst open and Storm rushed over to Luke's side, pushing against his leg, her tail wagging so hard it made a *thonk!* every time it slapped Luke's chair.

"Well, hey there, girl," Luke said, burying his face in the dog's neck.

Theresa caught Val's eye over the top of Luke's bent-over form, and Val could feel her compassion for their predicament. There would be no easy answers.

CHAPTER TWENTY-NINE

GIFT OF HONESTY

"*I*'m sorry your folks could only stay one night," Val said as she prepared for bed. "At least they got to watch Logan's scrimmage. I'm surprised the coach put him in at all, given he missed all the summer practices."

Luke pulled his sweatshirt off and threw it over the back of the chair, followed by his jeans. But instead of crawling into his side of the bed, he pulled open a dresser drawer and removed shorts and a T-shirt.

"Aren't you coming to bed?"

"Nah," he said, shaking his head. "It's been a long time since I could stretch out on my own couch and watch some television. We only get the basic channels out at the farm. I'll be back up in a bit."

Val watched him leave the room as she crawled into bed. He still had a haunted look in his eyes. She'd heard him tell his father he'd see him tomorrow, which meant Luke planned to leave again the next day.

They'd resolved nothing. How long would they continue to live in this limbo?

As long as it takes, a voice whispered in her head. *Can you live with that?*

* * *

She woke up to weak sunlight streaming around her bedroom curtains. Storm must have been sleeping on top of her right foot too long, because tiny pricks of pain shot upward as she slowly bent her leg, careful not to disturb the dog.

Luke's side of the bed remained pristine. He hadn't come back up.

She eased carefully out of bed, holding her breath when Storm opened one eye. The dog didn't normally go outside for another hour and Val didn't want to deal with taking her out yet. The eye closed again and Storm burrowed deeper into the rumpled comforter at the end of the bed.

Tiptoeing out of the room, Val used the bathroom and then headed downstairs to check on Luke. Soft snores coming from the family room made him easy to find. She slipped into the room, settled into the recliner next to the couch, and watched him sleep.

It was obvious that he was avoiding her. She understood. Avoidance was easier. But only in the short term.

He jerked awake. "Jesus, Val, what are you doing sitting there just staring at me? You scared the shit out of me."

"Sorry. When I woke up alone, I came down here to check on you."

He angled up on one elbow to better face her, rubbing the sleep out of his eyes with his other hand. "Have you been up long?"

"No. I've gotten used to sleeping alone, so the sun woke me, not the cold space next to me in bed."

"I honestly didn't mean to fall asleep down here," Luke claimed, stretching his head from side to side as if to unknot his neck. "This couch was not made for sleeping."

When she said nothing, Luke sighed and swung his legs around, sitting up. "Did you make coffee?"

"Luke, what are we doing here?" Val asked, ignoring his question.

He collapsed back onto the cushion with a sigh. "I don't have the faintest idea, hon."

His habitual endearment, along with the random crease across his cheek that matched the seam in the couch cushion, brought a small smile to her face.

"Have we totally fucked this up?"

Now his grin grew bigger than hers. "My wife, the potty mouth."

She shrugged, her smile fading. "Have we?"

He gave her question consideration before replying. "I hope not. I'd hate to lose this. Well, not *this*, exactly, because things between us have been pretty rough this summer, but you know what I mean."

She did know. They'd been together long enough that words weren't always necessary.

"Have you thought any more about moving to the farm?" he asked.

She stared at him. "Have I thought any more about it? Of course I've thought about it. I think about it every day. But, honestly, I made a decision about that even before I left Whispering Pines."

"And let me guess. The answer is still no?"

"The answer is still no. It isn't the right thing for me, and it isn't the right thing for our boys."

He leaned forward, elbows on his knees, hands clasped. "And what gives you the right to make that decision on behalf of our kids?"

"I didn't make the decision in a vacuum, Luke," she said, searching for how best to make him see things from her point of view. "I weighed the pros and cons of moving the boys away from here, from all their friends, from my family, from their school. And I asked them."

Luke bristled at this. "Val, you specifically told me not to talk to the boys about this yet, and then you go behind my back and turn them against me on it?"

Tamping down her rising temper, Val stood and walked over to the couch and sat next to her husband. They needed to have this conversation in private. She didn't want to wake the boys to a screaming match. "Luke, it wasn't like that. I was very careful to keep my thoughts on the topic to myself when I asked them about it."

"You do realize nearly every kid in the world would say no when asked if they wanted to move because of a parent's job-change."

He had a point. "Yes, you're right. But this is about so much more than a job, Luke, and you know it. This is moving from a decent-size town to a farm in the middle of nowhere. I'm not going to waste our time ticking off all the reasons I think it's a bad idea. You've already heard them from me, and I bet you've heard them from your mother, too."

"What does Mom have to do with this? Did you talk about it with her behind my back, too?"

"Hey, don't blame me. She's the one who brought it up, when you were showering upstairs yesterday. Luke, she wants to travel with your dad. To head south in the winter. To do all those things they couldn't do through the years because they were stuck on that damn farm. I don't want the same for us. I'm not sure why you would want it, either."

He shook his head in disgust and started to stand, but Val grabbed his arm, gently but firmly pulling him back down next to her. "We obviously aren't going to solve this today, Luke. Your feelings are still too raw about it, and I promised myself to hold my ground, too. But we need to talk about something else before the boys come down. Before you leave again."

"What the hell else is there to talk about?" he said, refusing to look at her.

"I want to talk about Kennedy. And I need you to be honest with me."

"Like you were honest with me about Ross?"

She sucked in a breath. "What the hell does that mean?"

"Oh, come on, Val. I'm not an idiot. There is obviously something between the two of you. How can you sit here and act all superior after you've been spending time with someone else out at the resort while I'm working my ass off at the farm?"

Her first instinct was to scream. Her second was to walk away. Neither option would help with their stalemate. Besides, as much as she hated to admit it, Luke wasn't totally wrong.

Her eyes snagged on the framed picture of last year's Christmas card, sitting on a shelf on the wall next to the television. The smiling faces of her family stared back at her, clueless as to the trials in the year ahead. Luke was an integral part of the family in that picture, and she couldn't throw it all away without a fight. She might not be able to help him realize how much he had to lose, but she had to at least try.

"I think we both need to take a deep breath and have a civilized conversation about this. It's far too easy to walk away from something, no matter how much it's meant to us in the past, when the going gets tough. I'll start. You're right. I like Ross. We're *friends*. For some reason, we connected, and we had lots of good conversations this summer. He was in a bad place and I think I was able to help him find his way through it. He helped me, too. Could it have gone beyond friendship? To be honest, yes. Very easily. But Luke, you have to believe me. It didn't. He respects the fact that I'm married. I wasn't ready to give us up . . . you and me."

"Are you going to sit here and tell me nothing happened? He never laid a hand on you?"

I refuse to live a lie, she thought, taking a deep breath. "I nearly kissed him once. That's all it was, nothing more. We both realized we didn't want to go down that path. And we didn't. I hope you decide to believe me, and to forgive me. I hate that I was even tempted. I should have been more careful."

She knew she'd been wrong to even consider anything more than friendship with Ross. She'd stepped outside of bounds, and it was up to Luke whether or not he'd forgive her. She couldn't change the past.

Luke rubbed his thighs, as if looking for a way to dispel pent-up energy, anger. His voice came out flat, but calm: "Thank you for being honest, Val."

She waited. It was his turn and they both knew it.

"This is hard, isn't it?" he asked, turning to her, a pained look on his face.

"It's only hard because it matters so much," she agreed, waiting.

He nodded, looking away. He seemed to be staring at the chalkboard he'd mounted for her in the adjoining room, but she couldn't be sure. "Apparently you are a stronger person than I am," he began, and she felt her heart split open.

Could she just run upstairs, jump back into bed, and pull the covers over her head? Pretend this conversation had never happened?

"Kennedy is gone. Her father passed away. She never did care for life on the farm, either."

"But I thought she was still around. You said she organized the fundraiser to help cover Alan's medical bills."

"She did." He squirmed on the couch. "This feels weird, talking to you about her."

"Well, so far I don't see anything too weird about it if she's just an old girlfriend."

He nodded. "It wouldn't be, if that were the end of the story."

Shit. She braced herself.

"I think Kennedy was feeling lost. She was so sad after her dad passed. I stopped over there after everyone had gone home a week or so after his funeral. She was trying to get things buttoned up, was struggling with what to do about an offer she'd received on their land. I tried to be a friend to her. It had been such a tough summer. First Alan, and then her dad . . ." His voice trailed off.

Val tried to put herself in the woman's shoes, tried to imagine how she'd been feeling.

"I'm so sorry, Val. I shouldn't have gone to her alone. I'll regret it until the day I die."

She didn't need any of the details in order to fill in the blanks. And now the burden of forgiveness was on her.

"Mom?! Dad?! What's for breakfast?"

Val jumped, startled by the sound of their son's voice. Noah, yelling downstairs on his way to the kitchen. She stood, her reflexes automatic.

Luke grabbed her hand, yanking her back down to the couch and to face him. A tear rolled down his cheek.

"I'm so sorry, babe."

She nodded. She had a pretty good idea just how sorry he was . . . about everything.

CHAPTER THIRTY

GIFT OF VINTAGE TREASURES

*V*al slammed her car door, nervous about the day ahead. The month of September had passed in a flash, and she breathed in the cooler air of October, detecting a hint of smoke and decaying leaves alongside the ever-present smell of pine.

Her sisters' first retreat of the season was in full swing. Renee had let her know the guest count that morning, as she would be serving both lunch and dinner. In between she had a small group meeting planned with four of the retreat guests to discuss healthy cooking options.

In my camper!

She'd brought the boys out to Whispering Pines two different weekends since school had started, putting the finishing touches on the place. They'd helped her scrub the exterior, too. Ethan had taken an example of a canopy she'd given him—from Pinterest, of course—and built her a collapsible one for the front of her camper. She loved the soft pink-and-white-striped fabric against the muted silver of the exterior. She mounted small, clear light bulbs around the canopy, adding a quaint touch, day or night. A large, patterned outdoor rug was rolled out in front and Lavonne had donated a small, black bistro table and chair set she'd picked up at a thrift store. Three glorious pots of orange, purple, and yellow mums completed the look.

In addition to the scheduled class, Val had asked Jess to include a note in their newsletter to the retreat attendees ahead of time, letting them know that if they had any old recipes that they'd like help with, to bring them along. Val thought it would be fun to see if she could help any of them recreate family favorites like she'd done with her grandma's sugar cookie recipe. She had no idea if any of the women would take her up on her offer. She'd find out at lunchtime.

Letting herself into the lodge through the front door, she could hear a low murmur of voices and an occasional shout of laughter. It was a welcoming sound. Following the voices, she made her way down the hallway, peeking into one of the gathering rooms. A handful of women were scattered about, visiting, journaling, and reading.

"Hi!" someone greeted her.

"Hello, everyone!" Val waved to the women. "Don't mind me. I need to get lunch going so you lovely ladies don't have to go hungry."

One of the women closed her book. "Wait, are you Val?"

Surprised, Val stepped farther into the room. "I am. I'm Renee and Jess's *much* younger sister."

This earned her a few chuckles.

The reader held up a hand. "There are quite a few of us here excited to see you."

"Really?" Val asked. "Why?"

"Because we brought recipes to work with you on!"

"You're kidding? I didn't know if anyone would even be interested. It was a test of sorts."

Another of the women chimed in. "Girl, my sisters and I have been struggling for twenty years with our mother's chocolate-frosted cookie recipe. We *think* we've tried every tweak possible, but they're never as good as Mom's used to be. If you could help us figure it out, next Christmas would be just like old times."

"You know, now that you mention it, I should have brought my grandma's old recipe box," a third woman added. "I didn't even think of it until you mentioned your sisters. My sisters and I actually fought over the box of recipes, since Grandma had been the keeper of so many family favorites. Can you believe it? We didn't fight over things worth money—just that one, sentimental thing. I ended up taking it home with me, but I've always thought it would be fun to make copies of them for everyone. But some are barely legible."

Val grinned. Helping to dig into a box of old recipes and decipher them sounded like the best kind of puzzle to solve. "If you don't live too far away, we should get together some afternoon. I'd be happy to look through them with you."

"You would do that?" the woman asked, clearly surprised at the offer.

"I'd love to!" Val said. "I'm sorry, ladies, I'd also love to stay and chat, but I have a meal to prepare. I'll be around through tomorrow, so catch me if you need my help with anything."

She turned to leave but then paused, turning back to them to add, "Anything cooking or food related, that is. But if you are having any trouble in your love lives, *do not* come to me for advice!"

"Duly noted," the woman with the cookie recipe said, giving her a thumbs-up. "No one can excel at everything!"

* * *

"I don't know if we should let Val play at our retreats anymore," Jess said to Renee as the three sisters gathered in Renee's living room after leaving their guests for the evening. "I think the women like her best."

Val took a sip of her steaming cocoa. The short walk over from the lodge had left her chilled. "You sound like you did when we were kids. Never letting me play with the two of you."

Renee tossed a marshmallow at her. She caught it, dropping it into her cup.

"Seriously though, Val," Jess said, "I think you're on to something with your healthy cooking and recipe revamp angles. Don't you?"

"It's starting to feel that way," Val agreed.

She'd spent the whole day talking with their guests, so many of them had questions. After dinner, a few of them had even tested things in the lodge kitchen with her. She didn't have all the necessary ingredients on hand, but they did manage to nail the chocolate cookies. The woman who'd brought that recipe had tears in her eyes as she moaned her way through the treat. And it had been as simple as swapping out buttermilk for the two-percent variety. Val knew it wasn't about the cookie itself. It was the magic of the memories it evoked.

"Tell us what you're envisioning," Jess prodded. "Have you thought about how you might be able to monetize this?"

Shrugging, Val admitted she wasn't sure yet. "But helping figure out old recipes seems to be where people have the most interest. I love teaching cooking techniques and pointers, too, but lots of other people are already doing that. Helping with recipes is more niche, more unique, I think."

Jess nodded, her business mind clearly clicking away behind her intense eyes. "We need to help you figure out a way to scale that."

"I'm all ears. Help away!" Val lifted her aching feet up onto the ottoman in front of her chair. "But maybe not tonight. I'm beat. And, frankly, tired of explaining the difference between baking soda and baking powder. Don't repeat this, but I'm afraid some of them have a long way to go before they can prepare a decent meal on their own."

Renee held up a finger. "Yes, but remember—that's why they're here. To improve different aspects of their lives."

"And we're happy to assist," Val agreed.

"Now, if we're done talking shop"—Jess set her mug on a nearby end table—"I have other news."

Renee smiled. "As long as it's *good* news, let's hear it."

"We set a date," Jess declared, clapping her hands together.

"To get married? That's wonderful!" Renee raised her mug into the air. "Here's to sealing the deal! When is this shindig going to happen and how big will it be?"

"We've booked the church back home for an evening Mass on December thirtieth."

"Really?!" Val asked, surprised. She'd expected a spring or summer wedding, maybe even here at Whispering Pines, like Renee and Matt had done.

Jess nodded, clearly excited to be marrying Seth in less than three months. "It won't be big. Family and a few close friends."

"Didn't Seth help Celia refurbish the stained-glass windows in that church?" Renee asked.

Jess's smile grew. "He did. Which is why we thought it would be the perfect place to get married."

"That is so romantic," Renee said with a sigh. "You're pretty quiet, Val."

Given how disenchanted she'd been feeling about marriage lately, Val was having a hard time mustering up much excitement. But that wasn't fair. She loved her sister and knew Seth was a great guy. This was a good thing.

"I'm sorry," she apologized. "I'm just tired. But this is *great* news, Jess. Why December?"

"We picked the holidays so Kaylee can fly home for it."

Val nodded, remembering that Kaylee, Seth's teenage daughter, lived in Texas with her mother and stepfather. Seth had never married the woman, but he was trying to maintain a solid relationship with his daughter. "I bet she's excited."

"Kaylee? She is over the *moon* about it!"

"Have you made any other plans yet?" Renee asked. "How can we help?"

"Well, about that," Jess said. "Don't think we're crazy. Hear me out on this before you say anything."

Val and Renee stole a glance at each other, curious. What was Jess up to?

"All right, I'll do my best to listen before reacting," Renee agreed.

"We want to stay out here, at Whispering Pines, in the Gray Cabin, for our honeymoon."

"What?!" Renee shouted, shock registering on her face. "Why in the hell would you want to do *that*?"

Jess caught Val's eye. "Didn't she *just* promise to listen before she judged?"

Val nodded, although she found Renee's reaction to be spot on.

"I know you still have some misgivings about that cabin, Renee," Jess admitted.

Renee snorted. "Misgivings? The thing is probably haunted."

"Don't be ridiculous. Remember Celia's letter, the one we found with our time capsule? She asked us specifically to show that little cabin some extra love. It had been her favorite when she was younger. She talked about how it was perfect for couples."

"Well, yeah, but that was before the old woman cursed it," Val chimed in.

Jess, the most practical of the three sisters, waved the notion away. "That's ridiculous. Ethan did a great job fixing it up, even added some insulation when he repaired the roof and some of the walls. Unless it's really cold, we should be able to stay in it. We can keep the fireplace burning and enjoy a few days of privacy. Besides, I feel like it's fate."

"What do you mean?" Renee asked, still clearly unconvinced.

"I was spending New Year's Eve out here by myself two years ago. That was the night I found the old paperback that mentioned Whispering Pines, even had pictures of the Gray Cabin, back when it was pretty. It looks like that again, now. I figure both me and that old cabin have come a long way in two years."

Renee sighed. "I still think you're nuts, but go ahead. Just don't blame me if your honeymoon dissolves into a big fight because the place has bad karma."

"Will you help me decorate it all cute and romantic, then, with candles and rose petals? The whole nine yards?" Jess asked, batting her eyes at them.

Val made a gagging sound and Renee burst out laughing at Jess's request. They knew she was teasing, but Val caught Renee's eye and winked. They'd have to do something to make it welcoming to a newly married couple. As long as there wasn't a holiday blizzard.

"Are you going to have a big reception or a dance or anything like that?"

Jess shook her head. "No. Neither of us want it to be a big, fancy affair. Just something small and special. Honestly, we just want to be married. The wedding will be nice, but it isn't our main focus."

"If it's a church wedding, I still think you should wear an actual wedding dress," Renee said.

Jess nodded, her eyes going to the blue trunk they'd moved from Celia's attic into Renee's new living room a few months earlier. "I really want to wear the dress we found in the trunk."

"Oh, yes, you must," Renee agreed. Standing, she took the decorative centerpiece off the top of the trunk, setting it to the side. Then she knelt down, fiddled with the latch, and opened the heavy lid.

A slight mustiness wafted into the air again. The wedding dress was folded on top. Renee carefully removed it, fluffing it as she held it high, allowing both Jess and Val a good look at it.

Jess got up off the couch to inspect it, running a light hand over the sweetheart neckline, an intricate pattern of tiny seed pearls covering it. "It *is* exquisite, isn't it?"

"Do you think it'll fit?" Val asked, eyeing the creamy satin fabric.

"Should I try it on?"

Renee grinned. "Oh yes. Come on. Let's go upstairs."

Giggling, the three of them headed for the stairs, Renee still holding the dress high. Once upstairs, Jess stripped down to her bra and panties. Renee and Val held the dress open carefully, and Jess steadied herself with a hand on Val's shoulder as she stepped into it. Together they arranged the bodice, skirt, and sleeves as best they could. Renee stood behind Jess, trying to figure out how the dress closed.

"There isn't a zipper. Oh my God, there are about a *zillion* tiny buttons. I'll just hold it closed for now so we can tell if it's close to fitting."

Val helped Renee pull the edges of the dress together in the back. The good news was the dress would close, with room to spare; letting the dress out might have been a problem. The bad news was whomever the dress was originally designed for must have had larger breasts than Jess. She looked so disheartened by the discovery, Renee and Val couldn't even tease her.

"This will never work," Jess insisted, looking down in dismay.

"I'll call Mom," Renee said, taking her phone out of her pocket. "She'll know what to do."

When Renee released the back of the dress, the ill fit in the front became even more pronounced.

"Mom, guess what? Jess and Seth finally picked a date," Renee said into her phone. "And she wants to wear the wedding dress from Celia's blue trunk."

A pause. Val wished she could hear what their mother was saying.

"Yeah, she can get into it," Renee reported.

"Jeez, thanks, Mom!" Jess yelled.

Renee shushed her. "Actually, it's too big. Do you think a seamstress could take the top in? Because right now Jess would need a six-pack of tube socks to make it fit."

Jess flipped her sister off and Val cracked up laughing, collapsing onto her back on Renee's bed.

Renee listened some more. "Okay, yeah, that would be great if you can get her over there tomorrow night. Say, sixish? We'll finish up here around four. Thanks. See you tomorrow."

The phone disappeared back into Renee's pocket. "Mom has a friend who's a wizard with alterations. We're supposed to send her a picture of what we're dealing with here"—Renee gestured to Jess's chest and the gaping dress—"and she'll try to line it up for the woman to be there tomorrow night. Mom didn't want to wait because she said her friend has some big overseas trip coming up sometime before Christmas, but she wasn't sure when. She didn't want to chance missing her."

Val groaned, still laying back on the bed. "An overseas trip? I can only dream. Do you guys know I don't even have a passport? I'm forty-three frigging years old and I've never been out of the country. Not even to Canada!"

"That *is* pretty pathetic, Val," Jess agreed. "You should make Luke take you to Italy or something for your twentieth."

"At this rate, I don't even know if there will *be* a twentieth," Val said, sitting up.

Renee came over and sat on the bed next to her, putting an arm around Val's waist. "Things still a little shaky, hon?"

Val nodded, but plastered a fake grin on her face. Tonight was Jess's—she wouldn't rain on the festivities with her own sad story.

CHAPTER THIRTY-ONE

GIFT OF SIGNS

*J*ess rode with Val to their parents' the following evening. They'd wrapped up their first successful retreat of the season. The wedding dress was draped across the backseat along with the christening gown.

"Renee had a good idea when she suggested we show the christening gown to Mom's seamstress friend. Maybe she'll know how old it might be," Jess said, turning down the radio after they'd finished their impromptu karaoke session to a favorite oldie-but-goodie by Meat Loaf. Val was glad none of her kids had been in the car to witness it. Their groans would have detracted from the fun. Or maybe added to it.

"I'm still curious about both dresses," Val agreed. "I wish there was some way we could figure out where they came from, or how they ended up in a trunk in Celia's attic."

"A *locked* trunk," Jess added, her head turning to take in the scene of a fender-bender.

Val moved into the far lane to give them room. The damaged vehicles had been pulled off to the side of the road, out of the way. Val wondered if Matt was one of the responding officers. It was possible, given the two units parked nearby with flashing lights. Renee had mentioned he was on duty.

"I hope that isn't a sign," Jess said.

"What?"

Jess gestured back toward the wreck behind them with her thumb. "That. The accident. I hope I'm not bringing bad karma into our wedding. Maybe both the old wedding dress and the Gray Cabin are a bad idea. We don't really know the history of either."

"Or maybe you just believe in second chances," Val offered, sparing a quick glance in Jess's direction.

"Good point. Without second chances, we'd all be screwed, huh?"

Val laughed. "We've all managed to find ourselves in need of second chances over these past few years. And we thought life would get *easier* as our kids got older."

"Guess the joke was on us," Jess laughed.

They rode on in silence for a few minutes.

"Wait. I might have an idea," Jess said, shifting in her seat to face Val. "Do you remember that old photo album that we found in the trunk along with the dresses and a few other things?"

Val shook her head.

"Oh, that's right—I was with Seth and Ethan when we found it. When we broke into the old trunk the first time."

Val laughed as she turned on her blinker. They weren't far from their parents' home.

"We thought it was weird that the album was in there. All of Celia's other photo albums had been stored in one place, and Dad had taken them to their house after Celia died, to keep them safe. When we found this other book in the trunk, we gave Mom and Dad that one, too, instead of leaving it in the attic."

It was starting to sound familiar to Val. "Hey, was that the photo album where you found that picture of Will and that Karen chick?"

"That's the one. Speaking of second chances, huh?" Jess let out a bitter laugh.

"What else was in there? Did you look through the whole thing?"

"Actually, no, I never did. It started with some pictures of Celia's eightieth birthday party. I thumbed through the rest of it a tiny bit, but I assumed everything else was from when we were adults. Maybe I was wrong about that. Maybe it wasn't in chronological order at all."

"Hmm . . ." Val turned onto their parents' street. Dusk was falling, but the sun was still peeking through tree limbs now devoid of most of their leaves. "Maybe we can take another look at the album tonight."

She parked on the street and took the smaller christening gown out of the backseat. "I'll carry this. You carry your dress. I don't want to be responsible for that beauty."

Renee pulled in behind them. Jess would ride back out to Whispering Pines with her and Val would head to their house with her boys. She hoped they'd give her more time before insisting they go home. They'd been here since Saturday morning, staying with her parents, while she helped out at the retreat.

Val led the way up the sidewalk to the house, her two sisters behind her. It was a beautiful, calm evening. A flash of red caught her eye as a bird swooped in front of her, startling her.

"Holy cow, that scared me!" she declared, a hand over her heart. "Did you guys see that?"

"I did," Jess said, a few steps behind Val. "Look. Up there on that branch over the porch. It's a red cardinal."

"Really, where?" Renee asked. "I don't see it."

Val could see the brightly colored bird, high up on a branch, looking down at them. It let out a loud squawk. Jess's hands were full with the draped wedding dress, so Val pointed the bird out to Renee with her free hand.

"I remember seeing one a couple of times last fall, out at Whispering Pines," Jess said. "They are so pretty, so *bright*. People say red cardinals are actually messengers from Heaven. A loved one that's died, coming to tell you something."

"That's right," Renee said. "I see it up there now. Harper kept seeing one with you, right? You tried to find her a red cardinal costume for Halloween but had to settle for a Toucan Sam one instead."

"Right," Jess agreed.

A memory flashed for Val as the red bird squawked above them again. There'd been a red cardinal in the woods that day, the day they'd pulled her old camper out. No one else had seemed to see it, but it had definitely caught Val's attention.

"I used to think it was Celia," Jess was saying, "swooping out to help me with the mystery of Will and Karen."

Maybe Celia is encouraging me, too, Val thought, ridiculous as that might sound. She smiled, tucking the thought away to explore later. *We all need our little secrets, our own little signs.*

The front door opened and Jake let Storm out. The dog rushed down the stairs, her energetic greeting imminent.

"Dammit, Jake, grab her! Jess, hold that dress up!"

Renee, the only one with two free hands, jumped forward to grab the rambunctious dog just in time. Storm greeted her with kisses, oblivious to the narrowly diverted destruction. "Yes, I love you, too, girl," Renee said, laughing and holding on tight while Jess got the wedding dress safely inside.

* * *

"Girls, this is my friend Bridget. You have her intrigued with this wedding dress of yours," Lavonne said, hugging each of them in turn. "Bridget, this is our bride, Jess, holding the mystery dress, and our other two daughters, Renee and Val."

Bridget nodded a hello, but it was obvious the vintage wedding gown had already snagged her attention. She had not yet noticed the christening gown, since Val had hung it high on a coat hook inside the front door when they'd come in.

"May I?" she asked, motioning toward the hanger Jess held in her left hand.

"Of course," Jess replied, handing it to the older woman.

Lavonne had mentioned her friend Bridget before, but Val had never actually met her. For some reason she'd expected someone older, maybe with an old-fashioned sewing tape draped around her neck and a thimble on her thumb. This woman was at least ten years younger than Lavonne, wearing expensive jeans and a cashmere sweater in deference to the cool fall air. And there wasn't a sewing tape in sight. Bridget walked into the living room, examining the dress as she went. She hung it from a portable stand, apparently set up for that exact purpose.

Lavonne turned back to her daughters and asked for a report on how the first retreat of the season had gone, giving her friend time to work. When Val told her of all the interest around old recipes, Lavonne was delighted. "I'm not sure how I can be any help to you with all of this, honey, but I'm excited to do whatever I can. I'm so proud of you. You are approaching all of this with a lot of creativity, working hard to figure out a way to build a business that fits *you* and your lifestyle. I know Celia would be proud of you, too."

Val felt embarrassed over her mother's praise. There was still so much to figure out, so much she had to learn. She'd hardly call any of it an actual business yet.

"Mom is right, Val," Renee chimed in. "You are on your way. Give it time. Things will start to come together."

She hoped Renee was right. "I did just think of a possible name," she said, thinking back to their arrival a few minutes earlier. "What if we called our business Red Cardinal Revivals, or something like that?"

Jess, who'd only seemed to be listening with half an ear as she kept an eye on Bridget in the other room, turned back to Val, a huge grin on her face. "Val, that's perfect!"

Their mother, however, looked confused. She'd missed out on their cardinal sighting and discussion. Jess explained and their mother's expression cleared. "Of course. Very clever. Too many family traditions die with the older generation. You can help revive those for people, Val."

"Correction," Val replied, "*we* can help revive them, Mom."

Bridget came back to join them. "Ladies, do you want to come in now and we can get to work?"

Nodding, they followed her in and settled onto the couch and loveseat. Bridget stood by the dress.

"I'm convinced no one ever actually wore this dress. When you examine the inside . . . the threads . . . there's no breakage or normal wear-and-tear whatsoever. As to the age of the dress, I'm no expert, but based on the cut, the style, I suspect it was created in either the thirties or forties. I did some research after your mother called me and sent me the pictures last night."

Jess nodded. "I really appreciate you taking the time to help us with this, Bridget. I haven't been able to stop thinking about this dress since we first found it in Celia's attic."

"The trunk it was stored in must have been air-tight. Its condition is remarkable."

Jess rubbed her hands together. "Do you think you'll be able to alter it so it fits?"

"In the bodice?" she asked, looking closer at the dress's structure. "It shouldn't be too difficult. Why don't you slip into it and we'll see what needs to be done?"

"Mom, where's Dad and Val's kids?" Jess asked. "I don't want to traumatize them if they walk in here on us."

Lavonne checked her watch. "After the close call with Storm and the dresses, your father offered to take them for ice cream. He's on strict orders not to bring them back until I call with the all-clear."

Val closed the curtains at the front window, effectively enveloping them in privacy. "That should do it."

Jess stripped down again and Bridget helped her into the dress. Holding the front in place while Bridget began working on the tiny row of buttons up the back, Jess looked toward the ceiling. "I sure wish there was some way to know the story behind this thing."

Val perked up at this. "Hey, Mom, where is that old photo album? You know, the one we found in the trunk with the dresses?"

Lavonne nodded. "It's in your father's office, with the rest of Celia's things we brought over from her house for safekeeping. Why?"

"Can you get it, please?" Jess asked. "Val and I were talking about it on the way over here. We thought maybe there might be something in there about the wedding dress or the christening gown."

Bridget glanced up from her work, her brow furrowed. "What christening gown?"

"There was a beautiful old dress, tiny compared to this one," Jess said, motioning down at the gown she was wearing. "It was folded away in the trunk with this. We actually brought it today to show you, too. Where did you put it, Val?"

Val quickly left the room to retrieve the dress. When she returned, Bridget sighed at the sight of it, her hands still busy behind Jess. "Oh my goodness. That is precious! And old. I bet it's much older than this wedding dress."

"Really?" Jess said, glancing back over her shoulder at the seamstress.

Bridget nodded. "I'll take a closer look once I have you pinned up."

Val gently laid the dress over the back of the couch, taking the album from Lavonne when her mother returned.

"Don't you girls remember? The album starts with pictures from Celia's birthday party. It was her seventieth or eightieth, I don't recall exactly. But I doubt there's anything in there about either of these dresses."

Jess jumped.

"Sorry, love, try to hold still so I don't poke you again."

"I don't mind the poke, just don't let me bleed on the dress," Jess joked to Bridget, then turned her attention back to Lavonne. "That's what I assumed, too. But I never looked through the whole thing. Maybe it isn't in chronological order. Have you looked through it, Mom?"

"Actually, no. She had so many albums. I bet there are at least thirty of them back in the office."

"Are any of those older?" Jess asked, squinting now.

"Well, sure, honey."

Jess let her head fall back.

Why didn't we think of that? Val wondered, mentally slapping her own forehead.

"Sounds like you ladies might have some answers to your questions right under your own noses," Bridget mumbled, her words the slightest bit garbled as she spoke around the stick pins she held in her mouth.

386

"Thirty albums? That sounds like a project for another day." Val sighed, disappointed they wouldn't get any answers yet tonight. Unless there was something in the album she held in her hands.

As Bridget continued to make tucks here and there on the dress, Renee and Lavonne commenting on how nice it looked, Val worked her way through the album. Unfortunately, it was in order by date. It started at Celia's party, the one they'd all attended, and documented trips and events from the last decade or so of Celia's life.

Val couldn't remember much about the party. She'd been there with Luke. They would have been newlyweds then, no kids yet. Those had been such fun years. Little in the way of responsibilities, some extra cash since they were both working. They should have done some traveling back then when they had the chance.

Almost as if Lavonne could read Val's mind, she asked Bridget about her upcoming trip.

"Our trip to Sweden, you mean? The one I'm going on with my daughter? We leave in late January."

"January? I had it all wrong," Lavonne said. "I thought you were going before the holidays. That's why I got you over here so quickly to look at this dress. I didn't realize your daughter was going, either. Is it just the two of you?"

Bridget stood back to get a better view of her handiwork. "No, it's actually a mother-daughter trip I found out about from the local community college. I'm taking a class on genealogy."

"Mom, quit distracting Bridget when she's trying to fix the dress," Jess said.

But Bridget's comments caught Val's attention. She ignored Jess. "A mother-daughter trip? To Sweden? That sounds *beyond* fabulous."

Bridget nodded, then touched Jess's arm. "Go look in the mirror on the door to the front hall closet. See if you approve." She turned to Val. "I hope it *will* be fabulous. My daughter has never been overseas. In fact, she needs to get her passport ordered this coming week. We can hardly wait. We plan to visit a number of our relatives we've never had the opportunity to meet before."

"Val?" Renee said, meeting Val's eye with a curious expression on her face. "This could be your chance. You and Mom should do something like that."

"Me?" Lavonne asked. "Us?"

Jess returned from the mirror, smiling. "This looks *great*, Bridget. Thank you! Yes, Mom, if the trip isn't full, you should see if you and Val could go. You're half Swedish, right? Don't we have relatives in Sweden, too? Val was just complaining last night how she's never even needed her own passport."

Val was beginning to feel stirrings of hope. "Mom, do you have any of Grandma's other old recipes, like the sugar cookie one I helped you with?"

Renee was nodding. "Heck, you two could go and write it off as a business expense! Bridget, do you know if there's room for anyone else on the trip?"

Bridget looked between the other four women in the room. "I certainly hope there's still room! It would be a blast to have Lavonne along. We'd have so much fun! And you, too, Val. I think you and my daughter are about the same age."

Val closed the album on her lap. There were no answers in it regarding the dresses. They'd keep searching for the history, for the story of the dresses, but maybe the real answer was in making new memories.

Regardless of what happened between her and Luke, he was still her boys' father, and he could be their sole parent for a while if she were to take a trip with Lavonne. While it would mean dipping further into her inheritance, Val had a feeling Celia would approve.

EPILOGUE

*L*ight snowflakes tumbled down from puffs of haphazard clouds. Brilliant snippets of blue peeked between them, allowing sunlight to illuminate the flakes like glitter.

Renee sighed. "It's a perfect day for a wedding." She held her face to the sun, attempting to catch a snowflake on her tongue and balance the large box in her arms at the same time.

"A wedding we are going to be late to if we don't get this cabin decorated," Val said, her mind jumping to her long list of things she had to do yet before driving to the church.

"Would you relax, Val? Jeez. Jess doesn't want any of us to stress over this. Besides, I already got started in here this morning." Renee pushed the unlocked door open.

"Really? Thanks. I thought we still had to do it all."

Renee shook her head. "No. Just some last touches."

"Why such a big box, then?" Val asked, nodding to the box her sister had just set on the floor.

"There's new bedding in here," Renee said, pulling the top of the box open.

The gleam of white satin puffed up when released, reminding Val of the clouds outside.

"Oh man, that's beautiful," she said, walking over to the box and removing a silky comforter, the fabric cool and sumptuous against her skin. "Brilliant, Renee."

"I could hardly leave the bed covered in the quilt that's been here since July, could I? Even if it's been laundered weekly. This needs to look like a bridal suite when we get done with it."

For some reason, Val's mind jumped back to the night she'd helped Matt bring a drunk and beaten Ross back to the Gray Cabin. The quilt would have covered him during his stays. Shaking her head, she pulled her attention back to Renee. She set the fluffy comforter on the couch and dug deeper in the box. "Good call. New sheets, too." Holding up a sealed white container about the size of a shoebox, she turned back to her sister. "What's in here?"

"Those are the preserved rose petals. Red, of course. We're going to sprinkle them throughout this place just before we leave."

"Get out! Oh my God, woman, you've thought of everything."

Renee laughed. "I tried. I know Jess acts like she's not much of a romantic, but Seth seems to be. This place isn't fancy, but that doesn't mean we can't make it special."

Val set the white box on the kitchen table. She hadn't noticed the large silver bucket already sitting there, flanked with two graceful champagne glasses. The silver piece looked old, and when Val lifted it she was surprised at its weight. "This looks ancient."

Renee snapped the folds out of the new set of sheets. "Come on, help me make up the bed back here. I stripped it this morning."

Val followed her back.

"It *has* to be old," Renee said, circling back to Val's observation. "Seth brought it over to the house, asked me to set it up in here, along with the glasses. Apparently his grandma saved them for him. The set belonged to his parents. It was from their wedding. Before his grandma died, she made him promise to use it someday. I bet she never would have guessed Seth would marry Jess. Remember how she was Aunt Celia's best friend?"

Val was surprised by the tears that welled in her eyes. She'd been feeling jaded in the romance department lately but the story behind the silver ice bucket was sweet.

Renee snapped her side of the fitted sheet into place like the pro she'd become, running a resort for the past two summer seasons.

Despite her best efforts, Val couldn't help the sudden onslaught of tears coursing down her face. Renee noticed and dropped what she was doing to rush to her side.

"I'm sorry, Val," Renee cooed, wrapping her into a warm hug. "I know this must be hard for you, with things still in limbo with Luke. But you put up a brave front."

Val hugged Renee back, resting her head against her sister's chest, too short to rest it on her shoulder. "I'm sorry if my makeup smears onto your shirt," she sobbed.

Renee only laughed. She didn't pull back. "You're just lucky I'm not dressed for the wedding yet."

They stood that way for another minute, Val breathing deeply in an effort to rein in her emotions. When she'd calmed, Renee released her, sat on the half-made bed, and patted the spot next to her. Val sat.

"Has something new happened? Did you guys make some decisions?"

Val used the sleeve of her sweatshirt to wipe at her ruined makeup. *Damn, why didn't I remember to use waterproof mascara, today of all days?* She'd have to redo it before the wedding. She considered how best to answer Renee's questions. While she normally shared nearly everything with her sisters, she didn't want to tell Renee about Ross or anything more about Kennedy. She supposed she was taking a page out of her mother's book, keeping those particular secrets to herself. Some things should stay between a husband and a wife. But she did feel the need to share her frustration over Luke's continued absence from their lives.

"Actually, *I've* made a decision. Ever since the boys and I came back from Whispering Pines, I've been suggesting to Luke that we see a counselor. He's been resistant. We try to talk, and sometimes those discussions go well. We usually agree on things related to the kids. We've even gone out for dinner a couple times when he's come to see the kids. It's times like that when things almost feel normal. But then he packs up on Sunday afternoons and heads back to the farm."

"And you aren't happy with this arrangement?" Renee asked softly.

"Of course not. Harvest is done now. I'm not exactly sure what he keeps going back to the farm for, but I've decided I'm not going to live like this anymore. He's invited to the wedding, of course, but I'm not even sure if he'll show. If he does, tonight is the night I'm giving him an ultimatum. Either he moves home for good, and starts going to counseling with me, or I'm going to file for divorce when Mom and I get back from Sweden."

Renee sighed. "I'm sorry to hear that, Val. But I can't say that I blame you. He's been gone too long. Unless both of you agree that this is how you want to live, as a couple, it's not fair to you."

Val nodded, but she couldn't let Luke shoulder all the blame. "I haven't been perfect in all of this, Renee."

Renee reached out and took Val's hand in both of hers, giving it a loving squeeze. "I know, sis. No one is ever completely innocent in these types of difficult situations. Hell, even Mom and Dad had their struggles through the years. But they managed to see their way through it."

"Wait, you know about that?" Val asked, shocked—if Renee was indeed referring to Lavonne's secret.

Renee nodded. "I don't think Mom knows that I know. A few years after Jim and I got married, we had some pretty serious issues come up in our marriage. I talked to Dad about it and he shared some things he and Mom had had to deal with when we were young."

"Mom definitely thinks none of us kids know anything about it— until she told me this summer, that is."

"She told you because of your issues with Luke?" Renee asked, searching Val's eyes.

Val knew she couldn't lie. "Not exactly."

Renee waited. Val debated. The fact Renee knew Lavonne's secret changed things.

With a sigh, she confessed. "Mom walked in on me in Ross's arms."

"What?!" Renee yelled, jumping off the bed. "I *told* Matt there was something going on between you two, but he insisted I was nuts. He is so damn blind."

Val hated that Renee had mentioned her suspicions to Matt, but it wasn't like she was in any position to question loyalties.

Renee paced the bedroom while Val stared at the ground, lost in her thoughts of the times she'd spent with Ross over the past summer. He'd been there for her when she needed a friend, someone who wasn't so invested in the other parts of Val's life, including her husband and kids. She'd skated at the edge of danger, but she'd managed to avoid it, for the most part.

"We didn't even kiss, Renee. Honestly, we probably would have if Mom wouldn't have walked in, but we didn't. And then we both decided it would cause too much pain if we let it go anywhere."

Renee stopped her pacing. "I'm really sorry if I'm to blame for any of this mess you find yourself in, Val. Ross was here because of Matt, because of their friendship."

Pushing up off the bed with a sigh, Val yanked her side of the fitted sheet over the corner, pulling it taut. "You have zero blame in any of this, Renee. Now, come on—we need to finish transforming this place from the Gray Cabin into the Love Shack, and we have a wedding to get dressed for. The clock is ticking."

* * *

The sun sets early in late December. By the time Jess and Seth and their wedding guests were gathered inside the church at five o'clock, darkness had fallen. The soft strains of a traditional Christmas hymn echoed through the old church, the recorded music soft and unobtrusive. As promised, Jess had kept things simple. Overhead lights remained off, casting deep shadows, but the bride and groom basked in the glow of candlelight and warm twinkling Christmas lights strung around a massive cut pine. White poinsettias lined the altar. Jess planned to leave the floral displays for the church to use as they saw fit. "What am I going to do with a bunch of wedding flowers?" she'd said when describing her vision for the altar to Renee and Val.

Val loved how the scent of pine gave a light perfume to the air; it was perfectly appropriate for Jess's wedding.

The priest was blessing the rings when she felt Luke's hand brush hers. When she looked up at him, he bent over to whisper in her ear. "You look beautiful tonight, Val."

She smiled at the compliment before turning her eyes back to the couple at the altar, but her mind was elsewhere. Thirty minutes before they'd had to leave for the wedding, Val heard Storm go crazy downstairs, and then she heard her husband's voice. *He came,* she'd thought, dropping the tiny diamond stud she'd been attempting to push through her earlobe and losing it in the carpet at her feet. She'd been on her knees, searching for it, when he'd come into their bedroom.

"What are you doing?" he'd laughed, dropping down onto his knees next to her.

"Looking for my earring" was all she'd said, and he'd looked with her until they'd found it. She'd stuck it through her piercing immediately, securing it with its back so she wouldn't drop it again, and he'd helped her to her feet.

There, on the dresser, was a business card for a marriage counselor. Luke must have put it there.

"We have an appointment on Tuesday," he'd whispered to her before turning away.

Little else had been said. They'd had to hurry. She noticed how handsome Luke looked in a new black suit and dress shoes. No cowboy boots tonight. His hair was trimmed and, if she hadn't been sure he'd never go for it, she might have thought he'd gone in for a manicure. His fingers and nails always looked so beat up and dirty, being a man who worked with his hands. Tonight, he was as well-groomed as she'd seen him in years. He'd made an effort.

She glanced to her right: their four sons looked handsome as well, Dave and Logan in suits, Noah and Jake in dress shirts and pressed black pants. While Jess had wanted simple, Renee and Val insisted everyone dress up. A holiday wedding called for some class.

Renee and Matt sat in the pew in front of them, similar to Sheriff Thompson's funeral, but this was in a different church and for a much happier occasion. Julie and Robbie stood beside them, Julie doing everything she could to keep little Harper quiet as she bounced the toddler on her hip.

Harper had played a special part at the beginning of the ceremony, dropping rose petals on the ground as she held tight to Seth's hand, entering the church together. Val could see the girl still had one of those petals gripped tightly between her chubby little fingers.

Across the aisle, Lavonne and George sat in the front pew, along with George's older brother, Uncle Gerry, and his wife, Letty. Behind them was Ethan and his girlfriend, Rebecca, along with Ethan's daughter, Elizabeth, and her boyfriend, as well as Ethan's sons, Dylan and·Drew.

One additional pew, the one behind Ethan and his family, held the only other guests. Grant Johnson was there, along with a woman Val didn't know, and Grant's daughter, Grace. Grant had been the twin brother of Renee's first husband, Jim. He'd formed a close friendship with the whole family, but with Jess in particular, so Val hadn't been surprised to see him at the wedding. She also knew that Grace was dating Jess's son.

Val turned back toward the front of the church, happy in knowing this small church, where they'd celebrated many family milestones, again held so many stories, so much love, as two of her favorite people pledged their love to each other.

Val knew it wouldn't always be easy for Jess and Seth—marriage never was—but with commitment, and maybe a little luck, they'd weather their own storms. Their kids would be there to help hold the family unit together. Nathan, Jess's son, stood next to Seth, acting as his best man. Lauren, her daughter, was Jess's maid of honor, and Kaylee stood beside Lauren, proudly acting as a junior bridesmaid.

Val noticed a smudge of red on Jess's dress. Looking up, she could see light from the moon as it shone through a section of the stained glass, reflecting down on the happy couple.

At the priest's instructions, Seth took Jess into his arms and dropped a light kiss on her lips. Val's eyes misted over. Luke must have noticed, because he laid his big, warm hand over hers.

* * *

"I did my best to keep Harper quiet," Julie insisted, laughing as they all reminisced over dinner about the scene the little girl had created earlier, at the end of the ceremony, when Jess and Seth were walking back down the aisle. Harper dove for Jess, Julie nearly dropping her at the surprise move. Unrattled, Jess had handed her small bouquet of white roses to Seth and dropped his hand, taking Harper into her arms. The three of them had continued their walk down the aisle, beaming with happiness and unfazed by their nontraditional exit.

Now they were seated in a private room in the back of a nice restaurant a few miles from the church. Val had offered to serve a family meal at the lodge, but Jess didn't want anyone to fuss. Looking around now, Val saw the wisdom in her sister's choice. This was nice, special. Everyone had ordered off the menu, and the food was delicious. As the talented wait staff discreetly cleared the dishes, Jess and Seth stood to cut the wedding cake, a pretty creation Jess had ordered from a woman named Mabel, a friend that ran a small bakery near the bookshop Jess had inherited a partial ownership interest in from Celia. Nathan now ran the bookshop.

It again struck Val how intertwined their lives remained, and how Celia's presence was still a part of their daily lives, even though she'd been gone for three years already.

While Val hadn't been as quick to do anything with her inheritance from Celia as her siblings, she was finally making some progress. She was heading to Sweden with her mother in three weeks, and they'd be learning cooking techniques from their distant relatives. She could hardly wait. Her brand-new passport was locked away in their safe at home, ready for her upcoming travels. Val hoped to fill it with the stamps from many future trips. After all, it was high time she started pursuing her childhood wish of traveling the globe, learning how to prepare brilliant new dishes.

Ethan stood to toast the newlyweds. Luke quickly picked up the bottle of champagne in front of them and topped off first her glass and then his.

Clearing his throat, Ethan raised his glass. "I just wanted to take a minute to wish this special couple the very best. Seth, you are a gutsy man joining up with this family, but I suspect you're up for the experience. Because I've learned something important in my nearly fifty years on Earth. Growing up, we all think that once we hit a certain age, all this family business is behind us and we'll head off and make it on our own. I'm sure for some people, that's exactly how it works. But not in this family. None of us have to go it alone around here. So welcome to the family, Seth."

Glasses clinked around the room and Ethan made a move to sit down, but then he stopped and held his glass high one more time. "Sorry. I forgot one important thing. Seth, I'll tell you the same thing I told Matt." This was met by a chorus of groans. They all knew what was coming. "Hurt my sister in any way, and you'll have me to answer to."

Glasses reluctantly clinked one more time around the room. People laughed as Ethan also pointed to Matt and Luke, making it clear the same still applied to them.

Grinning, Luke leaned in close to Val. "I'm ready to come home, honey. We have work to do, but I'm willing to put in the time and effort if you are."

She searched his eyes, and could read the sincerity there. She'd promised herself that tonight was the night she was done with the drama, and here was Luke, ready to step up as she'd hoped.

Leaning in, she met him halfway and kissed him softly. "It's about damn time," she whispered, to which he laughed out loud and caught her up in a more passionate kiss—much to the dismay of their boys.

Thank you!

Dear Reader,

I would like to thank you for taking the time to read **Choosing Again**. I am so grateful you selected it and I hope you enjoyed this fourth book in my Celia's Gifts series.

If you don't mind taking a few more minutes with this book, I'd appreciate it if you would leave a review. Reviews are extremely helpful and much appreciated.

Next up in the series is **Celia's Gifts** (Book 5). I decided we needed to wrap back in time and learn Celia's story!

For links to all my books and to sign up for my newsletter so I can keep you posted on new releases, please visit my website at

www.kimberlydiedeauthor.com.

Wishing you my very best,
Kimberly

CURIOUS ABOUT OTHER BOOKS IN
THE *CELIA'S GIFTS* SERIES?

I invite you to explore all the books in this uplifting, family-centered series.

Each book in the series highlights the impact Celia had while she lived and on the legacy she leaves to family members. Her nieces and nephews will face the inevitable struggles of mid-life while watching their children deal with the age-old issues of young adulthood. Will they survive broken hearts, broken homes, and abandoned dreams? These encouraging stories of family, love, and growth will inspire you.

Whispering Pines (Book 1)

A shocking job loss will force Renee to remember the beauty of new beginnings.

Summers at Whispering Pines defined Renee's childhood. Days meant swimming and sun. Nights meant ghost stories and campfires. Best of all, summer meant time with Celia, her favorite aunt. Through the years, trips to Whispering Pines would fade to memories.

Now Celia is gone and Renee's career is in shambles. How can she keep her family safe while she rebuilds their lives? Celia's final gift may provide answers, but there are risks. Why can't things be simple, the way they were when she spent summers at Whispering Pines?

Tangled Beginnings (Book 2)

Often the most difficult of choices can lead to the greatest of joys, but what if the stakes feel too high?

Jess is ready for a fresh start. Her twenty-five year marriage is over, her youngest is heading to college, and all she wants to do is retreat to

Whispering Pines. She's watched her sister Renee make the most of second chances, and now it's her turn.

But when her ex asks her to do the unimaginable, will his mistakes threaten to undermine her new chance at happiness? Long-buried secrets and new accusations tangle together, threatening to ruin reputations and lives. Threaded with romance, mystery, and ghosts from the past, this novel is bound to make you fall in love once more with the prospect of life, love, and forgiveness.

Rebuilding Home (Book 3)

A story of one man's struggle to rethink his vision of the the perfect family, true friendship, and what home really means.

When Ethan's wife walks out, his first priority is to protect his three teenagers from further heartache. He should have been a better husband. Now it's time to be a better dad. But a devastating fire changes everything. Suspicions and doubts threaten all he holds dear. When trust shatters, can old friendships guide him home again?

Follow Ethan on an emotional journey from fractured illusions, through tangled paths of hope and despair, to the renewed possibility of happiness and love.

Capturing Wishes (Book 3.5)

Children know the power of a holiday wish. Adults forget.

Virginia and Nathan make an unlikely pair. She's spent decades working in her beloved bookstore. He'll graduate from college in the spring. Both are at a crossroads.

Can Nathan convince Virginia it's never too late to chase her most elusive dream? It feels impossible, but no one should underestimate the magic of a Christmas wish.

Choosing Again (Book 4)

In the stillness of a warm summer evening, she'll summon the courage to change her life.

Val loves being a wife and mother, but she needs more. When the shrill ringing of a telephone in the dead of night splits their world into *before* and *after,* she's torn. With their home in chaos, she seeks refuge at Whispering Pines.

Well-meaning advice leads to a crushing revelation, and Val is devastated by the long-buried secret that threatens to tear her family apart. Is she destined to make the same painful mistake? Regardless of what she decides, this summer will change everything.

Celia's Gifts (Book 5)

Travel back to where this story begins and discover the answers to mysteries seemingly lost to the passage of time…

Fierce friendships, a fragile family, and a young woman's only sanctuary.

In the summer of 1942, a young woman's visit to the lake cottage of a friend will commence a series of events destined to weave her family's future to an extraordinary place for generations to come. The young woman is Celia, and that place is Whispering Pines.

Celia's Legacy (Book 6)

Because Celia's story was too big for just one book…

She only has one chance to leave the legacy her family deserves.

Celia sacrificed too much for her dream career, but retirement means freedom. She plans to relax and have fun at Whispering Pines...unless haunting memories threaten that dream, too.

She'll have to fight to keep her heart open through the hurt and loss that comes with aging. She may grow old alone, but she refuses to be lonely. She's learned valuable lessons along the way, and her family needs her hard-earned wisdom more than ever. Can she help Renee, Jess, Ethan, and Val avoid the regrets that tarnish her golden years?

This sixth book in this uplifting family saga will take you along on Celia's journey to build a legacy that's sure to live on for generations.

What more could a woman want?

For all of Kimberly Diede's books, please visit: www. kimberlydiedeauthor.com

CELIA'S GIFTS PREVIEW

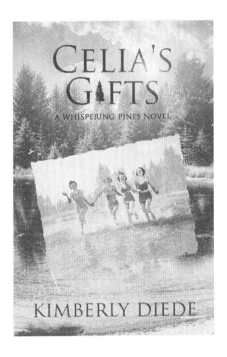

Celia's Gifts, Book 5

Fierce friendships, a fragile family, and a young woman's only sanctuary.

Intent on escaping the far-off echoes of war, plus the heat and humidity of a Minnesota summer, Celia tags along with college friends to a tranquil lake resort. She quickly realizes that one glorious month at Whispering Pines—filled with sun-splashed days and crackling bonfires under starry night skies—will never be enough.

Something about the resort pulls Celia in. Heartaches back home fade away. Here, she can be herself, even if she doesn't quite fit in. Her friends hint at dreams of exciting careers, but their focus is on nabbing the perfect husband. Not Celia. Her own father left them destitute, and she's vowed to never follow in her mother's footsteps.

But Celia can feel her steely resolve soften as she twirls across a crowded dance floor in the arms of a man she barely knows. Their whispered conversations last until pink washes a pre-dawn sky, causing Celia to reexamine everything. She's intrigued—tempted, even. But when catastrophe shatters the serenity she's found at Whispering Pines, she'll face an agonizing decision.

Travel back to 1942 as Kimberly Diede introduces you to a loyal, ambitious young Celia in this fifth book in her heartwarming series, Celia's Gifts. Immerse yourself in the loves and losses Celia experiences at Whispering Pines. Will unthinkable loss destroy her, or will she emerge stronger than ever?

Find links to your favorite stores on my website at www.kimberlydiedeauthor.com.

AN INVITATION

If you are enjoying the books in my Celia's Gifts series, please visit my website to join my mailing list for periodic updates on new releases and my other writing projects.

www.kimberlydiedeauthor.com

When you join my mailing list, be sure to watch your email for a FREE copy of my novella:

First Summers at Whispering Pines 1980

Fun fact: While writing **Choosing Again**, I was lucky enough to have actual recipe cards to reference. I've never personally tried these (I'm not the cook that Val is!) but I'd love to hear from you if you give either of these a try! You may remember these dishes from the family's Fourth of July picnic beginning in Chapter 11.

PICCALILLI

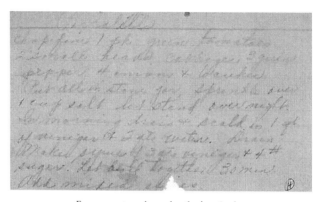

From my paternal grandmother's recipe box

Chop fine 1 pk green tomatoes, 2 small heads cabbage, 3 green pepper, 4 onions, 6 cukes Put all in stone jar, sprinkle over 1 cup salt, let stand overnight. In morning drain and scald in 1 qt vinegar and 2 qts water. Drain. Make syrup of 3 qts vinegar and 4 # sugar. Let boil together 30 min. Mix all.

LUSH SALAD

The lush salad recipe card was found in a recipe box that belonged to my Great Aunt Mary. Mary is the inspiration behind this series. You'll notice this one is dated 1967 and it is signed by Jessie B., a close friend of my aunt's. These treasures are priceless to me!

**1 pkg lemon jello, 1 cup hot water,
1 can tomato soup (undiluted), 1 tbsp chopped onion,
1 cup chopped celery, ½ cup stuffed olives (cut)
Dissolve jello in hot water, add soup. Chill. Mix in other
ingredients and let set.**

ACKNOWLEDGMENTS

I'm writing this "Thank You" section for **Choosing Again** on Memorial Day, May 25, 2020. Suddenly, we find ourselves trying to navigate through a dramatically changing world. Many questions remain as to what the future holds. But despite the uncertainty, there is still magic in losing ourselves between the pages of a book. For this, I am thankful.

I spent part of this holiday the same way I've spent every Memorial weekend for as long as I can remember. Growing up, I'd help my mom and grandma plant fresh flowers at the headstones of family members and friends that felt like family. Pausing once a year to show respect in this way always floods me with feelings: sadness over missing them, gratitude for the foundations they laid for my own life, and a poignant reminder that we all need to make the most of our days.

This year, both my father and my daughter Amber helped. We honored Mom and Grandma, along with others. I share this here because those two women showed me how to be a wife and a mother. They weathered the joys and sorrows of motherhood and reached milestone anniversaries with their husbands. None of that happens by accident. It all takes hard work. Thank you, ladies, for setting the example. You taught me the essential things in life.

As is the case with every book I write, I also owe a huge thank-you to my husband of thirty years, Rick, and our kids, Josh, Alecia, and Amber. Thank you for letting me *try* to be the best wife and mom I can be. Even when I fail, you know I love you all.

Thank you, again, to my editor, Spencer Hamilton, for helping me do justice to this amazing family that once existed only in my mind. Thank you also to Ivan Cakamura for your patience and creativity in designing another book cover for this series. You take the seeds of my ideas and grow them into beautiful works of art.

It was challenging to finish this book during such difficult times, but having many of my die-hard readers continue to tell me they can't wait for my next book gave me the encouragement I needed to keep my focus. Thank you to each and every one of you that gives of your precious time to read my stories.

ALSO BY KIMBERLY DIEDE

CELIA'S GIFTS SERIES

WHISPERING PINES (BOOK 1)

TANGLED BEGINNINGS (BOOK 2)

REBUILDING HOME (BOOK 3)

CHOOSING AGAIN (BOOK 4)

CELIA'S GIFTS (BOOK 5)

CELIA'S LEGACY (BOOK 6)

A WHISPERING PINES CHRISTMAS NOVEL

CAPTURING WISHES (BOOK 3.5)

FIRST SUMMERS NOVELLA

FIRST SUMMERS AT WHISPERING PINES 1980

ABOUT THE AUTHOR

Kimberly Diede writes contemporary novels that weave together family, hope, and romance. She writes family sagas, suspense, and women's fiction that you'll find hard to put down. She truly believes we are never too old for second chances at love and at life.

Kimberly enjoys spending the short months of her Midwest summers on the lakeshores of Minnesota and North Dakota. Nothing is better than time with her family at their cabin. Her love of tradition and all things vintage comes through in her stories.

Be sure to follow Kimberly on social media to catch glimpses of the junk she drags home to repurpose and to get updates on her latest books.

facebook.com/KimberlyDiedeAuthor
instagram.com/kimberlydiedeauthor
pinterest.com/kdiedeauthor

Manufactured by Amazon.ca
Bolton, ON